The Singing House

Janette Griffiths

BLACK SWAN

THE SINGING HOUSE
A BLACK SWAN BOOK : 0 552 99610 6

First publication in Great Britain

PRINTING HISTORY
Black Swan edition published 1995

Set in 11pt Linotype Melior by
County Typesetters, Margate, Kent

Black Swan Books are published by Transworld Publishers Ltd,
61–63 Uxbridge Road, Ealing, London W5 5SA,
in Australia by Transworld Publishers (Australia) Pty Ltd,
15–25 Helles Avenue, Moorebank, NSW 2170,
and in New Zealand by Transworld Publishers (NZ) Ltd,
3 William Pickering Drive, Albany, Auckland.

Reproduced, printed and bound in Great Britain by
Cox & Wyman Ltd, Reading, Berks.

For my mother

Acknowledgements

I'm grateful to Samuel Ramey for his advice in the early stages, to Ruggero Raimondi for offering to read the manuscript, to Paul Daniel and Opera North, and to William Morton and his fellow members of the Royal Opera House orchestra. I hope that all my musician friends will forgive me for any mistakes I've made in this fictional account of their world. Thanks also to Ann Vaughan-Williams for reading the first draft, and to Michèle, Philippe, Patrice and Gerald, my guides and companions through the world of opera for so many years now.

The Singing House

PART I
The Garden

Chapter One

On a December afternoon in the late nineteen fifties Rose Lorenzo sat in a church hall in north London and discovered the wonder that is music. So great was her joy, so brilliant the light cast by this revelation that little Rose wrenched a pearl from the swan brooch that she wore and pushed it up her nose. She was seven years old. Colour, light and music were in short supply in post-war England. But for the Sunday School's Christmas puppet show a kindly father had spent the morning wrapping coloured paper around the light bulbs, his wife had run up a set of small, red velvet curtains and the vicar had supplied a gramophone and a record of the music from *Carousel*.

Dah dah dah dee dum, da da da dah dah dee dum went the scratchy 78 and Rose squealed with pleasure. The other paler children all turned to stare at the half-Spanish girl whose father had dressed her in his mother's black lace mantilla and draped her in her jewels for the occasion. Rose would have stood out anyway. Her olive skin and rich brown hair (she had not yet grown tall enough to reach the peroxide on the Boots' shelf) distinguished her from the other girls. It even distinguished her from her sister Daphne who was blonde and slim and a wise enough nine-year-old to sit well away from her little sister and her flamboyant attire.

Dah dah dah dee dum, da da da dah dah dee dum went the music and Rose pushed that pearl all the way up her right nostril. She couldn't get it back down but the music was loud, whirling, all-embracing and she didn't care.

Once the red velvet curtains had closed and the

excitement was over, she didn't dare tell anyone about the lost pearl but spent many spare moments of her remaining childhood years trying to locate it and coax it back down.

When she was eighteen she told her sister.

'It's still up there,' she said. 'Perhaps I should get nose surgery.'

'Of course it isn't,' replied Daphne. 'You always dramatize, Rose. You must have sneezed it out within hours of shoving it in.'

'It's my nose,' said Rose.

Her Spanish father had been dead for ten years by then. He hadn't attended that long-distant puppet show, claiming that as a Catholic he couldn't attend a C of E affair. He had taken advantage of his family's absence to leap on his Lambretta and visit one of several mistresses scattered throughout the northern suburbs. When he heard about Rose's squeals of joy from her embarrassed mother he commiserated but that night he wrote a jubilant note to Claudia, a cashier in a Soho trattoria.

'My daughter is *my* daughter,' he wrote. 'They are all saying that she has an excessive over-reaction to music. In a polite English church hall my daughter screamed with pleasure because there was light and colour and beautiful sound.'

The Spaniard had neither the money nor the time to nurture the love of music in Rose. Within months of that brief and wonderful December afternoon he would have one grappa too many in Claudia's trattoria and ride his Lambretta under a Number 22 bus. Rose's youth thus placed in the hands of her shy, apologetic mother and her stern, no-nonsense sister, music and colour on such an overwhelming scale disappeared from her life for thirty years.

Those years passed. Losing her father so young made sensible Daphne anxious. She married Roger, a successful something in the City and had two sons. Losing her father so young made Rose fill the space he had left with dreams of extraordinary, imaginary men.

14

She did not marry. In order to hold on to a trace of that dapper little Spaniard full of song and fantasy, she studied Romance languages and became an interpreter.

In her mid-twenties she fell in love with a Spanish businessman at an olive oil conference. He talked of marriage but Rose discovered that he still had a wife. She wept for a week. The years went by. Her friends started to divorce. She would receive late-night phone calls from her peers wailing, 'Is this all there is?' Rose made soothing sounds and kept to herself the conviction that there was an invisible, intangible 'something more'.

But Rose herself was only convinced when the sun shone, when the right winds blew, when she felt young and invulnerable. On the dark, bare nights when she was weary and suddenly aware of the weight of years, Rose too was terrified that perhaps this was all there was . . .

Dah dah dah dee dum . . . a curtain had opened . . . a pearl had settled. But time passed. When forty loomed she let Daphne and even the divorcing friends convince her that she should marry. An appropriate man had appeared. Martin was divorced, wealthy, childless and good-looking. He seemed to like being married for he had done it twice before. Rose knew that she should settle down. A week before the wedding the muscles in her left shoulder locked tight. Wedding-dress fittings proved impossible because one half of her torso was now three inches higher than the other. Rose was relieved to be free of this formality and said she would buy something off the peg. During that same week she woke at 3 a.m. with crashing headaches. Some tumult seemed to break through the hours of darkness carrying within its calm eye a memory of an intensity of feeling that daily life with Daphne and Mother had diluted.

And yet in the clear light of that daily life she would look at the man she was to marry with affection and resignation – and she would look at her own greying hair in the mirror and no longer even dare to wonder about something more. She seemed powerless to stop the great rattling juggernaut of her life from sweeping her along.

On the day before her wedding it swept her to Leicester Square. Her shoulder had loosened sufficiently for her to hire a wedding dress at Moss Brothers. She had passed the age for billowing white satin and had been advised by her sister and mother to opt for something magnolia. They had also been keen on this same shade for the living-room of her new home. Or had that been apricot? Rose sat on the Northern Line, massaged her shoulder and wondered if she'd confused the two.

Two blocks from Moss Brothers she forgot all the polite pastels when she glimpsed an emerald green silk dress in a shop window.

'It matches your eyes,' said the assistant.

'It's my wedding dress,' said Rose.

'Isn't green unlucky?' asked the woman. 'How about this?' and she produced a delicate ivory silk.

Rose took the emerald green. A great wind was blowing through the West End that late autumn day. Rose had to close her eyes against the grit and litter that pelted through the air. The wind bore her towards the tube station – but the tube was closed because of a bomb-scare. Rose drifted down Floral Street. It smelt like a drain. She was reflecting on this irony when a gauntly handsome blond man approached her and stammered, 'Twenty pounds?'

'I beg your pardon!'

'Is that too much? Oh no! Oh dear! I told Eva I couldn't do this kind of thing—' He was fumbling in his pockets. Rose looked hard at him. She guessed that he was about fifty although his face was strangely unlined. He was casually dressed but perhaps aware enough of his good looks to know that the royal blue cords and pale blue cardigan were a perfect complement to his clear blue eyes. He thrust a piece of paper in front of her.

16

'I can't find my glasses and I can't remember what Eva said – I never could cope with figures and money. You'll have to tell *me* how much.' The wind was so violent that his voice was muffled by the whirling air and crashing billboards. In order to keep a firm footing on the pavement they both had to huddle against the blank cream wall behind them – the wall of the Royal Opera House. Rose hadn't even noticed the cream and columned theatre until she looked at the piece of paper and saw that it was a ticket to that evening's performance.

'You're trying to sell me a ticket! Oh my poor man – I hadn't understood at all.'

'Was twenty pounds too much?' The man had a strange, sad beauty. Rose could not look away from his eyes. She pushed the ticket back towards him. She saw now that the blank, cream wall was lined with people holding up bundles of notes.

'I can't go to the opera tonight.' She smiled and pointed towards the line of proffered five- and ten-pound notes. 'But it looks as though there are plenty of buyers.'

'I don't like the look of any of them,' he sniffed. 'You do have to sit with the person for over five hours, you know.'

'Five hours!'

'Of course. *Tristan and Isolde* lasts that long. Why can't you come to the opera tonight? I like the look of you.'

'I just can't. I've had a very busy day and I haven't been too well this week and – well if you must know – I'm getting married tomorrow.'

'Getting married?' said the man with a deep sigh of awe and wonder as if Rose had said that she was planning a one-woman expedition to the South Pole. 'Are you wonderfully happy?'

'Well, I—'

'I never got married,' sighed the man. 'But it must be the most wonderful thing a person can do, I suppose – is it?'

'I suppose so,' said Rose, uncomfortable under the man's clear blue gaze.

'You don't sound very convinced,' said the man. 'Are you full of trepidation – is that all part of it? I suppose it must be.'

'Yes, yes, trepidation is very much part of it,' said Rose. 'Perhaps you should be thinking about selling that ticket.'

'Oh I don't really care,' said the man. 'We paid for it months ago so the money is lost. I would *give* it to you.'

'I really can't,' said Rose and started to back away into the cold, buffeting wind. 'But I'm sure you'll sell it. Good luck.'

'Good luck to you!' cried the man. When Rose was almost at the corner of Floral and Bow Streets she turned back to look at him. He was standing with both arms hanging by his sides. From time to time he cast a forlorn gaze at the people holding up money. Then he stared off into the distance. A bell started ringing.

Rose took her wallet from her handbag and counted her cash. She took out a twenty-pound note. Before she could think any further she was carried on the wind and the sound of ringing bells to where the man still stood staring in front of him.

'Oh, I won't take money.' He did not seem surprised by her return. He pressed the ticket into her hand. His fingers were long and smooth and warm. 'It's in the amphitheatre, I'm afraid,' he said. 'We have to run up five flights of stairs.'

He was obviously used to this sudden last-minute ascent for he never once ran out of breath as they climbed.

'Are you passionately in love?' he asked as they started up the third flight of the red-painted concrete steps.

'You do ask some very personal questions,' puffed Rose. She wasn't used to such endless stairs. The bag containing her wedding dress kept getting caught between her legs. She gripped the iron banister and tried to regain her balance. She had no idea why she had turned round and returned to this impertinent man.

'I know – I can't help myself,' replied the man. 'Eva says I have no tact, but all the most interesting questions are the tactless ones – don't you think? *Are* you passionately in love?'

'Well – no.' Rose was unnerved by that clear, unblinking blue gaze.

'Shouldn't you be?' The man bounded on up the stairs.

'It hasn't always been a prerequisite to marriage,' panted Rose behind him. 'Romantic love is a recent invention – a product of poets, knights and troubadours.'

'Then what's the point?' said the man.

They had arrived in the amphitheatre. Rose, who suffered from vertigo, climbed the last step into that steeply raked upper gallery and thought for a moment that she might tumble head first into the red and gold auditorium that seemed to whirl and weave before her. She reached for her new companion but he was already settling into his seat. She sat down next to him at the end of a row.

'In that case I don't think you should get married,' said the man but in a tone so matter-of-fact that Rose thought he had offered to buy her a programme or a box of chocolates. She was about to decline politely when the prelude swept over them.

Chapter Two

The wind that had blown around Rose and the blond man as they huddled against the wall of the opera house had lost momentum as it crossed Europe. Somewhere over the Alps it lost all warmth too and as it wound around the mountain peaks it coated itself in snow. Now it blew into Vienna and draped that white coat across the city rooftops. This first snow of the winter blew onto the roof of the Figaro Haus where Mozart had worked on that opera. It settled around the spire of St Stefan's Cathedral and landed on all poor, debt-evading Beethoven's many Viennese dwellings. Out in bucolic Grinzing where Schubert and his friends would linger under the summer-vined trellises, white came in and covered the withered leaves. The wind scattered the last of its snow on the city cemetery where the great composers' graves lie: Haydn, Brahms and Schubert alongside Beethoven's stern obelisk and a simple plaque for poor lost Mozart.

Since the composers died, since the Emperors and the Empire died, since the first woman to dance a waltz and the first man to bake a Sachertorte died, Vienna had grown quiet, provincial, melancholy – a castle inhabited by a caretaker – brooding on her past.

Standing at the stage door of the Staatsoper and gazing out at the whirling white, the great bass singer Leo dalla Vigna reflected that Vienna's most glorious century, the nineteenth, seemed to have blown in with the blizzard. As he adjusted his scarf and hat and watched the slow progress of a passing carriage he let himself imagine that upon stepping outside he would find a world still inhabited by Verdi and Wagner. The thought pleased him but it was interrupted by Karl, the

20

artistic director of the opera house who had run from his office to intercept Leo at the stage door.

'Please think again, Leo.' He was not a young man and was out of breath and red in the face.

'I've thought enough,' replied Leo, tucking his scarf tightly into his coat collar.

'It's just one performance,' sighed Karl, looking for help from Fritz Schreier, the conductor who had also followed Leo to the exit but at his own pace.

'He's right, Leo,' said Fritz. 'It is just one *Giovanni* – then you pick up your fee and go home.'

'It's a vulgar piece of shit,' said Leo. 'I might expect something like this from some of your German houses, Fritz, but not Vienna.'

'Don't look at me,' said Fritz, who was musical director in Munich. 'The production's nothing to do with me.'

'We borrowed it from Berlin,' sighed the artistic director. 'The critics loved the concept of—'

'It's the Emperor's new clothes again,' snorted Leo. 'And none of you seem to see that the Emperor, like half the chorus, is naked! Well I don't like concepts.' He reached for the door-handle. 'I like *Don Giovanni*. I like Mozart—'

'I'm sure the producer does too,' said Karl. 'He just felt that by setting it in—'

'Producer?' Leo raised an eyebrow. 'You mean that organic carrot that's been telling me what to do all afternoon?'

'The man can't help the colour of his hair,' smiled Fritz. 'Anyway, what difference does it make for a performance? Let the thing go its way around you, pick up your money and go home to Bellagio and beautiful Kay.'

'Can't do that,' said Leo.

'Why not? It's just a job.'

'No it's not.'

'The intendant might sue this time.' The artistic director leaned against the wall and closed his eyes.

'Let him,' said Leo and walked out into the snow

towards the Sacher Hotel. Fritz and Karl stared through the stage doorway as the singer's Roman profile faded into the twilight.

'But he won't sue,' said Fritz.

'Of course not,' said Karl, turning to make his way back to his office where computers and faxes would go into action in an attempt to replace the departing Italian bass.

That winter as every winter, prized vocal chords made their way across the globe. From New York to Milan to Vienna the Great Voices flew from Great House to Great House, their owners wrapped in fur and cashmere, hats pulled tight over their ears, and coats and scarves wrapped firm around those precious lungs and larynxes.

'Air borne on air, that's all they really are,' Karl muttered to Fritz as they pondered possible replacements for Leo. They could have dismissed the celebrity of many great singers with a few terse sentences about the right management and a good publicity machine but they could not explain away the reputation of Leo dalla Vigna.

The conductor could recall the evening at the San Carlo in Naples when Leo appeared as Mephistopheles twenty-five years earlier. Fritz was still an aspiring violinist at the time and had not yet taken up his baton. And if Leo's personality was already big enough to overlap the stage, the young Fritz was not then the man he was to become. On that long distant evening he was simply a young man on holiday who had wandered into the opera house. Leo's performance had filled him with joy and energy and just a little envy.

Afterwards he had eaten in a pizzeria frequented by the artists from the San Carlo. There were about ten of them in a small alcove at the back of the restaurant. They were exuberant and confident, most of them Italian, and at home in the hot, pungent atmosphere of the little inn. They ordered dishes that weren't on the menu, sent back many of those that were and hauled the cook out of the kitchen to drink a glass of grappa.

22

Most of them were soloists and had poised, resonant voices that echoed across to Fritz, alone at his table for the tourist in the corner by the door. They had made him feel dry and cynical, emphatically a man of the North. Fritz Schreier had felt as he watched them that all his own life had been spent perched up in a few small corners of his head whereas these people seemed to live loudly and resolutely in every cell of their bodies.

Then he had noticed a centre of calm in the midst of their group. After a few minutes of staring that nobody there would have deemed impolite, he recognized Leo dalla Vigna accompanied by the most delicately beautiful blonde that Fritz had ever seen. His name, which Fritz had underlined on the programme, confirmed that he was Italian but where the others seemed to have their emotions (and how numerous these were!) spread across the surface of their being for all to see, Leo was serenely contained within himself. Even at twenty-three he was a great granite block of a man.

The blonde was his wife. Fritz, already prey to a lifelong weakness for luminous blondes, experienced another brief moment of envy for this man who within a year would receive a forty-five-minute standing ovation after his début at La Scala and go on in middle age to become a Kammersänger in Vienna and be awarded the Legion of Honour in France. Two years after that night in the restaurant he read of the death of the singer's baby daughter. Because he knew that his first encounter with Leo had changed the direction of his musical life and because he sensed that one day they would be friends, he had cut the small announcement out of *Il Corriere Della Sera*. Many years into that friendship, he realized with relief that Leo never spoke of his dead daughter to anyone.

Now Leo dalla Vigna dozed fully clothed on his bed in the Sacher Hotel, the score of Wagner's *Die Walküre* on the pillow next to his head. He had accepted the brief engagement at the Staatsoper in order to work on the role of Wotan in Wagner's great Ring Cycle with a discreet *répétiteur*. He had never sung a German role. He was a master of the Italian repertoire. And he was terrified of Wotan – that awesome, fatally flawed and self-destructive god of the Nordic gods. Leo had spent many secret months poring over the pages of monologue that Wagner had given the embattled deity. He had sat at home in his villa on Lake Como and played the score through on the piano, whistling the part to himself. He would never have dared express his secret belief that he and the doomed ruler of Valhalla were somehow linked to each other. Try telling a colleague over a cup of coffee in the canteen that you have an affinity with Wotan.

An afternoon spent being a Spanish philanderer and a morning spent secretly attempting to incarnate a miserable German god had drained Leo's energy. He was lonely and exhausted, weighed down by his characters and what seemed like a fruitless attempt to bring one of them to life. The *répétiteur* had been astonished at his command of the German language.

'Of course I can sing the German,' he had snapped. 'My mother was German. My name is Leopold – like one of those Emperors who used to run around here—' He had clicked his fingers trying to remember a distant history lesson.

The phone rang. It was his American agent in New York, confirming a concert engagement two years away.

'I also have a request here from the Friends of the Met for you to give a talk when you're over here next year.'

'I don't do talks,' said Leo.

'I know but you could do this one – it's a Christmas party thing – a charity do.'

'I'll write them a cheque for twice of what a talk would raise—'

'But they want to see you—'

'Why? They see me on stage.'

'Don't be obtuse, Leo. People like a little contact. A few questions and answers. You tell them a few anecdotes.'

'I can't tell stories.'

'Make something up. Learn it the way you learn lyrics.'

'I can't,' said Leo.

When his agent finally gave up trying and hung up, Leo went to the window and looked out at the snow falling down between him and the great grey bulk of the opera house. He did have a story but it was a story he could never tell to anybody.

He thought of calling Kay but he was lonely and a conversation with his wife would only make him lonelier still. He knew that Fritz would be with one of his women. He wanted someone to talk to and couldn't think of anyone in Milan or New York or Munich or any of the cities on his globe-trotting circuit to whom he could talk at that particular moment. He would have liked to talk to Wagner. He would have liked to pick up a phone and call the obnoxious, egocentric composer at his home in Bayreuth or *his* house on the lake in Switzerland and arrange to meet him for dinner at the Sacher. Wagner would appear in one of his favoured blue velvet outfits, drink too much champagne and insist that they both order the expensive Tafelspitz. He would, of course, leave Leo with the bill but it would be worth it. He would have talked to Wagner about their mutual *alter ego* – Wotan.

As far as the singer could make out the head god was having a mid-life crisis in *Die Walküre*, flailing around as so many driven ambitious men suddenly do in middle life. Leo wondered sleepily if Wagner himself had ever had such a crisis, but with the energy of genius, the composer had relaunched himself into life at regular intervals and at fifty was starting all over again with a young wife and a new family. An old familiar sorrow had just touched Leo at that last word when the phone rang.

'I knew you would still be here,' said a woman's

voice. 'I tried to get into the rehearsal room but there's a new doorman—'

'Clara, I was sleeping. I'm exhausted—'

'If you really wanted to rest you would have had your calls screened. Anyway when I saw the snow—'

Why didn't I have my calls screened? Leo wondered. Because I thought that Wagner might drop by for a drink? And instead, as so many times before, I get Clara. He hadn't seen her for several months now, not since a *Faust* in Paris. He wondered if she was still as thin. The older she got the thinner she got. Leo harboured a secret hope that one day she would be so thin that she would disappear from his life for ever.

'Shall I come up?' She wasn't about to disappear tonight.

'No, Clara, please don't. I told you I'm tired—'

'Well then, I'll wait in the bar. Shall I order you a drink? Whisky and water, isn't it? Or perhaps now you're changing your repertoire a white wine would be more appropriate? A Rhine wine?'

'Who told you that?'

'Now why should anyone have to tell me? I know enough about you and your career to understand that it's a natural development.'

'It's not proving that natural,' sighed Leo.

'But you can do it. We both know that. And when you do, you'll be the greatest Wotan this century has seen.'

'But I'm thought of as an Italian – a Verdi specialist. People are only comfortable when they can put other people in categories.' Leo paused, aware that he had slipped into Clara's old trap of alighting on the subject most dear to him at that moment and making him talk about it. And making him talk to her as a consequence. 'I must go, Clara. I need to catch up on my sleep.'

'I'm sure Wagner would have approved of your approach—'

'You don't yet know my approach.'

'It's your energy that he would have loved. Wagner

26

had it and he would have recognized it in you – that immense, raw, white-hot energy.'

'Well, that's all very flattering, Clara, but at the moment I don't even have the energy to come downstairs, so if you'll excuse me I think I'm going to get some sleep.'

'I can come up. We can have dinner in your room.'

'No we can't.' But the phone had gone dead.

Leo grabbed his room key, pulled his shoes on and ran out of the door, intending to waylay Clara at the lift and if necessary frog-march her back out of the hotel. Nothing in his education had prepared a man of his generation to treat a woman in this way. Neither his austere Protestant mother nor his gallant Italian charmer of a father would have approved of what he was about to do.

The corridors of the Sacher are lined with paintings by the Old Masters. Leo was familiar with every cherub, every Madonna, every red-faced, harddrinking Dutch farmer on the canvasses that lined the wall. He had never walked from his room without pausing to look at a detail of sky or a line on a face. Even on his way to a first night when he was sure that the occupants of each room could hear his heart pounding its way along the passage, he would find strength and serenity in the quiet, still worlds that another human hand, long since dust, had set out for him.

He didn't see any of the paintings tonight. He strode to the lift in a few seconds and stood in front of the doors. Three elderly Viennese women, clad in *Lodens* and damp feathered hats, were confronted, upon exiting the lift, with a seething mass of six-foot Italian bass. Two more lifts came and went, discharging German businessmen, a French pianist and the inevitable group of Japanese. Leo, his rage giving way to bewilderment, was about to return to his room when he heard the creak of the fire-exit door that opened onto the stairwell.

'I came up the stairs.' Clara was standing, panting,

behind him. She was thinner than ever. She wore a low-cut velvet dress. The row of sharp little bumps on her sternum made him shudder. 'Climbing stairs is good for the heart, I hear.'

And God help me, she is looking after her heart, thought Leo. He wanted to say, 'Don't, don't bother — just fade silently away,' but the thin, dark daughter of his long-dead impresario seemed to thrive on her regime of glasses of champagne, cigarettes and finger-sandwiches gulped down in operatic intervals as she traipsed from Milan to Munich to the Met.

She extended her cheek for a kiss. Leo didn't move.

'Have you got a menu in your room?' she asked. 'Or shall we go downstairs?'

'I told you, Clara — I don't want to have dinner with you.' For a second the smiling face quivered and looked as though it might crumple. 'I don't want to have dinner with anyone. I'm tired. I'm not hungry. I want to be left alone.'

'I bumped into the *répétiteur* coming down the Kärntnerstrasse. He told me that he was astonished by your German diction.' She was smiling back up at him.

'Well, he shouldn't be.' He had slipped right into the opening of her trap yet again. 'What the hell is he doing talking to you about all that, anyway? I don't want anyone knowing what I'm doing — not for the time being at least.'

'Oh, I told him that you'd talked to me about it.'

Leo lunged forward and grabbed the collar of the velvet dress. With the other hand he rang for the lift, praying that when it came, no pianists, no Japanese or American tourists would be witness to the sight of a celebrated Italian bass throwing a wriggling woman out of the Sacher Hotel by the scruff of her neck. But Clara had stopped wriggling; she had gone limp and slumped to the floor.

Leo bent over her, noting with relief that the elevator had arrived empty. He took the precaution of blocking it open with his shoe. Many, many times in the past he had been provoked to violence with Clara but he had almost always restrained himself. Now he had hardly touched her and she had passed out. But Clara wasn't unconscious. Her eyes had opened; the face had crumpled and Clara was crying. Leo, like a million other men before him, was undone by tears. He released his shoe from the elevator, letting it slide away, and put a reluctant hand on her shoulder.

'I was so happy when I knew you were going into the Wagnerian repertoire,' she wailed. 'I've had this dream of seeing you on the Bayreuth stage for years.'

So have I, thought Leo. He put his arm round her shoulder. Clara lurched forward, pressed her wet cheek against his beard and groped for his hand. Leo let her hold it for a few seconds then politely withdrew it and started trying to pull her gently to her feet. He had to get her out of the hotel corridor before the lift did disgorge a passenger. Clara didn't move.

'I've always thought that Wotan was what your voice was truly destined for,' she murmured as he tried to manoeuvre her limp body. Her breath smelt of stale tobacco. 'For years in my mind's ear I've heard your voice singing those great monologues – saying farewell to his beloved daughter. You would be immensely moving in that scene, wouldn't you?' Clara paused and stared up at him. 'My father knew that. I told him you'd be a Wotan one day. Everybody else had you down as just another great Italian bass—'

'I do know all this, Clara. Now let me take you downstairs. If you want to eat something, I'll have the waiter put it on my room bill but I must get some sleep.'

'There hasn't been a day in my life when I haven't imagined you on the Bayreuth stage.'

'Well, there have been plenty of days in mine when I haven't,' Leo snapped, wanting to add that his life, his career shouldn't have such importance to someone else. He was baffled by the devotion of all those loyal men and women who waited at stage doors in Vienna, Milan, London, Munich and New York, autograph books poised for a signature, asking breathlessly what the next role would be, when he would return to their town, how he felt about a certain production. The years went by and the same faces, pinched and pale in the harsh, white light of a stage door, would ask the same questions. Leo felt a mixture of gratitude and affection for most of them but he was relieved that they didn't have the access to him that Clara's family and wealth accorded her.

He took her down to the hotel restaurant and was about to call the head waiter and tell him to let her order what she wanted and put it on his bill when she started to cry again.

'Now what?' He tried to lead her towards a shadowy corner but she remained in the entrance. The head waiter saw his disarray and led them both to a table on the far side of the room.

Clara kept up a gentle sobbing until they were seated.

'It's just that I've really come all this way to ask a favour, not for me but for someone else. And now you're angry and I've ruined everything and I don't know how I'm going to explain it to them.'

And, as he had known from the moment he had heard her voice on the phone, Leo dalla Vigna found himself eating the Sacher Hotel's Tafelspitz not with Richard Wagner but with Clara Bartholomew. It was of little consolation to him that at some point during the meal they also spoke of Wotan.

Chapter Three

'Can I buy you a drink?' said Rose. She and the blond man were standing in the bar of the amphitheatre.

'Oh, I couldn't touch a thing,' said the man.

Rose ordered a glass of white wine from the bar.

'Well?' said the man when she turned to raise her glass to him. 'Well? Don't you have anything to say? Did you hate it? Did it unfurl too slowly for you? Was it like wading through sludge?'

'There were some slow passages,' said Rose. 'And for lots of the time I was adjusting to being inside this place – I've never been here before – I shouldn't be here now – I'm getting ma—'

'Married tomorrow. So you said. You could always leave if you don't like it.'

Rose swallowed her drink down in one go and ordered another one. She couldn't say to this stranger that when she'd heard the prelude, she had felt that it could go on for ever – as if it had always existed just alongside her, not quite audible but always present, suspended until that moment in a world just beyond her hearing. She didn't dare to express a vague suspicion that as the great ocean of sound had swelled beneath her and carried her up on it, her small, safe existence had receded into that dark, gale-blown night.

'Are you a musician?' she asked the man, hoping to turn his intense attention back to himself.

'No, no,' he sighed. 'Not any more. I never was really – I work in a travel agency – nothing very interesting. I book plane tickets, send people on safaris.'

'But you were a musician – what did you do?'

'Nothing much,' said the man, and turned away

31

from Rose to study an exhibition of framed photos of long-dead singers.

'We haven't been introduced,' said Rose, sensing that she couldn't pursue her questioning but wanting to say something. 'I'm Rose Lorenzo.'

'But not for much longer.' The man smiled and shook her hand. 'I'm Otto Winterbourne.'

'Do you come here often?' laughed Rose. 'But you do, don't you?'

'I've been coming here for almost thirty years. I've attended over twelve hundred performances. Eva knows the exact number. She keeps all the programmes in old suitcases and writes an account of what I thought of each performance in her diary.'

'And is Eva your wife?'

'I told you I've never been married!' snapped Otto Winterbourne. 'Eva is my twin sister. My identical twin.'

'She can't be your identical twin,' said Rose. 'You'd have to be the same sex—'

'Well then, she's the other sort,' said the man. 'I'm sorry but I'm not very good at making conversation during intervals. I hate intervals. It breaks the flow.'

'But you can't expect the average human being to sit for five hours—'

Otto wasn't listening. He had walked over to a small counter where he bought a programme which he handed to Rose.

'Here. Have this as a souvenir of your first time here.'

'Thank you.' Rose flicked through the pages. 'Why are there photos of Venice?'

'Because that's where Wagner wrote *Tristan* and that's where he died – in the Palazzo Vendramin on the Grand Canal. His wife Cosima held him in her arms for twenty-four hours after his death – think about that.'

Again those blue eyes held her gaze and again Rose found herself doing what he said. She tried to imagine Martin or Raul Fernandez, the Spanish businessman whom she'd once briefly loved, dead. All she could think of was the inconvenience that a corpse brought with it. Flies, evacuating bowels, doctors to provide certificates and undertakers to bring coffins. But somewhere in that same world where this extraordinary music resided was a love deep and unrelenting enough not to let go.

A bell was ringing. Once they were sitting alongside each other in the amphitheatre, Rose was free of the blond man's intense stare and could look around her. She noticed that a young child's torso was carved into the front of the boxes at her level and that as the rows descended towards the floor the child grew through girlhood to womanhood. She fell to studying her programme, scared that if she gazed too long, if she gave herself up to it, she would be sucked into this dark, enclosed universe and come to need it far more than it would ever need her. She studied the photo of Venice and thought of Otto's unsettling story of the composer's death.

Death gave way to sex with the return of the orchestra to the pit and the raising of the curtain. As the music washed over her a second time, Rose started to realize that she was in the middle of what felt like an enormous, invisible act of love-making. The two people on stage were fully clothed, were barely touching and yet the solemn, concentrated black-and-white-clad men and women in the orchestra pit were producing an orgasm of sound.

Thirty-two years after that afternoon at the Sunday School Christmas party, music brought ecstasy back to Rose Lorenzo, but the adult Rose was bewildered and overwhelmed by the emotion. Adults aren't allowed to squeal with pleasure in public places – or stick pearls up their noses. Rose was so unsettled by what was happening in the dark as the audience sat in silence around her that she knew she had to leave. Thankful to be on the end of the row, she slipped out and down the stairs into the light of the foyer while the orchestra yearned on behind her.

'Are you all right?' An usher in a burgundy jacket held out his arm.

33

'I can't seem to breathe,' said Rose.

'I'll take you to the St John's people.' Rose found herself sitting in a brightly lit room where a woman in a uniform was making her a cup of tea.

'You were about to faint,' she said.

'Low blood sugar,' muttered Rose. 'I haven't eaten all day.'

'I thought it was the music that made you swoon,' said a St John's man who was standing near the door. 'Young women used to do it a lot in operas in the nineteenth century. The prayer in Rossini's *Moses*, for example – now that always had them reaching for their smelling salts.'

'But we don't get it much now,' said the woman who wore much more make-up than Rose would have expected from a volunteer worker. 'Except when Placido or Carreras are in. Then you get the odd one or two.'

'I don't think I was about to swoon,' said Rose. 'I've been tearing around the West End all day and I wanted to get home but there's a bomb-scare and I got stranded so I came in here on an impulse. I shouldn't be here – I'm getting married tomorrow.'

'Then it's pre-wedding nerves,' said the woman.

'Pre-wedding terror,' said Rose. 'Utter terror. It hit me in there a few minutes ago. Is it normal to be so scared?'

'I wasn't particularly nervous when I got married,' said the woman. 'There again, I've done it three times so I suppose you get used to it.'

'I don't think I could go through this again,' said Rose, sipping her tea.

'Perhaps you don't really want to get married,' said the man. 'Perhaps you haven't found Mr Right.'

'I don't know,' sighed Rose. 'I don't seem to know anything about anything all of a sudden. It would all be so much easier if they gave you a handbook when you were born, or a blueprint or something, don't you think?'

'Babies can't read,' said the man.

34

'Have a biscuit,' said the woman. 'Have several.'

Rose finished the plateful.

'I would like to go back in now,' she said as the woman handed her a second cup of tea.

'Not now,' said the man. 'You'll have to wait until the end of Act Two. You see there's no gaps as such in Wagner – no little pauses for coughing, sneezing, stretching and the like. The punters all just sit in there – rigid!'

'I prefer *Trovatore* myself,' said the woman. 'There's more real tunes in *Trovatore*.'

A few minutes after the second act ended and the foyer filled with chatter and the clatter of coffee-cups, Otto appeared with a plate of sandwiches.

'How did you find me?' said Rose.

'I asked the usherette where the woman with the beautiful green eyes had got to. Did Wagner prove too much for you?'

'Is this – Him?' The St John's woman nudged Rose.

'Oh no, no – I mean he might be very nice – but no, not him, not at all.'

When Rose returned to her seat for the third act, she noticed the people around her for the first time. Apart from a few students there were a lot of grey heads. They behaved with all the rigidity of older English people, tutting and frowning when a latecomer obliged them to rise from their seat, but when the music started up again Rose saw the rapture on those lined faces. These people had sat through that invisible act of love-making that had driven her from the auditorium. And at the end of the opera when Isolde dissolved into death, a woman with a hair-net and a walking-stick wept. Rose was perplexed. These people understood such things. In such meagre lives as many must have had this could not be remembered passion. And so it must be imagined passion. Beneath the hair-nets and behind the dog-collars, were there such rich fantasy lives? Rose wondered. Or was it not so much imagination as something within each of them that only this music could reach?

At the end of the performance as the ocean of sound receded into the air, Rose sat next to Otto Winterbourne unable to think of a word to say. Out in Floral Street she prepared to consult her watch, say, 'I must catch the last train,' and make a quick escape but the blond man was racing ahead of her.

'Are you going towards the tube?' she heard herself saying.

'No,' he said. 'Not yet.'

'Oh well, I'd better.' She wanted to linger but she could feel that he was drawing away from her. His eyes were on a point beyond her shoulders, further down Floral Street. Then he seemed to remember her and again he fixed her with those clear blue eyes. 'But you don't regret coming?'

'Not at all. It was – I don't really know – it was – extraordinary. I can't judge the musical standards. Was it a good performance?'

'Well, Isolde is past it and of course nothing can compare with Bayreuth in '66,' replied Otto.

'And that was good, was it?'

The blond man was standing exactly where he had stood hours earlier when he had accosted her in the windy twilight.

'Good?' he said. He closed his eyes and leaned back against the cream wall. He extended his hand. Rose thought that he had belatedly decided to shake hers. She held out her own hand for a second time but Otto Winterbourne was rolling up the cuff of his blue cardigan.

'Feel my arm,' he whispered.

'What?'

'Feel my arm. Years after the event I still get goose-pimples at the memory of that evening. Look!' He gazed down at his own slender forearm. 'Feel!' Rose patted his wrist.

'You see!'

Otto's attention had wandered beyond her again. He rolled his sleeve back down and turned to walk along Floral Street.

'I must go,' he said.

'So must I,' said Rose, who suddenly didn't want to go anywhere. She wanted to say, 'Where are you going? Can I come with you?' But the man was moving away.

Rose felt in her handbag.

'Here's my card,' she said. 'It's got my current address and I've written my married address alongside it. Do look me up if ever you are in the area.'

'You'll be a bit far out at this married address. I don't move around London much – apart from coming here. Are you sure you should get married?'

'Of course – I mean – it's all arranged. We're having a very small ceremony – but even that takes all sorts of preparation – that's why my shoulder is lopsided—'

But the man's attention had drifted off down Floral Street again.

'Goodbye, Rose Lorenzo.' He clasped her hand. 'And good luck, whatever you decide to do.'

When Rose awoke the next morning, she noticed that her shoulder had stopped aching for the first time in weeks. She went to the mirror and saw that the slight hunch had gone. Then she remembered that it was her wedding day. Without waiting to eat breakfast or even make some tea, she picked up the phone and made three phone calls – to Martin, to her mother and to Daphne. Between each call she leaned back against the wall with her eyes closed, took a deep breath, then picked up the receiver and dialled again.

Daphne was out. Rose guessed that beautiful, organized blonde Daphne would be at the hairdresser's where she herself should have been on such a day – but she had forgotten to make an appointment. She decided to walk to the salon. It was over an hour away but the brief conversation with Martin had left her pacing the apartment and chewing at the skin around her fingernails. Far better to plunge her gnawed hands into her pockets and walk through the cold November air past trees and houses and strangers.

When she arrived in front of Gianni di Firenze's salon window, she saw Daphne sitting in front of a mirror as Gianni wove pearls through her sister's thick, yellow tresses. Pearls again, and in a more appropriate place.

The blonde head turned to face her.

'Rose! What are you doing here?' She read her sister's lips through the glass.

'I'm not getting married.' If only I could turn away now, thought Rose, and walk off into the wind. But Daphne followed her. She strode straight out into the High Street with her pink towel still around her shoulders and half her head dappled with pearls.

'What do you mean?'

'I can't,' said Rose. 'And I can't explain.'

'Is there someone else?' Daphne had to hold on to the towel with one hand and the pearls with the other.

'I don't think so,' said Rose, gazing down the High Street deep in thought. 'Something else, more than someone, but I don't know what.'

Daphne burst into tears.

'I just read in a magazine that at your age a woman has more chance of being blown up by a terrorist bomb than of getting married. And I was imagining the four of us getting together to rent one of those Tuscan villas where you always need loads of people and I was so glad that you were going to be an even number instead of odd – always bloody odd – and now here you are—'

'You really must stop reading those women's magazines, you know. Can't we go inside somewhere?' Rose took her sister by the arm and led her to a pizzeria across the street.

'Have you told Martin?' said her sister. 'What did he say?'

'He said, "Did I need time to think?" '

'And of course you do! That's all you need is a few days to get over your nerves.' Daphne started to remove the pearls from her blonde braids.

'Well, I said that perhaps that might help and he said

that he couldn't give me time. He felt that at my age I'd had time enough.' Rose watched as her sister released the last pearls and her blonde hair fell onto her shoulders.

'Oh, Daphne, why are you so blond and proper and pure and English?' she blurted out, feeling suddenly unclean, dark and devious. 'Why can't my life follow a nice, straight line the way yours has?'

'Because you run it off the rails at every opportunity,' said her sister. 'Because you are Father's daughter, because you got the Spanish blood and I got the English. Most children of mixed marriages are half and half but when nothing of our father manifested itself in me – well, he must have been feeling neglected, left out – so he poured himself into you.'

The waitress brought their coffees.

'You're wayward and difficult, Rose,' said her sister. 'What do you want?'

An answer came to Rose's lips but she couldn't say it – not sitting in the pizzeria drinking coffee with a sister still clad in a bright pink towel. She stared unseeing at the Saturday shoppers in the wind-blown High Street. I want something that is contained in that music, she thought, and stirred her coffee and ignored her sister who was still talking on the other side of the table. I've never experienced it but I know about it, just as last night's old ducks with walking-sticks knew.

'And, of course, it's all right being alone in winter,' Daphne was saying, 'but wait until the light nights come.'

Rose thought she had said, 'White knights' and leaned forward, keen to hear the rest.

'When the long summer evenings are here, there's no place for a lone woman – on holidays, at barbecues and the rest—'

'There is a lifetime between here and next summer,' said Rose with such conviction that she surprised herself.

'And you've thrown away your last chance of having

a child,' said Daphne. 'A woman is only a quarter as fertile at your age, anyway—'

'Then I'll have to do it four times as often!'

'Who with?' smiled Daphne, triumphant.

'I don't know,' sighed Rose.

'You have no idea of what you've done, have you?'

'Probably not. I want to go home, Daphne. I want to be alone and think, or perhaps not think. I just want to sit quietly for a few hours.'

'But your home isn't going to be yours in a few days. Have you thought about that?' said her sister.

Rose hadn't. She hadn't thought beyond the enormous energy that not doing something involved. Her sister was right. Her belongings were due to be moved out to her new home the following week. And in impatient, cramped London a new tenant would be carrying his tea-chests and suitcases up the stairs as hers were carried down.

'Would you like to stay with us?' asked her sister.

'Thanks but I'll work something out,' said Rose.

She went home by taxi. The driver seemed to think she was a tourist and took it upon himself to point out places of interest along the route. Rose leaned forward and slid the glass partition open, wishing that she could stay for ever inside the warm cab. Perhaps they could just drive on like this for days, years, with the cabbie naming the landmarks as they sailed across the planet, giving her good solid facts about unmoving, unchanging things of stone. Rose thought of how much she'd always envied those brave, fictional souls who could ride their lives off into the sunset. Oh, the euphoria of sudden change, and oh, the consequences – the barren wastes to be crossed alone, the ravines, the dark woods that lay ahead.

When she stepped out of the warm taxi a light sleet was slanting in on the east wind. The digital clock on the taxi's dashboard said four o'clock. She should have been sitting down to her wedding high tea. She turned her back on the freezing flurries as she paid the driver and walked inside. I won't bend body and soul against this wind, she thought as she was buffeted along the front path. I'll let it carry me where it will. Not for the first time that day, Rose had the conviction that she had embarked on a journey. And yet she had returned to her very ordinary rented apartment where nothing more awaited her than an evening of phone calls carrying the disarray and disapproval of her friends. Once inside her flat, she took the phone off the hook and put the emerald dress in a long plastic wrapper from the dry-cleaners.

Now, she thought as she hung it up in the wardrobe and fought off an increasingly familiar wave of terror and exhilaration, now anything can happen.

Chapter Four

That first snowstorm of the winter had missed the town of Bellagio on Lake Como where Leo dalla Vigna's villa lay on a secluded headland. A lot of weather missed Bellagio, the pearl of the Italian lakes as the tourist brochures liked to call it. This had influenced Leo's choice in renting a villa there twenty-five years earlier. The common cold lurking behind a loved one's smile, the weather outside and the air-conditioning inside are a twentieth century opera singer's preoccupations. When Leo sang his first season at La Scala, he had moved his young American wife into the villa on the lake. Once he had established a name for himself, he had intended to move out and take her back to one of the dull but strangely comforting towns in his home province of Emilia Romagna.

Then their small daughter had died and Kay had refused to leave the only place that the child's brief life had touched. Leo had been desperate to get away from the oversized, ornate house with its one small ghost and its marble staircases, its damp rooms staring out on the sullen lake, its blind stone statues and what he considered to be ludicrous topiary. How he hated the green privet hens that greeted him each time he came back from Milan or Vienna or London. But his excuse that the rent was too expensive had become invalid when he had been taken on by Clara's father, the great impresario, and secured contracts at the Met and La Scala.

Leo had continued to dream of Emilia Romagna. He missed the human scale of towns like Parma and Bologna; he missed the Marie-Thérèse yellow of Parma and the arcades of Bologna. He even missed the giant plastic wedges of Parma cheese that lined the country roads to advertise its most famous export.

As a Verdi bass he had thought it only natural that he stay in the region that had fathered the old Maestro. He had even considered buying a small estate near provincial little Bussetto, the town that had fostered the composer. He had naïvely imagined having more children, settling in a rambling house looking out on the Po valley; there was even a dog in the scenario and mushrooming trips in the autumn. He would be a wise, kind father and pass his music on to his children. Sunday afternoon pilgrimages would be made to Verdi's villa at St Agata. With his children he would relive that first thrilling moment when he had walked into that stuffy, dark Victorian interior and stood in the room where the old man had breathed life into *Don Carlos* and *Otello* and *Falstaff*. In his old age he would give master-classes at the little opera house in Bussetto.

It took many years for Leo to realize that it was always autumn in these dreams – always the time for the turtle-doves to gather on the wires and for the mushrooms to be gathered in the woods – always these imaginings were tinged with the pink smoke of an Emilia Romagnan harvest. And when the dreams didn't become reality, he privately comforted himself that he was still in the deep green high summer of his life – that autumn was still too far down the road, that all was still possible.

But the other children could never be born now. During that first year of grieving he and Kay had made desperate love in their efforts to replace the dead child and failed. When they learned it could never be, sex for sex's sake seemed pointless. He had suggested that they adopt. Kay refused and drifted away from his body towards beautiful infallible objects. She filled the villa on the lake with fine carpets, Sèvres vases, and English antique furniture.

Leo dreamed less and less of those flat, friendly plains further south. He acquired a passing interest in astronomy which permitted him on his brief

43

homecomings to seclude himself in a room at the top of the house and stare off into the heavens. One night he calculated that the window where his expensive telescope was situated, pointed directly towards Leipzig, birthplace of Richard Wagner. This became a small and secret justification for the direction he hoped his career would take.

Unbeknown to Leo, one of his youthful ambitions had been realized as he slept through that snowy night in Vienna. The silent villa had acquired a dog. Kay had returned from a trip to an antique-dealer friend in Como with the friend's miniature Pekinese tucked into the pocket of her sheepskin jacket. The antique dealer was off to live with his lover in Eton and had just discovered that the dog could not accompany him. Kay had been terrified of the wheezy little life that had suddenly become her responsibility. She tucked it carefully into her pocket and then almost sat on it when she climbed into the car.

The next morning when she woke, Kay was still not sure that she would keep it. She hated the way its heart beat so close to its chest wall and she thought the wheezy breathing would drive her to distraction. She hadn't thought about Leo's reaction. Leo had dreamed of a dog that would walk for miles across the Po plain with him – a dog that would swim in the streams where he had swum as a boy. The Pekinese had very short legs and asthma-like panic attacks when taken near water. But Kay was feeling rebellious. Leo, she said to herself, is not here enough to notice if I had a pet hippopotamus in the bedroom. She locked the dog in the house and went out for her morning swim.

The villa had a V-shaped wooden deck on the tip of the headland just in front of the library window from which Kay could dive straight into the frigid blue water below. Kay swam naked and she swam in all weathers. The lake never froze enough to prevent that first elegant swoop into its waters every day at 8 a.m. Even in the depths of winter when the night still lapped against the wooden deck and she could barely

44

make out the water below, Kay would dive. She knew the peak tourist times when a speedboat might whip past her but they rarely came this far away from the comforting babble of the village resorts. The colder the water and the weather the more Kay liked it for she had been raised in Minnesota where the snow rose three feet high and lasted six months long.

She donned a pair of rubber sandals and a red towelling bathrobe and walked across the deck enjoying the spring in her stride as the rubber hit the wood. A few feet from the tip of the headland, she flung off the bathrobe and skipped out of the sandals. Today Kay did an elegant back-flip, and if the little dog that gazed mournfully at her from the window had been interested it would have seen that the same pale blonde hair grew between her legs, that she had a taut flat stomach and just one small, round, dark-pink nippled breast.

Kay was convinced that the almost invisible scar where her right breast had been would disappear completely if she continued to freeze her body in the glacial winter waters of the lake. When the water had started to warm in the spring after the operation, she had found herself imagining that with summer warmth and blooming the breast might grow again.

She stayed under the water for a long time. This was also a morning ritual. When she re-emerged she knew that her first sight would be of the distant mountains on the far side of the lake. She knew every change in the colour of those summits. That first morning view was underlined by the freezing water, lapping around her chin. In winter when the cold had taken her breath away and her teeth chattered as she came up to the surface and trod water, the lake lay leaden grey, the sky as leaden above it and the mountains dirty white in the distance. In spring when the water was a gentler blue a line of pink and orange azaleas stretched along the banks of that distant shore. They looked almost luminous in the young fresh light of the new season, and most definitely frivolous – these exuberant blooms slipping in between the stern mountains and the solemn wrinkled lake.

Today the water was gold. The retreating sunrise still shed gold on the cream façade of the house. Yellow leaves of birch and russet leaves of beech had settled on the surface of the water. Kay had to pick a birch leaf from her mouth as she surfaced. But she couldn't see the mountain. She rubbed her eyes and realized that she must have got turned around after the back-flip. Two anxious black eyes were staring back at her from her bedroom window. For the first time in twenty years, Kay cut her morning swim short. She scooped up her sandals and robe and ran back to the house and the small shivering dog in the bedroom.

When the young American music student who worked as odd-job man arrived an hour later, the sound of his key in the latch was greeted by another, louder sound for the first time since he took the job. Like several of his predecessors John Tillson had been bitterly disappointed by the silence of the great singer's house. He had been eager to take up the part-time post, imagining himself waxing the floors to the accompaniment of the death of Boris Godunov or feather-dusting the chandeliers to the champagne aria from *Don Giovanni*. But every time he saw Leo, the man had a suitcase in his hand and was either headed up to the big dark bedroom upstairs that was not included in John's chores or out of the door into an airport-bound taxi.

On one of the many days when both Leo and Kay were absent John had taken the opportunity to study the library where they spent their evenings, if they chose to spend them together. Outside his college library John had never seen a room with walls so densely lined with books. But where was the music? he wondered. There was, he knew, a grand piano but this was up in the music-room on the first floor that was out of bounds to John. Anyway he was looking for recordings – to see what the man listened to, whom he admired. He had not understood that, as with so many people who make music, Leo felt very little need to listen to it.

Even the seventh of December, the feast of Saint Ambrose, the patron saint of Milan, that marks the opening of La Scala, had passed through the villa in silence. John had been thrilled to be hired to work at the dalla Vigna household just weeks before this date. He knew that Leo was playing Philip the Second in Verdi's *Don Carlos* and he'd nurtured a vague dream of witnessing some part of the preparations but Leo had decided to stay in Milan for the duration of rehearsals rather than risk the icy, treacherous drive along the lake shore. Kay had been busy with the purchase of an Elizabethan tester bed that was being sent from Stow-on-the-Wold in England and seemed to occupy all her time with phone calls and papers from Customs. John had waited patiently but when December the seventh had come around and *Il Corriere Della Sera* had featured interviews with the Maestro and the producer, he had lingered over piling the logs up in the grate and waited for Kay to leave for Milan or at least turn on the radio.

'Are you not going to Milan, Mrs dalla Vigna?'

'Hah! The seventh of December at La Scala is *una brutta serata*,' laughed Kay and seeing his puzzled expression had added, 'You had better get to work on your Italian, John dear. That means literally that it is an ugly evening. All those politicians, all those dowagers drooping under the weight of their emeralds, all the high-class tarts, not to mention the hysterical Milanese queens; no, no honey, I have been to enough of those to last me a lifetime. So has poor old Leo.' She went on quickly, seeing the disappointment on John's face, 'He's always glad to be on the other side of the footlights so he doesn't have to get too close to that lot. And *Don Carlos* is so gloomy.' She was, John noticed, talking faster and faster. 'All that Spanish Inquisition stuff and heretic-burning. And anyway, I couldn't go because – well – no, come and see.' And she had led him to a large room at the end of a corridor.

'It was delivered this morning – you know what shippers are like – they can never say exactly when they will come.' She opened the door.

'A four-poster!'

'No, John – a tester bed. That carved panel at the top is called a tester – that's what differentiates it from a four-poster. It is an Elizabethan tester bed.' Her pale face and blond hair stood out against the sombre brown wood. 'I know it sounds silly but because it is just here and new and in a strange place after travelling all over Europe with its four hundred years of history being bashed around by the movers, well, I didn't like to leave it.

'Now of course, Elizabeth was on the throne at the same time as Philip of Spain,' she had said as they walked back into the kitchen. 'That means that this bed was being carved by skilled English hands while Philip was brooding on his problems down in the Escorial. You must remind me to tell Leo about that when he comes home tomorrow. It will please him.'

John, who was quite literally entranced by his employer's beauty, was also a good God-fearing American boy and this last loving thought for Leo had pleased and reassured him. All was well in this big, beautiful house but, he had noticed, Kay made no attempt to turn the radio on that evening. And the house remained silent through all the months that followed.

This late autumn morning, however, as he opened the door, he was greeted with a loud repeated 'Yap!'

The yap got closer as Kay opened the kitchen door.

'I just made some coffee, John. Would you like some?' Kay had always just made coffee, and always offered him a cup as he walked through the door. He put his battered leather case down in the entrance hall and walked towards the kitchen.

'Do you have a lesson today?' Kay poured him a large cup of weak American coffee.

'No, just practice – I'm going to my teacher's house to practise on a grand – the upright in my room makes the most awful sound.'

'Yap!'

John knew now that this sound was in the kitchen. Kay ignored it.

'What a pity our grand isn't downstairs. Then you could take a couple of hours in the afternoon and play on that. I'll have to talk to Leo about getting it moved down one day. It seems a crime for it to sit up in that damp room on the lake—'

'Yap!'

Kay had frequently offered to get the piano brought downstairs; the piano stayed upstairs. He let her voice fade into the background and focused on that other, more alien sound. It was coming from behind the enormous old-fashioned cast-iron range.

'I wasn't going to tell you about this because I don't want you saying anything to Leo.' Kay pulled a small, beige, wheezing Pekinese out from the window-ledge behind the range. As she came closer, John could smell hot fur. 'I want it to be a surprise for him.'

'For his dinner?' said John. 'Mrs dalla Vigna, you've just about cooked that little dog.'

'Oh, I don't think so,' said Kay looking very, very hurt. 'I just wanted it to be warm.'

John ran his hand against the dog's hot rump. He knew from Kay's wounded expression that he must not pursue the subject but he stepped back towards the cooler end of the kitchen and succeeded in drawing Kay and the overheated little dog with him.

'I got him from that young Italian count who has the antique store down in Como,' she was saying. 'He refused to tell me his name, saying that I must rename him without any prior influence so that he would become truly mine – well, ours—'

The phone rang.

'Will you get that?' Kay was holding the dog tight against her chest.

Clutching it to her heart, thought John, and he wanted the thought to be cynical; this was, after all, a rich, spoiled woman with nothing to do but fret over a yappy dog. But the thought turned out to be tender and full of affection. John adored his employer. At night he had strange troubling dreams about her but he never let himself think of them during the day. He picked up the phone. It was Leo.

'Hello, Signor dalla Vigna.' Kay pointed to the dog and pretended to zip up her mouth with her thumb and forefinger.

'Ciao, John, is my wife there?' John always felt a thrill when he heard Leo on the phone. Operatic basses invariably have the most impressive speaking voices and Leo's warm, grave, resonant tones always made him want to prolong the conversation. Kay was signalling to him that she was not available and that he should say just that.

'She's out by the lake at the moment,' John improvised. 'Shall I call her or can I take a message?'

'Tell her I called from Vienna – we've had a blizzard and I'm stranded at the Sacher.'

'Why isn't he at the Bristol?' whispered Kay who was listening to the conversation. John shrugged. He wasn't about to quiz Leo on his choice of hotels.

'I have a couple of days before I head back to London so I may break the journey with a night at the house. I'd like to stop and pick up my snow-boots. It's a pity I couldn't get out last night. The *Tosca* tenor chartered a small jet to get him down to La Scala. I could have begged a lift off him.'

John Tillson loved these conversations. He could guess at the identity of the tenor. Legendary Italian tenors, private jets, La Scala – just to hear these words uttered in that splendid bass voice at the end of a long-distance phone line, he would have swept a thousand floors and carted a hundred tons of aubergines and tomatoes back from the market.

'Why doesn't he just buy new boots?' sighed Kay. Her right hand was clamped over the dog's flat, wrinkled black nose.

John shrugged again.

'Tell her I'll call first thing in the morning when I know which flight I'm on,' said Leo and was gone.

'He'll be on Austrian Airlines,' said Kay. 'We always go through the ritual of wait-listing on Alitalia but he doesn't trust them – they're Italian like him, you see.'

When Kay released the dog's nose, it had a sneezing fit that went on for so long that they both became convinced that it would die of some horrible Pekinese version of asthma. Kay placed the dog on a cushion on the floor and they both peered at it, and occasionally at each other, as the little body writhed and shuddered. When it did finally stop, the dog seemed none the worse for its dramatic experience and fell asleep on the cushion in the middle of the kitchen floor, snoring loudly.

Chapter Five

When Clara returned from Vienna, she had to enter her house by the back window. A pile of newspapers had fallen in front of the door six months earlier and prevented her entering the house by the traditional method. Clara had become adept at loosening the putty on the pane and clambering into her dining-room. On the first of many such entrances, she had put her high-heeled shoe through a Louis XV chair, ripping the red velvet and forcing the springs to the floor. She had never quite found the time to call in an upholsterer and the chair had remained in its precarious place by the window. Many an unsuspecting great conductor and celebrated singer had sat in that chair, their backsides sliding to within inches of the floor and their arms and legs poking out of the top in a cloud of dust.

Clara landed in it now, but because she was wearing her winter boots her foot didn't get enmeshed in the usual tangle of velvet and springs and she could bounce off and onto the Persian rug, narrowly missing an open can of cat food. Clara's Siamese had moved in with the people across the street months earlier but she had continued to buy the food in the hope it might return.

It was only three o'clock but the house was already November gloomy. Even she had to admit that the smell of cat food had become overpowering. She had filled three large plastic bags with opened Whiskas tins, the contents of overflowing ashtrays and mildewed newspapers when she found an article on Verdi and the father/daughter relationship in an old Covent Garden programme. She raked through the piles of music magazines, found other articles on the same theme, and sat down to read them among the piles of rubbish. Only after midnight was she ready to climb into her unmade bed.

Once into her nightdress, she picked up the phone and started to dial Otto. She had rung the number and dragged a sleeping stranger from his bed when she remembered that Otto was no longer on the phone. She rang directory enquiries, got the number of the Pakistani who ran the late-night grocery store at the end of Otto's street and rang him. Once she had informed him of the urgency of the situation and ensured that he would trudge through the cold night to Otto's house, she continued her reading. At ten to two the phone rang.

'Clara! A charming Muslim gentleman has just knocked on my door to inform me that I should call you regarding my mother's death,' said Otto at the end of a poor line. 'His teeth were chattering with the cold. His voice trembled with sympathy. How could I tell the man that his concern was much appreciated but twenty years too late?'

'I've got a special guest for you. I just had dinner with him in Vienna at the Sacher,' said Clara. 'He's agreed to come to that little society thing of yours.'

'Not him? Really? He'll come and give a talk? To the OAS?'

'Sunday night. You'd better be ready—'

'Sunday night! I'll never—'

'And get that sister of yours to freshen the place up—'

'That's uncalled for! She does her best—'

'This is a man who stays in suites at the Crillon and the Sacher. He won't want to find one of your sister's long white hairs in his wineglass. And make sure there's some decent food. None of the bridge rolls and sweet cheap Riesling your little society usually serves.'

'If we're such a squalid bunch down here, why did you do this for us?' asked Otto. 'If we're so lowly, why did you waste your time getting him to come down here?'

'Because I feel sorry for you.'

'Oh, that's cruel.'

'Do you want me to cancel it then, Otto? It's no skin off my nose. If you must know I think you do a good job with your little music club—'

'Stop calling it little! We've got lots of members,' Otto's voice echoed through the sleeting London night.

'Most of them on Zimmer-frames as far as I can make out,' said Clara. 'You'd better start a new membership drive before the current bunch keel over—'

Otto wasn't listening.

'Do you really think I do a good job?'

'Excellent.'

'I'll do a wonderful interview with Leo. I've followed every inch of his career. And because he never gives talks there's no chance of repetition. Are you sure he'll come?'

'At seven p.m. on Sunday evening.'

'But he'll want a fee, won't he? Can we afford him?'

' "Give the takings to Cancer Relief," he said. Can you manage that?'

'Of course.'

'Oh, and he wants me to be on the platform in a sort of chairwoman capacity,' said Clara.

'You? But I usually do that.'

'Well, we'll both do it. I can be a kind of back-up in case you dry up.'

'But there's so much to say. It's such an honour,' said Otto. 'I won't dry up.'

'It wouldn't be the first time,' said Clara.

'That is so cruel—' Otto started to say but Clara interrupted.

'I might be able to get you tickets for La Scala.'

'Not the opening? Not the seventh of December?'

'Probably in the orchestra stalls – so make sure that Eva doesn't wear her crêpe knee bandages and her Hush Puppies.'

'Oh, I will, I will,' said Otto trying to calculate the price of air tickets and hotel rooms. He didn't dare refuse the seats but he knew that Clara had no notion of his limited resources.

'And I've brought you two Sacher cakes fresh from

the Sacher itself. I thought they would be a nice addition to the Leo evening.'

'But they won't keep that long,' said Otto, relieved to deal with a small familiar subject like cake and abandon the column of figures that was erecting itself in his head.

'I've put them in the freezer. The chef at the Sacher said I could.' Clara knew that the cakes were still downstairs in her flight bag, but she was suddenly tired of Otto. 'I'll talk to you before Sunday,' she said, and as the voice at the other end started to thank her again, she hung up, pulled the covers over her head and slept.

During the night, Siegfried, the Siamese, climbed in through the still-open dining-room window, prized apart the white box from the Sacher Hotel and devoured both cakes. He stayed in the house just long enough to vomit on the Persian rug, then left and returned to his comfortable new residence across the street.

Chapter Six

Leo dalla Vigna sat at the kitchen table of his Bellagio villa reading the *Corriere* in a frayed, brown towelling dressing-gown that kept falling open to the waist and revealing the black hair on his broad chest. The singer's informality and the reverence that the young American had for him were a dangerous combination for John Tillson. Petrified into silence, he clutched the coffee percolator and prayed for Kay to come in and fill the kitchen with her blondness and her light and talk about tester beds and Sèvres vases. But Kay had rushed out of the house before his arrival. The Pekinese had had another sneezing fit the previous day and been packed into its basket and driven off to the vet's, where it had spent the night. Kay had phoned John to say that she was going to collect it and that he should say nothing to Leo because she wanted to surprise him with the dog when she came back.

'Are you making coffee, John, or just hugging the pot?'

John put the percolator on the table. He knew that Leo wasn't comfortable when he poured his coffee for him, but even approaching the table entailed looking right at his employer who was absorbed in the sports page of the *Corriere* and hadn't noticed that his dressing-gown had now gaped even further open to reveal denser black hair below his navel.

The man was quite naked beneath the old brown robe John realized, and prayed for Kay to come in. His fellow students were fascinated by the intimacy with the great singer that John's job offered him.

'Does he have balls down to his knees?' a horn

player from Naples once asked. 'I always imagine basses as being hung like cart-horses.'

'I've never seen him naked,' John had replied, praying that he never would. He had been thrilled at the prospect of getting closer to Leo and Kay. Now it made him uncomfortable. His friends' bawdy teasing brought out the puritan lying just below the surface in John. He felt protective of Leo and wanted him to remain an almost mythical figure. He repelled his friends' questions, fearing that something of the aura that surrounded the singer would evaporate, that the *double entendres* and the salacious references would spill over and soil even Verdi himself.

'But he is one big old boy, isn't he?' insisted the horn player.

'He doesn't have an ounce of fat.' John's voice sounded high and reedy as he defended him. 'He is just kind of massive. It's all solid.'

'Sure but that still means that pretty little blonde lady must have to get on top,' added a young baritone. 'And ride the big old guy like a brewery shire-horse.'

John, to his shame, had often thought of this. Leo's near nakedness brought an image of Kay's pale beauty, pink and vulnerable beneath all that flesh, hair and muscle. Or on top, as the baritone had said, riding him and loving it.

Some mornings, Leo smelled of an expensive cologne. John had spent a Saturday morning in a Milan department store, sniffing at the flacons on the male cologne counter, and had identified it as being by Christian Dior. He had used his healthy, blond, American good looks to charm the sales girl into giving him a sample and then decided that wearing the same cologne as Leo was 'sappy' and tucked it away in a drawer. One day, he had leaned over Leo to hand him his mail and noticed that this smell seemed to emanate from the man's thick neck, from some warm point beneath the grey-flecked beard. He imagined that rough beard rubbing up against Kay's soft breasts and was envious and deeply aroused.

From where he stood by the sink, he could see out onto the deck with the lake and mountains beyond. Great grey clouds covered the peaks.

'I think there's snow headed this way,' he said to Leo. The *Corriere* rustled.

'No word of it in the weather forecast,' said Leo, scowling at a map of Europe. 'We don't get snow down here.'

'I know those clouds, Signor dalla Vigna. When I was at college in New York State, they meant blizzards.'

Leo put his paper down and came to stand at the window next to John.

'*Che bello! E quasi Wagneriano.*' John was used to Leo reverting to Italian whenever he expressed enthusiasm. He wanted to tell him that he had missed the point, that he was trying to warn him of the gathering snowstorms, of all their implications of delayed aircraft and closed roads. John kept a close watch on Leo's schedule and knew that he had to be in Covent Garden the following day.

'But it's coming this way,' said John.

Leo put his broad hand on the American's shoulder.

'This isn't your Midwest, John. I've never seen snow here.'

John waited until he could politely slip away from Leo's grasp and walked towards the front door. He knew that he would never get used to the more tactile Italian society. Just that morning a ticket-collector on the ferry had put his arm around him to apologize for a delay on the boat from Como. And a woman had stood so close to him in the line at the bank that he thought she was about to climb on his back. Only Kay had a similar need for space around her, he had noticed. And it was Kay that he sought now as he busied himself with shaking out the front-door mat.

An hour passed. He had done all the meagre chores that he could find to fill the time and still Kay didn't come. John's actual duties in the house were vaguely defined.

'Nothing that would harm your hands,' was all Leo had said when Kay introduced him. A cleaning woman came in three times a week and scrubbed floors and bath-tubs. She had access to the upstairs rooms where John had never set foot. He often thought that he earned his salary for being an amiable American presence always willing to go on a shopping trip or to filter telephone calls.

As he stared out of the window at the green privet hens by the wrought-iron gate and watched for the grey BMW to round the corner, he realized that he had never been completely alone in the house with Leo. He couldn't have said if that realization had come before he heard Leo's voice echoing down the staircase, or if the first notes had set his brain to thinking that, because Leo was alone in the house, he had taken the opportunity to sing.

At first he sang no recognizable aria, just ran through a few vocal exercises, but as John tiptoed across the hall and seated himself halfway up the staircase, Leo launched into Philip's great aria from *Don Carlos*: *Ella giammai m'amò*. He accompanied himself on the piano – that perfectly tuned grand that Kay had so often promised to let John play. Leo played very well indeed, John was forced to admit, and the old familiar envy was about to spring up when Leo's voice seemed to fill the stairwell and the hall and pick up all his grubby, mediocre feelings of resentment and jealousy and sweep them away. He felt his neat blond hair rise on the nape of his neck until he thought the back of his head had been lifted clean off. And then he felt only what the lonely old king was feeling: all the bleakness and desolation of power bought at the price of love.

When the aria was over, silence descended once more on the house. John guessed that Leo must be sitting gathering his forces to start again. He waited on the stair, his head turned towards the music-room, trying to guess what would come next. Then he heard the sound of Leo's brisk, heavy footsteps in the

59

corridor. He scuttled off down the stairs and hid in the small telephone alcove in the stairwell. Kay had decorated it in green brocade with two green silk upholstered benches that faced each other, saying that she wanted it to feel like the inside of a sedan-chair. She had succeeded and John had never been able to order cheese from the grocer or phone a plumber without expecting liveried footmen to pick him up and whisk him down the driveway. Now he sat on one of the benches and held his breath.

'John!' he heard Leo's voice at the top of the stairs. 'John! Are you still around?' John couldn't have said why he didn't reply. He felt like . . . what did you call the aural equivalent of a voyeur? Because Leo never sang in the house, he felt guilty listening to him, as though he had crept upstairs and peered through the keyhole to the bedroom. He heard Leo walk to the window. He guessed that he was looking to see if his bike was still there and remembered with relief that he had chained it to an iron rail on the other side of one of the privet hens. He listened as Leo coughed, cleared his throat several times and went back to the music-room.

When John heard the piano again, the sound was more muffled but he didn't dare leave the alcove. Leo's voice was muffled too and for a few seconds John's mind struggled to recognize the piece that he was singing. Not a late Verdi, certainly not an early Verdi, not a Puccini, nor the French repertoire that he had heard the singer didn't care for. Leo was singing in German and he was singing Wagner.

John slipped out of the alcove and stood just below the banister. He had been right. Leo was singing Wotan's farewell to his erring daughter Brünnhilde in *Die Walküre*. The young American stood, tensed against the stairwell, not daring to move. Leo didn't sing Wagner. Leo was an Italian bass, as far removed from the dense dark forests and the ecstatic summits of Wagnerian opera as were the flat farmlands of his Emilian homeland. What had old man Verdi himself said of Wagner's music? 'Write *that* music under *this* sky?'

But Leo was singing that music under a sky almost halfway between the two composers' homelands. And he was singing it magnificently. His diction was perfect and it seemed to John that he brought the carefully built line of Italian bel canto to Wagner and rendered it more beautiful than any of the numerous recordings the young American had listened to in his days at college. He'll never sing straight through it, thought John. He'll never *get* straight through it, but Leo sang on, passing through the rapturous moment when Wotan realizes that by bestowing vulnerable humanity on his goddess daughter he is making possible a new world order, to the tender poignant strains of his final farewell to the only person he has ever truly loved.

As soon as the last note faded, John crept from the house on trembling legs and ran towards his bike. He had to tell somebody what he had just heard. He climbed astride the bike and rode in a very crooked line towards the Bellagio ferry.

Leo didn't hear him leave the house. He was sitting immobile at the piano, astonished by the beauty of what he had just done. This was not vanity. Like so many celebrated interpreters of music and drama, Leo knew when he had given a poor performance and he was equally aware of having produced something of beauty. He didn't believe in self-deprecation because he didn't believe that what he did was entirely himself. His better performances always left him with a feeling of standing back with the audience, as enraptured as they by what had just issued from him. Once in a recital in Vienna, when the applause had gone on to the point where he suspected it of being self-perpetuating, and he had no soprano or conductor to share the tumult with him, he had found himself wanting to hold up his hand and say, 'It is not Leo dalla Vigna that you are applauding. Understand this. It is something that exists independent of me, something that I have in my care that I can convey to you.'

Now in his vast, silent house on the lake, there was no audience, no orchestra, just Leo and his piano and the music of Wagner. He had sung through the farewell without the text and was again astonished to realize just how well he knew the piece. He had been working on it in secret for several months, and two days before in Vienna it had seemed set to elude him for ever. Now almost unbidden, in the late autumn half-light, Wotan had welled up from within him. He forgot to turn on the light as he sat in the darkening room with the last yellow rays of the weak November sun disappearing behind the distant mountain. Hardly able to believe what he had just done, he decided to play through the farewell again, peering at the score in the dark room, too absorbed in the music to remember to stand up and turn on a light.

Kay's BMW drew up only minutes after John left. The Pekinese had been given a tranquillizer for the journey home and was sleeping soundly in the pocket of her sheepskin coat. She saw the unlit windows, their shutters still open to the cold mountain air, and was disappointed that the young American had gone without seeing her and the dog. She had decided upon a name for her pet on the drive home and had wanted John's opinion. And where was Leo? He had taken an early morning flight from Vienna and headed for bed to catch up on his sleep only minutes after kissing her hello. He's probably been called away to some god-damned theatre, thought Kay, but when she turned off the car engine, she heard his voice coming from the music-room. He was singing a piece of music she had never expected to hear in her home.

She let herself into the house, pulled the dog's basket from under the green brocade bench in the alcove and bundled the sleeping dog into it. Then she ran upstairs and turned on the light in the music-room. Leo stopped singing immediately and turned to face her. There was tenderness in his expression but Kay was sure that it sprang from what he had been singing.

'You can't leave anything alone, can you?' She

couldn't bring herself to step across the threshold and enter the music-room. She never entered the music-room. 'Onward and upward, that's my Leo. It's like some awful greed of the ego to always be accomplishing, accomplishing. Can't you ever fail?'

Chapter Seven

Rose kept the phone off the hook for most of the week following her cancelled wedding, only replacing it when she had to call to make an appointment to visit a flat. One call did manage to slip in on the Thursday morning during one of those seconds when the receiver was back in place. Rose stared at the telephone in astonishment. When she picked it up a male voice said, 'So you didn't get married.' She knew immediately that it was Otto, the blond man with the goose-pimpled arm. 'I think you were wise,' he added.

'Oh, I don't *think* so,' said Rose. 'I *feel* I did the right thing – in my bones or guts or wherever that kind of business goes on – but as for thoughts and logic – I definitely don't *think* so.'

'Well, then you have done the right thing. Listen, I was calling to say that I run a little music club – we have talks, slide-shows and the like – and I thought that perhaps I could have Eva put you on our mailing list.'

Rose was disappointed. She didn't know what she had expected but this man was linked in her mind with grand staircases, velvet curtains and chandeliers – not mailing lists.

'That illustrates my point about the right thing,' she said. 'From the weekend I won't have anywhere to live because I didn't get married. This place is already rented out to someone else. I won't have an address as of Sunday.'

'Then I can't send you an application form?'

'Where to?'

'Oh – right – yes, it is a bit of a problem, I suppose—'

'Just a bit,' sighed Rose.

'Why don't you come to tea?' said Otto. 'Eva will light a fire and make something. Can you drive?'

'You live near a tube, don't you?'

'Oh yes, the end of the District Line. I was just wondering – can you drive?'

'Yes, but I haven't got a car in London.'

'That's all right. I never learnt, you see. My attention span could never take in all the different visual stimuli, lights, dogs, mothers with prams, cars coming at you . . . And Eva's got arthritic knees. Why don't you come tomorrow at four o'clock? But you can only stay for two hours because we're going out in the evening – to *Don Carlos*, the old Visconti production at the Opera House.'

'But I've got an appointment to visit a flat at four—'

'Four is the only time we can manage,' said Otto and continued to recite the address. 'There's no phone number. I'm calling from a box. We had a slight altercation with the GPO and they cut us off, so don't be late because you won't be able to warn us.'

'But I have to visit a flat—' Rose repeated but Otto was gone.

At three o'clock the next afternoon, Rose realized that she had five minutes in which to decide between tea with Otto and Eva and viewing a flat near her mother's house in Staines. Less than a week earlier she had told herself anything could happen but, as in most lives, nothing had. And now the gaunt blond man with the unnerving blue eyes had invited her to tea. Rose wanted to go, not because she was attracted to him – she didn't think she was – but because he seemed to have such definite convictions about the few quivering strands of her life that he had glimpsed: 'You shouldn't get married!' 'You've done the right thing!' Rose needed to hear such certainty. There are in this world, she knew, straightforward souls who can surge towards each new goal, unfettered by chains of doubt and feeling. She knew she wasn't one of them. She had made a brave move, the right move, she still thought, but now she was scared and lonely. The future seemed to contain nothing but estate agents fiddling apologetically with keys and locks, and flats with small stains on the carpet.

She took the tube to Richmond at the end of the District Line. She walked towards the river and took out her A–Z. She didn't need to. She could hear the house as soon as she turned the corner into its street. A vast, deep male voice was booming out of the windows and echoing across the municipal gardens and the wide, winding river. Rose imagined it sailing above the Thames Valley, drowning out the sounds of the jet engines on the runway at Heathrow airport and landing with a thump in the Queen's drawing-room at Windsor Castle. And if she has any taste she'll keep her windows wide open, Rose thought, as the rich, dark voice wrapped its warmth around her.

The house was very ordinary – an end-of-terrace, slightly dilapidated, imitation Georgian. Rose was disappointed. Again she had been thinking of the gaunt man in terms of opulence – colonnades and gilt edge. And if the house sang, its music was a recording, she realized. In spite of the let-down, Rose walked towards the corner dwelling without ever once taking her eyes off it.

There were two doorbells. One had no name and the other said 'OAS'. The initials looked sinister. She tried to remember where she had seen them and then tried to fathom what they could mean. Otto and his Arthritic Sister? Odd And Solitary? The house was singing so loudly that there seemed little point in trying either of the bells. She was feeling tempted to bend down and call through the letter-box when the door opened and two voices said, 'Hello!'

Eva had a bulging apoplectic troll of a face. Where her brother looked as if he might just decide to sink into his body, the sister seemed to be struggling to burst out of hers. Otto was standing behind her. Above and beyond them the bass singer was off again – a bleak and solitary rumbling it was, accompanied by a lone cello.

'Rose, dear!' He ushered her in and raised his eyes to the ceiling. 'King Philip sits alone in his study overlooking the Escorial and contemplates *his* solitude.'

'Who said anything about solitude?' asked his sister.

'Well, I just thought that Rose here was probably feeling a bit alone—'

'You talk a lot of cock, Otto,' said Eva. At least, Rose assumed it was Eva. 'I made a ginger cake – you're not funny about ginger, are you?'

'No, no – that would be lovely.'

Inside, the house was only slightly rumpled. Somebody – Rose could not yet decide which of the twins – had attempted to keep the carpets clean and put new covers on worn armchairs. As Rose had expected there were photos of people in operatic costume; she glimpsed a group of women with horned helmets, a man in fur with an eye-patch and spear, Maria Callas in an Empire dress, poor Parisian lovers in the snow, a woman with three chins wearing a kimono, and a handsome black man in a white nightie strangling a blonde.

'*Ella giammai m'amò*,' said Otto, squeezing her shoulder as Eva took her coat. ' "She never loved me." King Philip is admitting to himself what he knew all along: that young Elizabeth de Valois, the French princess that he has forced into a political marriage, could never love the grey old man that he has become. Probably the finest moment in all of Verdi. Sometimes I think *Don Carlos* is his finest opera – even though you're supposed to say *Falstaff*. What do you think? I bet you're going to say *Otello*.'

'I don't know,' said Rose. 'I told you I don't know anything about opera.'

'Well, there's nothing wrong with liking *Otello*,' said Eva as if Rose's future tastes had been decided for her. 'Come and sit down and tell me why you didn't get married.'

'You've only got two hours, remember!' cried Otto.

'Won't you be joining us?' said Rose.

'For a minute or two later on. The OAS is having a

67

very special guest this weekend and I've got lots of preparing to do. You should have become a member, Rose. You don't know what you'll be missing.'

'But I won't have an address—'

'Perhaps you should come anyway. It's at seven p.m. on Sunday. At first I was going to talk on Fathers and Verdi but now that we've got this—'

'I'll be moving on Sunday,' said Rose.

'Where are you going?' said Eva.

'I don't know,' sighed Rose. 'That's the problem.'

'You should have got married,' said the sister. 'Whatever do you think will become of you now? At your age you'll sink to the bottom of society like a stone.'

'Not these days,' said Rose. She wanted to sit down. 'Could I have that tea, please?'

Eva led her into the large sitting-room.

'Like a stone,' repeated Eva. 'Was he that bad?'

'Yes,' Rose lied.

'We've got a room that we used to rent in the basement here,' said Eva. 'Why didn't you tell her about our room, Otto?' she called to her brother in the kitchen. The music was still playing.

'Because it's for students.' Otto's head appeared through a serving hatch. 'Because she's a woman, a lady, and anyway we haven't been able to rent it for years.'

'And why not? Because not everybody wants to listen to five different versions of the death of Otello over their breakfast while you decide whether Toscanini really did have the edge on the others. Even a music student can't put up with that racket all day, every day.'

'I don't really want a room,' said Rose. 'I was thinking in terms of a flat.'

'You might not be in a position to be fussy,' said Eva. 'I charge fifty pounds a week and it's got a gas ring and you'll have the bathroom to yourself – so it's almost a flat.'

'Oh, but it's not for you, Rose,' said Otto, reappearing through the hatch. 'Not that I wouldn't love to have you but it's for a young girl. It's very basic.'

'Could I see it?' said Rose.

'Of course,' said Eva. 'Oh, and there's no telephone. Otto had a punch-up with—'

'I know. That's all right. I don't have anyone I want to call right now—'

'Solitude, you see!' cried Otto's voice. He had vanished back through the hatch.

'I'm rather proud of it,' said Eva. 'It's an intelligently conceived little space – much more in it than you would expect.' She went to a drawer and took out a key. Rose followed her back outside and down a staircase at the rear of the house. The key opened some french windows that looked out on a small lawn scattered with leaves from a lone beech tree.

'These are all wrong,' said Eva, pulling open a pair of long, red velvet curtains. 'Otto says they're exactly the same colour as the ones at La Scala. I think they make a small room look even smaller. I've got some nice floral Laura Ashley things upstairs that I found in a sale.'

By intelligently conceived, Eva meant that the bed was up a high, straight ladder just two feet from the ceiling and that the space under the bed was given over to a sink, a fridge and a hotplate. There was an upright piano, a small table, a chair and a stool.

'Well?' said Eva.

'I don't know. Would you mind if I spent a couple of minutes on my own in here? That way I can see how it feels.'

'As you wish,' said Eva. 'I'm going to chop some logs. There's snow on the way.'

'Do you think so?' asked Rose.

'Absolutely,' said Eva and strode off to the bottom of the garden in the twilight. Once she was gone, Rose put her coat and handbag down and tried scaling the ladder. When she got to the top she realized that she had neither the courage nor the agility to go back down. The house sang on. The bass had been replaced by an ardent duet. Rose lay alone on the bed, listened to the two singers and thought, Well, they won't get what they long for either.

After a few minutes, she clambered gingerly down the ladder and went upstairs to tell the twins that she would take the room.

'Well, I suppose that's good if you think you can stand it,' said Otto. 'When are you coming?'

'On Sunday – in the afternoon.'

'What a pity – that's our big day – otherwise I would have offered to help you move, but on Sunday it's impossible.' Otto was standing on a stool in the hallway, straightening out a portrait of a horse-faced woman who wore a sumptuous dress of silk and rhinestones.

'Annaliese Hartman as the Marschallin,' he said. 'Before she went on to the heavy-duty Isoldes and Brünnhildes. Isn't she beautiful?'

'Well perhaps, in a Germanic sort of—' Rose squinted up at the photograph. Her heart was pounding from the shock of making a decision. Her mind was scrambling to visualize her belongings and boxes, and staircases and transport.

'Not conventionally beautiful, of course! Not like some boring little cover girl – but think of all that one woman encompasses.' Otto's finger caressed the woman's profile. 'I used to take her roses every time she sang Isolde. White roses because Isolde means white or fair. The first time I actually got to hand her a bouquet – it was at a stage door in Munich – I couldn't take my eyes off her throat.' He ran his finger across the throat in the photo. 'In there, inside those few inches of flesh, bone, cartilage and muscle were contained the Marschallin, Turandot, Isolde – it was all I could do not to reach out and touch her throat.'

'Better to just give her the flowers,' said Rose.

'She was our Isolde last week,' said Otto, satisfied with the position of the photo, and resting a hand on Rose's shoulder as he climbed off the stool.

'And you didn't tell me I was seeing such a wonder?' said Rose. She was surprised at how much comfort was contained in the brief contact with Otto.

'But you weren't!' cried Otto. 'The silly old cow is past it now. Why the fuck can't they see when it's time to stop and give up with dignity?'

The doorbell rang. The twins stood in the hallway, stared at the door and then stared at each other.

'She's early,' said Otto. 'I won't answer the door until four o'clock. She can sit on the step and read a newspaper or something.'

'Don't be ridiculous,' said Eva. 'You can be civil for an extra fifteen minutes.'

'I'll take Rose on a tour of the house.' He turned to Rose. 'You won't want to meet her.'

Eva had opened the door. Rose saw a thin dark woman of her own age. There was no sign of the winter's day on her expensive clothes. Rose guessed that she had come in a taxi, and felt suddenly, absurdly envious of the stranger. The woman exchanged a brief greeting with Eva, then patted her aside and stared at Rose.

'And who is this?'

Rose felt like a hospital patient wheeled out to be visited by a member of the royal family.

'I'm Rose Lorenzo.'

'Spanish or Italian?' asked Clara, looking more intently at Rose.

'Don't go getting excited, Clara,' said Eva. 'She's just a new lodger. She's not some late-developing diva, she's not a singer or a society hostess. She's nobody for you to be interested in.'

'And where are the Sacher cakes you promised us?' said Otto.

'I was burgled,' said Clara, turning her back on Rose and apparently taking Eva's advice that she wasn't worth her attention.

'They burgled your cake?' asked Eva.

'Yes, yes, they broke in.' Clara wasn't about to admit that she had omitted to replace the window pane. 'They ripped open the beautifully tied boxes and stole the cakes.'

'Why would they rip open the boxes?' said Rose, but no-one was listening.

'And they vomited on my Persian rug,' said Clara. 'They do that deliberately. They're Marxists and they want to show contempt for people who have worked hard and done well.'

'But you've never worked a day in your bleeding life!' cried Eva.

'They do it all the time,' Clara insisted. 'Vomiting over people's beautiful belongings.'

'No, no, not vomiting,' said Eva. 'They shit on things as a statement – I've heard of that.'

'Please, Eva!' cried Otto. 'You know how I am about bodily functions.'

'And they shouldn't have opened the boxes,' insisted Rose, feeling her voice float away unheard towards the steamy kitchen. 'Why would a burglar run through the street with a sticky cake in his arms?'

Clara ignored the question and turned to Eva.

'It's political – they're hateful wretched people and they're trying to make a statement.'

'Why would they make a statement with a Sacher cake?' sighed Rose but Otto and Clara had turned their attention to a pile of leaflets about the talk by the great singer, and Eva had returned to the soup that she had been making in the kitchen.

'Well, I'll be going.' Nobody acknowledged Rose's departure. 'See you on Sunday.'

'Aren't you coming this evening?' Clara looked up from the pile of printed programmes. 'Isn't Otto bringing you along?'

Otto blushed. 'I'm sorry, Rose, but this late in the day a ticket would be impossible.'

'There's nothing to apologize for,' said Rose. 'I'm not really in a state of mind to be going to the opera—'

'But you would love it, Rose, and you would see a living legend on stage in one of his greatest roles. I would give you my ticket—'

'No he wouldn't,' called Eva from the kitchen. 'He

wouldn't give up his seat if our mother's life depended on it.'

'Our mother's dead so the question doesn't arise,' said Otto.

Eva had finished with the soup. She wiped her hands on her apron and followed Rose into the passage.

'If you give me a cheque for a week's rent and a week in advance, I can give you the key now,' she said.

She was removing from Rose all possibility of second thoughts or backtracking. She wrote Eva the cheque and a few seconds later found herself standing outside the french windows with the key to her new room in her hand. As soon as she stepped through the red velvet curtains she vowed to herself that none of her friends or family would ever be invited to her shabby new dwelling.

She sat in silence on the only chair and stared out at the beech tree. This was not a room that was open to improvement or transformation. She had no impulse to paint its walls or rearrange its few bits of furniture. This room seemed to be telling her that it was to be taken as it was, for its physical aspect was of little importance compared to how it sounded. More hitherto unknown music swept down to the basement room. And as Rose sat alone, the new song of the singing house filled her, not with the restless almost physical longing of *Tristan*, but with a resigned autumnal sense of the weariness of all wanting.

As long as the music played, Rose sat and stared. Already the winter's day was slipping into night and the room was growing dark but only when the music stopped could she deal with practical considerations. When silence returned to the room, Rose decided that since her decision was now made, she must adjust to the bed up the ladder. The trick, she discovered, was to remove her tights. That way her bare feet gripped onto the rungs and she didn't slip. The trick to coming down was to start by facing outwards, get the arches of both feet firmly planted on the first rung and then gently swing the body round and descend. On her

73

second attempt she missed a rung and fell to the floor with a crash. She landed with equal force on her right elbow and knee. As she lay on the floor, she noticed the dust around the corners of the room and she felt the freezing draught that blew through the half-inch opening at the bottom of the french windows. What have I done? thought Rose. The pain in both limbs was acute; her energy was gone. Rose sat and sobbed tears of regret and apprehension.

And then the song came to her again. Rose now knew that it was the same opulent, autumnal sound that had filled the room minutes earlier but the voices were different. The three people upstairs had, apparently, finished with soup and cake and burglars and were comparing different versions of the same piece of music. The music played and played. Rose stayed where she was, rubbing her knee and elbow. As long as the sound filled the basement room, Rose could believe that in spite of the draughts and the dust, she had done the right thing. She dreaded the silence. But when the music stopped this time, she heard a rapping and a woman's voice calling, 'Miss Lorenzo, Miss Lorenzo.' She made no move to answer but sat and listened to this strange voice that seemed to have been sent by some vicious demon to remind her that in spite of all the preparations and dreams and plans of the previous months, by her own doing, she was still Miss Lorenzo.

'Miss Lorenzo, please do answer,' said the voice. 'It's about tonight.'

Rose pulled herself to her feet and peered at the red velvet curtains. They were completely opaque and gave her no hint as to who was behind them. She hesitated for a few seconds but when a fist slammed against the window-frame, she gingerly pulled back the curtain and saw Clara.

'What is it?' said Rose, opening the door and remembering as she did, that her eyes were red and swollen from crying.

'I've got a ticket for you for tonight – if you still want to go.'

'Oh, I couldn't – it's late and there's so much to—'

Clara was easing her way into the room. Rose had issued no invitation but already Clara was through the doorway and looking around her.

'How can you stand to live in such a confined space?' she said.

'I haven't tried yet.'

'Are you a mature music student or something? I mean why here?'

'Why not? Look, I am grateful for the invitation but it is such late notice—'

'No it's not, you've got plenty of time. I don't have the ticket on me but I'll be in the Grand Tier so you can— No, better still, I'll leave it at the box-office.'

'I am tempted,' said Rose.

'Then it's yours.' She rolled her small dark eyes in the direction of the bed up the ladder. 'Better than sitting in this little dump all night.'

'Is it an expensive ticket?' said Rose. 'I've heard about opera house prices and—'

'But I'm giving it to you!' said Clara. 'I could see how disappointed you were about not going.' She looked hard at Rose's red eyes.

'I wasn't upset about that,' said Rose.

'And I thought that if it meant that much to you, then I was sure I could help. Anyone would be disappointed to miss an evening like tonight—'

'But I wasn't upset about that—'

Clara was already halfway out of the door. She had suddenly tired of this strange weepy woman as she had tired of Otto on the phone a few days earlier.

'What was the music that was playing upstairs?' Rose called after the thin figure as it headed out of the cold, shadowy garden.

'The last of Strauss's "Four Last Songs",' replied Clara, not bothering to turn round.

'Why "last"? Last what?' Rose called after her but the figure had vanished. Rose stood on the cold damp lawn in her bare feet. She was strangely pleased with that word 'last'.

Chapter Eight

'What is so wrong with preparing Wotan?' Leo was back in his frayed brown dressing-gown and sitting on the edge of his double bed. Kay was in the adjoining bathroom, standing in front of the basin, removing her eye make-up. The tap was running. It had been running for no purpose as far as Leo could make out for at least ten minutes. Kay always let the water run and run; and as the years had gone by, Leo, who considered himself a frugal Italian peasant at heart, had become exasperated by her American extravagance. 'After Kay does her ablutions,' he had said to John one day, employing a word he remembered from an English lesson years earlier, 'the level of the lake drops by about fifty centimetres.'

'I told you – it's some horrible form of pride that makes you want to prove to everyone that you are not just the best in your category; you have to muscle in on everyone else's category too.' Kay was cleaning her teeth now with an electric toothbrush. Leo gave up any attempt to talk to her while she was in the bathroom and took his robe off and climbed into his bed. Kay's double bed was only inches away. They had devised the separate arrangement years earlier when the young Leo was just beginning a life of fretting about colds and draughts and had wanted the second bed as a safe haven from anything Kay might be carrying when he had a crucial performance the following day. Imperceptibly he had made the bed his own; he couldn't have named the day when he had gone straight to the second bed by the bedroom door. Kay had never acknowledged the move.

'I'm very, very tired, Leo.' She sat down on her bed.

76

'I was driving around in appalling traffic coming up from Como and there was freezing fog rolling off the mountains and I didn't expect to come home and hear that.'

'And what is so wrong with *that*?' Leo had bought Kay a silk négligé in a shop near the Ponte Vecchio in Florence a month earlier. Tonight she had put it on for the first time. Because of her operation and her scar, she was careful to wear the outer robe tightly closed around her long, slender neck. Leo was thinking how beautiful she looked but he knew that his own private triumph singing the German composer's most ecstatic music was the main cause of his sudden desire for a wife with whom he hadn't made love in several years. He hadn't even had a woman in several months but had been too preoccupied with his new role to notice the physical lack.

'I said, what is so wrong with that?' He could speak more softly now that she was within feet of him.

'Not Wotan.'

'Why not Wotan? And don't say I'm overreaching myself, Kay. You were a singer. You were ambitious—'

'Because of Brünnhilde, because he has a daughter—'

'What?'

'You heard me.' Kay was looking past him out at the lake through the window. Leo got out of bed and walked naked to the window and closed the shutters. He pulled the robe back round him and sat down next to his wife.

'Kay, this is ridiculous. Like you just said, I'm a boring old bass. I do priests, kings and fathers. I've been a father in Verdi operas and it didn't bother you—'

'Because of all the love – all the love that pours out of him, out of the music for her, his daughter, I couldn't stand it.' She looked away from him. Leo reached for her pale, slender body and held her to him. She didn't react to his caress. He kissed her neck and started to undo the blue silk cord at the top of the négligé. Kay wrenched her body away from him.

'Don't patronize me, Leo.'

Leo put his arms back around her and held her frail body tight against his.

'And it's goddamned Wagner,' she sighed. Leo released her. She smoothed out the négligé and slid back to face him from a few feet across the bed. 'People who love Wagner are sick – emotionally crippled. They can only live their emotional lives through his music.'

Leo was tempted to say that people whose emotional pleasure came from a Sèvres vase weren't necessarily doing much better but he was stopped by his guilt, his belief that Kay's attachment to all the inanimate objects that filled the house was a consequence of that one isolated act of his, all those years ago in the numb hours after his daughter's funeral.

'You just don't like Wagner, Kay,' he sighed. 'You're certainly not alone in that.'

When Leo had met Kay all those years earlier at the Accademia Chigiana in Siena, neither of them had any interest in the Wagnerian repertoire. They were the two most promising students of their year. Kay's voice was destined for the vocal trapeze acts of the Donizetti, Rossini and Bellini repertoire. The beautiful, hardworking American girl was the centre of attention for all the Latins at the school but Kay was too busy studying to notice them, and if she noticed the self-contained, grave Leo a little more, nothing happened between them until a couple of years later when they were both appearing in *La Bohème* in Stresa – Leo singing his one big aria to his coat and Kay dying of consumption. After five performances of the Puccini opera, they were married.

The local critics had been unanimous in their praise for those first performances of Leo's; they had acknowledged that Kay had a perfect voice but said that she was unsuited to the lush emotion of Puccini since she seemed to have understood little of life and suffering. 'She moves through this opera,' said one local paper, 'like an office girl pushing a lunch-tray along a canteen counter.'

'But what can I know of life and suffering?' she had sobbed over breakfast that morning to Leo who seemed to have been born knowing everything about everything.

Before any of the critics from the big, prestigious opera cities like Milan or Naples could pass judgement on Kay, she found that she was pregnant. With the birth of her daughter and the rush of joy that accompanied the feel of the child's damp hand on her belly, Kay felt that she had finally learnt all there was to know about love. Within seconds she was to learn all that there was to know about sorrow when doctors had taken the malformed child from her and returned after several silent hours to say that she would not survive her first year.

She had looked to Leo, had reached for his hand and thought that she saw in his eyes at that moment, a withdrawal, a closing of a curtain as if he had made an instant decision that this child who would pass so briefly through their lives could not be allowed to make any emotional claims on a young ambitious man who needed all his energy and emotions for his career. She prayed that she had imagined it but Kay was convinced that for him the sickly child in the incubator had already been written off. And when she had flown the child from specialist to specialist in New York and Washington and Los Angeles, Leo had been rehearsing *Don Giovanni* in Bari and had not been available. By his return, the baby was already dead.

Now over two decades later in the bedroom where the child had been conceived, Leo stroked Kay's blond hair, noticing for the first time that the pale yellow was giving way to white.

'I'm bored with the same old repertoire, Kay. I've still got a dozen or so good singing years ahead of me. I can't face filling them with Philips and Borises. I need a challenge.'

'Don't you ever get tired of pretending to be people? Doesn't it ever strike you as just plain ludicrous for a middle-aged man to be dressing up, painting his face and play-acting?'

'Every day of my life,' said Leo. 'Without the music it would be pointless but I need the music, Kay.' Leo wouldn't have dreamed of saying that his face-painting and play-acting had paid for the tester bed that seemed to bring his wife the same joy that Wotan's Farewell had just brought him. Since she had ceased to sing, Kay had shown a distaste for opera. Leo had sensed her unspoken message – that truly terrible, unbearable things happen in life, and that to simulate them on a draughty stage for three hours before going out into the night to eat a pizza was cheap mockery.

'I want to sing Wotan.' Leo rose and walked towards the corridor. When Kay had burst into the music-room, he had abandoned his piano so quickly that he now remembered that it was standing open in the dark room with the window ajar and all the humidity of the lake seeping in.

Once inside the room, he closed the door and sat down at the piano. He lifted the *Walküre* score gently off the stand and sat in the dark, fingering the pages and whistling the sleep motif to himself.

'Yap!'

Leo heard a scratching against the door. Something was flinging its small self against the wood. He closed the piano lid, put the score back in its place and went to open the door. A small, beige Pekinese hurled itself at his ankles.

'What the—' He bent down and picked up the wriggling animal. He found himself facing a snorting, squashed black muzzle. The dog peered back at him, its eyes so markedly protruding that at least a half-inch of white showed above each brown iris giving the little animal an offended almost demented expression.

Kay's pale, blond face appeared behind the snuffling little dog. Her slender fingers reached up and pried it from Leo's hands.

'What the— Where did it—'

'That young count who runs the antique business

gave it to me,' she said, hugging the animal to her. 'I had no choice in the matter, he just foisted it on me. I wanted to surprise you with it when I came back and then—'

'*E proprio brutto*,' said Leo, gazing down at the panting Pekinese and caressing its neck in spite of himself.

'Don't call it ugly – it's a pedigree. Giacomo is going to send me its papers.'

'Papers won't stop it being ugly,' laughed Leo, still stroking the dog. 'Unless we manage to wrap them round its head. Oh, *mamma mia*, you're ugly!' He lifted the dog out of Kay's arms and held it up in front of him.

'I know what you're thinking, Leo,' said Kay. 'But I'm not. I'm not one of those silly women who wants a little yappy toy dog, like the old divas. It's just kind of landed in my life – but maybe one day I could go in for breeding them – it would give me something to do with my time.'

'It's another object,' sighed Leo, rubbing his large thumb across the dog's velvety black muzzle.

'No, no,' said Kay. 'Not this time. It's living, breathing—'

'Rasping and snorting, more like. Why couldn't you get a big solid dog that I could at least walk in the woods when I'm here? I'd have loved that.'

'Like Wagner with his Newfoundland, I suppose!' Kay retrieved the Pekinese. 'Poor Leo. First you think you're Wotan – now you think you're Wagner himself!'

'I just said I'd have preferred a boisterous big dog instead of some yappy thing that I'm scared of stepping on. Kay, dear,' he ran his hand along her thin shoulder, 'isn't this some terrible cliché that we're falling into? The thwarted parents giving their love to this, this poor ugly thing.'

'Fuck you, Leo!' The dog plopped to the floor. Kay knelt down to pick it up. 'It isn't a thing – it has this tiny heart that beats so rapidly. Feel, feel.' She pulled Leo's hand to the dog's upper belly. 'It terrified me at first but now I don't mind it. Don't you understand this is progress for me?'

Leo crouched down on the floor alongside her, aware of how cold the tile was on his knees. Kay made no attempt to move. He realized that she was crying. He watched her in silence then gathered her and the dog into his arms and set off along the corridor back towards their bedroom. If Kay considered this ugly little creature a form of progress, he asked for nothing more. Kay so rarely cried and she never really laughed either. For years it had seemed to him that as long as she was away from the theatre, and at the house or an auction-room, she would remain relentlessly good-humoured and smiling.

In the first years after her child's death, Leo had been scared by her abnormally even temper, and when the small, malignant tumour had appeared in her breast, he had felt that all his fears had been confirmed. After the operation, when the doctors declared Kay healthy, he had believed that more than a tumour had been cut out. He wanted to believe that with it was gone all the guilt, all the silent reproaches, all the bitterness. Six months after her mastectomy, a plastic surgeon in Milan had described a new procedure that would allow doctors to rebuild Kay's missing breast. Leo had been jubilant, had felt that the perfectly timed arrival of this new surgery was proof that healing and a new start were possible.

Kay had refused the surgery. At first Leo thought this was some deep-seated mistrust of Italian medicine and had flown in a surgeon from New York. Still Kay refused. She wants to wear that missing breast like a battle scar, he had let the thought whisper itself in his brain and then banished it. For months he carried brochures and pamphlets on cancer and stress tucked into his libretti as he flew around the world and had finally persuaded Kay to attend a support group run by an American woman in Como. She came home after the first meeting and told him a story of a plump Swiss German matron who had put her arm around her and said, 'What are you fretting about, Liebchen? It solved all my problems. When my Heinz starts to look at me like a love-sick cow and I'm feeling tired, I take out my prosthesis, throw it at him and say, "Here, darling, you go play with that."' Kay had giggled when she told the story but only for a few seconds. It was a light nervous giggle that betrayed her bewilderment at the older woman's indifference to physical perfection. Leo had laughed out loud and found himself envying old Heinz.

A week later, Kay dropped out of the group and came home and said to Leo in her matter-of-fact way that she had never even believed in a link between stress and cancer. As she made them both a late-night cup of coffee, she said she believed in a wild, raging, mindless fury sent by the Fates to hurl pointless, unmerited pain at unsuspecting passing humans. And now here was a Pekinese, dropped into their life by the whim of a count from Como. Leo decided that he should be grateful for small, beige, snuffling mercies, and set Kay and the dog gently down on her bed.

'What is its name?' he said, running his hand along the dog's warm back.

'He said I have to rename it – that way it would be truly mine – ours.'

'What have you come up with?'

'Nothing yet,' said Kay, who had picked a name but was waiting to test it on John Tillson.

'I'll think about it while I'm in London,' said Leo, his hand leaving the dog's back and caressing Kay's thigh. She slipped her hand under the dog's belly and deposited the animal on the floor beside the bed. They both heard it grunt and sigh and then, apparently, sink down in a sleeping heap. Leo continued to stroke Kay's thigh. He felt shy, ill at ease; other women's bodies had warmed to his hand since the last time he had touched Kay in this way. He stroked on, hardly daring to break the hypnotic silence by lifting the silk nightdress or un-doing his bathrobe. Kay reached out again and turned out the bedside light, then he felt her hands reaching for the belt on his robe. At the same time he reached out to undo the négligé and slip the nightdress over her head but she seemed to be tightly wrapped in both. He couldn't find flesh anywhere, just silk, what felt like yards and yards of silk. He reached back down for the familiar thigh but in the moment when she had turned out the light Kay must have smoothed the sumptuous garment back down around her. He could feel her hands reaching for him as his robe fell open but still he tried to touch her body.

'I don't care about the scar – it makes no difference to me,' he whispered. 'You're my wife.' But the silk resisted and her hands had found him. In the space of a few seconds, Leo had to battle with his own very raw sexual arousal, his disgust for the form this ostensible act of love was taking and his knowledge that to reject Kay's slender fingers now would destroy this fragile truce that the sleeping dog seemed to have procured. He lay back against the headboard and came in her hands.

Chapter Nine

'Who is Clara?' Rose, Eva and Otto were squeezed into a tube train.

'She's a rich, spoilt, silly cow,' said Otto.

'Not silly,' said his sister. 'Rich, yes, spoilt, probably, but not silly. Her father was one of the top impresarios in the opera world over twenty years ago. He had been part of the allied forces that bombed Milan and La Scala during the war. He'd grown up in the Italian community in Clerkenwell—'

'The compass-makers of Clerkenwell,' said Otto.

'He loved Italian opera,' said his sister.

'And the poor man had to destroy the thing he loved—' added Otto.

'But afterwards,' Eva went on, 'he stayed on in Italy, helped rebuild the theatre and then started up his agency. He did very well, well enough to open an office in London. He invested his money very wisely and made a fortune.'

'But he wasn't all money-making and show-biz glamour like a lot of today's agents,' said Otto. 'Not all cheap trimmings and flash—'

'Oh no,' said Eva. 'They say he really loved the business – and he seems to have passed it on to his daughter.'

'I don't believe *she* really loves the music,' sniffed Otto.

'You're so envious you don't want to give her credit for anything,' snapped Eva. 'I think she's lonely – like a lot of spoilt rich women.'

'Didn't she ever marry?' asked Rose.

'Of course she married!' sniffed Eva. 'Of course she married. To a musicologist—'

'But that wasn't glamorous enough for her,' said Otto. 'So she divorced him only a couple of years after marrying—'

'You don't know the reason,' said Eva. 'You're just surmising—'

'But it didn't work out?' said Rose.

'Relieved, are you?' asked Eva. 'Reassures you, does it, that marriage isn't such a good idea?'

'No, no, not at all—'

'But what you haven't understood is that a woman who has been married and divorced is not considered as peculiar as a woman who's never married.'

'Look how peculiar our Eva is,' Otto winked at Rose.

'And whose fault is that?' said his sister.

Rose *was* disappointed to learn that Clara had been married. She felt more isolated than ever and wondered if she would notice if she herself became 'peculiar'. She thought of the dark woman's expensive clothes and taxis to the suburbs and was filled with an envy of things she had never wanted.

'Surely Clara's money doesn't come from her ex-husband? An academic wouldn't have that much—'

'Of course not!' said Eva. 'There was some long-drawn-out business about her inheritance but the upshot was that she got it. Wealth has isolated her as wealth so often does, and left her with too much time on her hands.'

'So she just drifts around the world going from opera to opera,' said Otto.

'So do we when we can afford it,' added his sister. 'Otto's jealous of her unlimited resources. If he had her money he'd do the same.'

'Not behaving the way she does, I wouldn't.'

'As I just said, she's got too much free time – if she were slugging it out on the Northern Line with the rest of the world by day, she'd have less inclination to roam around at night.'

Eva and Rose sat down in two vacant seats.

'And how did you get to know her?' asked Rose.

'You mean, why would some upper crust heiress

bother with a couple of dried-up old farts like us?'

Because that was what she did mean, Rose couldn't reply.

'She used to be interested in Otto – years ago,' said Eva.

'Otto and Clara?' said Rose.

'Not romantically! When Otto had his little singing career and she thought he might become something—'

'So Otto was a singer!'

'He made a feeble stab at a singing career – years ago.'

'Not that feeble!' hissed Otto who was hanging on to a strap a few feet away. 'I came fourth in a competition once.'

'Once,' said Eva. 'It was our parents' fault. We were born when they were quite old and already a bit gaga. They got it into their heads that he was gifted – and now here we sit in the suburbs with our record collection and the music society and the vicars and the Zimmer-frames.'

'You miserable old bag.' Otto slid into the newly vacant seat next to Rose and hissed across her at his sister. 'Why do you bother coming to my events if that's what you think? Why do you waste your precious time making sandwiches and pots of tea? I'll tell *you* why, Rose—'

'Please don't,' said Rose. The train pulled to a stop. Rose wondered if she still had time to give back the room key, squeeze out of the train and run away to – to what? There seemed to be nothing else to do but ride this hot overcrowded tube train to the opera house.

'I'll tell you why,' Otto repeated. 'Because her life is so empty – she's got nothing else to do.'

'And why is it empty, you vicious little shit? You tell me why it's empty!' At that moment a pregnant woman boarded the train. Otto jumped to his feet to give her his seat and, to Rose's relief, was sucked into the crowd near the door where his response, for he had supplied one, was rendered inaudible.

*   *   *

Leo dalla Vigna sat alone in his dressing-room. Alongside him on a table was a Spanish-style top hat that he was convinced was a bad fit and liable to slide down over his eyes in the middle of his entrance. A dresser had promised to bring him pins and hair-grips, and in waiting for him Leo had transferred all his anxieties about his performance onto the hat. He scowled at it and waited. His ear was tuned to all the footsteps that passed along that basement-level corridor on Floral Street. He welcomed the first visit of the stage manager, glad as ever to be in the cosy familiarity of Covent Garden, and finding the polite, familiar Anglo-Saxon faces to be a soothing contrast to the passions and mayhem of La Scala or the icy intrigues of Vienna.

On the corridor above him, he knew that his Elizabeth de Valois, a young Italian soprano, was vomiting into the toilet bowl. But he also knew that for her that wretched ritual marked the culmination of her stage fright. After that she would be serene, whereas he continued to sit in silence and solitude and fret about his hat.

He made a last attempt to attach it himself, gave up in exasperation and sat watching the feet of the pedestrians who passed above his window on Floral Street. He was feeling a moment of envy for the tube-bound, pub-bound, scuff- and grubby-shoed workers who had finished their working day, when the dresser appeared.

'You took your time.' Leo was rarely rude to employees but in the hour that he had spent in the dressing-room, he had decided that the hat was too high, too wide, too hot, and that, as a result, he would not only make his entrance feeling sweaty and stifled before he had even begun but would also have half his face covered.

'You're putting it on backwards, *signore*,' said the dresser, gently taking the hat and placing it on Leo's head. 'I would have come and helped you but I know how you like to do it yourself.'

'Fifteen minutes,' said the stage manager over the speaker in the room.

'What was I thinking of?' said Leo. 'You'd think I'd never sung it before.'

The dresser, who knew that Leo wouldn't need his hat for at least another forty minutes, put it back down on the dressing-table, smiled and prepared to withdraw until he was needed.

'What was I thinking of?' Leo sighed to himself, aware that in the midst of struggling with the hot hat, he had been thinking of names for the ugly little dog back in Italy. He had decided that the punched-in muzzle and bulging eyes were distinctly un-Italian and had been rooting around through Shakespeare and Restoration comedy for a fitting title for a creature that panted and yelped and dribbled.

'Do you know how many times I've sung this role?' he said to the back of the departing dresser. 'Almost a hundred.' But the dresser was already gone and Leo was left alone with the unnerving number and the even more unnerving realization that the seeking of dogs' names was his admission that his life with Kay was set in this lonely, sterile pattern. She, he now knew, had recognized almost two decades ago that there would be no child, no more family, whereas he had not thought beyond the next role, the next theatre, the next triumph. That scene in their bedroom when he had lain sticky and stifled with her hand around him, with the dog snoring on the floor, that had been her triumph.

'Five minutes,' said the stage manager over the loudspeaker.

King Philip II, and therefore Leo dalla Vigna, makes a silent first appearance on the opera house stage in *Don Carlos*. Verdi's stage directions require that the old king accompany his new young queen in a stately procession and that the young Carlos bow before '*lo sguardo sospettoso di Filippo*'.

Leo had a long wait for this moment. This being

grand opera, the tenor and the soprano had to find each other in the forest of Fontainebleau and declare their love. A page had to appear and tell Elizabeth that she was to marry the old king. A whole act would start and end, and his colleagues would be settling in on stage before Leo had even opened his mouth. He ran through phrases from his aria, '*Ella giammai m'amo*' – 'she never loved me', and found himself thinking of Kay and feeling utterly perplexed. There had not been a moment in the past twenty years when he could reply with certainty that she loved him. And yet she had never expressed a desire to be without him.

Before he could push his own heart to the frightening question of whether he loved her, he ran through another difficult passage in the opera. By the time he came to the aria a second time, he had succeeded in replacing Kay's image with that of the young Italian soprano who was on stage by now and wrapped in the arms of the tenor. Leo had sung with her before and enjoyed the physical contact with her healthy, uncomplicated beauty. He didn't desire her but took pleasure in her youth and enthusiasm. Her blondness was reminiscent of the young Kay, but she was ruddier, more robust and straightforward than his enigmatic wife.

Leo liked the feel of his young compatriot's full and heavy bosom when she took his arm to make their entrance. A mention of her name in Vienna or New York and he would immediately recall the smell of her rather cloying, vulgar perfume mixed as it always was during a performance with the round ripe smell of her sweat. He even knew the smell of her breath more than that of clean, brisk, elegant Kay. For she slept those three feet away from him and cleaned her teeth and rinsed her mouth with what seemed to be half the water of Lake Como whereas young Giulietta had clutched him and trembled and sobbed and sweated as often as seven times a month counting dress rehearsals. The bond was one of sweat and tears if not blood, and only with the advancing years had Leo succeeded in detaching himself from love affairs made, not in heaven, but in the artistic administrator's office when the cast lists were drawn up.

The dresser returned to the dressing-room and adjusted Leo's cape and hat; he heard the young Bulgarian baritone who was singing Rodrigo make his way along the corridor for his cue, and then the stage manager knocked for the second time that evening. Leo rose and followed her familiar black-clad back up the stairs along the long, cream corridor and into the wings.

Even though Leo, like Kay, had come to believe only in blind, mindless fate, he still crossed himself before he stepped out into that spotlit cube. The soprano slipped a hand under his and the warm, familiar weight of her breast settled onto his forearm. A sceptre was placed in his other hand and an assistant stage manager armed with a score and a torch to read it by, signalled his cue. 'Suspicious expression' settling onto his features, King Philip II and his young queen stepped out onto the stage.

Leo had time after this act to go down to the canteen. There was a long interval and he was not due back on stage until the grandeur and splendour of the Auto-da-Fé scene when Philip would be crowned and every soloist, chorister and acting extra who had donned a costume in Covent Garden that evening would be up on stage with him. Philip would enter, stately and isolated, amidst the brass and brocade, the strings and silk. In the meantime, he pushed his tray along the canteen counter, opting for a weak cup of black coffee and a dried-up Danish pastry. The Bulgarian baritone in the queue behind him ordered a large plate of Irish stew and joined Leo at one of the non-smoking tables at the back of the room.

'How can you eat that now?' said Leo, scowling at the overflowing plate of meat and potatoes.

'I can eat anytime,' said the baritone, wasting no time in shovelling the food onto his fork for he was back on stage within minutes of curtain-up.

'*Puzza*,' sighed Leo, wishing that the man would take the strong-smelling dish elsewhere but the baritone just took the Italian utterance as a cue to lean forward and whisper a few words back to him in Italian.

'You've heard about—' he dropped his voice even lower and hissed the name of a prominent German bass-baritone.

'What about him?' said Leo.

'The voice – completely gone. From one day to the next, he woke up and nothing, nothing – *muto* – *muto* . . . He can speak but that's all.'

They both sat in silence, contemplating this piece of information. Every few years a story would go round the great opera houses about a singer who woke up one morning to find that his or her voice had abandoned them. That just once or twice these stories were true, sent a chill through the two men.

'It must be some temporary complaint,' said Leo, spooning more sugar into his coffee. He knew the man well and couldn't recall his being ill for more than a few days in his career.

'That's what they hoped at first,' Dimitri Dimov went on, whispering in between forkfuls of meat and potatoes. 'But it's official now – well, not official – they haven't told the press, but he's out of the Ring in Munich next month.'

'But he might be better by next month,' said Leo, spooning another sugar into his coffee and stirring the thick, syrupy mix. At the mention of the Ring in Munich, he'd lost all desire to drink it.

When he looked back up, his nose nearly banged against the Bulgarian's who had already finished his stew and was wiping gravy off his beard. He had drawn even closer to Leo.

'They've asked me to do it,' he hissed.

'You? Do Wotan?' Leo pushed the coffee aside and tried to lean back to a place where the Bulgarian's beard wasn't tickling his chin and where his warm, meaty breath wasn't gusting across his face. He would have enough of that in the next few hours. 'Aren't you a bit young?'

'Wotan was young in *Rheingold*,' said Dimov. 'Anyway, they are desperate – that's not why they picked me, of course – they might have taken somebody a bit older but no-one's available.'

'What about—' Now it was Leo's turn to lean forward. He ran through the names of one Englishman, two Americans and a few lesser-known Germans.

'Not available!' cried Dimov.

'Don't you think it's more for a bass-baritone?'

'Fischer Dieskau did it in Salzburg!' said the Bulgarian triumphantly.

'I know and I didn't like it,' said Leo. 'I didn't know you knew the role.'

'I did it in Sofia two years ago.'

'In Bulgarian?' Leo raised one eyebrow. He was suddenly hotter than he had been on stage all evening.

'Of course not. I did the whole cycle in German.'

'And you feel ready for Munich? A German-speaking audience – Wagner in his own country?'

'*Certo!*' concluded the young Bulgarian. He got up to leave. 'Must go. Ciao! Ciao!'

Leo reached over for the gravy-stained dish and placed it on a neighbouring table. He sat in silence for a few more minutes, then got up and made his way along the corridors to his dressing-room.

On the other side of the proscenium arch, Rose, Eva and Otto were sitting, drinking coffee on the concrete stairs that led to the amphitheatre.

'Lousy seat, eh?' was all Otto said when Rose squeezed through the crowd to join them during the interval, for if Clara was in the Grand Tier, her gift to Rose had been a distant two-pound bench in the upper slips. 'It's too bad – the production looks as good as it sounds. Sumptuous costumes and colours. Pity you can't see it.'

'Pity you *can* hear it,' said a tall man with three hooped ear-rings in his right earlobe.

'What does that mean?' asked Otto.

'The mezzo soprano is so very vulgar,' sighed the man.

'I think she's just right,' said Otto. 'A real tigress.'

'She's vulgar,' the man said to Rose. 'You should have seen Verrett or Bumbry – now they were Ebolis.'

Otto drew in his breath. Rose had seen the same expression on his face in the tube only hours earlier. Otto was on the verge of another altercation, she guessed, and excused herself and went to buy a programme. She set about putting faces to the voices. She was not enjoying the opera as much as she had hoped. She was frustrated with her limited view of the stage and she found the unknown score difficult to get into her ears on a first hearing. It sounded as dark and sombre as its setting in the grim Spanish court at the time of the Inquisition. One voice had reached out to her, had found her up in the top of the slips and wrapped its warmth around her but what else could Rose expect of the much-vaunted Leo dalla Vigna? She was looking for his face in the programme when Eva and Otto came over to her. The man with the three ear-rings was with them.

'Sandwich?' asked Eva and handed her half an egg sandwich that she pulled from a plastic bag. 'I always make them up at home. They're a criminal price here.'

'Of course, I saw dalla Vigna in the early days at La Scala,' said the three ear-rings, 'when he was doing the Mephistos and that Boris—'

'We saw those too,' said Eva, her mouth full of egg sandwich. 'So none of that crap about how much better he was when we weren't there because we were.'

The hooped ear-rings trembled.

'Let's say that he is just a few centimetres past his peak then, shall we?' said the man.

'No, no, we won't say that,' said Otto. 'In his case I think his peak will prove to be a vast and lofty plateau like the Table Mountain that we used to learn about in geography. I think he'll stay up there for quite a while yet.'

'Sentimental drivel,' replied the three ear-rings. 'That's the trouble with the Covent Garden crowd. On the Continent, where I live for half the year, we wouldn't let these goats out on stage.'

'Well, why don't you bugger off back there?' said Eva.

Bells were ringing again. Rose made her way to her perch high above the house. She had dressed flimsily and was getting a cold. She spent what remained of the opera in dull incomprehension, struggling not to cough or sneeze and only forgetting her discomfort during Leo dalla Vigna's great aria at the beginning of Act Four. In her dark blind little corner she was entirely at the mercy of the sound coming first from a solo cello in the orchestra pit and then from the voice of Leo dalla Vigna himself.

She had never heard sounds so bleak and dark and yet so rich and beautiful. But of course, that's what I would think, she reminded herself. I've been primed. It's exactly what Otto told me to think. Still, the voice was comforting, and even if its message was one of despair, its sheer enormity and depth made her feel safe and secure for the first time in days.

When the stage manager cued Leo on for his solo curtain-call, carnations rained down on his head from high up in the side-galleries. The people in the orchestral stalls took their cue from the occupants of the cheaper seats and rose to their feet. Leo had never cared for the long-drawn-out solo bow; he was embarrassed by the hand-on-heart or arms-held-open-to-the-auditorium gestures of many of his fellow Latins and tended to leave the stage a few seconds too soon, trailing behind him a smattering of stray applause that frequently left the next singer out at a disadvantage since the audience had not had time to take a second breath and build up its energy, and was still hoping to see more of Leo. Tonight he bent down and picked up a few of the fallen carnations. With his free hand, he gestured to the orchestra, realizing too late that this being London, a city of last trains out to the suburbs at

11.43, the players had already left and he was thanking an empty pit.

'So this is where you were going when you rushed off last week,' said Rose. Otto was clutching a small, leather-bound book to his breast. He and Eva were standing on either side of a black bollard in front of the stage door. Rose was standing a few feet away, raking around in her bag for her tube ticket and trying to look as though she wasn't with them. When she had longed to accompany him on that wind-blown evening less than a week ago she had imagined something so much grander than this huddled crowd of middle-aged autograph hunters.

'You actually wait out here for autographs?' she whispered. 'I didn't know people really did this.'

'But don't you want to keep a trace of what you have just seen?' replied Otto. 'How can you just walk out of here and get into the tube and be with all those smelly, everyday people with their halitosis and their cheap paperbacks and their Walkmans?' A sudden ripple of activity around the door distracted Otto's attention. He left Rose and Eva and surged forward.

'He waited twenty years for Renata Tebaldi but he just missed Callas on her way into the theatre in Rome the night that she walked out after the first act and the scandal went as far as the Italian parliament,' said his sister who remained standing by the black bollard.

'It's the Spanish tenor,' Otto called over to them, flicking through the leather book for an empty page. 'Give me the Mont Blanc pen, Eva! Give me the Mont Blanc pen!'

Chapter Ten

As Leo's taxi made its way through the traffic to the south-west suburbs, the driver regaled him with stories of English soccer – 'Because you're Italian.' The driver told a good tale. Even though the Anglo-Saxon names meant nothing to Leo he found himself following the games with interest and envying the cabbie his ability to tell a story. That's what the audience at the music society would be waiting for, he knew, from the days when he gave such talks to opera fans around the world. They would sit politely through the questions about his training and his choice of repertoire but they would be waiting for the anecdote, the personal memory that would draw them into that inaccessible world beyond the proscenium arch. And, despite his years of experience, Leo never succeeded in giving them what they wanted. He was too intense, cared too deeply for the truth to exaggerate a mishap or embellish a triumph in order to give it shape and drama or humour.

He did have that one story that he would like to tell but this was no amusing account of disaster backstage. Oh, there was humour in his tale but it was bleak – because the story that he could not tell was a macabre black farce. For twenty-five years he had carried it within him, longing to tell someone and finding no-one until he had come to believe that it was a story that would only end with his end.

The taxi pulled up outside a house in the south-west suburbs. Leo was scowling at the shabby façade, wondering why he hadn't resisted Clara's pleading back in Vienna, when the ageing blond twins whose names he could never remember came running down the path to meet him. The taut, pale face of the brother seemed to confirm that he was right to come, that he owed this relative stranger an evening of his precious free time, but before he could ask himself why he had incurred such a debt, the male twin thrust a twenty-pound note into his hand.

'Let me settle up the cab fare,' said Otto.

'All the way from the West End, oh no you bloody well don't,' retorted his sister.

'But we said we'd pay expenses,' said Otto.

'I've already paid it,' said Leo.

'But that was part of our—'

'It doesn't matter,' replied Leo. The sister was nodding agreement. Because she looked so English and stern, Leo couldn't resist an impulse to take her thick, calloused hand gently in his and kiss it.

'Hmmph,' sniffed Eva and went inside. Leo turned to the male twin and shook his hand firmly. That finer, softer hand was shaking so violently that it slipped from his grasp.

'Bring him into the kitchen and give him a glass of wine,' Eva's voice echoed from the hallway.

'Not the kitchen,' Otto shouted back.

'Of course the kitchen – the poor man spends enough of his life in sterile hotel rooms.'

Leo hurried up the steps. He wanted a glass of wine. The thought of the coming evening when he would be out on that platform, exposed to all those adoring eyes, with neither cape nor feathered cap, kingdom nor character to hide behind, made him more nervous than a score of first nights in the great houses.

The kitchen was bright and warm and smelled of minestrone.

'Soup,' said Eva and thrust a steaming bowl at him.

'And wine,' she added and handed him a glass of red wine.

Leo studied the label on the bottle.

'Barolo,' he said. 'Excellent choice. I've got several cases of this in my cellar.'

Eva didn't respond to this flattery.

98

'Sit him down, Otto. Sit him down!' she said to her brother who lunged forward and with those still shaking hands grabbed Leo by the forearms and pushed him onto a rickety kitchen chair.

The kitchen was hot. Still wrapped in his navy blue cashmere coat, his black scarf and his trilby hat, Leo felt that his bulk filled the room, as though he was a bear that had stumbled into a cramped human dwelling.

'Take his coat and hat, Otto! You should have done that in the passage.'

Otto didn't give Leo time to stand up but grabbed at the coat and started to pull it from his shoulders.

'Just a minute,' said Leo, trying to rise from his seat but getting caught in the tangle of Otto's arms. He felt his hat being whisked from his head and his scarf unwound from around his neck. He managed to stand up just long enough to feel his coat being dragged out from underneath him and then he was pushed back down by the now familiar trembling hands. Otto pulled up a chair and sat next to him.

'I thought we'd go over some of the subjects that we'd discuss in our little forum.' He took a clipboard and some paper from the table drawer.

'Forum?' said Leo.

'Well, that's my name for it,' Otto blushed. 'Since both Clara and I will be questioning you—'

'Both of you?' Leo raised one eyebrow. 'I was told that it was your society and that I was your guest—'

'And, of course, you are.' Clara was standing in the doorway. Immaculately dressed in expensive clothes and with hair and make-up that had, apparently, come straight from the salon, she looked almost handsome. 'Otto just thought that it would be less taxing for him if we shared the questioning.'

'But you said—' Otto was reaching for his papers. 'But you said—' he stammered a second time. A bell rang in the hallway.

'Doorbell, Otto,' said Eva.

*　　*　　*

99

Rose had spent the day moving. She had arranged for her furniture to go into storage and packed up just her books and clothes. All through the long, weary morning of sorting and stacking she prayed for something to happen that would give her an alternative to the tiny room and the increasingly terrible twins. But her hands continued to sift and pack; her back bent to lift and set down; her arms carried boxes into a rented car; her feet walked her back and forth until her old apartment was empty. At some point in the morning Daphne had overcome her disapproval and sent Ben, her twelve-year-old, to help Rose pack. Most of the back-breaking work was already done but still she was delighted to see the blond boy.

She hugged him to her as she stood in the doorway of the old, empty flat. Dearest favourite nephew Ben, she thought, the son I never had, the son I should have had. He brought with him a note from Daphne saying that he had to be back for dinner and rehearsals for a school play. Rose looked enviously at the white piece of paper, the clear handwriting, Daphne's safe structured world and thought, None of that will ever happen to me now.

Still, she and Ben drove to the twins' house and despite her vow never to let a member of her family see her shabby room she opened the french windows and watched with wry relief as Ben put down a box of books and scaled the pine ladder.

'You're going to sleep up here, Aunt Rose?' he said. 'Brilliant.'

Only when they had unloaded the last box did Rose notice that her lone chair was missing and in its place was her second note of the day. This one was from Otto.

'I needed the chair for our meeting,' it said. 'If you have a spare teapot, I want that too, and the stool if you wouldn't mind carrying it up at seven o'clock.'

'I've been carrying all bloody day,' said Rose, and marched upstairs to say as much to Otto. But far, far more than that, she wanted to say to both twins: 'Here is my nephew. I do have family. I'm not this isolated, abandoned soul that you imagine. Here is someone who is my flesh and blood, almost my son – he should have been my son but no matter. Somebody close to me has done the normal, healthy, conventional thing and reproduced themselves and this wonderful blond boy is the result – so there!' But inside the house Maria Callas was singing a florid, intricate solo, the twins didn't answer the doorbell and Ben had to go home to his school play.

At seven o'clock Rose clambered up the backstairs clutching her teapot in one hand and carrying her stool under her arm. She tapped on the kitchen window but still got no response. She went to the front door, set the stool down on the doorstep and sat on it. She was exhausted. She had caught cold and taken a flu remedy. She wanted nothing more than to climb into bed and sleep and sleep. Even the teapot seemed heavy. She set it down between her feet, closed her eyes and sat in the dark of the December night for a few seconds before ringing the bell. Had she arrived five minutes earlier, she would have found the front door swinging open, as Otto had left it in the excitement of greeting Leo. But this unwitting invitation had been issued to Clara, who walked in and slammed the door behind her.

When she did ring the bell, she got no response. She sat back on her seat and debated picking up her odd cargo and retreating to her room. Then she heard the gate open and voices coming up the path. The members of the OAS seemed to be arriving all at once. She still didn't know what OAS meant.

'What do those initials stand for?' she asked a tall blonde woman who was about to ring the OAS bell.

'Operatic Appreciation Society,' replied the big blonde.

'Oh,' said Rose, and repeated the name to herself. 'But that's not quite right. Surely that would make the appreciation operatic as opposed to the society—'

The rest of the group was coming up the steps. Again

there were a lot of grey heads, sensible winter coats and boots and a dog-collar or two. There was even a woman with a Zimmer-frame. The door opened and the big blonde woman swept on through. Rose just had time to rescue her teapot before the others pushed past her. She heard mutterings about the front row and knew that these genteel music lovers would trample any obstacle between them and those coveted seats.

When she did enter, Otto greeted her with a hurried kiss and, 'Such excitement, Rose – the great man is in my kitchen.' He grabbed the teapot, left her with the chair and disappeared along the passage. He shut the door tight behind him. Well, that's out of bounds, thought Rose, who had started to follow him, curious to see a great man in a suburban kitchen. She dragged the stool into the living-room, which was lit tonight by a roaring log fire in the grate and splashed with colour from red and white tiger tulips that stood in opulent bunches in fine cut-glass vases around the room. The grand piano had been polished and the fire's glow reflected in its lid. Three chairs had been placed next to the piano and on a small rosewood table in front of them stood a carafe of water, three glasses and a plate of smoked salmon sandwiches.

As Rose struggled to squeeze her stool into place in the back row, Eva appeared from the kitchen with a tray of red and white wine. She handed them briskly to the occupants of the front row, motioning to them to help themselves to the salmon sandwiches. At first none of them moved for fear of having their precious seat stolen from under them. Then the big blonde woman who had introduced herself to her neighbour as being a *répétiteur* from a provincial company and was too large and loud to lose her seat to anyone, helped herself to a handful of sandwiches and passed the plate along the line.

Every seat in the room had been filled except the one that Rose herself had carried in. She was glad to be in the back row, where she could sit with her legs under her and raise herself up to look over the heads of the crowd at the 'great man', if great man he was. Eva was serving wine to her row. She served Rose a glass of red without seeming to recognize her. Rose had just felt the warm glass being shoved into her hand when there was a rustle among the front rows and the door opened and Otto, Clara and Leo dalla Vigna walked in. Her ruse of kneeling on her seat was of little benefit to Rose for everyone in the room sprang to their feet and started to applaud as soon as Leo's broad silhouette appeared in the doorway. Rose herself was too tired by a day of carrying boxes to move, so she sat at the back, behind the clapping crowd and waited.

When the applause subsided and the rows of grey heads sank back into their seats, she saw the man himself. It took Rose a few seconds of staring at him before she realized that she had never seen a man quite like this in her life. She had spent years on the Continent amongst men of similar dark colouring; men who had the same taste in elegant, English clothes; men of the same age group whose beards and brows were streaked with grey, but she had never seen a man of such immense and immediate presence. He looked grave and wise and solid. Even as the applause washed up on him and he smiled a diffident smile of acknowledgement, there was a stillness about him that seemed to calm and still the excited members of his audience.

At the same time, Rose felt a shudder of recognition, felt that she had always known this man. Watching him from her corner, Rose experienced that confusing mixture of familiarity and discovery that she had felt the first time that she heard the music of *Tristan*, as though this man had always been there, just a breath away, but not seen until this moment.

Otto was on his feet, making a long introduction. He listed Leo's roles, recounted his triumphs. Rose learned that an ovation at La Scala can last forty-five minutes and that one man can be brought back for three dozen curtain-calls. As Otto warmed to his subject, recalling glorious evenings of earlier decades in Milan, Vienna and New York, Rose sat and looked at the man and thought: I have always known you.

As Otto concluded his introduction, Rose became aware of Clara. She was wearing the kind of designer dress that Rose had glimpsed in hotel display cabinets. She had never wanted such clothes, but now she found that she was comparing them to her own grubby overall and she was studying the smooth whiteness of Clara's skin and measuring the inches between the intense brunette and the broad dark man on her left.

Rose heard Otto say, 'Ladies and gentlemen, what an honour it is to welcome Leo dalla Vigna.' She heard the applause start again, saw a few of the more zealous members leap to their feet a second time and sit back down just as quickly. She realized that she was still clutching the glass of red wine and, forgetting the warning against alcoholic beverages that had accompanied her double dose of flu remedy, swallowed the dark, dry Barolo down. Within minutes the pale green rug rose up to meet her. She tried to concentrate; the room oscillated. Otto was asking Leo questions about his early days at La Scala. Rose wanted quite desperately to hear what this man had to say but her mind had started to whirl around inside her head, taking in the speakers' words and flinging them pell-mell into dark, unreachable corners of her brain. But if she could not follow the sense of what Leo was saying, she could still hear the sound of his words. And as the room revolved gently around her, she felt her spirit reaching out and anchoring itself on his voice. Not for the first time she found comfort and security in this voice so vast and deep, seeming to encompass hope and sorrow, to create a safe haven within the space that it filled.

In between his questions, Otto had programmed appropriate excerpts from Leo's recordings. From time to time his slender and now only slightly shaking fingers would press a button and the singing Leo would fill the singing house. During those moments it seemed to Rose that Leo could disappear into himself, unaware of the adoring eyes on him as he listened to his own voice. Just once he shook his head briefly as if trying to quell the music that welled up within him.

Then weariness overcame Rose. She felt her head lurching forward and made a conscious effort to pull it back. But her feverish brain wanted rest and soon she succumbed and let her chin loll forward and be lulled by the sounds of Otto's soft tenor and Leo's bass as they talked and Leo's recorded voice sang. From his seat at the front of the room Leo looked out at the audience and saw that one member had fallen fast asleep. And this was not a weary grey head that slumped forward but a blonde woman. Again he rued his inability to tell a tale, again he envied the cab-driver who was probably sailing back over Hammersmith Bridge by now, his tales of own goals, cup finals, million-pound transfers unfurling behind him.

Leo was sorting frantically through his twenty-five years of opera experience, hoping to find a tale that would arouse and amuse the blonde and all the smiling grey heads around her, when he noticed that Clara had drawn her seat closer to his.

She smiled at him so warmly that for a moment he thought that he had unwittingly shown wit and that this was the result. But he looked to the blonde and she slept on. During the first half-hour of his talk, he had forgotten Clara. In his introduction, Otto had described her as one of the society's patrons and she had responded to this with an uncharacteristically shy smile. Now she looked beyond Leo to Otto who had dropped his papers on the floor for the second time that evening.

'Perhaps I could come in here and ask Signor dalla Vigna some questions,' she said to Otto's blond head as he rummaged around on the green carpet. 'Am I right in thinking that you met your wife, the wonderful American coloratura soprano Kay Lindstrom at the Accademia Chigiana in Siena?'

Leo noticed that at the mention of the word 'wife', the whole room seemed to lean forward several inches. How hungry they were for details of his private life and how determined he was not to provide them. But he couldn't say, No, no, he hadn't met his wife in Siena. And to launch into a discourse on how he disliked allusions to his private life would sound pompous, an over-reaction to what was, ostensibly, an innocent question. Besides, Otto was sitting back up and beaming encouragement and he very much liked Otto whose eyes shone when he spoke of Verdi and Wagner and whose hands trembled when he spoke to Leo. When he was out of this painful spotlight and standing in the kitchen with a glass of wine in his hand, he planned to take Otto aside and tell him that there was no need to tremble for him; that he, Leo, was just an ordinary man who had been given an extraordinary voice; that he was a channel for the truly great composers' work. And if the night went on and the frowsy blonde sister served up some more of that soup that still smelled so good, he would say that the trembling hands, the quake in the voice, all the misplaced adulation isolated him, the undeserving singer, and made him feel quite desperately lonely.

Clara was waiting for an answer.

'Yes, we both went to the Accademia Chigiana,' he said and without stopping for breath, 'it is a fine school. Some of your finest singers went there. Gwyneth Jones, I think—'

'But your wife's career came to a tragic halt with the death of your daughter,' continued Clara.

'I not talk about my private life,' said Leo, his English failing him for the first time in years.

'Of course not,' smiled Clara and turned a page in her notebook. The audience sat back, their interest receding along with the promise of witnessing the great man's emotional disarray.

'She must miss singing,' Clara added, in a conversational tone, addressing her question solely to Leo.

'You'll have to ask her,' he replied, and the brief exchange brought the audience forward in their seats yet again.

Rose woke up. The atmosphere in the room had

changed. When she had drifted off, only minutes earlier, the people around her were displaying a generous, almost cloying enthusiasm for the man on the platform. They laughed at the smallest witticism, smiled a hundred smiles of encouragement as he answered the simplest question. Now their adoring indulgence had given way to tension. They were all staring at Clara, who had apparently taken over the interview. She still looked as poised and unruffled as when she had entered the room but Leo was changed. Rose could see that. He was sitting forward, legs apart, his forearms on his knees, 'like a boxer waiting to come out of his corner', thought Rose. Something terrible was about to happen to the man on the platform and there was nothing she could do to stop it. But what could happen in Otto and Eva's warm and lovely room with a fire in the grate and good wine in the glasses?

'Looking through this long list of roles,' Clara continued to leaf through her notebook. As she held the page aloft in a squint of middle-aged long-sight, Rose felt a second of sympathy for her. Then Clara found what she was seeking; the squint turned to a smile and Rose went cold inside. 'I see that after all the priests and elders, after Moses and Mephistopheles, the one role you have made your own is King Philip in Verdi's *Don Carlos*. You, the long bereaved father, could bring to the music of the estranged father such depth of feeling—'

'I not talk about private businesses,' said Leo, feeling his English slip irretrievably out of his grasp.

'Oh, but I was talking about your professional life. About the unique ability of the true artist to transform private grief into creative triumph. Whole theses have been written about Verdi losing his wife and daughters to typhus and yet going on to write some of the most poignant father/daughter encounters in the operatic repertoire. You, as an interpreter of his music, must have gone through a similar process.'

Leo looked hopefully towards Otto but he was still

shuffling through his papers. Now his whole body was trembling.

'If memory serves me correctly,' Clara smiled on, 'your little daughter was not even a year old at her death. She passed through your life so briefly and yet you have gone on to become the supreme father interpreter of opera—'

Leo rose. In spite of his bulk he seemed to make no noise as he moved.

'And what courage it must now take to tackle the Wagnerian repertoire.' Clara's voice was unchanged. She intended, apparently, to continue the interview as if her subject were still seated obediently alongside her. 'And especially in what must be the most tormented and loving father role of them all – Wotan.'

At the mention of 'Wotan' the grey heads that had been fixed on Leo, now turned to each other as they expressed pleasure and surprise. Leo paused but he had vowed not to turn around. He strode down the aisle and still his broad, dark form seemed to make no sound, but as he left the room, the lid on the grand piano slammed shut, sending a cut-glass vase full of tulips and a plate of smoked salmon sandwiches crashing to the floor.

Otto dropped his clipboard and ran after him. His departure was a cue to the members of the OAS to move. They rose from their seats but were unsure of where to go. The big blonde salvaged a salmon sandwich and said the evening was better than anything she'd seen on *Wogan*. The others drifted towards the door and hovered, their lined faces crestfallen but their waiting bodies revealing the hope that lingered – that the great man would return, the vase be repaired and the evening go on as before. Only Eva proved that she knew better by appearing with a dustpan and brush and sweeping away the shattered glass almost as soon as it hit the floor.

Rose knew as soon as he had risen from his seat that she had to get to the singer. She jostled past the hesitant group at the door, sending the woman with the Zimmer-frame lurching forward and pausing just long enough to set her back into place. She dared to go right through the door that had restrained the OAS members but found only an empty kitchen. She continued through to the hall and there she saw Otto and Leo, standing in the dark by the front door. The sight of the singer, only feet away from her, froze Rose to the spot. Leo hadn't seen her; his attention was directed towards Otto into whose hand he was thrusting a wad of notes and saying '*Per i fiori*.' As her eyes adjusted to the dark, Rose saw that Otto was gazing up at Leo, opening and immediately shutting his mouth as if he were trying to talk underwater. Leo opened the door to leave and in the stream of orange light that poured in from the street lamps, Rose saw tears on Otto's cheeks. The singer, who was perhaps also seeing those tears for the first time, reached out and gripped Otto's slender shoulders in his large hands. He squeezed him so hard that the blond twin was raised several inches from the ground. As he was brought up to eye level with his idol, Otto turned his face away, holding his head stiffly to one side, apparently ashamed of his tears. Leo set him gently back down and walked out of the door.

Rose ran after him. She knew that she should go to Otto but he was slumped unmoving against the hall wall whereas Leo was striding down the garden path and motioning to a taxi. She caught up with him at the gate. The taxi was slowing down. Rose prayed that it would ride on by but as she clutched at the elbow of the navy blue cashmere coat, the cab stopped. Leo turned and saw for the umpteenth time in his career, a woman looking beseechingly into his eyes. His first instinct was to slide into the role he had played at so many stage doors: prepare to accept praise with grace and modesty, and answer the usual questions about future plans. But those other questions in the warm and lovely room only seconds earlier had seemed to Leo to strip all his roles from him, even this the most familiar one. He felt exposed and vulnerable and could obey only the primitive urge to flee. He turned away from the woman but in that same lurid light that had revealed Otto's tears, he saw that she was the blonde who had vexed him so deeply by sleeping through so much of the evening. He had last glimpsed her, slumped in her chair, as Clara had moved warm and smiling towards him. He stared down at her in silence.

Rose's eyes were on a level with his beard and his thick neck wrapped twice in a black woollen scarf. His bulk thrilled her. His eyes were brown and gentle and were gazing quizzically down at her. The cab honked its horn. Leo made to walk towards it, then turned back, grasped both her hands in his and said, '*Grazie, grazie mille, signora* – you have the *cortesia* to sleep through *tanta ignominia*!' And he was gone through the gate and into the taxi.

Rose stood in the empty street, aware at first only of the warmth and smoothness of the hands that had just held hers. Then, as she deciphered the tangled sentence and realized that she had been thanked for being asleep, she saw a triangle of light coming from the front room of the singing house as the corner of a curtain was raised and then left to drop back into place.

PART II
The Staircase

Chapter Eleven

The great winds of the autumn gave way to the great snows of winter. What started as a light sleet that wan December morning in London, spread and rippled and thinly coated France, then folded back upon itself and covered the whole continent. White and silent, this second, strong, confident snow of the winter settled on the tops of the pine trees, sifted down and draped the forest floor, wrapping itself around every branch and twig. Slow, heavy and deliberate, it fell without ceasing, muffling the rooftops of the great singing houses in Northern Italy, Germany and Austria. This was no vulnerable, ephemeral snowfall. As lakes froze and cities shivered, as winter tumbled and swirled across the frigid continent, billions of flakes waited to follow the billions that fell.

Clara awoke with the first fall of sleet, put yet another plate of meat out for the cat, packed a large expensive suitcase and took a taxi to the airport to catch the dawn flight to Milan. Her sleep had been perturbed and restless. Again and again in her dreams her hand lifted the green brocade curtain to reveal a pair of hands holding other hands, lit by an orange street light. Now, as she bundled her expensive clothes into the suitcase, her only thought was flight towards the Continent and the singing house that was La Scala. Clara was first out of Great Britain and over the Channel that morning, carried, although she didn't know it, on the waves of the winter storm that gusted around the plane.

Rose lay up in her high little bed and thought that she could hear the silence of the snow. But there was no snow last night, she remembered, and there is no

113

reason for there to be snow this morning. She reached for the diary that she kept under her pillow. There were few entries for the year. Nothing, not even her wedding plans, had seemed important enough to write down. Now it seemed important to say that it was snowing. She lay back on the pillow in no hurry to rush to the window, quite sure of what she would find outside and wanting nothing more than to listen to its silence.

There was a knock on the pane. Rose did rush now, wrapping her robe around her, sliding down the ladder, hoping that it was Otto. He would be distraught, still stunned by the collapse of his carefully planned evening. She would comfort him and in the consoling, they would come to talk about that dark, elusive man who had brought his stillness to the singing house. But it was Eva who stood outside the door in her overcoat and boots, holding an umbrella over her head as the sleet swirled between them.

'Let me in, Rose,' she said. 'I have to ask a favour.'

Leo had awoken in his Savoy Hotel suite that morning to find that he no longer felt lonely and homesick. The desolation that had swept over him in the warm and welcoming suburban room only hours earlier had gone. He ordered a full English breakfast and only when he had emptied the plate did he start to feel some guilt about the adoring, innocent members of the OAS whom he had abandoned the previous evening. He also wondered whether he should deny Clara's outburst about his plans to sing Wotan. No, no, there was no point in denying it now. Besides that may explain why he felt so much better this morning. Now that it had been said, now that his secret ambition was out in the open, his assuming of the role ceased to be a dream and became a fact.

He was also bound for Milan where he was to rehearse for the opening performance of the season in Verdi's *Attila*. When he arrived at the airport to take a mid-morning flight, the thickening snow had finally proved too much for the English authorities and his plane was delayed by several hours. The benign mood of the Savoy suite stayed with him, however, and as he sorted through a batch of assorted phone cards and prepared to call both his agent and home, he marvelled at the beauty of the teaming flakes that filled the glass panel of the departure lounge.

He called Kay first. She had awoken to find that the first blizzard in a decade had covered her diving deck. These days the brisk pad out to swim was not her first act of the morning. Before that she had to let out the nameless Pekinese but this morning the dog had turned around after two seconds and trotted forlornly back inside, its fur and black nose covered in thick white flakes. Kay had just armed herself with a broom and an umbrella when the phone rang.

'This blizzard is everywhere,' Leo replied when she told him of the snow in Bellagio. 'You can't swim in this.'

'The lake's not frozen.'

'But you'll catch your death just walking out of the house.'

'I'm a tough Midwestern girl,' said Kay.

'Well, at least have John sweep the deck,' he said, and Kay smiled. There was something strangely exciting about her husband's choice of words.

As Leo stood in the snowbound terminal, tapping out his Milan agent's number, Rose and Eva stood waiting for the kettle to boil in the phoneless house by the Thames.

'I forgot to take my stool back,' said Rose. 'Nowhere to sit . . .' she shrugged.

'We've got a proposition for you, Rose,' said Eva, leaning on her closed umbrella as if it were a shooting-stick.

Rose shuddered. 'Proposition' was a potent word, carrying with it an offer of change and of new possibilities. It also implied that a decision would be expected of her and Rose had awoken that morning wanting nothing more than to gaze out at the snow and dream and drift. But Eva's life consisted of actions and decisions; in her world there was always wood to be chopped, soup to be made, tickets to be obtained and performances to attend.

'It's my knee,' said Eva, and reaching down, grabbed her left knee and held it up in front of them both. 'Feel it,' she said. 'Feel how knobbly and arthritic it's become.'

Why did these twins insist on thrusting their limbs at her to be felt? Rose wondered as she gingerly tapped Eva's knee. Why couldn't they just occasionally have some of the English reserve about physical contact?

'We want you to drive us around Europe,' Eva went on. 'What with my knees seizing up again and Otto unable to drive, but he said you do. We will pay petrol and hotel rooms – we don't stay anywhere very fancy, mind you – you'll just have to pay food and any other expenses. And we'd let you off the rent for as long as we're gone.'

'Where exactly do you mean by Europe?' asked Rose, whose first thought was that she wanted to stay right where she was, alone in her room, gazing at the now thick snow falling on the beech.

'La Scala, La Fenice, and the Staatsoper.'

'You want me to drive to Milan,' Rose replied, trying to work out what the other names meant.

'And Venice and perhaps Munich or Vienna,' said Eva. 'I intend to draw up an operatic circuit and sell the idea as a package to Otto's employers – link hotels with tickets to performances, have Otto give his little talks – and finally make some money doing it. We need to supplement our income, you know, before we're both too old—'

'How is Otto?' asked Rose.

'Reading maps,' replied Eva.

That was no answer, thought Rose, but she was relieved to know that he wasn't weeping or fighting with the phone company or experiencing any of the woes that the twin brother seemed subject to.

'I'll have to consult my diary about the trip,' said Rose.

'All right,' said Eva and stood and waited.

'I'll – I'll let you know when I've looked at it.'

'Look at it now,' said Eva. 'We want to leave tomorrow at dawn.'

'Tomorrow? Oh, I could never be ready for tomorrow—'

'Why not? What do you do with yourself all day?'

'I've got some translating work to do,' lied Rose. 'And I'm coming down with the flu. Yes, the flu – I'll need a good week to recover.'

'You haven't got the flu. You've got a cold,' said Eva, turning to leave. 'But it's up to you – we've made the offer. One way or another we have to leave tomorrow. If you don't drive us we'll have to find our own way.' And she limped out of the french windows and into the snow.

She wasn't limping when she came in, thought Rose. She picked up her diary, intending to continue where she had left off when the older woman had appeared at her door but the names of La Fenice and La Scala sang from the blank page. Red plush velvet, crystal chandeliers, fat Latin ladies, dapper little Latin men, French perfumes, marble staircases, cloakrooms that might actually contain cloaks, domes dominating an ancient skyline, royal boxes, winding corridors, stage doors, curtains rising, curtains falling, flowers tumbling from the gallery, formal bouquets, a thousand lights blazing, a thousand lights dimming and everywhere, everywhere, music and voices. Soprano voices soaring to the ceiling, tenor voices carrying them aloft – air issuing from a sweaty Italian, or a stocky Spaniard, from the plain humble bodies of fallible, earthbound people, swelling and surging upwards: perfect, sumptuous, all-embracing human sound. And off in the back of her mind, like the distant rumble of an avalanche, Rose recalled the voice of a bass singer.

A few hours later she scribbled a note to her mother, posted it, returned to the house and knocked at Otto and Eva's door. Nobody answered but the door was

117

open. She let herself in. Otto was sitting on the pale green carpet in the front room, surrounded by yellow Michelin maps and red Michelin guides. Only her stool remained, marooned at the back of the room where she had left it the previous evening. When she walked towards Otto she saw a circular greasy stain on the carpet where the sandwiches had landed.

'I knew you'd come,' he said, unfolding a map of Europe. 'I'm plotting a route that has no ugly sights, no autobahns, no factories – a route that only passes through beauty.'

'Don't talk such crap, Otto.' Eva put her head through the serving hatch. 'With a blizzard blowing all over Europe, you'll go on the autoroute like everyone else.'

'I can't drive up mountains,' said Rose, sure that for Otto, mountains, peaks, crags, ravines, anything dramatic, romantic and menacing must represent beauty. 'I've got vertigo. And I'm not used to driving in snow – don't we have to put chains on the tyres or something?'

'Eva's taken care of all that this morning,' said Otto.

'No mountains, Otto,' said Rose. 'Besides, if you want to work out a circuit for a conducted tour of the great opera cities, you don't want to be wasting time scaling the Alps.'

'Conducted tour? Is that what Eva told you?' Otto sat back on his haunches. 'Poor old cow,' he whispered. 'She's trying to convince herself that's why we're going. Truth is we go every year. It's a pilgrimage. We pay our annual homage to the ghosts of the great composers and we pursue the great voices. That embarrasses Eva. She goes but she's ashamed, so every year she comes up with this spiel about making a profitable little business out of what she calls our "hobby". Stamp-collecting is a hobby, train-spotting is a hobby. But this—' he traced the route to Milan on the map, 'we actually have tickets for the opening of the season in La Scala. Muti is conducting *Attila*. And Leo, our Leo, is in the title role—'

'What happened last night, Otto?' said Rose.

'Fucking Clara causing fucking trouble again, asking personal questions, stirring up the fucking muck.'

'And where are our first-night tickets for La Scala coming from?' Eva's head reappeared through the serving hatch. 'From fucking Clara, that's where, Otto. You're an old whore for accepting her offer.'

'But she has access to things and people,' sighed Otto, 'that I can only glimpse at.' The serving hatch slammed shut. He smiled wanly at Rose. 'It's true. She's my lifeline to all that. I thought that with my little society I might get a few invitations, the odd first-night ticket, but it never really happened whereas that spoilt cow has it all. Why shouldn't I accept the odd offer, Rose? Why shouldn't I?'

'I don't know,' said Rose, who had been hoping to learn more about Leo.

'Listen, Rose, listen and then you will know,' said Otto and, selecting a record from his collection, he placed the needle halfway across the disc and sat back, eyes closed. A tenor sang, a soprano responded.

'Nowhere in life is emotion so raw, nowhere else in any art is "I love you" said with so much boiling passion. That's *Masked Ball* – no masterpiece, in fact it's a rather ordinary middle Verdi but oh, the feeling—'

Otto hummed along looking straight at her, searching her eyes for a response. He took Rose's hand. She tried to look away but had to leave her hand where it was, resting limply in his. Was this some clumsy attempt to tell her that he loved her? The music stopped.

'I thought – no, no, I didn't think,' Otto corrected himself still gripping her fingers, 'I truly believed that I would be singing that one day – up on a stage, the orchestra before me, the soprano in my arms. But my voice was more of an Irish tenor, not fashionable now, not Italianate enough. I spent a year in Italy trying to build it, make it more dramatic. I used to tell people I got a scholarship but I didn't. Eva got a part-time job and she and my parents paid and for a while it helped but I didn't have it, you see, Rose. I just didn't have it.'

'And you've accepted that? You don't mind any more?'

'Mind what? That the door to that world is closed to me for ever? Of course I mind.'

'Why?'

'Now there's a daft question—'

'No, no, it isn't,' said Rose. 'Do you really think there's that much to be said for fame? And we all know about fortune.'

'It wasn't the fame or the fortune – I've just told you, it was the music.'

'Well, you've still got that.'

'Perhaps, but not in the way I wanted.' Otto sat back and listened to the old vinyl record that was playing itself out behind him. 'You can't know what it feels like to have one's voice sailing over a full orchestra, to be at one with that vast sound. I only had a glimpse, a key-hole peep, but I do know . . . And to walk onto a stage with an audience full of kings, princes, heads of state and know that none of them can do what you are about to do.'

'That sounds like ego to me,' said Rose.

'That's as may be but I worked so hard for it, thought I was destined for it. I even came fourth in a competition once – and in the end I just wasn't good enough. But I can't stop loving it, Rose.'

The declaration of love was made. 'You're lucky to have something that matters that much,' said Rose, relieved not to be the object of that love. 'Some people go through their whole lives not having a passion for anyone or anything. Millions of quite bland, polite lives run their course and expire without ever knowing passion.'

'Oh, I couldn't imagine that,' said Otto, quite matter-of-fact now. He tapped her hand. 'But you do see why I prostitute myself to foul old Clara, don't you?'

'Perhaps.'

'Not perhaps, Rose. You must see. *You* must. I saw you last night. I saw you run out into the street. That's

120

why I knew you'd come on our journey.' He walked to the window. The street lamps had gone on. Rose could see the enormous snowflakes streaming down the column of light. 'Whatever Eva says, we will take the loveliest roads. I'll tell you stories of Verdi and Puccini, Wagner and Strauss, of the great singers and the great houses. You're so lucky, Rose – what I wouldn't give to be able to hear *Parsifal* or *Falstaff* again for the first time – to have it all ahead of me.'

He put another record on as the twilight faded. With this invitation to a journey the snow and music seemed to intertwine and stretch out across the old continent. The music of the dead composers, the music of a dead world seemed to re-emerge through the blanketing snow – a world inhabited by Otto, Eva, Leo and Clara, by the queues of people freezing in front of Covent Garden, La Scala and Vienna, and, increasingly, by Rose herself.

Chapter Twelve

Next morning Rose drove the twins' car through the morning suburbs and towards Kent to the accompaniment of Siegfried's Funeral March from *The Twilight of the Gods*. Otto put the cassette into the player, announced its title, climbed in the back of the car and stretched out under a blanket; Eva sat in the front, opened a map and announced that she would navigate. Within five minutes they were both asleep and didn't wake until the car joined the queue at the ferry.

'I sent him a bill,' Eva announced as she opened her eyes and stared at the lines of cars around her.

'Oh, Eva, no!' wailed Otto. 'Say that you didn't! Say that you're joking!'

'I billed him for the broken vase and the carpet cleaning. I sent it care of La Scala, by registered post.'

'How could you?' moaned Otto. 'How could you blame that poor man? You should have sent it to Clara. The cow has the money to pay and it was her fault.'

'He's right,' said Rose.

'She knows Leo will pay,' said Otto, sitting back in his seat with a sigh, picking up his papers and pushing his reading glasses back up his nose. 'He's got a reputation for being honourable. I'm embarrassed by you this time, Eva – I am – he gave me a hundred quid to replace the tulips and the vase, and in cash. But you can't ever leave things alone, can you?'

Eva had opened the map and was running her finger down the Autoroute du Sud.

'We'll break the journey somewhere around here.' She held the map up to Rose. 'If that's all right by you. I've worked out the best route and marked it in yellow. You can look at it in the cafeteria.'

'Will we have dinner on the ferry?' said Rose.

'Oh, Eva and I never eat on the boat – we have to stay out in the fresh air on top or we both get migraines.' He rummaged in a small bag and pulled out a few sheets of paper. 'This will give you something to read after you've studied the route. These are transcripts of talks I've given on various aspects of Verdi, Wagner, Mozart. I do feel we rather threw you in the deep end with *Tristan* and *Don Carlos*. These are very simplified explanations for people who don't know anything.'

Once they had parked the car and made their way up the stairs to the main floor, the twins did keep on going past the warm, carpeted cafeteria and out onto the deserted deck. They went straight to the front of the boat, donned two plastic, hooded macs that they pulled from a travel-bag and sat with their legs on the rail in front, staring silently through the snow towards an invisible horizon. Once or twice Eva leaned forward and pulled Otto's collar up to keep the snow out, stopping to wipe a stray flake from his eyebrows.

What have I done? thought Rose, as the big boat sailed away with the snowswept twins before her and the White Cliffs of Dover behind. And again she saw the dark silhouette making its way towards a taxi. And she knew that even were she deprived of sight and hearing, her feet would still go in one direction. She turned away from the winter lights of Kent and stared, with the twins, towards the frozen continent before them.

Otto was true to his promise of filling the car with composers and singers, arias and stories. Eva was true to her vow of keeping them on the efficient, wide roads that would carry them south to La Scala. They drove past filling stations and hypermarkets. There wasn't a château in sight but it didn't matter because the snow furred and blurred the concrete and the plate glass.

They broke their journey in a two-star hotel at the spot that Eva had marked on the map. In the morning Rose came down to breakfast to find Otto making a call from the pay phone at the reception desk.

'But you promised—' Otto's smooth skin was tinged pink. He repeatedly wiped one hand on his jacket. 'But when I checked with the woman at the box-office, she said—'

Rose tried to concentrate on the map of Italy that Eva had left with her the previous evening but seconds later Otto's voice rang out through the small lobby.

'She hung up on me! The cow cut me off in mid-sentence!'

Rose knew that he was referring to Clara.

'That bitch! That fucking bitch!' He sat down at Rose's table. 'Well, you definitely don't have a ticket for La Scala,' he glared at Rose. 'Trouble is, by fighting for *you*, by trying to help *you*, I've upset the cow and now I'm not sure that we have one either. Fuck her! Fuck her! Fuck her!' Otto yelled at the indifferent French hotel walls. 'She's done this before. She did it for Domingo in Vienna. We got there – we had a special air fare where we had to fix the date of our return. She knew that but she went and got tickets for another performance so we either had to cough up a couple of hundred quid in extra fare or miss Placido.'

Rose was wondering just how expendable her presence would be on anything but the driving part of the trip. She was deeply disappointed that she didn't have a ticket for Leo dalla Vigna's performance in *Attila*. She had wrapped her emerald green dress in layers of plastic and placed it lovingly across the cases and bags in the back of the Escort.

'It snowed again during the night,' she said, rising to leave, longing to escape the small room that was taut with Otto's tension. 'I'll have to scrape the car off.'

Eva was already in the car-park. She was so heavily bundled up in a headscarf, shapeless woollen coat and fur boots that, had she not been scraping vigorously at the windows of their car, Rose wouldn't have recognized her. The twin sister's untidy blonde hair was already caked with falling snow. She had started the car and left it running; Rose had to make her way through a cloud of exhaust fumes and wet, stinging snow to get to her.

'Otto is having some kind of crisis in the dining-room,' she told his sister.

'So what's new?' Eva reached into the car and turned on the rear windshield-wiper. 'Who's lost their voice this time? Which fat cow has decided she'd rather sit at home in her villa and eat chocolate?'

'Clara seems to have reneged on getting your tickets.' Rose took a second scraper from the boot and started to work on the windows on her side.

'Oh, she does that all the time,' said Eva. 'It's part of the ritual.'

'So she will come through with the tickets eventually?' said Rose, relieved that her seat in La Scala was about to be restored to her.

'Maybe, maybe not. Who really gives a bugger?'

'Your brother does!' Rose wanted to add, I do, but because she never knew how Eva would react, she was reluctant to confide her true feelings to her.

'Sod 'em all, I say,' said Eva, banging her gloved hands together to remove the excess snow.

'You can't mean that,' said Rose. 'You've been doing this for so many years, travelling to all these opera houses, helping Otto when he had his career; it must have value.' The exhaust fumes were pouring out between her and Eva. Because Rose couldn't see the older woman's face through the snow and the smoke, and because the engine's roar half muffled her voice she felt safe to probe more deeply than she would dare had they been able to see and hear each other clearly.

'You've got it arse-upwards!' cried Eva. 'It has value because I've done it. If I admitted to myself that Otto's great music is just air and ego, all the years I've given to it would be diminished.'

'But some things are worth giving your life and energy to.' Rose's thoughts floundered around in the snow and the smoke. 'Great music must be – it must.'

'Hmmph,' snorted Eva, and walked away to get the bags from the lobby.

Their journey towards the Italian frontier was laborious. The snow-ploughs hadn't cleared the smaller roads to the autoroute. A car had skidded into a snow-filled ditch and two others had spun to a halt on the ice patches that lay invisible beneath the unending white.

Otto insisted on putting Siegfried's Funeral March back into the cassette player. Rose asked him to remove it, saying that it was music that demanded one's full concentration.

'I am concentrating,' he replied.

They had just reached the autoroute and the first stretch of clear road in two hours when Otto declared that they would have to get back off and find a pay phone.

'I must send a bouquet to Jessye for her opening night in Vienna.'

'But we just got on the autoroute.' Rose looked to Eva for support.

'Then we'll just have to get back off,' said Eva. 'Anyway, I want to make a phone call, an urgent call.'

'Who to?'

'To Clara.'

With the mention of the word 'Clara' and the knowledge that her precious ticket lay in the absent woman's possession, Rose obediently followed Eva's directions to the desolate little village five kilometres up the road.

The blizzard was so dense that the only light visible in the village square came from a boulangerie in the far corner under two pollarded plane trees. Their truncated stumps had accumulated a half-dozen inches of snow at each tip; they looked to Rose as though a dark woodland giant had, on a frivolous impulse, given himself a manicure and was holding his hands up to survey the result. Otto got out of the car and walked to a phone-booth that loomed and receded in the whirling white. Rose and Eva watched from inside the Escort as he ordered the bouquet and had it addressed to the diva without once referring to an address book. Then he returned to his seat in the back of the car and told Rose to drive on.

'What about my call?' said Eva, opening the door and swinging her plump knees to the outer edge of the passenger seat. The snow blew into the car, entering their mouths and noses and rendering them all speechless.

'You're not really going to call Clara?' said Otto. But Eva was gone through the snow to the phone-booth.

The wind and snow gusted into the Escort. Rose reached forward to close the door but Otto wanted to watch his sister's conversation. The booth had misted up and Eva's eerily immobile silhouette appeared and disappeared between squalls of snow. She had the receiver to her ear but the conversation seemed so even-keeled that Otto concluded that she wasn't talking to anyone.

'She's just pretending to talk to her in order to placate me,' he announced after they had been watching her for about five minutes.

'Why does she do that?' Rose was asking the question not just for the snow-blown moment in the phonebooth but for the whole of the twins' lives.

'She always has.'

The smugness of the word 'always' revolted Rose. Sitting in the freezing Escort with the door open, watching a doting sister pander to her spoilt brother's whims, she realized that she too was placating Otto. She leaned forward and slammed the door shut. She turned the engine on to warm up the car. Had spoilt, capricious Otto been in the phone-booth, she would have been tempted to drive away and leave him in the frozen desolate village, standing between the dark giant's manicured hands for ever. She stared ahead of her, expecting his chin to appear somewhere near her ear as he issued an order to reopen the door but a hand clutching a cassette appeared instead.

'The "Siegfried Idyll",' said Otto. 'Imagine, Rose, if you will, Christmas Day, 1870. In the Wagners' villa at Tribschen on Lake Lucerne, Cosima is furious. It is her

127

birthday and she has been complaining to her diary that there is no sign of a present from our Richard—'

Wagner again, thought Rose. I thought we'd heard the last of him when we set foot on Latin soil. She closed her eyes and sat back in the driver's seat.

'Unbeknown to old Cosima, however,' Otto went on, 'the maestro had been rehearsing his orchestra to play this piece on the double staircase when she emerged from her bedroom on Christmas morning. Has any more beautiful gift ever been given a human being?'

Rose was about to say that finding a whole orchestra outside your bedroom door when your breath smells and you are in dire need of a pee might not be every woman's idea of a birthday present, but Otto had pushed the cassette into the machine and, of course, he, and Wagner, had her again. She had been expecting an ocean of ecstatic sound or the brassy pomposity that she thought came with the earlier works. She had not been expecting the tenderness, the serenity that filled the car.

'It was also a gift to Cosima for the birth of their first son, Siegfried.' Gentle and serene as the music was, Otto's words filled Rose with pain. How far she had travelled from England and Daphne and Martin and Ben, the son she would never have, the son she should have had. These barren twins had sucked her into a black hole that contained nothing but notes, sounds, rhythms, voices. Nothing she could hold in her arms the way she had once held the splendid Spaniard or even Martin; nothing that she could see and love the way she loved Ben's blond head and his thin tanned legs. She kept her eyes tight closed; from a long way away in the back of the car she heard Otto's voice calling, 'Bullfinches! Bullfinches!'

A flock of bullfinches had settled onto what she had come to think of as the giant's fingertips. Their raspberry-red breasts were lit from behind by the warm yellow light of the baker's window.

'A flock of flying rubies,' said Otto. The bullfinches had nestled in the smooth deep layers of snow on the tree stump and in the thick Vs of snow between the branches – at least a hundred birds and most of them the flamboyant red males. The baker's light through the cascading flakes illuminated the poor pollarded plane tree and made it glow ruby-red and gold and white – an instant Christmas tree on the desolate, winter-locked square. More and more birds gathered and now it seemed that the tree was draped in red.

A flurry of wind sent the snow tumbling, lumpen and heavy from above. The red birds rose as one and flew off into the blizzard. Eva crossed the few yards from the phone-booth. They had both forgotten her.

'Well, that's that sorted out,' she said.

'Did you get the tickets?' said Otto.

'You mean did I get the tickets back? We already had them—'

'Well, did you?' asked Otto.

'Yes I did.'

'See, Rose, I told you magical things would happen—'

'What's magical about it?'

'What Otto means—' Rose started to say, but Eva didn't wait for her to finish her sentence.

'Magic! Bollocks! I talked to Clara like a human being if you must know – treated her as I would treat a normal person—'

'And you got the tickets?' said Rose, thinking that yes, the bullfinches had for a magical moment formed a curtain, like the velvet curtain of Covent Garden and the one that awaited and would open onto Leo dalla Vigna at La Scala.

'Oh, I didn't get *you* one,' said Eva. 'I got ours back but there was no talking her into coughing up a third ticket. She says that there was never any question of a third ticket in the first place.' Eva picked up the map and ran her finger along the Route Nationale. 'If Rose drives fast enough we could be in Milan for supper.'

'At the Santa Cecilia!' cried Otto. 'Onward, Rose! We'll have fettuccine alla siciliana and a bottle of Barolo to celebrate *Attila*.'

129

Chapter Thirteen

'Snowman!' cried Kay when she opened the door to John Tillson that morning. The young American had cycled through the blizzard. He was caked in snow; it covered his cycle cape and clung to his boots; his hair was thick with it and his eyelashes were tipped with it. His vision was blurred as a result and only when he stepped into the thick heat of the hall and the snow slithered onto the mat, did he see that Kay was still in her dressing-gown. But dressing-gown wasn't the word for what his employer was wearing; John knew that a more elegant, feminine word was needed for the high-necked, flowing silk robe. Kay looked like one of the operatic heroines she had long since declined to portray. '*Rosenkavalier*' – the title of the Strauss opera slipped into his mind. Not Kay's repertoire, it was a role that would never have suited her voice – this Viennese wife who took a young man as her lover. But as he stepped into the villa and the snow fell from his eyes, John thought that Kay had deliberately dressed like that.

'I'm late for my swim,' she was saying and when he turned around from hanging his frozen cape on a hook by the door he saw that she was holding out a broom and an umbrella.

'Would you go out right now and sweep the deck down?' That brief promise of imminent seduction had slipped away like the snow onto the mat. 'I was all set to go out there and do it myself,' Kay went on, 'but Leo seems to think that sweeping the deck holds some horrible threat for me. Dear Leo.' John was filled with resentment of this absent husband who with one order issued from an airport lounge or a four-star hotel could impose his silent presence between the beautiful blonde woman and himself.

'You're not going to swim in this weather, are you, Mrs dalla Vigna?'

'That's what my husband said,' Kay laughed. 'You men from warm climates are all a lot of— Oh, but John, you are soaked right through! There's water dripping from your sweater sleeves.'

John looked down at the circle of puddles that had formed around him on the mat.

'What can I do for you?' Kay's brow had furrowed. John guessed that for reasons of her own she was avoiding the obvious, intimate solutions of a hot bath or warm clothing. He grabbed the broom from her.

'I should probably sweep the deck while I'm still wet – I couldn't get any wetter.' And he was gone out towards the lake, his dripping feet leaving a trail on the marble floor.

When he came back a quarter of an hour later, he saw that Kay was clutching the sleeping Pekinese. She had changed into an emerald green woollen dress. She looked beautiful; he was filled with disappointment.

'You poor thing!' she cried, as he paused by the french windows and shook the snow on his hair and shoulders back onto the newly swept deck. 'I don't know what I could have been thinking of – you must get into some warm clothes. I've run a bath for you, and I've hung an old track suit of Leo's inside the bathroom door. Now you run along and get yourself warmed up and I'll make some coffee.'

John Tillson didn't move.

'Where exactly is the bathroom, Mrs dalla Vigna?' He had only ever used the handbasin in the downstairs toilet and although he was sure that Kay wasn't about to send him up to the forbidden territory of the first floor, he couldn't think where there could be a full bathroom downstairs.

'Oh, you poor thing!' said Kay for the second time that morning. 'Come with me.' She turned away from him and, as she turned, John realized that he could hear the sound of running water and that it was coming from above. He watched as her feet scaled the first few steps of the great staircase. Soaking wet and still cold, he started to follow her.

'The best part of love is climbing the stairs,' he had once been told by a French flute player. But he was only being guided upstairs to the bathroom; the quote was irrelevant. Still he pondered on its truth as he followed Kay's slim ankles up the long staircase. John's experience of love was limited to two awkward liaisons with girls at his music college back in the Midwest. He found the Italian girls so earthily, sensually beautiful that he was too intimidated to know how to approach them. If climbing the stairs was a metaphor for anticipation, John felt that he had been ascending a staircase since his arrival in Italy. Only now, as he watched Kay's legs as they moved rhythmically against the emerald wool of her dress, had he found a focus for that anticipation. But he was sure that the Frenchman was wrong. Doing it was better thought John, still hardly able to envisage such an act with the elegant blonde woman before him. He repeated the crude phrase inside his head. Doing it, doing it, doing it with Kay had to be better than this aching, dizzying ascent of the stairs.

They had arrived in a corridor. Kay turned to the left and led him along. They were virtually in the dark. All the doors on one side of the passage, the lakeward side, John calculated, were closed – except one and that had blown open when they reached the top of the stairs. They were approaching that door now. Kay's pace accelerated as she swept past. John tried to slow down long enough to look inside the room. He saw that it was the music-room. He glimpsed a grand piano by the window and cabinets that contained precious papers under glass and even had a curtain that could be pulled to protect the documents from the sun. John saw busts of the great composers: Wagner on a stand by the window, his face turned towards the lake; Beethoven and Mozart next to the piano and Verdi in an alcove on the wall. It seemed to John that this was the most beautiful room in the house, not just because it contained a piano and therefore music but because the objects in this room were linked up to something greater than themselves, whereas all the beautiful pieces that Kay displayed existed wholly for themselves, and were, as a consequence, solitary and forlorn.

He tried to linger but Kay swept on, up the corridor to an open room where the sound of running water thundered ever closer. This room was on the other side of the house, and when John followed Kay inside, he saw that the windows looked out on the topiary that Leo so despised. The privet hen, its head made lopsided by an uneven settling of snow, seemed to be peering in at him with a lascivious wink. The bathroom was magnificent. Standing amidst the steam and the warmth John couldn't take it all in but saw that the bath was marble and sunken and that it was surrounded by mirrors.

'Leo hates this room, says it looks like Versailles,' said Kay, gesturing towards the mirrors. 'But I wanted to open it up – I think it worked.' Only as Kay went on to point out clean towels and fresh bars of soap did John realize with some disappointment that this was a guest bathroom. It was a completely neutral room. There would be no chance in here for him to sample some of Leo's cologne or discover if Kay shaved or waxed her legs, took the pill, or if either of them suffered from migraines or haemorrhoids. He could see in a glance that the hoped-for bathroom cupboard of personal intimacies was bare.

'That's Leo's track suit,' said Kay, pointing behind the door. 'He only wore it once when he thought that he should jog – he never did, so it's in immaculate condition.' She refrained from remarking on the difference in their sizes but, as John looked at the length of the legs and the width of the shoulders, he felt once more the old resentment.

'Take your time,' he heard Kay saying. She had

133

walked to the doorway and seemed in a hurry to leave. 'I'm going to have my swim now.' And she closed the door behind her and was gone.

John turned away from the track suit and looked at the bath. It was full now. There was no bath in his lodgings – just an erratic shower in the Italian style that sprayed all over the tile floor. Here the sunken bath was long and wide enough for two but he didn't have to think about that because it wasn't *their* bathroom. Kay had thrown some bubbly concoction into the tub; he would never have dreamed of using such things but the water was hot and fragrant and generous. John could think of nothing better than luxuriating in that bath – but not yet.

He wanted to go back and have a long look at that music-room. Of course he was particularly interested in the piano, he told himself, but he did want to examine the contents of those glass cabinets, and perhaps look at the view of the lake. He waited until he heard Kay's footsteps descend the stairs and cross the marble floor. Then barefoot but still in his soggy clothes he raced out into the corridor. It was darker than before. John realized that the light had come from the doors of open rooms and now they were all shut, but he raced on along the corridor, unconcerned because he knew which door led to the music-room. It was locked. He hardly registered the disappointment of not seeing the piano and the cabinets; he was too busy trying the handles of other doors on the same side of the corridor. He rattled and pulled at them all; they were all locked. Every door on the lakeward side had been locked – in the few seconds that he had stood in the bathroom his view out to the lake had been blocked. He tried the doors again, each door, any door; the piano and the precious papers were long forgotten. He had to get into a room where he could look out of the window, at the lake, at the snow, at the mountains . . . at Kay. When he came to the last door and found that locked, he flung his wet body against it and admitted to himself that his whole frenzied mission in the dark corridor was to watch his employer undress for her morning swim.

'Voyeur' and 'Peeping Tom' were not words that the God-fearing Lutheran boy had ever applied to himself, and even as they surfaced he chased them away with the argument that he had to keep an eye on the lone, eccentric woman out there trying to swim through a blizzard.

Back in the bathroom as he stripped off his soggy clothes, he cursed Kay for installing the multitude of mirrors – he could see his smooth, muscular, naked body diminishing almost into infinity. And he could see his erection, pink and enormous and pathetic, glaring back at him from mirror after mirror after mirror. He wrapped a towel around himself, ignoring the absurd bulge below his waist and sat on the closed toilet lid, feeling the cool of the porcelain against his back. His hands had slipped below the towel; he was about to wrap his fingers around his penis and pull when he saw the skylight. It was a surprising addition to the classical architecture and on any other day he might have continued to sit and pull absently at his erect organ, contemplating all the while the pros and cons of such a structure in the elegant villa. But this skylight faced lakewards. He looked around the room and saw a wicker chair. He placed it under the sky-light and hauled himself up.

The towel dropped away. John's head was up above a beam on a level with the window. He was vaguely aware of his erection, throbbing away below him in the bathroom, but forgot it in his search for a way to open the snow-covered skylight window. He found a metal handle concealed in one corner. He pulled it to one side and pushed the window open. The snow was still falling but lighter now. He was disorientated and didn't know which way he was looking. Then, through the snow, his eyes focused on the deck. Kay was walking along it in her robe. She stopped at the edge – he gripped the wooden ledge of the window. She stepped out of her robe and John saw that she was quite naked. He ejaculated there and then, felt the semen whoosh through the air and heard it land with a sticky slap on the marble floor.

'Yap!' The Pekinese came tearing into the bathroom, sniffed at the blob of semen, then tore into the chair leg. John felt himself falling through the air. His last sight was of Kay's long white back, of her perfect rounded buttocks as she prepared to dive. He landed on the floor and bruised his knee, but he didn't care. The dog licked his nose as he reached for some toilet paper to wipe up the mess on the floor. Bruised and naked as he was John even rolled and romped with the little dog. He was in ecstatic good humour. He had just seen what he'd known he would see – that his employer was the perfect goddess who had filled his dreams since the day he met her. No longer caring about right or wrong, indifferent now to the absent husband whose track suit loomed above him, John plunged into the hot, fragrant water.

Chapter Fourteen

After his conversation with Kay, Leo had tried his agent's number but it was engaged. He would have to wait until he arrived in Milan. Leo was disappointed. Once he made a decision about something he liked to act immediately. Who knew what could happen during the hours that he would be suspended in mid-air over the Continent? He had always been pathologically superstitious about anything connected with his craft but today that same happy calm that had come with the winter morning stayed with him. A few hours delay would make little difference, he decided. And the familiar, reassuring stillness settled upon the big man as he sat back down in the executive lounge and opened his *Attila* score.

Attila had not been the opera scheduled to open La Scala's season but La Scala's schedule had been thrown into chaos a month earlier by a stage-hand and scene-builders' strike and, with only a week remaining before December the seventh, the management had chosen to open the season with a revival that centred around Leo – a singer whose volcanic energy would make a rather tired old production look brand-new.

When Leo arrived at the Grand Hotel Duomo late that December afternoon, he found a request for an interview from the arts section of the *Corriere* and an urgent fax from his agent.

Leo had spent so much time in the departure lounge at Heathrow that all his earlier energy had left him. He had a long-held theory that departure lounges had accumulated a million travellers' boredom and frustration and that their air was hung full of these dreary, contagious emotions. He intended to have a bath, go straight to bed and talk to no-one in Milan until the rehearsal the next day. It was, therefore, an irritated Leo who stood at the reception desk with the messages in his hand. Even as he sifted through them, wide brow furrowed under his snow-flecked hat, the phone rang for him at reception.

'Your agent,' said the receptionist.

Leo looked around at the crowded hotel foyer and decided to take the call in his suite.

'I've been trying to get you all day,' he said, closing the room curtains on a floodlit view of the spires of the Duomo. Before his agent could reply, the singer told him of his desire to sing the Munich Ring.

'There isn't going to be a Munich Ring,' said Roberto, his agent.

'But I can sing it! I've been preparing it in secret for months!' cried Leo.

'So I've heard,' said his agent. 'And thanks for keeping me informed, Leo.' If Leo was the most talented artist on Roberto Manzi's books, he was also considered to be the most wayward and complicated.

'There isn't going to be a Munich Ring – they've cancelled their Ring Cycle. And before you go taking it personally, it's not because Leo dalla Vigna has expressed a desire to sing it but because they've got problems with their curtain—'

'What do you mean their curtain?'

'Their curtain – their stage curtain! Apparently they went out and got themselves this hi-tech curtain. It's computer-operated and has taken to opening and closing itself at odd moments. You know those things weigh a ton and could be lethal. It appeared before the end of *Aïda* the other day and almost gave her and Radames a swift and preferable alternative to death by suffocation—'

'I don't understand,' said Leo.

'Do you think I do?' said Roberto. 'Do you think they do? Anyway, they are scaling down their Ring because they feel that they can't take on a whole cycle with a capricious curtain liable to signal the end of the world long before Wagner intended it. Now they've sent to Japan where the thing comes from and, if they can get the technicians to work on it in time, they may just do one evening – probably a *Walküre*.'

'That's fine,' said Leo, single-minded as ever. 'That's the Wotan I'm most in sympathy with. The *Rheingold* Wotan doesn't have the emotional heft—'

'It's not fine at all,' said his agent. 'You know I handle Dimov. And they've asked him to do it.'

'Has he signed a contract?' said Leo. 'Has anything been put on paper?'

'I'm not going to answer that, Leo. Don't ask me to be unethical.'

'He's young. He's got years ahead of him,' said Leo. 'Does Munich know I'm available?'

'Why? Do you intend to tell them?'

Leo didn't answer. He was fond of Roberto. He had been with his Milan agency for almost as long as he had been with Clara's father's successor in London. He was deeply loyal to the two men and had no idea of the hair-tearing exasperation that his independent, enigmatic personality engendered in both of them.

'Why would Munich settle for him when they can afford me?' said Leo.

'Only you, Leo, could make a statement like that and not sound conceited,' sighed his agent. 'Look, why don't you leave it with me for a few days and I'll see if I can do some schedule-juggling.'

'I'm going to sing it,' said Leo.

'Munich may decide not to do it,' said Roberto, praying that the curtain would stick closed for ever. 'Let's have dinner after the dress rehearsal on Wednesday and we'll see where we are then.'

Once he had hung up the phone, Leo felt a surge of relief and with the relief came energy. The thing was said and therefore the thing was real and would be done. He forgot his plans to stay in his room that evening. He felt restless and in need of company. Even though he knew she could not join him and did not really want her to, Leo called Kay. But she was

139

standing at the window that looked out on the privet hen, clutching the Pekinese in her arms as she watched John Tillson cycle away down the drive in Leo's track suit. She was too absorbed in watching his halting progress through the snow to pay any attention to the ringing phone.

Leo took out his address book and thumbed through it. In spite of his celebrity and the deep sexual attraction that both his voice and physique held for women in two continents, Leo had only a small collection of telephone numbers that he would call on a lonely evening between rehearsals or performances. Early in his career he had decided that any woman drawn from inside the theatre presented too many dangers and complications. He did, however, choose several of his mistresses from the women who mysteriously appeared in his dressing-room after a performance. These were rarely the truly devoted fans. The stage doormen armed with lists of authorized visitors and the labyrinths of stairs and long, distant corridors kept them huddled in patient groups at the stage door.

The women who strolled past the doormen and into his dressing-room were of a different race. They were beautiful and their men had money and status. They displayed an elegant enthusiasm for the performance but, Leo knew, would never applaud until their palms ached or cry 'Bravo' until they were hoarse as he had done so many years before for Christoff and Siepi.

Such women were convenient for Leo since they frequently resurfaced at record company receptions or opera house galas. They were often bored, and happy to be bedded by King Philip II or Mephistopheles. During a brief period when he had added *Don Giovanni* to his repertoire, these sleek thoroughbred women had seemed to multiply before his eyes.

Leo often felt the whole weary ritual to be sapping away at his humanity. The suspicion that the throngs of adoring women might even increase according to the role he was singing had confirmed his fear: that none of them were interested in him, Leo, whose daughter had died one cold day in spring and had been buried when the mad wind, the Föhn, was blowing over the Alps. Sinking into the dark warm depths of their bodies, Leo often imagined that a moment would come in the hours after love-making when he would finally be able to tell one of them the story of the day of the funeral. Stroking a Milanese countess's auburn tresses one summer night, he had almost started but the countess had nuzzled up to his warm naked chest and asked him if he knew the secret of Maria Callas's dieting success and the moment was lost for ever.

The countess's number was still in his book. Her city apartment was only five minutes away by taxi and Leo knew that at this time of year, her husband was off with his polo ponies in Argentina. Leo recalled her huge, soft white breasts with some affection but out of a quirky deference to Kay, he decided to flick past her number and seek a woman of less statuesque proportions.

He picked up the phone and called Natalia, the ex-wife of a Russian language coach at the theatre. An exuberant half-Italian, half-Russian brunette, she lived in a chaotic apartment with two St Bernard dogs and a parrot that could recite Rossini. She invited Leo for dinner and he accepted although he had no intention of eating until he returned to the peace of his hotel room later that evening.

The snow was still falling when he stepped out into the street and hailed a taxi. He wrapped his scarf twice around his neck and pulled his hat well down over his forehead. With the night so white and the streets of Milan so empty and lonely, the divorcée's comfortable apartment beckoned to him like a slightly greasy beacon. Besides, if her breasts were of no consequence, Leo had mentally classified her as having the finest arse in Italy and it was with the pleasant anticipation of sinking his fingers into her big creamy buttocks that he rode the lone taxi through the winter's night.

When he rang the bell to her apartment, a high-pitched squeak responded.

'The parrot has learned to imitate the microwave,' said Natalia, greeting him with a long kiss below his right ear. She was wearing a yellow silk kimono. Leo saw that her sleek black hair was damp and that her skin still bore traces of white body lotion. He also saw that she was clutching a dish-cloth and a large saucepan.

'Come into the kitchen while I put the dishes away.' She led him through a cluttered lounge lit only by the burning logs in the fire.

'So you've had dinner?'

'Of course I have. You know full well the invitation was a formality.' She smiled up at him. She had aged comfortably, thought Leo. He liked the mass of fine upward lines at the corner of her wide brown eyes. He liked the thought that he had lain with her long before those lines had appeared. 'You never once stayed to dinner in the past,' Natalia went on as if she had sensed that his thoughts had strayed backwards. 'Why on earth would you start now?' She finished arranging the dishes and took his coat, scarf and hat and put them over a chair in the kitchen.

'Now we can sit down and have a vodka.' He followed her into the warm half-light of the lounge.

'Ping!' screeched the parrot.

'I liked it better when it did Rossini,' said Leo.

'So did I,' laughed Natalia and Leo saw that she was naked under the kimono. He went over to the old grey parrot's perch and started to sing the Calumnia aria from *The Barber of Seville.* The parrot peered at him quizzically and after a few bars it joined in.

'Vodka?' Natalia held out a full tumbler.

'No, thanks,' said Leo, and leaving the parrot to sing on, went to sit on the couch.

'You are such a stoic, dear Leo,' she said, and plopped down into the armchair at right angles to him.

'Where are the dogs?' said Leo.

'Gone to Russia with Sergei.'

'What visions that conjures up!' laughed Leo. 'Old Sergei on a sledge being drawn across the tundra by his St Bernards.'

'I'm thinking of going to join him,' said Natalia solemnly. 'I'm homesick.'

'I used to be homesick,' said Leo, surprised to hear the words on his lips.

'You travel too much – it's a ridiculous way of life,' said Natalia. She poured herself a second vodka.

'I was homesick at home.'

'Crazy Leo,' she laughed, and drew one foot up onto the chair. The kimono fell open and Leo's eyes went straight to the thick dark patch between her legs. 'I saw your home in an architectural magazine at the hairdresser's last year.' She was hugging her knee to her chin. The dark patch had spread open. Leo glimpsed the moist pink slit protruding from black hair and leaned forward and pulled her to him. 'Sick of a home like that!' she laughed. 'Crazy Leo!' She slid onto the couch alongside him and pulled off his sweater and undid his shirt buttons. Within minutes they were both naked but as Leo turned to roll on top of her, he felt a sudden weariness and closed his eyes.

'We're getting old, Leo,' he heard Natalia say, and felt the roughness of that patch of black hair against his belly as she straddled him. He sat forward, pulled her to him and kissed her hard. She was a robust, energetic lover. He knew that he could thrust and pump her down on him with none of the fear of crushing her that he had always felt with Kay.

'*Calumnia*,' sang the parrot.

When Leo had come a second time and was lying back on the couch thinking that there are as many different kinds of sex act as there are people, she said, 'What's this I hear about you going all Wagnerian?'

'What do you mean?' Leo shifted away from her.

'Leo! You are terrifying when you glare like that!'

She sat up and pulled her kimono around her. 'I'm just repeating what I heard the other day – that you've been preparing Wotan. Why do you want to bother with all those endless monologues – all that German to learn—' She yawned and stroked his damp belly.

'Where did you hear that? When?'

'*E un venticello*,' said the parrot.

'A couple of days ago from a friend at the *Corriere*.'

A few days ago – then the word had come from Clara or Kay. But Clara kept her secrets preciously until she could use them to her own advantage. That left Kay and as he reached for his clothes and started to dress he became convinced that this minor sabotage of all his months of work had to be Kay's vengeance.

'Why are you so worked up about keeping things quiet anyway?' sighed Natalia.

'I am pathologically superstitious,' said Leo. All the good humour of the morning in London was gone. The familiar loneliness had returned. Leo wanted to be back in his anonymous hotel suite with a dull, solid steak sandwich en route to him from the kitchen and the scores of *Die Walküre* and *Attila* for his only company. He took Natalia's hand and walked her to the door.

'*Calumnia*,' screeched the parrot.

'You could stay a bit longer.' Natalia stopped within feet of the doorway. 'At least pretend this was a social call.'

Leo took Natalia in his arms and hugged her tight.

'Will you be at the opening night?' he asked her.

'*E una brutta serata*, all those corrupt politicians and high-class tarts,' smiled Natalia. 'I'll be at the dress rehearsal though. We could have dinner afterwards.'

'I'm having dinner with my agent,' said Leo.

'I guessed you'd say something like that.'

Leo hugged her again.

'Good luck in Russia,' he said on impulse, suddenly sure that he would never see Natalia again.

'Hah! Now you've said it – it becomes real!' cried Natalia and opened the door for him. 'Goodbye, Leo dearest – *in bocca al lupo*! What a stupid thing that is to say – you should be saying it to me – *in bocca al orso*!' And blowing him a kiss down the corridor, she closed the door.

'Ping!' cried the parrot.

Chapter Fifteen

Clara tied a headscarf under her chin and headed out into the Milan snow to dispose of the third ticket for the opening night. She knew that she could get a good price for the ticket from any of the concierges at the better hotels. She also knew better than to linger in the public areas of the Grand Hotel Duomo. She planned to reappear in Leo's dressing-room after the *première* when the exhilaration of his triumph and the great bass's innate generosity would erase any rancour he may feel towards her. And even if he did prove hostile, Clara intended to persist. As a spoilt, unlovable child she had resolved that even if the rest of the world did not want her, the rest of the world was going to have her. In the playground of her Swiss boarding school the plain English girl had trudged relentlessly after the groups of children who fled from her. Because she knew that her resolve would never falter, she could be equally sure that her small prey would eventually give in. Being included in the game of jacks or netball, being part of the group was what counted to Clara; she accorded little importance to the value of being *wanted* to participate.

When she came home lonely and friendless from that boarding-school, her father's house was often filled with exuberant, demonstrative singers. With their extraordinary voices they could express what adolescent Clara considered to be her unique pain. And they were never cruel or cold to the whining, ungracious child. They couldn't afford to be.

Thirty years later, she trudged through the Milan snow, quite sure of her place in the operatic world that she loved so dearly. If like Spanish tenors and Italian sopranos before him, Leo did throw her out of his dressing-room on December the seventh, she would bide her time and reappear at some other point in his calendar. In the meantime her priority was to dispose of that spare first-night ticket. Clara pushed past an elderly woman with a poodle in a red woollen coat and walked through the doors of the Grand Hotel e Di Milan.

'Verdi died in that hotel,' said Otto as the twins' Escort passed along the street only seconds after Clara. 'The people of Milan knew that the old Maestro was about to leave them for ever and they put straw down in front of the window so that he would not be disturbed by the sound of horses' hoofs. Silence was the only gift they could give to a dying man who had filled their world with such beautiful sound.'

The Escort had broken down minutes after they had rejoined the autoroute in France. They had spent the afternoon in a café next to a service station. Eva went outside to keep an eye on the mechanic and Otto traced Verdi's career for Rose.

'Three hundred pounds!' said Eva, emerging from under the car. 'And he's not swindling us. I looked for myself.'

'Three hundred pounds?' Otto wrinkled his brow and stared up at the fluorescent strip-light in the ceiling. He looked as if he were struggling to understand just what three hundred pounds was. 'Three hundred pounds?' he said slowly.

'I told you the car needed replacing months ago but you wanted to spend the money on the summer festivals.'

'Can't we put it on a credit card?' Otto's gaze left the overhead light; he beamed at his sister.

'We'll have to drive all night and save on hotel bills,' said Eva.

'That's all right,' said Otto. 'Rose won't mind.'

Rose hadn't minded. The further south they drove, the louder the call of the great singing house in Milan became. Otto had described the crystal light of its chandelier and the feel of the stone wall on the cold grey mornings of queuing for gallery seats and Rose had come to understand that he loved the stocky, muscular stone building as another man might love a woman. And with the conviction of a lover he set the image of the theatre before them like a mirage, always waiting just ahead of them in the snow.

They drove across the border and into Italy just after midnight. At some point in the frozen dark Rose had insisted on stopping the car and sleeping. Otto remained awake, saying that the thrill of seeing the Italian language on a billboard prevented him from sleeping. While Rose and Eva dozed he recited the advertising slogans to himself, '*Altissima, Purissima, Levissima – Acqua Minerale Naturale . . .*'

They had stopped for breakfast an hour outside of Milan and when they drove into the city proper, Otto had reached the golden old age of the Italian composer.

'He was supposedly in retirement, was done with the wretched, corrupt world of grand opera for ever and then Boito, the rebellious young composer who had earlier led an anti-Verdi campaign, came to him and talked him into *Otello* and there he was, seventy-three, with his greatest masterpiece. But it wasn't over; he said that he was finished with composing for ever and then he produced *Falstaff,* a comic opera. Can you imagine that at eighty, Rose? A benign last wink at an absurd world. '*Tutto nel mondo è burla!*'

They had entered the city of Milan. Rose was struggling to stay awake and alert at the wheel when Otto's chin appeared on her headrest and he announced: 'Verdi died in that hotel.'

Rose slowed the car down just long enough for them to gaze at the hotel. 'He died in the room on the first floor just below the word Milan', said Otto. 'On 27 January 1901 at 2.50 in the afternoon. He left strict instructions for a funeral without music but the Milanesi couldn't bear it. When his body was transferred from the Milan cemetery to the house of rest that he built for his artists, the people of Milan burst into the Hebrews' Chorus from *Nabucco*: "Va Pensiero".'

'Here's La Scala,' said Eva. 'Just in case you hadn't noticed.'

The wind had picked up and was blowing thick snowflakes against the windscreen. Rose switched the wipers on to rapid, and consequently the great theatre appeared and disappeared through the snow and the sweeping motion of the two blades of rubber. She saw stone porticos with cuffs of grey slush at their base and then the theatre was gone. She saw a terrace, its four round lamps shining through the Milan morning, and then it was swept away. She saw a dull, neo-classical façade, ochre walls, a frieze showing a god or goddess driving a chariot and then the snow blanked it out, a taxi behind her honked its horn and they were forced out of the piazza and into a narrow street beyond.

The first person Rose saw in Milan was Leo dalla Vigna. She had glimpsed anonymous figures as the Escort had driven into the city through the remains of the December dawn but they were just silhouettes bent against the wind or huddling at bus-stops breathing little clouds of body warmth into the frigid air. She hadn't looked into anyone's eyes until she bumped into Leo dalla Vigna coming out of the Grand Hotel Duomo.

When she and the twins had arrived in the Via San Raffaele, Rose had moved to unload the bags.

'Oh, we can't afford this place,' said Otto. 'We're booked into a cheap hotel behind the theatre but Clara is friendly with the concierge here – she should have left us our tickets. You wait with the car.'

Rose had been happy to wait. Otto had left the 'Siegfried Idyll' playing on the tape-deck. She was irrationally happy to be in Milan, jubilant to be in the winter city. She stepped out of the car and into the city, wanting to put her feet on its frozen ground and mark her arrival. The street was empty. The snow fell.

Leo dalla Vigna walked out of the Grand Hotel

Duomo and paused to tighten his scarf around his neck. Rose saw him, saw the broad silhouette, the wide-brimmed, snow-flecked hat and did exactly what she had done in the London suburb. She ran to him. She ran with no hesitation and no doubt. Leo was the embodiment of her deepest most constant thought since that evening at the twins' house. All through Europe she had avoided the thought, refusing to even look at it but the figure in front of the glass hotel door filled her with certainty. Rose ran, slipping on the snow, steadying herself on the wing-mirror of a Fiat but never once taking her eyes off the broad figure that had stopped to examine a wad of papers.

She reached out and touched his arm. Months, years, later she would remember the smooth warmth of the cashmere, how thick the bulk of the fabric was and how far away his flesh and blood had seemed. He looked down at his arm and her hand, clutching the navy blue material. His eyes travelled slowly along her arm to her breast and her face. Still the snow fell between them. Already her ungloved hand was cold and numb. Leo said, '*Signora*?' He hadn't recognized her but then why should he? How many hundreds of women pursued him at stage doors throughout Europe? He was glaring down at her, his gaze so intense that she lost all courage and let her arm drop to her side. She said nothing, could think of nothing to say but could not summon up the will to move away. '*Signora*?' said Leo again. How beautiful was that voice. How well she remembered it.

Then Leo reached out and wiped a large flake of snow from a lock of blond hair on her brow. Rose shut her eyes for the second that his hand rested on her damp forehead and in that moment she heard his voice again, talking more rapidly now and in Italian.

'*Mia figlia e morta*,' he said. '*Sopolta un giorno di nebbia*.' Rose understood Italian but not well enough to avoid the laborious task of translating each word as the singer uttered it. 'My daughter is dead. Buried a day of fog.' She opened her eyes and looked up at Leo.

He was still gazing earnestly down at her. 'But I could not have prevented it. And when it was done—' He stopped and shook his head with that same spasm that she had seen when he was listening to his own singing voice in Otto's living-room. Then she had understood that he was reining himself in, trying to keep in check the music that welled up within him. Now something else had welled up and again he held it back. The moment was over. He smiled down at her; a practised professional smile now of a performer awaiting praise. Rose complied.

'I saw you in *Don Carlos* at Covent Garden. You were wonderful.'

'Thank you, thank you, *signora*.' Rose was reaching for a pen, going through the mechanical actions of the admirer faced with the admired. She held out the pen and shrugged to signal that she had no paper. Leo took a sheet from the wad of messages still gripped in his hand and scribbled, 'Leo dalla Vigna. *Attila*, La Scala.'

Then he reached out, shook her hand, said, 'You must not stand around in this snow – you will catch cold,' and was gone.

Rose continued to stand in front of the hotel doors, clutching the paper in her hand and watching his slow progress along the Via San Raffaele towards the Galleria Vittorio Emmanuele and beyond to La Scala.

'Was that who I think it was?' Otto came through the same glass doors. Eva was behind him examining the contents of a small buff envelope.

'*Now* who is hanging around for autographs?'

'What did he say? Was he on his way to rehearsal?' Otto stepped out into the street, shielded his eyes from the snow and gazed after the dark silhouette disappearing into the Galleria. 'Even just walking in the street, he has something, a presence – a magnetism that normal mortals don't. How lucky you were to bump into him all on your own. What did you say?'

'"I saw you in *Don Carlos* at Covent Garden. You were wonderful",' intoned Rose, slipping the piece of paper into her pocket. She wanted to look at it more closely when she was on her own.

'That's original,' said Eva. 'I'm sure you made an unforgettable impression with a line like that.'

'I wasn't trying to make an impression,' said Rose. 'But he said something very strange – in Italian. He was looking right at me but it was as if he were talking to himself. He said, "*Mia figlia e morta*," – "My daughter is dead,"—'

'*Rigoletto*,' said Otto. 'The hunchback's daughter dies in *Rigoletto*.'

'But it's a baritone role,' said Eva. 'He never sings that.'

'I told you – he didn't sing!' said Rose, sorry that she had even mentioned the puzzling outburst. 'The poor man isn't an opera singer twenty-four hours a day—'

'Oh yes he is,' said Eva. 'Shows how little you know.'

'Of course, his daughter did die,' said Otto. 'But it was years ago and he never ever talks about it. You saw that at our meeting the other evening. Oh, that bloody awful evening.' The blond twin leaned against a parked Fiat and rubbed his index fingers under his eyes, dragging the thin skin into thick creases above his nose.

'Anyway, it was a lifetime ago,' said Eva, taking her brother gently by the elbow and pulling him towards the Escort. 'The child only lived a short while.'

'Came in, looked about, didn't like it, went out,' said Otto as they climbed into the car. 'I saw that once on the country grave of a two-day-old baby. It probably made a wise decision. What is there to stick around for?'

'Music?' said Rose.

'Yes,' said Otto, with little conviction. 'Perhaps – it makes it bearable.'

'Not that Otto really likes music,' said Eva. 'He likes opera – high notes, raw emotion, guts pulled out and spread all over the stage. Put him in front of a string quartet and he'd be asleep in seconds—'

'You mean-spirited old cow!' cried Otto. 'What are

Wagner and Strauss if not some of the greatest musicians who ever lived? Just because you never really enjoyed it and only tag along because your own life is so bloody empty!'

'And whose fault is that? Why is my life so bloody empty? Whose fucking hopeless career monopolized the best years?'

'You never had any best years, Eva!' Otto turned to Rose who was sitting in the driver's seat, her hands folded in front of her, staring at the snow piling up on the windscreen.

'Even music isn't worth this! Trailing round Europe with a tone-deaf bag of tweed and mothballs! Waiting for fucking Clara to deign to sell me a ticket! Two hours bliss and two months of misery. That country baby had the right idea, Rose, I tell you. If I'd had the chance I'd have pissed off within minutes of setting foot in this place. What is there to stick around for?'

'Love,' said Rose, still gazing out at the snow on the windscreen.

'What a peculiar thing to say,' said the twins in unison.

Chapter Sixteen

'Everybody knows,' said Leo to Kay in Bellagio. He was calling during a break in rehearsals.

'Everybody doesn't know because everybody doesn't care.' In the warm kitchen overlooking the lake Kay lit her first cigarette in twenty years. 'Stockbrokers, brain surgeons, soccer players, homeless people don't really lose any sleep over Leo's career plans.'

'So you don't like the role – you've got a private problem with it. This is no reason for – for—' Leo sought the word in English.

'What are you talking about?'

'You know.' Leo leaned against the wall with his eyes closed. 'I'm tired of being guilty, Kay, of eternally paying for – for things that happened two decades ago. It's easy for you now, sitting up there in the villa with your Sèvres vases and your Elizabethan beds.' This was treacherous territory. Leo had sworn that he would never illuminate this obvious if ugly truth: that his one despised act the afternoon of the funeral had provided the wealth that allowed Kay to mourn for ever in great material comfort. 'What would our lives have been if we'd had to bear my failure and our daughter's death? Because she would have still been dead, Kay, no matter what—'

'You never say her name. Have you forgotten it?'

'I can't. I can't, Kay. And I can't be guilty for ever. I even thought you seemed happier lately so why did you do this?'

'For the umpteenth time, Leo, do what? What have I done?'

'Told somebody at La Scala that I was preparing Wotan.'

154

'This is about goddamned Wotan – about a fucking role? Oh no, Leo. You're not going to find a way of blaming me if that goes wrong – I suppose you're still planning to do it?'

'In Munich.' Leo whispered the city name into the phone, aware of the absurdity of this sudden secrecy but unable to stop himself. 'At least it's not definite but there's a good chance of a *Walküre* – replacing Metzner.'

'What's wrong with old Hans?'

'Long story. But like I say, it's not definite so I don't want to say too much—'

'Oh, I have no doubt you'll do it. Another triumph for big Leo. Here he is finally playing God – what he knew he was cut out for all along. But don't rush it, Leo. We all know what happens when the mountaineer gets to the top of his last mountain—'

He plants a flag, thought Leo, and images of Wagnerian swords and spears sprang up in his mind.

A *répétiteur* put his head around the door. 'Signore, we have all been looking for you. Rehearsal started back up ten minutes ago—'

'I have to go,' Leo said to Kay.

'You owe me an apology. Falsely accusing me of sinking so low—'

'Come to the opening,' said Leo. 'Just this once, Kay—'

'Can't leave the dog.'

'Oh, that's right, the dog. I thought of a name for him,' said Leo, who until then hadn't known that he'd named the demented Pekinese. 'Otto,' he said. 'I think it's perfect. Otto.'

'Where did you get that from?'

'I honestly can't remember,' said Leo, who honestly couldn't remember. 'I must go, Kay.'

And Leo hung up and left his wife sitting in the kitchen, smoking her second cigarette in twenty years and wondering if three inches of snow on the front steps were excuse enough to call John Tillson in to sweep on his day off. For two hours she would sit and stroke the Pekinese and wonder. For those two hours, Leo would be lost in song. As the weariness of the winter morning wore off and the pot full of coffee warmed and woke him, so the singing would seem to Leo to pull all the stray tattered edges of his life together. When he sang a great role, when King Philip or Boris and most recently and most powerfully of all, Wotan, issued from his mere human body, it seemed to Leo that he dissolved and came into perfect harmony with the air around him. For that last half-hour while members of the chorus knitted and a *répétiteur* looked at his watch and wondered about lunch, Leo felt perfectly in place in the world.

While Leo sang, Clara trudged back to her hotel, a Gianni Versace bag in one hand and her handbag still containing the spare ticket in the other. Nobody had been willing to give her the price she wanted for the seat but she was unconcerned, sure that it would more than recover its value on the night. Now she was on her way to tea at the Biffi Scala. She stopped in the Galleria to examine a rack of postcards. She found a rare photo of La Scala in the snow and bought it. But when she sat down in the café, she realized that she had no-one to whom she could send the card. Clara might well know the great singers and conductors, be recognized and allowed backstage and into dressing-rooms, but she also knew that none of them were waiting for a friendly word from her. What puzzled looks a 'Having a lovely time. Wish you were here.' picture postcard would receive from a Pavarotti, a Muti or a Carreras.

Clara did have a concerned and loving stepmother in Hampshire whom she had never forgiven for marrying her father. She had steadfastly refused to acknowledge that the same stepmother had fought a long and difficult battle to provide Clara with the inheritance that now paid for her airline tickets and hotel rooms.

She put the postcard on the café table, left the message side blank, stamped it and addressed it to Siegfried Bartholomew.

'That's the Biffi Scala,' said Otto, clutching Rose's arm. They had checked into their small hotel behind the theatre an hour earlier and had decided to take a short walk before catching up on their sleepless night in the afternoon. 'Maria Callas used to go in there looking for Visconti. She had a crush on him and used to make a point of removing her glasses when she walked in – so that she'd look more graceful and attractive – but then of course she couldn't see him—'

'Let's go in there and have a nice strong coffee,' said Rose, who was still groggy from her sleepless night.

'Oh no, we don't go in places like that,' said Eva. 'Much above our means. I got a Thermos filled in the hotel and we still have some sandwiches left from the journey.'

'But I want to feel as though I'm in Italy,' sighed Rose. 'I'll pay.'

'Oh, well, if you really insist—' Otto was already studying the menu. 'But it is six thousand lira for a coffee, Rose. That's six pounds you're spending on a couple of drinks—'

'She's not spending anything on me because I'm not coming,' said Eva. 'I want to change some money at the bank and they close in the afternoon.' She walked off towards the Galleria.

Otto and Rose chose a table by the entrance. They didn't see Clara sitting at a table in the corner.

'Tell me about Callas and Visconti,' said Rose. 'Did she really fancy him?'

'Oh yes. The foolish woman didn't have a clue when it came to men. In that case, as I'm sure you know, she was flogging a very dead horse.'

'Visconti having a distinct preference for—'

'That's right, but the poor woman had never been given a chance to be a woman – just a singer, you see. So she wouldn't have known about that kind of thing—'

'What about you, Otto?' The place where they sat was dimly lit. Otto was seated at right angles to Rose so that she could ask the question and look straight ahead, look, in fact, at Clara's narrow back a few yards away from her.

'Oh, Callas never met me! So our love affair was ended before it began, you might say.'

'That's not what I meant,' said Rose. 'Do you have any distinct preferences?'

'That's an audacious question.' Otto had leaned forward and to Rose's surprise was looking right at her. There was not a trace of discomfort or embarrassment on his long, friendly face. 'But no, no, I don't share Visconti's proclivities.'

'Oh, well – good.' Rose scooped the foam off the *cappuccino* that had just been placed before her. 'I mean it's nice to have that cleared up.'

'I like the way you scoop the foam off your coffee as soon as you get it,' said Otto. 'I, alas, always try to save it until last but by the time I get to it, half the bubbles have popped and it's gone. In case you hadn't noticed, Rose, that's a metaphor for my sex life. I can never seem to plunge, if you'll excuse the expression, into the here and now. Always waiting for some distant perfection shimmering on some far-off shore.'

'Tristan and Isolde? Cosima obsessively holding the dead Wagner for twenty-four hours? Don't you think the oversized quality of opera might have spoilt you for ordinary human love?'

'If it has, I'm not sorry,' smiled Otto.

'Or, and this isn't necessarily my view,' said Rose, 'cheap psychology would say that you've perhaps suppressed some other feelings—'

'Oh, no, I don't fancy boys – never have. I know that the opera houses are full of homosexuals worshipping their divas – whole theses could be written about that – but to be honest, Rose, I don't seem to need much sex, not the thrusting, sweaty reality of it, at least. I expect there are a lot of people like me out there but nobody talks about us because it's not a very fashionable way to be.'

'But isn't opera really all about sex? All that sweat and tears and exultation. Have you ever—'

'Of course. Of course. But a long time ago – and not that much. I even fell in love once, in my callow youth in Siena. All very distant and unrequited. I'll tell you about that one of these days—'

'Tell us about what?'

They hadn't seen Clara get up from her table and walk towards them. 'I am so terribly sorry about that ticket.' She squeezed Rose's hand and smiled hard at her. 'But you should try some of the hotel concierges. They may have something. Of course, it's probably the most coveted ticket in Europe so it will be at least triple the usual price—'

'How much would that come to?' said Rose.

'At least eight hundred thousand lira?' Clara looked to Otto for confirmation.

'It seems to me that I could buy a house with that,' sighed Rose.

'Not quite,' said Otto, 'but you must count on paying at least three hundred pounds.'

'I can't afford that!'

'Oh, I know, Rose, I know, my dear.' Now Otto squeezed her hand. 'I'd give you mine but—'

'Shut up, Otto.' Rose turned to Clara. 'Isn't there any other way? What if I went to the box-office and tried there? Perhaps there will be a return.'

'Oh, you are sweet,' smiled Clara. 'Isn't she sweet, Otto?'

'She's lovely.' Otto didn't smile back. 'She's a good, good friend. Listen, can't you get her a ticket? Don't you know anyone?'

'If I did, I would, but I don't,' Clara shrugged. 'But let me know where you're staying and I'll get in touch if anything comes up.'

Otto took out a piece of paper and wrote the hotel name, address and number with deliberation. He handed it to Clara who held it away from her and squinted at it before putting it in her handbag. Rose remembered that squint, remembered how she had suddenly felt well disposed to Clara on that now distant evening in London when Clara had struggled to focus on the question on her clipboard. But the question had been wicked, Rose also remembered. Or had it? That evening had been buried in the winter snow and she recalled only a slam of a grand piano lid, silence and Leo dalla Vigna's hands on hers.

Leo walked through an almost silent theatre, a theatre that dozed in the long afternoon between morning and afternoon rehearsals. He was hoping to find the one German member of the music staff with whom he could comfortably work through his Wagner piece. He wanted to arrange a short session with him before he returned to his rehearsal. He had gone to his office and found no-one. Now he wandered through the slumbering theatre, past the closed door of a wardrobe department where a sleeping seamstress's nose lurched towards the fur tunic of a Hun. Leo walked on, consulted his watch and scowled in exasperation at the absence of any of his colleagues. Singing his way along the silent corridors, he stomped past the side of the stage where a couple of stage-hands snoozed against a cardboard ravine.

'They deign to come back to work five days before the *première* and already they're asleep,' he said to the sleeping figure of the prompter in the prompt corner.

'*Cosa*?' the prompter leapt to his feet. 'Ah, Leo, what are you doing here?'

'Looking for Manfred, and hoping to rehearse.'

'Manfred is out to lunch. Everybody is out to lunch. You should be out to lunch, Leo.'

'I wasn't hungry.' Leo fumbled in a breast pocket for his rehearsal schedule. 'Look, I'm due back this afternoon at 2.30.'

'Never 2.30, not at La Scala,' smiled the prompter. 'Five o'clock at La Scala. Here in Milan we accord the digestive process the respect it deserves – you know that, Leo. And anyway,' he pointed to the piece of paper, 'it's tomorrow. Look—'

'I can't see that – these past two months I've needed glasses for reading.'

'Trust me,' smiled the prompter and handed him the paper.

'Then I shall go home,' said Leo. The prompter smiled his approval, assuming that Leo meant to go to the Grand Hotel Duomo, but Leo was referring to Bellagio.

There was a thin layer of ice under the powdery snow that covered the steps of the villa. He skidded forward as he turned his key in the lock and found himself precipitated into the waiting arms of Kay who was standing in the silk négligé just behind the front door. She disguised her surprise with a yawn.

'You've been sleeping too?' Leo leaned down to kiss her. 'There is so much to do in an afternoon. What is it about everyone here that they have to sleep it away?'

'It's the weather,' sighed Kay.

'I thought you liked snow,' said Leo. 'The front step is treacherous, by the way. You should get the boy to sweep it.'

'His name is John,' said Kay.

'I'll do it beore I take my coat off,' said Leo, and depositing his bags on the marble floor, grabbed a spade from the closet and disappeared back outside. Kay went upstairs, put on her beige trousers and sweater, came back to the hall and gazed sullenly at the vigorous figure of her husband as he accomplished the task she had saved for John. The young pianist had said on the phone only minutes earlier that he had an important lesson but would do his best to come out later that evening. 'That is, if you don't mind my coming in the evening, Mrs dalla Vigna,' he had added. And Kay had said no, no, she didn't mind, and that she would make them some dinner – and that he shouldn't worry if the snow got too thick – there were so many spare bedrooms in the house . . .

Now her husband was out there shovelling the snow and making what she felt was unnecessary noise as he smashed the layer of ice below it.

'There,' he said, as he came back in, and to Kay's

astonishment, he swept her into his arms and held her cheek to his frosty beard. 'Dear Kay, I don't know what has happened but for a week now, I have felt so wonderful!'

'That's nice for you,' muttered Kay.

'A sense of relief, of healing. Oh, Kay.' He took her hand and led her towards the warmth of the kitchen. 'I didn't mean to sound so hard this morning on the phone. When I said that I wouldn't accept feeling guilty any more, what I think I meant was that finally I am facing what you had the courage to face all those years ago—'

'Please, Leo, not now.' Kay pulled away from him and set the coffee-pot on the stove.

'This sounds ridiculous, embarrassing, almost – I wouldn't say it to anyone but you—' Leo took his coat off, put it over a chair and went on talking, staring out all the time at the frozen white mountains beyond the lake, '—but there is a feeling of release in this role that I'm about to do—'

'So you're definitely going to do it?'

'Looks like it,' said Leo, and again he pulled her to him. 'Darling Kay, I have to keep moving on. I don't have your pleasure in – in—' he gestured hopelessly towards a French faience on a shelf, '—beautiful things. The mad wind was blowing that day, Kay. The Föhn was blowing, you remember that, Kay. We heard it in our bed the morning of the funeral. We hadn't slept and the dawn came and the Föhn came—'

'What happened to Hans?' Kay withdrew her hand and set out two coffee-cups.

'Uh? Hans?' Leo pressed down on the sides of his broad face with the palms of his hands as if he could squeeze the identity of the forgotten Hans from the depths of his memory.

'You said you'd tell me what happened to Hans, that it was a long story. Tell me now.'

'Not so long,' sighed Leo, and sat down at the kitchen table. 'His voice went.'

'Just like that?' said Kay, and suddenly sympathetic

162

to the absent singer, sat down next to her husband. 'Poor Hans.'

'Come down to Milan for Saint Ambrose night.' Leo had sensed the softening in Kay and seized his opportunity. 'Come for the dress rehearsal tomorrow. I'm having dinner with Roberto – he'd be happy to see you.'

'All right,' said Kay.

'You mean that? You really will come?'

'Yes, yes – if I say I will, then I will.'

Kay went upstairs and changed back into her négligé. When she came out of the bedroom, she heard Leo behind the closed door of the music-room. He had wasted no time in taking his music up to the big, humid room on the lake.

'It wasn't really for you, anyway,' she sighed as she paused outside the door. And she found that she was strangely excited by the idea of John Tillson arriving while her husband took his own pleasure alone at the piano in that hated room by the lake. I could take him into the room downstairs and undress that lovely young body and dumb old Leo would just sing on to himself up there, she thought, and paused on the bottom step, rubbing her hand over the whorled wooden base of the banister. She had never dared voice the thought that had been in her head for weeks now, but as Leo sang on she ran her hand around the diminishing wooden circle and said to herself, 'I could take that pretty Midwestern boy and screw the shit out of him right there on the tester bed while dumb old Leo gives himself a hard-on with no help from anyone but Richard Wagner.'

'Yap!' She had forgotten the Pekinese, had locked it in the big comfortable room that opened out onto the deck when she had thought that John might call. Now she wanted to hold it while she kept her silent vigil.

Kay went to sit at the window of the formal dining-room that they never used. From there she could see the gate that Leo had left open and the sweep of the snow-covered driveway. Her eye scanned a distant curve in the road at the dark edge of a small pine wood. She knew at exactly what height the bicycle would turn the corner. She watched for the caped figure cycling behind the single headlight. But John Tillson was also sitting at a piano in a small auditorium in Stresa. He had been called in to replace a fellow student stranded in the blizzard on a road further north. John was playing a Schubert song, accompanying a not very talented singer. He wasn't thinking of Kay. Unlike Leo, he wasn't in any way aroused by what he was playing. John was too nervous, too intent on his score to think of anything but the notes and his fingers.

Kay waited until the little dog grew restless. Then she fed him and put him back in the room with the tester bed. She took out the meals that had been cooked and frozen by the housekeeper, opened a bottle of wine and waited for Leo.

He was late down to dinner; he had lingered in the room he loved so well with the company he liked best: Verdi, Wagner, Mozart, Rossini and Beethoven. When Leo stopped playing, he turned as he had done a thousand times before, to the treasures that he had accumulated over the years: original manuscript scores, a letter from Verdi to Boito, a pair of Wagner's reading glasses. Leo took this last item from its place under a glass cabinet and held them gently in the palm of his hand. They had a surprisingly modern electric-blue metal frame – unlike the grandfather wire frames that he was about to acquire. He had never dared to touch them for long but now he unfolded them and placed them on the end of his nose. He studied his reflection in the mirror by the window.

'For God's sake, Leo!' Kay was standing in the doorway.

'It's not what you think,' Leo laughed, and the good mood still upon him, he removed the glasses, put them back in their cabinet and followed Kay downstairs to dinner. He noticed when he entered the kitchen that the bottle of wine was half-finished and that there was a stale smoke smell that he put down to Kay's long wait for him to appear. He decided not to comment; he was too happy to be home, to eat his dinner in his dressing-gown and sop up the sauce with a big chunk of bread without attracting the attention of half the restaurant.

Kay's attention was on the snow-covered driveway; her eye still held that dark curve in the road; still she waited for a single lamp to ride through the night. When Leo got up halfway through the meal to get the Fortnum's Christmas puddings that he had brought from London, she thought, How grey the hairs on his chest are becoming.

And as he read out the instructions on reheating and serving with brandy butter, she drifted away back to the window in the dining-room. Leo opened a bottle of grappa and took it into the lounge where he stoked the fire and waited for Kay to join him, but she didn't. And when she abandoned her vigil at the window and went upstairs, Leo was already in bed and fast asleep.

Chapter Seventeen

Leo awoke the next morning to the sound of Kay's voice in the bathroom, singing a song from a Broadway musical. Across from the bed was her suitcase, open for the first time in a decade and half-packed. Leo had never wanted the apparent devotion that so many of his colleagues' wives displayed. He was baffled by their ability to trudge from theatre to theatre, joined like Siamese twins to their spouses and never seeming to need a life of their own. He liked his solitude, had a grudging admiration for Kay's independence and knew that by refusing to run after him his clever wife sometimes made him want her.

She didn't swim that morning and Leo didn't see her until a half-hour before they were due to leave when she came downstairs looking magnificent in a mink coat that Leo hated. He too had taken more time with his clothes that morning although he could not have said why. He was bent over in the hallway, lacing a new pair of shoes when the Pekinese appeared out of nowhere and flung itself at his foot.

'Well, well, and where have you been hiding?'

'You didn't ask to see him,' said Kay, coming back inside from a brief walk with the dog to the main gate.

'Yes, but I named him,' said Leo, as the dog ran round him in circles. '*Buon giorno*, Otto. What will you do with him while we're in Milan?'

'Oh, but he's coming with us and I'm still not sure of that name.'

'To the hotel?'

'Of course, Leo, people do it all the time.'

'They do?' He tried to recall the last time he had seen

a dog in a hotel corridor. He had felt the tension in those three words, 'Of course, Leo', and was weighing the consequences of refusing to take the dog against those of a week in a hotel room with the Pekinese who was now circling the hall, charging and sinking its teeth into his shoelaces.

From where he stood, all he could see was the waddling backside and the whites of those bulging eyes. But its muzzle was velvety black and soft; Leo had a fond memory of holding the ugly little dog. He decided that it, too, would go to Milan, and to reinforce his decision, he bent down to the demented bobbing head.

The Pekinese, who had been about to fling its body at the toe of his shoe, saw his hand and seemed to change course in mid-leap. The small eager head sprang up to greet Leo's wide palm, which landed therefore with far more force than Leo had intended. The dog let out a howl that was surprisingly loud for its size and seemed to shrivel onto the floor below him. When he bent to gather the little dog up, he saw to his horror that its left eye had popped out of its socket. The animal had gone into shock. It lay sprawled but stiff on the floor; the eye hung above its cheek. Leo wondered for a panic-stricken second if he could somehow stuff the eye back in before Kay noticed, but Kay's slender fingers had appeared from nowhere and were reaching to feel the heartbeat of the petrified dog.

'I don't believe you did that! How did you do that?'

'I patted its fucking head, for God's sake, Kay.'

'Oh shut up, Leo! I'm trying to think.' Kay closed her eyes, clenched her fists and shook them. 'This can happen, I read it in a book on Pekinese. Oh, what did they say? What did they say to do?'

'I'll call the vet,' said Leo. 'Is there a vet in town?'

'I put his number in the book just two days ago,' said Kay, not looking up from the rigid dog.

A minute later, Leo heard himself saying, 'We have a Pekinese here whose eye just popped out.'

167

'It happens with these dogs,' said the vet. 'Poor overbred little bastards. Get it here within twenty minutes and I can save the eye.'

'But I have to leave for Milan. Can't you come here?'

'*Attila*!' said the vet, who had recognized the address. 'I don't care for early Verdi, Signor dalla Vigna, it's too—'

'Well I do,' said Leo. 'Listen, if I pay for a taxi can you come up here?'

'I have appointments at my office. Of course, *Don Carlos* is a different proposition – a truly grand work—'

'I'll drive him in on my way to the theatre,' said Leo and hung up. Within seconds he had somehow gathered up all his belongings and stuffed them in the Mercedes while Kay made her way very slowly to the car, the little dog wrapped in a blanket in her arms. She refused to relinquish the Pekinese. Even as she struggled to climb into the car from the slippery driveway she would not let go of the dog and its eye which she held with no trace of disgust like a jewel in her hand.

At the vet's Leo sounded his horn until an assistant ran out and scooped the dog from Kay's arms.

'We'll wait here until they call us. I'd rather avoid small talk with that vet. There's still a chance we can be in Milan in time for lunch.'

'But I'm not going to Milan now,' said Kay, climbing out of the car. 'How could you think I would?'

'But doesn't he just have to stuff the eye back in?' said Leo. 'I was about to do that myself when you went all hysterical on me.' He was irritated now, aware that fate had flicked a wrist, his wrist, and stolen from him what he sensed was his last chance at reconciliation with his wife. Kay was standing by the car. A few light flakes of snow dropped onto her mink coat. She made no move to bend towards the car when she spoke, obliging Leo to wind down the window and crane his head up towards her.

'Come to Milan, Kay – please.'

'It's out of the question,' she said. 'God, you don't have any idea, Leo, do you?'

'It seems I don't,' said Leo, and he rolled up the window, turned the ignition and roared away towards Como and the A9 into Milan.

Chapter Eighteen

When Rose went down to breakfast she found Eva studying a map of Northern Italy and making mileage calculations on her napkin.

'You're not planning to go anywhere today, are you?'

''Course not, but there's Venice and Vienna and Munich to think about. Somebody's got to plan ahead.'

'Today? With your big evening coming up? If I had a ticket I don't think I could think past curtain-up.'

'Oh, as far as I'm concerned today's already been and gone.'

Then give me your ticket, thought Rose. Let me sit in your stalls seat. Even if I don't understand half of what you do, dear old Eva, I will gaze on that stage with twice the love, believe me. Your spoilt magical brother has made that theatre into a mirage that has slipped away each time I've been in sight of it. And that mirage contains what may be another mirage but I have to sit in that theatre this evening and look at him up on that stage in order to know.

'What will you do while we're in the theatre?' asked Otto, pouring himself another cup of tea.

'I haven't thought about it,' said Rose.

'I know what I'd do,' said Otto. 'I'd lie down in the snow outside and roll and kick and scream until they let me in.'

'Then thank Christ it's poor bloody Rose, and not you, who hasn't got a ticket,' said Eva.

'I'm going for a walk,' said Rose, who could no longer stand the assumption that she would be left outside. She went to her room to get her coat and count her money; she had a vague hope of bribing Clara into finding her a seat. When she stuffed the notes into her coat pocket, she felt a piece of paper. She pulled it out and read, 'Leo dalla Vigna. *Attila*, La Scala.' She sat back down on the bed and gazed at the bold, confident scrawl.

'*Sepolta un giorno di nebbia,*' she heard him say again. 'Buried on a foggy day.' And now the strangeness of the statement sank in, and she knew as she had known when the words were uttered that this was no line from a libretto.

She stared at the paper again. She had always wondered why people sought autographs. She had always sensed that the thrill lay in the proof of physical contact. That celebrated or notorious hand had for a few seconds touched that scrap of paper. That noble or evil brain had for perhaps not even a fraction of a second been engaged in the act of putting words onto paper. But it was in the knowledge of physical contact that the real pleasure must lie. Of course, once the possessor of the autograph turned it over, scrutinized it, gazed at it as Rose now did, their imprint overlaid the other. The paper became tatty, grubby, as their dreams crowded around the hastily scrawled name on the page.

Rose decided to fold the paper and put it in the bottom of her suitcase. There was writing on the other side. In taking a sheet from his wad of messages, Leo had given her what she now saw was the last page of a letter. I will have to find him and return it, was Rose's first delighted thought, but when she read what was written on the page: '. . . *as long as they put someone much younger than Frau Hartman in the role of your daughter, we will see a confirmation of what my father and I knew all along. With apologies and much love, Clara*' she realized that the sentence was so slight that to make a point of returning it would be ridiculous, would make it look like the excuse to see the man again that it really was. But those last words, those last words, '*much love, Clara*', sent her into a squall of confusion and hurt. And yet he had discarded them . . .

Rose read the sentence again and again, '*your daughter . . . what my father and I knew . . .*' She could hear Leo's words as he stood on the Via San Raffaele, '*Mia figlia . . . sopolta un giorno di nebbia.*' Fathers and daughters again. Not for the first time, she felt left out of life. She sat in the gloomy, thin room and wished that she could remember more of her own father, as if a memory of the carefree Spaniard who had ridden out of her life and under a Number 22 bus might fill in the blank page of Leo's letter.

She decided not to look for Clara. Stumbling upon her name seemed to Rose to be a STOP sign held out to remind her that, for reasons she still could not understand, Clara came and went in a world that would not allow her to bask for even a second in the light of its vast chandelier.

She avoided Otto and Eva for the rest of the morning and chose instead to visit the Duomo. Rose had not been raised with any religious faith. Her father had been a long-lapsed Catholic who was not averse to lighting candles when feeling anxious about the outcome of a new love affair or business gamble. He'd had a long-standing affinity with St Rita, patron saint of hopeless cases, and it was with the hope of finding her that Rose now entered the great cathedral.

When she failed to find St Rita, she lit a candle to the Madonna instead and prayed for a ticket to see Leo. Superstition told her that this might not be an acceptable request so she covered herself by praying for the well-being of her mother, sister and Ben. Roger, Daphne's husband, could look after himself. Then she sat down in a corner and worried about money.

The leave of absence that she had taken for her wedding and early weeks of marriage had permitted her to come on this journey. It had also used up most of her savings. Within a week she must return home. Tonight would probably be her last chance to see Leo. She could not think beyond that moment, could not imagine life beyond that instant when he would be standing before her again. She counted her cash, allocating three hundred pounds to pay for her ticket. The amount seemed so enormous, so extravagant, so decadent, that her fingers shook with embarrassment as she counted out the equivalent sum in lira and folded it into her wallet.

Outside in the piazza, Eva bumped into Clara. This was not unusual, for on such a freezing winter's day the travellers' circuit was limited to La Scala, the protection of the soaring glass Galleria and the arcades that bordered the shops in front of the Duomo. The two women met near the steps to the Duomo. The snow had abated and the winter afternoon sky behind the white spires, parapets and ascending saints was dark blue and pink. Drab grey clumps of pigeons surrounded their feet.

'Did you get the tickets?' said Clara, who had stopped to buy a bag of chestnuts from a vendor.

'Yes,' said Eva. 'Did you get our cheque?'

'Yes.' Clara cracked open a chestnut. She didn't offer one to Eva. 'Aren't you going to thank me?'

'No,' said Eva. 'We paid good money for them. Anyway, you owe my brother an apology for the mess you made of his discussion evening.'

'Rubbish,' said Clara. 'It needed livening up. I hate the cloying, sycophantic tone those affairs always have – everybody laughing at feeble jokes and asking the same old questions. Besides, why can't your brother look after himself? He's almost old enough for a bus-pass.'

'He worked very hard on that evening,' said Eva. 'It meant a lot to him.'

'It wouldn't have happened if I hadn't persuaded Leo to come.' Clara finished the chestnuts and threw the bag to the ground. Eva picked it up and deposited it in a waste-bin.

'Why did you get Leo to come?'

'You know why – because I feel sorry for Otto.'

'He doesn't need your sympathy.'

'Oh, I think he does,' smiled Clara.

'Have you got any real friends?' The dumpy blond

173

twin stared hard at the thin dark woman before her.

'Have you?'

'That's the point,' said Eva. 'Do you want to end up like me?'

'Oh, I don't think there's any chance of that,' laughed Clara.

'You'll come unstuck one day,' said Eva.

'I doubt it – that's a myth that people like them put around,' she nodded in the direction of the Duomo, 'in order to make sure people like you behave.'

'You deserve a lonely old age.'

'The way my trust fund works I'll be richer than ever so I probably won't have one – sorry to disappoint you.' She linked arms with the older woman and walked her towards the vast, soaring entrance of the Galleria. The sudden show of affection threw Eva into disarray and even though she had intended to walk through the Duomo she found herself being led back towards the opera house.

'You see, Eva, you mustn't believe all they tell you. I learnt that a long time ago. They also tell you that it matters *why* someone wants you – I don't think it does – why should I care if they want me for my money as long as I've got them? It seems to me that a lot of relationships that are based on so-called true love don't hinge on much in the long run.'

Poor arthritic Eva, who knew nothing of true love, could find no reply and with her terrier tenacity she returned to her first thought. 'You should apologize to Otto. You could buy him a drink after the show tonight—'

'Why?'

'Because it would make him happy,' said Eva.

'I've got other things to do,' said Clara, still clutching Eva's arm in hers. 'There will probably be a reception tonight. If you were in my place, what would you rather do? Go to a gala reception or have dinner with you two?'

Eva withdrew her arm. 'You spiteful cow,' she said.

'Your trouble,' Clara went on, 'is that you've got no

imagination. You can't answer that question because you can't imagine any other life than the one you've got. It's probably a blessing,' she added. 'Anyway, I intend to go to the reception where I'll have plenty of company. The sensitive, artistic, musical types who think themselves above money are very good at sniffing it out and hanging around it – probably because they're always in desperate need of the stuff. Wouldn't you like to go, Eva? Imagine gallons of champagne, tons of smoked salmon and caviare—'

The twin sister's face was screwed tight as she tried in vain to stretch her imagination.

'I have a duty to my brother,' she said finally, as though she had taken Clara's invitation seriously.

'Duty's not a word in my vocabulary,' smiled Clara.

'At least you're honest,' said Eva.

'I like you, Eva,' said Clara. 'Not enough to waste an evening having dinner with your brother, but I do like you.' And she disappeared into the afternoon crowds that paced the mosaic floor of the Galleria.

At six o'clock Eva knocked on Rose's door with a foil package.

'I managed to stretch out some Parma ham from the OAS evening,' she said, and unpeeled a layer of foil to reveal a dry-looking sandwich.

'You stretched it all the way to Milan?' groaned Rose.

'That's right – I thought you might want a snack before we leave.'

Rose declined. She didn't see the twins until they were all due to leave for the theatre that evening.

'You look beautiful, Rose,' said Otto, when she joined them at the reception desk. 'I mean, you usually look very nice, of course, but that's such an elegant dress.'

'It was going to be my wedding dress,' said Rose.

The twins backed away from the folds of emerald silk.

'Oh no, not your wedding dress. Do you think you should?' said Otto.

'Obviously or I wouldn't be wearing it, would I?'

Holding onto Otto's arm for the brief five hundred yards that led to the theatre, Rose forgot that she might only be walking as far as the entrance. When they rounded the corner, however, and saw the crowds, the barricades, the *carabiniere* in full uniform ushering in the VIPs and the forlorn group along the side wall hoping for a last-minute ticket, she was suddenly aware of the hopelessness of her quest.

'I'll wait with you,' said Otto. But for the minutes that he stood alongside her, Rose could feel his impatience. His longing to walk onto the marble floor of the foyer under the warm light of its chandeliers lay between them as solid as a stone wall, through which she found it impossible to make any conversation. After a few minutes of uncomfortable silence she said, 'Why don't you go on in? Nothing's moving here. We'll arrange to meet by the entrance in the interval if I do get a seat, and if I don't, well, I'll treat you to dinner.'

'Oh, all right – if you're sure, but don't give up until the last minute,' said Otto, and already his gaze was on the main entrance and his steps were turned away from Rose.

A light snow had started to fall. Rose found herself pushed back behind the barricades. Taxis and limousines were depositing elegant women and sleek, bored men at the front door. Rose wondered where Leo was and answered her own question with the thought that he was hidden somewhere in the heart of the big stone building. She tried to imagine just what he would be doing at that moment and realized that she knew nothing of his world. Such desperate longing for such an unknown being was absurd, she knew, and a sudden moment of shame sent her backing away from the theatre. But all the time her eyes were on the floodlit edifice in front of her. La Scala. What had Otto said it meant? The staircase. Rose knew that there was no other path open to her but the journey on up the invisible stairs that extended from Floral Street across snow-swept Europe to this great theatre and beyond.

She pulled her collar up and scanned the arriving crowds, praying that in one of the bejewelled hand-bags or mink pockets lay her ticket.

Leo's first act upon arriving in his dressing-room was to put on at least part of his costume. But because his Attila outfit consisted of a loose-fitting pair of cotton pants and a fur cape flung over his bare chest, he wrapped his old towelling bathrobe around him while he waited for the make-up man to arrive. He didn't recognize the young man who knocked on the door with his brushes and paints. And when Leo enquired after the old Venetian who had made his face up for years, he was told that he had died. Leo sat in gloomy silence while the young man painted dark lines down the sides of his nostrils. Even within the great singing houses that stood as rock solid and central to each European city as its cathedral, change was happening faster than Leo could follow. Dressing-rooms were suddenly re-situated in dark, hitherto unseen corners of a theatre, familiar stage doorkeepers died, the whole extravagant, enormous Palais Garnier in Paris now echoed only to the sounds of ballet dancers' feet as a new unlovable building took its place. Leo was feeling old.

The make-up man was brushing dark powder over the few grey hairs that had appeared at the top of his chest. Leo felt older still. The young man had finished his work. Gathering up his brushes he rose to leave. Then he turned and, with the tip of his finger, very lightly rubbed some excess colour from just above Leo's nipple.

'Beautiful chest,' he muttered so softly that Leo wasn't sure he'd heard him.

'What?'

'*Niente, niente, signore.*' The young man was standing in the doorway. He started to walk away, hesitated, and with a cruel little smile, whispered to Leo, 'In my dreams, *signore*, I am free to imagine anything — anything.' Then he was gone.

Leo sat down hard in front of the mirror. He felt strangely violated. He knew that his stage presence incited more than just a reaction to his singing voice but he was used to the more discreet fan worship that awaited him at a chilly stage door. There, a lingering handshake from a genteel widow or the stammered request for the umpteenth autograph was the most aggressive overture he could expect. But this whispered insinuation in the intimacy of his dressing-room, this reminder of his responsibility for the dreams he kindled in others had unsettled Leo. He was still sitting lost in thought when a delivery arrived from the stage door.

Along with the usual telegrams and flowers from well-wishers was a cage containing the moth-eaten parrot last seen in Natalia's apartment.

'Ping!' it greeted Leo as it was borne into the dressing-room.

'No, no, *non questo*!' said Leo, and sang a few bars of the parrot's only aria. The parrot lifted a foot, winked and settled in to sing along with him.

There was an envelope tied to the top of the cage. Leo pulled it off and was about to open it when the Spanish tenor appeared in the doorway.

'Are you all right?' said the tenor.

'Me?'

'*Si*, terrible sounds are coming from in here.'

Leo pointed to the parrot on a table behind the door. The tenor leapt back into the corridor.

'It's as old as the hills and quite harmless,' sighed Leo.

'Feathers!' cried the tenor. '*Mamma mia*! Feathers!'

'It hasn't got many.' Leo folded his hands across his naked stomach and studied the decrepit bird.

'But I'm allergic,' wailed the tenor and disappeared back into his room to the disappointment of Leo who had been settling in for a conversation. He tore open the envelope that had come with the cage.

'Caro Leo,' said Natalia's big wobbly handwriting. '*I am going travelling. Perhaps I will wind up back in*

178

Russia. You get the parrot because he likes you. And I trust you to look after him. I liked you, Leo. I suppose I loved you but alas, I couldn't trust you to look after those feelings. You can have no idea of how much I waited for you, how the landmarks on the years that I have known you were those days when you came to town. That was how my life was divided up. Leo is here for Don Carlos or for Giovanni. Leo is jetting in for a concert Boris. Leo is opening the season at La Scala. After all this time you could have at least called me at some point during the week but you didn't. You never do. It's not the end of the world by any means but it will be nice to know that I can be somewhere else and get on with my life while you are singing in Milan. Addio, mio Leo. *I hope we don't meet again.'*

In a second of lucidity Leo pictured Natalia hesitating over that last sentence; superstitious Natalia would have been convinced that writing those words would make them come true. And for a second, he was sure, she hadn't wanted that. But the words were on the paper and Natalia was gone and what saddened Leo the most was the knowledge that he wouldn't miss her much at all.

There was a knock on the door and an old man's smiling face appeared. Leo reached over and felt in his trouser pocket for a couple of 10,000-lira notes.

'Buona sera, Maestro. Sono il capo del claque.' The old man's habit of announcing his own rather dubious occupation had long since ceased to irritate Leo, who just wanted to give him his money and send him on his way. Paying the leader of La Scala's claque was little more than the perpetuation of a tradition. Leo feared nothing from a group of organized booers. He closed the door behind him, put a towel over the cage to silence the parrot and waited for his call.

Clara arrived in the piazza and made her way towards the forlorn group waiting against the wall for a returned ticket. As she approached with the precious third ticket in her hand, there was a rustle of excitement, eager men and women rushed forward, but after a few words they shook their heads wistfully and returned to their place in the queue.

From her place on the other side of the barricades Rose watched Clara trying to sell the ticket that had so briefly been hers. The crowds were thinning out, the ushers were beginning to close the great doors to the foyer. Rose could stand it no longer. She squeezed through the barricade and approached Clara.

'How much do you want for that ticket?' By looking innocent and hopeful she must surely shame the wealthy Englishwoman into selling it at an honest price. But Clara showed neither embarrassment nor surprise as she turned, smiled at Rose and said, 'Eight hundred thousand lira.'

'Oh, sod those bloody zeros,' said Rose, all innocence and most of her hope gone. 'How much is that?'

'Four hundred pounds.'

'Oh! Oh no, I can't. I just can't,' sighed Rose. Clara shrugged. 'But the bell is ringing. What will you do if you don't sell it?'

'Nothing,' smiled Clara. 'It's all the same to me.'

'Then surely you wouldn't mind reducing—' Rose stopped. The humiliation that she had intended for Clara had come to rest on her. She was ready to cajole, persuade and beg for the ticket. She opened her purse and counted her money, aware of Clara's gaze on her ringless fingers and her short unvarnished nails.

'That's all my cash,' sighed Rose. 'I haven't got any more.'

'I didn't ask for any more,' smiled Clara.

'I changed four hundred pounds into lira when I got to Italy. That's it—'

'Then you must have known unconsciously that that was the amount you'd need.' Clara smiled and held out the ticket.

'Three hundred and fifty – I'll give you three hundred and fifty,' said Rose. 'Look, they're closing the last doors to the theatre. If I don't take it you won't get anything for it.'

Clara shrugged and put the ticket back in her bag.

The bells were growing fainter; the warm yellow lights from the foyer were slowly being blotted out as the ushers closed the last doors. With a trembling hand Rose counted out the money and placed it in Clara's hand. As the bells stopped ringing, Rose and Clara walked into La Scala together.

Chapter Nineteen

'I went back to the concert hall the next morning at dawn.' John Tillson poked the log fire. Kay's face glowed pink in the flames' reflection. 'I couldn't sleep – I was so excited.' John was still excited but the cause had changed. Here he was sitting in that big chair by the fire – Leo's chair. Kay had called and asked him to come to the villa, not to sweep a deck or run an errand but to watch her husband's performance on the television. John was thrilled but he also sensed a subtle upgrading of his status. The previous evening he too had been applauded. He had stood on a platform and taken a bow. True, it was a very rapid bow for a performance of a couple of minutes accompanying a not very distinguished singer but even if Kay was not aware of it, John felt that he had earned his seat in that large comfortable chair by the fire.

'But when I got back there, of course, the doors were all locked and litter was blowing across the empty piazza. I waited for a café to open and had a cup of coffee and tried to bring it all back into my mind but I couldn't. The emptiness was louder, if you see what I mean. Will it always be this eph . . . eph—'

'Ephemeral?' said Kay. 'Yes it will. You produce a few beautiful sounds, just a few and not every evening at that – not even the greatest artist can do that – the audience flings its adulation at you for a few minutes, you're high as a kite. Then they walk out into the night and wonder whether they'll have the pizza or the fettuccine and you on your side of the stage do the same. And it's all over until the next time, if there is one. Talking of pizza, I made one—'

'Oh, you didn't have to do that, Mrs dalla Vigna.'

'I used an American recipe,' said Kay. 'With a crisp crust instead of the bread dough. Would you like to eat it now or shall I save it for the break?'

'Well, I am real hungry. I couldn't eat all day – the excitement kind of took my appetite away.' John's energy was ebbing away as he spoke that sentence. Kay's dismissal of his excitement, her confirmation that it would never be more than those few fleeting minutes in the footlights had squelched his own euphoria. When she went out of the room and returned with a bottle of wine, he leapt to his feet to help her open it. 'If you were down in Milan I guess you would be drinking champagne by now.'

'Oh I never drink any alcohol when I go to the theatre. It blurs your concentration.'

'But you don't mind not concentrating tonight?' John heard himself say the sentence, heard the one-raised-eyebrow tone of the seducer in good God-fearing John Tillson's voice and blushed to the roots of his blow-dried hair. Kay didn't reply. She didn't even seem to have noticed, for she was pressing the buttons on the remote control. She had produced the television from out of the broom cupboard minutes earlier. John had been disappointed to see that it was a small portable model. He had also been trying to find a way of politely suggesting that they remove the thick layer of dust that covered its surfaces. Now, embarrassed and excited by his own daring, he took the remote control from Kay's hand, brushing his fingers against hers, and placed it on the table.

'Mrs dalla Vigna – I'm a musician and I'm not real sure how these technological things work but,' he motioned towards the TV, 'I think there's some business of invisible rays going from the remote control to the set. Now with all that dust—' He ran his finger across the screen.

'Oh, who cares anyway!' Kay poured herself a glass of wine. 'I've seen enough Verdi to last me—'

'Oh, but I care!' John blurted out. 'I don't care what you say about it being a *brutto serato*.'

'*Brutta, brutta serata* – feminine, John.'

'*Brutta,* then. I would have given my right arm to go.'

'You'd make a pretty silly pianist with just a left arm.' Kay had emptied her wineglass. 'Anyway, you should have said something. Leo could have arranged a ticket. Even as late as yesterday we could have given you mine.'

John guessed that this offer was as empty as the long-standing invitation to play the piano upstairs. He didn't let himself imagine that with a few simple words addressed to his employers two days earlier, he could be sitting in the red and gold auditorium in Milan. Instead he fixed his attention on the television. While Kay poured herself another glass of wine he ran the sleeve of his sweater over the dusty screen. Then he saw the dangling wire.

'You haven't plugged the TV in, Mrs dalla Vigna! It's not plugged in.' John took the plug and pushed it into the socket. The closed scarlet curtains of La Scala appeared on the screen. The camera tracked backwards and showed the first members of the audience filing into the auditorium. A commentator holding an unwieldy hand-microphone made a rapid announcement.

'Oh look, Kay! Oh, I'm sorry, Mrs dalla—'

'Kay's fine,' said Kay. 'That name is a mouthful.'

'They're interviewing Leo!' John was too excited to bother with any more formalities. Leo's heavily made-up face appeared on the screen; he was making a familiar pronouncement about the merits of Verdi's early works.

'Ridiculous costume,' said Kay, as the camera panned around the dressing-room.

'Oh, I don't think so – I mean you can't really make Attila the Hun elegant and—'

'It's a good thing he still has such a wonderful body,' Kay added, as she went in search of the pizza.

John Tillson suddenly lost interest in defending Leo's appearance. He scowled at the screen and decided that the man was too tall.

*   *   *

In her seat in the stalls Rose sat with her eyes closed, gripping the armrests as though she were in an aircraft flying through a turbulent sky. But this turbulence was all within Rose. She had attained the coveted place but in doing so had handed all her spending money over to Clara. The humiliation was so great that Rose could hardly take anything in. She wanted to say, 'I'm in La Scala; I did what I knew I'd do, I've climbed the staircase,' but her mind was interested in nothing but that figure: £400. She wanted to look at the auditorium, the crystal chandelier, the plush red, the gold carvings on the wedding-cake tiers of boxes but her mind was saying, That's almost a month's rent, that's a week's holiday, and you've paid it to look at a man you hardly know. Rose was awash with humiliation. I can hardly feel myself living this, she thought, and tried to repeat a sensible sentence to herself – a sentence that would rein in all the mass of frazzled emotion that was spilling out of her.

'Well, now we'll see what all the fuss is about.' There, she muttered it to herself again. It was the kind of thing Daphne would say if somebody shot her into space and landed her on the moon. But Rose had seen enough of Leo in that one brief evening at the twins' house to know what the fuss was about. She couldn't scale her excitement down and become Daphne. She gave in and let the whirlpool of sensations spin her around: the smell of Havana cigars and French perfume in the foyer, the etched old-world Italian faces, the random sounds from the orchestra pit that had mingled with the sound of her own feet, the last feet to enter the auditorium and make their way down the centre aisle. The orchestra was still tuning up. An A from the oboes and there was the maestro's sleek head, close enough for her to lean forward and stroke. Contain yourself, Rose. Thank God for the dimmed lights and the dark in which she sat. Oh, stop my mind, still my heart and my mind, she prayed. I can't take anything in.

A chorus of Huns, shaggy and resonantly male, had wandered onto the stage. Rose could see Otto and Eva on the other side of the aisle. Otto was staring straight ahead of him, his hands clasped on his lap. Eva looked as though she was sitting in a bus-shelter waiting for a Number 22. And I must look as though I've plugged myself into the chandelier, she thought. Lots of spear-waving up on stage. Something's about to happen. Concentrate, Rose, think about the story. What the hell is the story? Leo. There he is. Leo.

Clara had kept her favourite seat for herself. It was in a front-facing box just below the royal box. She had sat there on many a first night and knew that the occupants usually included a politician from Rome, his beautiful Hungarian mistress and a few of his friends. She also knew that the politician was on trial for corruption and assumed that she would have the six seats to herself. She walked along the curving red passage until she found the usher with a key to open both her box and its corresponding dressing-room across the corridor. She motioned to the young man to open the door to the dressing-room first and saw with some disappointment that a mink coat was already hanging there. She changed into her evening shoes and removed her own coat and only when the oboes were sounding their A did she signal to the usher to open up the door to the box.

The beautiful brunette mistress had already taken her seat. She, too, had apparently assumed that she would be alone and had spread herself across the two front seats, but when Clara appeared she smiled a warm smile of welcome. She had stretched her plump thighs over the second of the six piano stools that lined the box and she took her time removing them and returning the seat to Clara. All the while she smiled and looked intently at her new neighbour. Clara didn't need to look too closely at her. She had seen her face in gossip magazines throughout Europe and knew that the woman had wealth and influence that were inde-pendent of her imprisoned lover. She also knew that the brunette beauty invited the great and the good to her Sardinian summer home that Clara longed to visit.

The conductor had taken his place. Clara applauded. Her neighbour yawned loudly and said, '*Che noia questa musica.*'

'What do you come for if it's boring?' said Clara.

The woman smiled, 'Sorry, no speak English – I Hungarian.' Clara had read that too.

'*Perche venire?*' Clara repeated in her poor Italian. The woman shrugged, stretched her legs out onto another stool and smiled a long, languorous smile.

'It's not boring,' Clara said. 'Not boring at all.' But once the lights had dimmed, once the thrill of seeing Rose empty her purse for the ticket started to fade, once the anticipation of seeing who occupied the boxes was blotted out by the dark, Clara found that her own enthusiasm wavered and flagged. The Hungarian yawned and scratched all through the opening bars. At one point she dug Clara in the ribs to point out a clock with Roman numerals that marked out five-minute intervals above the stage.

Then Leo appeared on the stage and both women fell silent. At some point during his opening aria, the Hungarian woman pressed her thigh against Clara's thin, silk-and-sequin-clad leg. Clara had her opera-glasses focused on Leo and did not therefore have a free hand with which to repulse her neighbour.

'Never, never have I known a night like this,' said Otto, when he and Eva met Rose in the foyer. She was standing in front of a massive, strangely blank-looking bust of Toscanini.

'He always says that,' said Eva, and went off in search of the toilets. Neither of them expressed any interest in how Rose came to be inside the theatre.

'Did you see Leo's entry?'

'Yes,' said Rose, who had glimpsed Clara on the far side of the foyer.

'Total command from the minute he steps onto the

stage. Enormous presence. Even when he's silent, you're aware of him. And the voice seems to me to have more heft, more body—'

'Certainly a lot of body,' muttered Rose. She wanted to flee the approaching Clara. She didn't want the dark Englishwoman's presence to enter into her dream of La Scala and she mumbled an excuse about queuing for the toilets and walked away across the crystal-lit hall. She was surprised to discover that it led into the theatre museum; the galleries full of pianos, portraits, old scores and costumes were still open and filled with members of the audience.

Rose spent the rest of the interval alone wandering from a model of Chopin's hands, to Liszt's piano, to Verdi's bronze bust, to Toscanini's reading glasses and a photo of Wagner's death-mask. She thought of Cosima who wouldn't let her genius go and she tried to reconcile that long lost world with the bored tanned men who gazed unseeing on each exhibit and the over-made-up women whose heels clicked across the floor around her. And she understood that when she had handed Clara all her cash, it had been in a quest for something that lay, not in the glittering auditorium, but here amongst the long-dead musicians.

Up in the villa on Lake Como, Kay carried two empty plates back into the kitchen and returned with a bottle of cognac. John had moved to sit on the floor. She was stretched out on the couch. They had watched the first act in silence. John's was the silence of intense concentration. Kay was quiet because she didn't want to wake the Pekinese. She had brought the dog down from its basket where, with its eye safely back in its socket, it was sleeping off the shock of its encounter with Leo's hand.

'Wow!' said John, as the last notes faded from the warm room.

'You'll have to enlarge your vocabulary if you intend to get famous and give interviews like old Leo,' said Kay.

'Sorry, Mrs dalla— Kay, but wow! Was that beautiful! Old man Verdi had such rhythm. And that ensemble at the end of the act. How could he do that, keep it all together and yet swooping and weaving?'

'When Victor Hugo saw what Verdi had done with his play in *Rigoletto*, that was the thing he said he envied most – the ability to have four people all expressing themselves separately and simultaneously.'

Kay was surprised to find that she still remembered so much about a world she had chosen to ignore. She poured John a glass of cognac. He reached up to take it then rose and went to sit back in Leo's chair. Kay was sorry that he had moved away. She would have preferred him to remain where he was with that perfect blond profile in her line of vision. Now, in her husband's chair, he looked so small, so childlike. Poor John, the enthusiasm that she was trying to share, raking around in the memories of her musical training, that enthusiasm made him look even more immature.

Leo. He was back on the screen, seated at a banquet table on the stage, glaring out at them. Kay felt suddenly ridiculous. She left her cognac untouched, excused herself and ran upstairs. The Pekinese awoke and waddled after her. Alone in her bedroom, she lit a cigarette and switched on the wide-screen TV that she watched most evenings. Up in her room the set was plugged in and she could always work the remote control. She tuned into an Italian game show.

John finished his cognac and poured himself another one. He wasn't concerned about Kay's whereabouts. She had obviously just gone to use the toilet. He would have liked to do the same but he couldn't bring himself to move from the TV screen. He took advantage of Kay's absence to turn up the volume. Leo was singing '*Io tel dono*' to the soprano. John, who had the libretto propped on his knee, saw that this translated, 'I give him to you'. He drained the glass of cognac and thought hazily how appropriate the phrase was. If Kay didn't come down soon, he would go to look for her. He felt that Leo's chair had added to his own stature; he seemed to be growing into it and he was exasperated that Kay was not witness to this novel feeling of confidence and expansion. He could wait no more and started to walk towards the great staircase. He swayed, wobbled, steadied himself on the banister and made his way up the stairs.

There was so much noise in the usually silent house that at first he found it hard to locate Kay's room by sound. Leo's voice thundered up from below. Chorists echoed him, the tenor and soprano joined in. But soon he heard the even louder sound of canned laughter along the corridor. As on his last excursion to the upper reaches of the house, all the doors were closed. He remembered his old urge to see the music-room and paused trying to remember which door led to that sanctum of Leo's where the cold marble composers gazed sightless at the lake. He tried the first handle he came to. It opened immediately and there he was, standing in front of the grand piano. The room was ice-cold. He fumbled for the light switch but he couldn't find it. He walked forward in the dark, swaying even more as the brisk air hit him. He was aiming for the dark bulk of the grand piano, not quite sure what he would do when he reached it but with a vague drunken notion of laying his fingerprints over Leo's and playing better than the older man ever could. But the piano lid was locked shut and the key was gone.

John was unperturbed. The hollow laughter at the end of the passage reminded him that he was on his way to Kay. He turned around and headed back to the door, sorry that he had not had the foresight to turn on a light in the hall. He bumped against a cabinet as he blundered around in the dark, cold room. The cuff of his jacket caught on Wagner's nose. As he lunged towards the door, the bust tumbled to the floor with a crash. John stood petrified in the hall. His first instinct was to shut the door tight, in a vain attempt to block out the damage. He couldn't bring himself to go back in there and look at what he'd done.

Leo sang on. The hoots of laughter from the other TV

lured John on. He wondered, but only fleetingly, why Kay had turned on another channel. Too soon he was outside her door. He tried to compose himself. The last time he had been up on the first floor, he had ejaculated onto the bathroom marble at the mere sight of her perfect buttocks. Alcohol, he knew, slowed down the sexual response and for this he was grateful. He was only too aware that he was trying to replace Leo dalla Vigna in Kay's bed and body and he knew instinctively that Leo was a wonderful lover.

Kay hadn't heard the crash. She was cleaning her teeth with the electric toothbrush, letting the water run into the sink as she always did. She didn't hear John knock on the door and only when the sound of Leo's voice burst into the room did she turn and see the young man inside her bedroom leaning against the closed door.

'Why did you change the channel, Kay?' Oh, she was sorry she had told him to call her Kay. It sounded ridiculous.

'I didn't,' she lied. 'It just happened to be tuned to that one when I switched on the TV. You can change it back.'

'Oh, I don't think we want to watch any more TV.'

'I might,' said Kay, reaching for the remote control and rapidly switching back to Leo. 'You shouldn't be in here, John,' she said.

'I wondered where you'd gone. I was concerned.'

'Why don't you sit down? She pointed to a chair as far away from the two beds as an object could be and still be in the room. The two beds. Of course, now he had noticed those. He made no move to sit in the chair, but just stared at the two beds – the one rumpled where Kay had been sitting on it and the other immaculate, empty and untouched. Kay remained in the doorway, feeling somehow safe and respectable because she was still in the bathroom.

'John, either you sit down or you go back down-stairs. Why don't we both go into the kitchen and I'll make you some coffee?'

'Please don't send me away.' He was walking towards her. He looked so young and guileless that when he sat down on Leo's bed and held his head in his hands she found herself sitting alongside him and putting her arm around his shoulders.

'Why is he so good?' Kay heard him say. 'Why is he always so good?' At first she didn't understand what he meant but then she realized that Leo was still singing out at them from the TV.

'Not always,' she said gently.

'Oh yes, always,' said the young man in her arms. 'Always good, always powerful, always musical, always sexy, always fucking perfect.'

'Not perfect, John, far, far, far from perfect.' The young man sat with his eyes closed, his hands resting on his knees now. Kay stroked his blond hair, her hand sliding slowly into the small hollow at the nape of his neck. This is all I wanted all along, she thought, just to hold his perfect, young clean body. With her other hand she lowered the volume on the television. Leo glared out at her. He or Attila was looking betrayed but all Kay could feel was the silken hair, the warm skin. He is like a child, she thought. Like a child and yet she sensed a stirring and she knew that the moment was threatened.

'I thought of a name for the dog,' she whispered. 'I wanted to share it with you before I told anyone else.'

'Oh yeah?' John didn't look up but there was a thickness to his voice that Kay knew only came with desire. Please not that, she thought. That's not what I wanted at all.

'Yes, yes, I wanted your approval – I trust your judgement,' she added.

'You do?' Still the thickness filled the voice and he was straining to turn and face her. She tried to stroke on but his neck had hardened now. He was staring into her eyes.

'Winston,' she said, and laughed a false tinkling laugh.

'Why Winston? Who's Winston?' He obviously had

no idea and Kay suddenly felt very old. Her hand dropped to the bed. Beyond John she could see Leo in close-up, his mouth wide open. How grotesque opera becomes on TV, she thought, and then John lunged at her. He pulled her face to his. She smelt the pizza, the cognac, the wine and then she felt his tongue pressing against her closed mouth. His hard young body felt wonderful and for a moment Kay relaxed, opened her mouth, let her tongue touch his. But this young man had a young man's haste and a drunken young man's clumsiness. Already he was fumbling at the collar of her blouse. Kay didn't notice immediately. She had closed her eyes and forgotten everything but the feel of another tongue on hers. Then she felt his long, slender, usually so graceful fingers sliding underneath the blue silk. She tried to withdraw but it was too late.

'What the hell?' She opened her eyes and saw the look of horror on John's face. His features were twisted with disgust. He was holding his precious hand aloft, away from his own body as though it were contaminated. Then he saw Kay looking right at him and she saw the effort on his face as he struggled to soften those rigid muscles and mask his dismay.

'Oh, Mrs dalla Vigna – I didn't know – I couldn't know—'

'Get out,' said Kay, walking to the door and holding it open. 'Get the hell out of here right now!'

'Oh, I am so sorry. It's all right. It doesn't matter—'

'I said get out! Just get the fuck out!'

John stood up, opened his mouth to speak but ran instead past Kay, past the closed door of the music-room, down the stairs and out of the house.

On the silent TV in the bedroom, Leo walked out from behind a scarlet curtain and took a bow. Applause echoed up from the abandoned room downstairs.

Chapter Twenty

Clara had formulated her own philosophy about sex at her boarding-school. Flesh was flesh, and in the dark, gender wasn't that important. As far as the physical sensations were concerned, well, there was usually damp wiry hair to fumble with, then warm flesh which in either case got wet at some point, quivered uncontrollably for a few seconds and got wetter still.

When, during the second act, her Hungarian neighbour slipped her hand between her thighs, Clara did not discourage her. A chorus of Huns was stamping around a dangerously raked stage and Leo wasn't due back on for several long minutes. Clara spread her bony thighs, closed her eyes and leaned against the back wall of the box.

When after a shared bottle of champagne during the second interval, the Hungarian woman took her hand and made it plain that she expected her gesture to be reciprocated, Clara extended her own hand and rummaged absently around in the woman's thick pubic hair until the Hungarian gasped so loud that the maestro stopped the orchestra in the opening bars and turned his sleek head to glare at an innocent spectator in the stalls.

At the end of the performance the two women exchanged business cards in their dressing-room. The Hungarian murmured an invitation to Sardinia. Clara replied that she didn't care for summer resorts but was flushed and exhilarated when she joined Otto, Eva and Rose in the foyer.

'Why don't I take you all backstage?' she said, and smiled at Eva.

'Me? Backstage? Oh, but I'd love to!' said Otto who

had avoided Clara until that moment. Now he took her arm and, forgetting Rose and Eva, let her lead him out through the departing crowds into the night. Rose tried to follow but was hindered by Eva who had taken *her* arm and whose arthritic knees made for slow progress past the cold wall where the forlorn group of ticket hunters had waited a few hours earlier and around the corner to the stage door.

Another group of people waited there. Amongst them Rose recognized the man with the three hoops in his right ear whom she had last seen in the amphi-theatre bar at Covent Garden.

'Avoid that lot,' whispered Otto. 'Or they will start thinking they can come too.' But the man with the three ear-rings had seen them and was waving to Otto. He came towards them, his arm around a younger, petulant, blond man.

'Same old faces everywhere,' said the older man. 'This is Marco, a friend of mine from Mantua.' Otto ignored the two men. He was looking beyond them at Clara who was talking to the stage doorkeeper and seemed about to disappear down La Scala's inner corridors and out of sight.

'What a wonderful evening!' said Rose.

'*Non tanto*,' sighed Marco from Mantua. 'It is always sad to hear a great voice on the decline – to hear the winds of time, *come si dice*? creaking in the rafters.'

'Whose rafters?' cried Rose.

'Come on, Rose.' Otto was tapping her on the shoulder. 'Clara has cleared things with the doorkeeper.'

Rose saw the shimmer of silver and sequins dis-appearing down the corridor. She turned her back on Marco and his companion but the older man grabbed at her elbow.

'Are you going to the dressing-rooms?'

'We have an appointment with Signor dalla Vigna,' said Otto, and took Rose by the hand. The older man did not release his grip.

'Take me,' he said softly. 'Even if you can't take Marco, take me.'

'Bugger off,' said Eva, and once again Rose felt her hand on her elbow and felt herself being pushed past the doorkeeper's lodge and out into a courtyard.

'Run, Rose, run,' said a breathless Otto. 'Through that door there or we'll lose Clara.'

Rose started to run but slowed down once she was through the door and in a short low corridor.

'If she has offered to take us, surely she won't run away from us,' she said to Otto.

'Oh, you never know with Clara,' he replied. 'She's very moody.'

'Well then, to hell with her,' said Rose. 'If she can't do a straightforward kindness, what's the point? And anyway, how come she is even allowed in there after what happened at your house?'

'I told you she knows the right people. Oh please, Rose, please,' said Otto, tightening his grip on her hand. 'I've never been back here before. My place is on the other side of the stage door. This is unknown territory – think of all the legends that have walked these corridors.'

'Or corridors like them,' said Eva's voice behind her. 'The place was bombed by the Allies during the war.'

'By Clara's father, if I remember rightly,' said Rose.

'Yes, but he didn't want to,' said Otto. 'He didn't *mean* it. Just think, Rose, Verdi walked these corridors, so did Puccini, so did—'

Rose had stopped listening and slowed her pace to a halt. The corridor was lined with music-stands; in a corner lay an abandoned pile of Huns' torches. As they turned a corner and plunged deeper into the labyrinth of backstage passages, Rose realized that the splendour of the evening was slipping away with each step. With each step the illusion faded. She felt Otto pulling at her upper arm. Against her will, she was being dragged out of the enclosed, perfected safe world that she had inhabited for the last three hours, and being flung into these corridors with their cold unforgiving lights and their steep, sudden staircases.

Rose stood still. Otto tried to drag her along the corridor.

'Please, Rose, please. If I lose sight of Clara, it's all over.' She felt the pressure of Eva's short plump arms on her shoulders.

'I'm not sure I want to go any further.'

'But why not?' whined Otto.

'Because this evening was beautiful. I think it was complete in itself.' Rose spoke very deliberately, discovering her own thoughts as she voiced them. 'I don't think I need to see some fat tenor taking his make-up off.'

'The *signora* is right.'

Leo. He had appeared around a corner, still clad in his last-act costume. How thick and crude his Hun's make-up appeared in close-up, Rose thought, as she stepped backward out of Otto's grip.

'But only up to a point,' Leo continued. 'The lady is right not to want to get too close to an illusion but, *signora*, perhaps you did not notice, the tenor is not fat.'

'Oh, but of course he's not, *Maestro*.' Otto rushed forward to shake Leo's hand, but the singer was hardly aware of the slender fingers on his. He had recognized Rose and was peering quizzically down at her as he had done in the suburban sleet and in the Milan snow.

Rose was aware of his bare chest, only inches from her silk wedding dress, glistening with beads of sweat on the tawny skin and the black hairs. She had a sudden urge to reach out and run the tip of her index finger across his nipple but when she held out her hand it was to shake his and say, '*Buona sera.*'

The broad, smooth palm that enclosed hers was a familiar memory by now. Rose felt, as she had felt in London, the warmth, the solidity of the man whose hand she continued to grasp until Otto edged his way in front of her.

'What a stunning performance, *Maestro*! Tell me,

when will we have the pleasure of seeing your Attila in London?'

Leo scowled down at the blond twin. The effort to force himself into the mould of the great opera singer and answer the old, tired questions seemed to him to be almost physical. Then he remembered the affection he had for the timid twin and smiled.

'I can't remember my plans off-hand but give me a few minutes to get changed and get this mess off, then come along to my dressing-room. Even you, *signora*.' He winked at Rose and disappeared up a flight of stairs.

Within minutes they were on the short corridor of the male principals' dressing-rooms. Most of the doors were open and little groups of people seemed to be waiting before each one. Rose found herself standing with Otto and Eva in a queue to see the Spanish tenor.

'What am I doing here?' she said to the twins.

'Oh, shut up, Rose!' said Otto. 'I'm sorry but, please, if you don't want to be here – if you think all this is sycophancy or whatever the word is, well, you know the way to the hotel. We'll see you at breakfast in the morning.'

'I'd never find my way out of the theatre,' replied Rose without any hesitation. 'I'd probably wander and wind up stairs and down corridors for hours and days and weeks and years and be found a forgotten skeleton in a silk wedding dress decades from now.'

Clara came out of the end dressing-room. She was carrying a large cage. Inside it sat a parrot with moth-eaten gaps in its grey feathers.

'Ping!' it yelled at the people in the corridor. Clara saw the twins and Rose and walked towards them, holding the cage aloft, a triumphant smile on her thin face.

'A little present from Leo. Isn't he beautiful?'

'Lovely,' said Otto. 'Clara, where did you go? We thought you were taking us down to the dressing-rooms—'

'And I thought you were following me,' said Clara,

staring into the cage and making clicking noises at the parrot. 'Anyway, you seem to have done very well on your own.'

'Yes, well, we have been inv—' Otto was cut off in mid-sentence by Eva who stepped forward and poked a calloused finger through the cage.

'You won't be able to bring this thing into England,' she said as the bird nibbled her fingertip. 'There's rules against it you know.'

'Oh, I'm sure I'll be able to work something out,' said Clara. 'Right now, my big problem is what to do with it tonight. We're all going on to a big reception – Leo and the singers and I that is – and of course the maestro – and, well, I can't very well take this poor boy along, can I? I suppose one of you wouldn't consider dropping it off at my hotel. You will be going straight back, won't you?'

'No,' said Eva. 'No, we won't. We have other plans too.'

'Oh, oh really? Anything fun?' But her attention had already wandered beyond the twins and Rose to a group of Italians in elegant evening clothes who were muttering something about the big reception and making their way towards the door. Without a good-bye, she swung the parrot away from Eva and headed down the stairs.

'If it's going to be a long wait, I think we should get in line for Leo,' said Eva, and walked towards the group of people waiting outside the closed door.

'Queue up?' Rose was reluctant to follow the twins. She sat down on a small sofa outside one of the rooms. She felt suddenly humiliated to be standing in a line waiting for a man to deign to open his door and speak to her. 'And why the fuck has he given Clara a parrot?'

After about five minutes, Leo opened his door and two elegant Italian women walked out. Rose glimpsed Leo's arms, clad now in a pale blue shirt, as they held each woman in turn; she heard his voice murmur farewells and rise in greeting to the next people in the queue. He seemed to know them too. How many people in how many theatres throughout the world were on such cosily familiar terms with this elusive man whose broad, dark shadow had drawn her through the snows of Europe to stand in wait for him?

She continued to wait, studying the people in the line in front of her, trying to label them, to tidy them away into small corners of Leo's life so that they would become less threatening. Here, going in now were an elderly, slightly down-at-heel Italian couple. The wife clutched an old-fashioned camera which she had scrutinized at regular intervals, even holding it up and shaking it at one point. They came out all smiles and more farewell hugs after only a few minutes and were replaced by a very young, very beautiful Italian girl whose smooth olive skin and thick, black, ringleted hair made Rose feel hopeless and desperate.

She must be a music student, she told herself, an aspiring soprano or whatever. Her interest must be wholly professional. But the minutes the nubile young woman remained on the other side of the door were the longest of the evening for Rose. And only when she came back out and Rose heard her address Leo with the formal '*lei*' and shake his hand did she relax. Still the queue went on. Still the cries of greeting and familiarity filled the corridor. All these people and all the hundreds like them in Munich and Vienna and New York have a head start on me, thought Rose. They all know far more about Leo and about his world than I, who have, after all, only squeezed his hand on three occasions and exchanged a very few words ... Just how many words have I exchanged with him? Rose fell to counting while Eva and Otto talked about Mont-serrat Caballé with an elderly Argentinian in front of them.

She had calculated that she had addressed precisely fourteen words to the man behind the door when that door opened. Leo was standing there, his face slightly raw from where he had removed his make-up. He was clad now in grey wool trousers and that pale blue shirt.

He saw the three of them in the queue for the first time and, with a brief apology to the Argentinian, ushered them in to his dressing-room. Only when he had closed the door and walked over to a pile of towels and clothes on a seat did she notice that he was barefoot. He saw her gazing at his feet and shrugged.

'I've been getting dressed in between visitors,' he said. Rose wondered just how many clothes he would therefore have been wearing during the long minutes that the nubile young Italian had been in the small cramped room with him. And the room did feel small and cramped with the four of them standing in there. It smelled of sweat and a cologne that Leo had sprinkled liberally over himself before opening the door for the first time. She heard him mutter, '*Scusi*,' and sit down on one of the two chairs to don his socks. Rose found herself staring at his feet. How white and exposed they looked and what an intimate act this was. In what circumstances did a woman usually watch a man put on his socks? A man to whom she had said just fourteen words?

'So kind of you to invite us, *Maestro*.' Otto sat down on the seat opposite Leo and pulled out a leather-bound autograph book and a Mont Blanc pen. Leo pointed to his feet and smiled and finished pulling on his socks before he took the book and scrawled his signature on the page that Otto held open.

'And when can we expect to see you in London?' Otto blushed to the top of his bow-tie.

'Not for at least three years,' smiled Leo.

'Three years!' cried Rose. 'We might all be dead by then!'

'It is absurd, *signorina*, I agree with you, but alas it is the way the great houses work.'

'How can you live like that?' said Rose. 'Most of the time I don't know what I'm going to do a half-hour from now—'

'But what you do is of no consequence to the world, Rose,' said Otto. 'Thousands of people wouldn't be disappointed if you didn't show up for an engagement.'

Before Rose could think of anything to say to that, she heard her name on Leo's lips.

'Rose,' said the bass and smiled at her for the first time. He turned to Otto.

'Who can say what is really of consequence in this world, *signore*? What I have just done has disappeared into the air, without a trace. If you went into the auditorium now, you would find the cleaners sweeping up the rubbish under bright lights that show how worn the fabric is on the seats. You won't find any notes, any sounds, any feelings. Where do they all go?'

'Oh, I didn't mean any offence to Rose,' said Otto. 'None at all. And anyway, the sounds are all there suspended somewhere, I'm quite sure of that. We just don't have the capacity to hear them.'

'Unlike dogs,' said Eva. 'Dogs can hear all sorts of things we can't.'

'It's got nothing to do with bloody dogs!' said Otto. 'That's a completely different thing.'

'But dogs can hear better,' retorted Eva. 'Any fool knows that.'

'And why, pray, should some bloody cocker spaniel be able to hear the long-dead voice of Maria Callas when I can't, you silly cow? I'm not talking about frequencies, I'm talking about – about different dimensions, about—' Otto saw Leo gazing at him and blushed again.

'About time being a dimension in which we can travel around?' said the bass gently. 'It is a comforting thought to imagine that nothing – nobody, is ever really lost.'

That last sentence threw the awkward little group into silence until Eva coughed and said that if they wanted any dinner they should be getting going before the restaurants closed.

'Have you a restaurant in mind?' Leo asked Rose.

'Nothing definite.'

'Then try the Santa Cecilia. It's just around the corner and stays open very late. A lot of the artists use it.'

'Will you be eating there?' said Otto.

'Alas, no. I have to go to a reception,' said Leo. 'I won't eat nearly as well as you.'

Again they stood in a moment of uncomfortable silence until Eva thrust her hand forward and said, 'Well, good night, sir.'

Leo ignored her hand, put his arm around her neck, pulled her to him and kissed her on the cheek. For the first time since Rose had known her, she saw the dumpy blonde woman blush. Leo had moved on to shake Otto's hand and then he turned to Rose.

'Good night, Signora Rose,' he said and reached forward to kiss her on each cheek. She raised her chin to receive his kiss and felt his lips on her neck just below her ear. He lingered longer at the second kiss. Rose could smell his cologne and a rounder, Mediterranean smell beneath his beard. She could feel the warmth of his skin under the roughness of the dark hair. She wanted to return the kiss, to brush her lips lightly against the dark, sombre face but she was in the wrong position and could only make an absurd pursed lip movement into the air of the hot, cramped dressing-room.

And then they were back out in the corridor as the Argentinian squeezed past them and greeted Leo. They followed other people leaving other dressing-rooms and soon they were out in the icy street.

'He's got a wife, you know,' said Otto, as they paused under the arcade to pull their coats tighter around them for it was snowing hard again. 'She's one of the most beautiful women I've ever seen – a natural blonde, tall and slender with the most incredible cheek-bones. And she was a musician.'

'Why are you telling me this?' asked Rose. The three of them set out across the Piazza della Scala, very gingerly putting one foot in front of the other, for a layer of ice lay concealed under the new snow and their evening shoes had no grip on the skating rink that the square had become.

'I thought you might be interested,' said Otto.

'Well, I'm not. That's his private life. It's the

musician, the singer, that interests me.' She skidded towards the great bronze figure of Leonardo da Vinci but righted herself in time.

'Of course,' said Otto and taking Eva's arm, led them towards the side-street where the light of the restaurant was the only bright spot in a darkened arcade.

Rose paused in the entrance, blocking the twins in the doorway. She was surprised to find the restaurant only half full. And the people who sat at the starched white-linened tables looked like businessmen or commercial salesmen and their wives. They were not what she had been expecting.

'All gone to the reception,' said Otto, answering her unspoken question and pushing her forward for the second time that evening. This time he pushed her into the dining-room. A waiter seated them at a table in the corner. Otto ordered fettuccine with aubergines and black olives for all of them. And they sat in the silence of starched white linen.

'This place is like a morgue,' said Eva.

'I told you they are all at the reception,' said Otto. 'Of course, I said all the wrong things in there,' Otto went on. 'I always do. But usually it's harmless rubbish about where they are singing next – not dogs. Why did you have to bring dogs into it, Eva?'

'And why did he give Clara a parrot?' said Rose as the waiter brought the bread-sticks. 'I mean, did he actually go out to some Milanese pet shop and pick it out? I find that hard to believe – it was so mangy-looking. And why a parrot? And most of all, why any kind of gift? What was she even doing anywhere near him after what happened at your house?'

'Perhaps it was symbolic,' sighed Otto. 'Anyway, I've already told you she has some kind of charismatic hold over these people.'

'She doesn't strike me as being very charismatic,' said Rose.

'Well, you're jealous, aren't you?' said Otto. 'I mean, there she is, parrot and all, at some wonderful gala and here we sit.'

'Not that we'd have any business at one of those dos,' said Eva. 'What would we say to all those distinguished musicians? It's not our place.'

'Not our place at all,' sighed Otto.

They sat on in the starched white silence. None of them said another word until the pasta was served. When the plates of fettuccine were placed before them, for just a few moments, Rose forgot the desolation in which the evening seemed destined to end. There is no reason for me ever to meet that man again, she thought, as the waiter's hand removed her empty plate. He has, after all, a wife – an extraordinary beauty – a natural blonde, a musician.

Rose felt a sudden urge to reapply her make-up. As she stood up to go to the bathroom, Otto took her hand and squeezed it.

'Thank you so much for buying us dinner,' he whispered. 'Eva would never have let me come here at these prices.'

'Oh my God!' Rose clapped her hand across her mouth. 'I've got no money!'

'But you said you'd treat us!' Otto released her hand.

'I intended to but I spent all my cash—'

'How humiliating! How could you do this to us? Oh, the shame!'

'If she hasn't got any money, she hasn't got any money.' Eva pushed her half-eaten plate of pasta away. 'Didn't you know before we came in here?' she hissed.

'It was the ticket,' sighed Rose. 'I paid four hundred pounds for it.'

'How much?' said the twins in unison. 'You're mad!'

'Please don't remind me – I couldn't face the thought of not going in—'

'That's almost a month's rent,' said Eva. 'That's a week's holiday—'

'Please don't, Eva.' Rose rummaged in her bag. 'Perhaps I could put it on a credit card – there's no money in the account but I could cover it when I get back.'

There was a sudden ripple of applause in the half-empty restaurant. Everybody except Rose turned towards the entrance. Eva and Otto lost interest in her dilemma and started clapping. The waiter had put down a small glass bowl of Parmesan cheese and was clapping. The cook came out of the kitchen and clapped and cheered. Rose knew who was standing in the doorway. She sat back in her seat and joined in the applause. Only after a few long seconds did she dare to look towards the door where Leo stood smiling towards them, a few flakes of snow on his wide-brimmed hat.

Chapter Twenty-One

'We have to leave,' said Eva, as Leo pulled up a chair and sat down next to Rose.

'Not already?' said the singer.

'We seem to have less money than we thought,' said Eva. 'Spent it all on theatre tickets.'

'Please don't, Eva,' whispered Otto.

'It's all right, I've found my credit card,' said Rose.

'But I came to buy you dinner,' said Leo. He took Eva's hand and kissed it. 'I remembered after you left that I owe you some money for the carpet cleaning—'

'You got my letter?'

'Please, Eva, no,' said Otto. 'He doesn't owe us any money.'

'It is my pleasure. Now will you all have dessert?' Leo called the waiter, asked for menus and a plate of pasta for himself.

'They have an excellent walnut tart,' said Leo.

'I can't digest nuts,' said Otto. 'I've heard rumours of a Verdi festival in Parma, opening with a *Don Carlos*. Will there be any chance of seeing you there, *Maestro*?'

'I haven't been invited,' said Leo. 'What about the ladies? Don't you want dessert? And some coffee or a grappa later on?'

Rose didn't reply. Since the moment that Leo had walked into the restaurant, handed his coat and hat to the waiter and walked directly over to their table, the scene seemed to be moving in slow motion. She was watching the banal but quite extraordinary sight of this man walking towards her from a long way away. And Rose feared that if she said too much her words would be slow and slurred like an old record played at the wrong speed. Already there was the building up of a shared past. He, Leo, had left a reception to join her. And now as they sat within inches of each other, he was referring to the quite astonishing concept of 'later on'.

'Can't somebody open a door or window in here?' Eva's voice came to Rose, not in slow motion and not from a long way away but right next to her where the older woman was fanning herself with the programme.

'But it's freezing out there,' said Otto. 'Signor dalla Vigna will not want to sit in a draught.'

Eva pushed her chair away from the table and stood up so violently that all the cutlery on one side fell to the floor and a bottle of mineral water rocked and was only saved by Leo's broad hand which had been reaching for a bread-stick.

Rose watched as the twin sister made her way towards the toilets. Eva was muttering what sounded like a stream of obscenities but the two men had resumed their conversation so only Rose heard the 'all go fuck themselves' and the 'bunch of arse-holes' punctuating the by now familiar operatic small talk: 'And will you abandon *Attila* and *Moses* completely now that you are taking on the Wagnerian repertoire?'

Rose left Otto listening with rapt attention to Leo's reply and followed Eva into the toilets. She found the older woman bent over a sink, her head awkwardly crooked to receive the full blast of running water from the cold tap.

'Menopause,' she gulped as the water flowed over her. 'Can you splash some on the back of my neck?'

'But of course,' said Rose, responding more to the first statement than to the request as she cupped her hands and splashed the icy water over Eva's plump pink skin. The front of Rose's silk wedding dress was soon soaked but the older woman just said, 'Don't stop, don't stop. I got so hot at the table, I thought I was going to hit someone. It comes up from your back and just floods over you.'

'Of course,' said Rose again. 'Of course.'

'Stop saying "of course". You can't have any idea what it's like until it happens. But it will come sooner than you think.'

'Of course,' said Rose absently. Now that she knew that Eva was all right her attention had wandered back to the dining-room.

'And this is only part of it,' said the head in the basin. 'Then there's the flooding and the vaginal dryness—'

'Oh!' said Rose. The idea of Eva even possessing a vagina shocked her into scooping the cold water with a vengeance. She gazed down at the damp plump neck on the rim of the sink. She had never thought of Eva as a woman, just a solid and efficient provider of soup and theatre tickets. Poor old duck, she thought as she sloshed more water over Eva's head. It took the extinguishing of that womanhood for anyone to notice that you'd ever had one.

'You don't have to overdo it!' Eva's head reared up out of the basin. Rose had soaked her blonde hair. Efficient Eva walked over to the hand-towel machine, unhooked it and tore off a long strip of striped fabric which she wrapped around her head.

'I'm knackered,' she said. 'I want to go back to the hotel. Will you walk with me?'

'Didn't you order a walnut tart?'

'Sod the tart,' said Eva. She turned towards the door. Rose waited for her to remove the hand-towel turban but when she did pause it was to say, 'Once I calculated how many months of my life have been wasted on preparing for a motherhood I knew I would never experience. They really should come up with a system where the people like me could be told in advance that they are going to sit the whole long bloody dance out. It would save getting the ball gowns out of the moth-balls; it would save all the false hope.'

But you surely never owned a ball gown, not even a metaphorical one? thought Rose. And did you ever hope?

Eva opened the door and made her way down the

small passage that led into the dining-room. She apparently intended to wear the turban across the restaurant and the piazza and into the hotel. Rose caught up with her, intending to offer her her evening shawl in its place but when the two women reached for the door out of the corridor, Rose saw that Eva was weeping.

'Wanna go home,' she sniffed, and passing wordlessly by the table where Leo and Otto talked on, she walked out into the snow. Rose knew that she should follow her but she also knew that once she left the restaurant, she could not be sure of returning. She went to the table and sat back down. Leo didn't acknowledge her return. He was staring at the door that had just closed behind Eva.

'Why is your sister crying?' he said to Otto.

'Eva never cried in her life,' said her brother.

'Well, she's crying now,' said Leo.

'Yes, she is, Otto,' said Rose. 'And she's walking through that blizzard.'

'We must go after her,' said Leo.

'She's going to the hotel,' said Rose. 'It's just around the corner. I'd have suggested a taxi but it's too close.'

'But we can't leave her alone like that,' said Leo, standing up and walking towards the door.

'It's all right, damn her,' said Otto. 'I'll go. I'll go.'

A sheepish Rose followed the two men to the door of the restaurant where Leo insisted on flagging down a cab and giving the driver a hefty tip in advance to pick up the woman just yards away under the colonnades. He bundled a bemused Otto into the back seat, shook his hand and walked back into the dining-room.

'What was wrong with her?' he asked Rose as he sat back down to the plate of pasta that had been placed in front of him.

'Advancing years, diminishing womanhood, sudden realization that her life might have been wasted.'

Now that the others were gone, now that just she and this man remained at the round table in the corner, Rose found that the earlier unreal sensation had vanished. Otto's departure seemed to have taken with it the myth, the legend that was Leo, and left in their place a wise, solid man who listened gravely to her explanation and said, 'Ah.' He scooped a forkful of fettuccine into his mouth, chewed on it, swallowed it down and leaned towards Rose. 'One morning in each of our lives, it seems to me that we wake up and there it all is, perched on the edge of the bed, so to speak, grinning malevolently at us – the advancing years, the diminishing manhood or womanhood, the sudden realizations – they all seem to steal in overnight . . . overnight . . .'

He poured himself a glass of wine and gazed past Rose at the door which was closing now on the only other diners who had remained in the restaurant: the elderly couple from the queue at the dressing-room. When they saw Leo looking in their direction, they were suddenly flustered and excited; the old woman gave him a girlish wave; her husband tipped his feathered cap. Leo saw neither of them. He was too deep in thoughts of passing time to see a door close or open. The couple realized that they were being ignored; the woman's old face fell; the husband shrugged and muttered an insult to the stinging snow that pushed its way into the entrance as the door swung open.

'What wonderful English you speak,' said Rose.

'It is because I have sung so much at the Met and Covent Garden,' Leo lied and refilled her wineglass.

'Oh, but that wouldn't make you that fluent. People can go back and forth to a place for years and never get beyond the vocabulary that serves their basic needs,' said Rose with the assurance that came from being on her own professional territory. 'Either you have an excellent ear, which I suppose you would, being a musician, or you must read a lot.'

'I have a good ear and I do or rather I did have a great love of English literature, in the days when days were longer and I had more time.' Again Leo fell to contemplating the passing of time as he studied the face of the young woman in front of him. She was about a decade younger than he was, he calculated, not disarmingly, terrifyingly young like some of his more recent leading ladies whose peach skins and clear eyes could kill all his conversation dead in seconds. She dyed her hair, he noted, and not very efficiently either. He looked at the faint traces of brown and grey at the roots and remembered how proud he had once been of Kay's natural pale blonde hair, of how proud Kay herself still was. And for the first time in his life, he was aware of the absurdity of being proud of what was no more than a whim of genes and nature. There was greater merit in Rose's rather clumsy struggles with a peroxide bottle, he decided, and liked her even more.

'Another reason for bilingualism is, of course, the constant use of two languages in the home,' Rose went on, feeling uncomfortable under the big man's scrutiny. His eyes had been on the top of her head for far too long.

'You certainly seem knowledgeable on this subject,' said Leo.

'I'm an interpreter,' said Rose. 'English, French and Spanish.'

'Ha!' said Leo with a broad smile, and sat back satisfied in his chair as if that simple statement had settled everything. 'So, people tell you things and you understand them.'

'That's a nice way of putting it,' said Rose. 'But most of the time they tell me very boring things – the market price of olive oil, the advantages of extending the TGV to Madrid.'

'I knew you would,' said Leo.

'I beg your pardon?' said Rose.

'I knew you would,' said Leo again and reached across the table and patted the tips of her fingers. Then he withdrew his hand and flicked his head slightly as she had seen him do twice before – once to quell a rising surge of music and once in front of his hotel just two days earlier, to quell something that she sensed was more sinister.

'Don't you think that most people tell other people boring things?' he said, rejoining the conversation where Rose had left it. 'The only good conversations I seem to have any more are with Wagner and Verdi. Tell me something that's not boring, Rose. Are you married?'

'No,' said Rose.

'But you have been?'

'No,' said Rose, feeling as though she was failing an important examination. 'But I almost was. I decided at the last minute that it would be a terrible mistake, cancelled everything and came here instead. In fact,' she added, the fourth glass of wine and the proximity of Leo's dark brown eyes making her garrulous, 'I'm wearing my wedding dress.'

'It is very beautiful,' said Leo, studying the emerald silk so intently that Rose felt once more inhibited. 'But it's all wet.'

'Oh, that,' sighed Rose. 'I was sloshing water over Eva's neck in the toilets.'

'Ah,' said Leo.

'You are married,' Rose heard herself saying.

'Yes,' said Leo and suddenly regained his interest in the plate of pasta in front of him. Rose watched, fascinated by the vigour with which he downed the fettuccine. Flecks of tomato sauce fell onto his greying beard. He wiped them away with the wide, white linen napkin. She wanted to ask him, 'Is your wife as beautiful as they say? Why did you give Clara a parrot? Why did you come here to this humble restaurant tonight when half Milan is at your feet?' And she wanted to close her eyes and rub her own smooth cheek up against the roughness of that greying beard.

'I was so hungry for some decent food,' said Leo in answer to her third unspoken question. 'There was one of those buffet things at the reception. Lots of champagne and people queuing up to shovel all sorts of incompatible dishes onto one plate. I hate buffets. Shall we order that walnut tart?'

Otto had appeared in the doorway. He was snow-covered and breathless. Rose calculated that he must have flung Eva into the hotel entrance and turned right around to be back in the restaurant so soon. She also calculated that she had about thirty seconds in which to say anything else to Leo before Otto's long legs crossed the tiled floor.

'Why did you give Clara a parrot after what she did to you?' she heard herself say.

'I shouldn't have done that,' sighed Leo.

'What did she do to you that night at Otto's house?' said Rose more urgently. 'What happened exactly?'

'One day I will tell you,' said Leo. 'I will tell you the whole story. It will be a change from olive oil and the TGV.' He too was studying Otto's progress to the table. 'Can I call you, Rose? Where are you staying?' He took a small card bearing the name and address of the restaurant from the ashtray and handed it to her. 'Write it on the back of here – quickly.'

Rose had already taken a pen from her handbag. She wrote the name of the hotel and the number which she took from a brochure she had picked up at the reception. She slid the card across the table and into Leo's hand. The tips of her fingers were still thrilling to the brief contact with his when Otto pulled out a chair and sat down between them.

Chapter Twenty-Two

Clara had followed Leo out of the reception and through the frozen Milan streets to the restaurant under the colonnades. She had seen him enter, heard the applause that greeted him and then she had waited, planning to follow him inside a few minutes later. She was not surprised at his departure. She knew that Leo never lingered at these society occasions. She also knew that the weary Leo would not put up much resistance if she sat down at his table and talked about Wotan. He would be reticent at first, would pour himself a second glass of wine and not offer one to her, but Clara knew that if she persisted, and she always did, she would ignite a spark of interest in the solitary Leo. She had waited in the entrance to the restaurant until the applause died down and the other diners went back to their meals. Then she had pushed the door to the dining-room open, and she saw Leo sitting down at a table with Rose.

She had slammed the door shut and run out into the street along the sheltered pavement under the arcade until she got to the hotel. There, she retrieved the elderly parrot that she had left with a bemused receptionist and ran back out into the snowy night. She didn't know where she was going but she sped along the narrow streets, swinging the cage so violently that the terrified, squawking bird was flung off its perch and crashed against the bars. Clara ran on until she reached a small, deserted piazza where a half-frozen fountain still dribbled a trickle of water into an icy basin. She smashed the layer of ice with her one free, bare hand and threw the cage into the water. It sank down but bobbed back up to the surface. The old

215

parrot proved agile and alert enough to avoid a soaking. It leapt to the upturned side of the cage and clung on upside down as the shallow water in the basin settled around the base.

'*Calumnia*!' it yelled at the departing Clara but she didn't look back. 'Ping! Ping! Ping!' it cried with ever-decreasing volume as the lone woman left the piazza and walked calmly back to her hotel.

For an hour, Clara was satisfied and almost happy. She imagined Leo's face when he saw the abandoned parrot. She felt vindicated. Only when she was drifting into sleep did she realize that there was no reason for Leo ever to see what she had done.

Remorse and the sudden realization of the pointlessness of her act woke her at 3 a.m. She dressed quickly, pulled on her snow-boots for greater mobility and walked out into the empty streets. At first she couldn't remember just where the tiny piazza was located and she went around the same blank, frozen block of buildings three times, almost giving up in frustration when she saw the alley that led to the square. The night was so cold that the thick snow that had fallen earlier had frozen onto the layer of ice below. She slipped and slid, lunging at parked cars for support, cursing Rose as she lost her grip and lurched onto her knees in the stinging snow. But she didn't give up. Some vague thought of her lost cat and the recurring reminder that Leo had given the precious bird into her care pushed her into the piazza. The little square was silent. Clara's finely-attuned ear knew immediately that the last trickle of water on the fountain had frozen solid. The one lamp that lit the piazza was so dim that at first she could see only the dark shadow of the fountain in the centre of the cobbled square, but as she advanced the moon came out and she saw the frozen stream of ice gleaming white in its frigid light. She had entered the piazza on the wrong side to see the parrot. She was still several feet away when she saw the cage, locked into a newly formed block of ice. She stopped and started to recoil.

'It's all Leo's fault,' she muttered to the indifferent, shuttered buildings around the square and she turned and ran, still sliding, still skidding, back down the alley-way and towards the hotel. Behind her in the square, snow fell on the stiff and somehow smaller body of the old parrot, lying silent now on the bottom of the cage where it would be found at dawn by a baffled Milanese street-sweeper.

Back in her room, Clara decided to go to Milan Central Station and buy a ticket to any one of the great opera cities. She would soothe herself with some distant end of the repertoire where Leo never ventured. She might even wangle a ticket to the Domingo *Otello* in Berlin. Names of composers and cities and singers whirled in her head as she bundled the silver sequinned dress and her thick wad of money into her suitcase.

An hour before Clara's dash to the fountain, Rose and Otto had passed along those same icy streets. They had sat with Leo until a desperate head waiter had placed two bills on the table. Leo had swept up the bills and paid them, swept up Otto and Rose and despatched them into a taxi, shaking a euphoric Otto warmly by the hand and kissing Rose, but much more formally than he had kissed her in his dressing-room. As the taxi pulled away, Rose had turned and watched as the big man walked through the empty street to the Grand Hotel.

'What a contrast to three hours ago,' murmured Otto, watching Rose watching. 'And yet it is almost a law of nature that always it must end up like this.'

'Walking alone through the dark,' said Rose.

Rose was woken the next morning by the sound of a man's voice in the hallway outside her room. The voice was deep and resonant and talking in Italian. She rushed to the door. When she opened it she found Otto deep in conversation with the fattest couple she had ever seen. Individually, the man and woman were simply obese but the sum of their enormous parts filled the doorway, blocking all light from the corridor. The deep resonant male voice belonged to the fat man,

217

Rose realized with crushing disappointment.

'Alberto and Stella Marchetti,' said Otto, kissing Rose on both cheeks.

'No kisses, Otto. I'm hardly awake,' said Rose.

'Former illustrious members of the La Scala chorus,' continued Otto.

'We was thinner then,' boomed Alberto.

'Alberto's face and body were as beautiful as his voice,' bawled Stella.

'Why are they shouting?' Rose whispered to Otto, who was pushing his way into her room. The fat couple followed.

'Chorists always do,' said Otto. 'Why aren't you dressed, Rose? We have to leave for Venice within the hour.'

'Venice?' said Rose. 'You didn't say anything about Venice last night.' Because the room was small and narrow and because the chorists were so fat, they were all standing in an absurd single line with Rose pressed against the table by the window, Otto and Stella along the unmade bed and Alberto squeezed in the doorway at the rear.

'*Venezia, la Serenissima,*' sighed Alberto from the back of the queue.

'Yes, yes, I know that,' said Rose and drew back so that she could look Otto sternly in the eye without banging her nose against his. 'I can't go to Venice within the hour.'

'Why not – you've got nothing to do here.'

'Yes I have,' said Rose. And to herself she said in silence: I have to wait for a call from Leo. What else is there to do in the world?

'What you got to do?' said Stella, sinking down onto the little bed.

'Why are these people in my room?' Rose didn't bother to whisper this time.

'They're Italian,' said Otto. 'They have a completely different sense of spatial relations. You may have noticed this when you queue up in the bank – they tend to like to get very close.'

Alberto had squeezed past Otto and taken Rose's hand in his.

'Come, *signorina, presto, presto*, if we are to be in Venice for lunch.'

'We?' said Rose. 'Are they coming too?'

'But of course. They are going to help us get tickets to La Fenice. Alberto knows someone.'

'I know many people,' said Alberto.

'But how do you know Alberto?' said Rose.

'Oh, we were at the Accademia Chigiana together in that one brief summer that I thought I might be a singer.'

'Where Leo studied!' said Rose. 'I remember that from the talk at your house.'

'Yes, but I wasn't there at quite the same time—'

'Leo dalla Vigna!' cried Stella.

'*Che grande cantante!*' cried Alberto. '*Che grand' uomo!*' And for a moment Rose thought that he was going to cross himself. They all stood or sat in silence, hushed by the invisible presence of Leo.

'I can't go to Venice this morning,' said Rose. 'And if I did, would we come back to this hotel afterwards?'

'What on earth for?' said Otto. 'There is nothing else to see in Milan.'

Oh yes there is, thought Rose, oh yes there is.

The phone rang. Rose started towards it, paused and turned to her three visitors.

'If you don't mind?' she said. She couldn't talk to Leo with the three of them squashed in alongside her.

'Oh, we don't mind at all,' said Otto and remained right next to her. 'But do be quick if we're to be in Venice for lunch.'

'At the Taverna la Fenice,' sighed Alberto. 'You don't really eat good nowhere in Venice but this place will do.' And he too remained in place smiling at Rose.

Rose picked up the phone. It was Daphne.

'Rose, dear, I have been so worried—'

'How did you know where I was?' said Rose.

'Mother said she got a note saying you'd gone to La Scala so I called all the cheapish hotels in Milan. I'm calling from Roger's office so we don't have to worry about the bill. Are you all right?'

'Yes, yes, I'm fine – hold on just one minute.' She turned to Otto. 'It's my sister.'

'Get rid of her,' said Otto. 'It's your old life, Rose. Come with us to Venice.'

'She's not my old life – she's my only sister.'

'Oh yes, sisters,' sighed Otto. 'I suppose we're manacled to them for life but get rid of her anyway. She'll still be around when you come back – they always are.' He had turned his attention to Rose's half-open suitcase and was fingering the emerald silk dress that lay over a chair.

'Don't touch that,' said Rose.

'I was just going to fold it,' said Otto. 'I'm a good folder.'

'Oh, all right. Look, Daphne, I can't talk now—'

'You have to, Rose. Your boss is wondering why he hasn't heard from you.'

'I'm not due back for two weeks,' said Rose.

'Next week, Rose. You're due back next week. Why don't you make your way home – you've been to La Scala by now, haven't you?'

'Oh yes,' said Rose.

'Then fly back.'

'I can't,' said Rose. She turned her back on the chorists and Otto and whispered into the receiver. 'I can't come home, Daphne. I'll talk to my boss but in the meantime can you put five hundred pounds in my current account? Mother will give you the number.'

'Five hundred pounds! What are you doing out there?'

'I can't explain,' whispered Rose. 'Please do it, Daphne. I'll pay you as soon as I get back.'

'God help me if Roger finds out,' said Daphne. 'He thinks you're unstable.'

'What's it to do with Roger – it's your money.'

'You have no idea of what being married is about,' sighed her sister.

'How could I?' whispered Rose. 'On that subject, have you heard anything of Martin?'

'Why? Do you regret what you did?'

'No, not at all, but I feel guilty.'

'You don't need to. Roger's already seen him with another woman.'

'He didn't waste any time.'

'Men don't,' said Daphne. 'Oh dammit, somebody here wants this phone.'

'You won't forget the money?' said Rose, but her sister had muttered a rapid goodbye and was gone.

While she had been talking to her sister, Otto and fat Stella had folded her dress and her shawl and placed them gently inside the small suitcase. Alberto was sniffing at a bottle of perfume on the ledge above the sink. He squirted some into the air.

'Gem,' said his wife. 'Van Cleef and Arpels.'

'I know that,' said Alberto and squeezed the nozzle at the silk handkerchief in his breast pocket.

'Can't we go to Venice tomorrow?' said Rose.

'It's *Don Giovanni* tonight,' said Alberto.

Otto had put his arm around her.

'He has a wife, you know.'

Rose closed her eyes and leaned back against the formica table. She was suddenly aware of her unwashed state. Her mouth felt stale; her eyes felt dry and swollen.

'I want a pot of tea and I want to be left alone to wash and pack. If you can take care of that, Otto, I will take the lot of you to Venice.'

'Love you, Rose,' whispered Otto as he ushered the chorists to the door.

'Oh, please don't,' replied Rose, but the three morning visitors had already squeezed back out into the corridor.

When Rose came downstairs half an hour later, Eva was going over the bill at reception.

'How are you today, Eva?' said Rose.

'Fine,' said Eva, not looking up from the bill.

'I left Otto and those dreadful chorists loading up the car. They both talk so loud I can't hear myself think.'

221

'Chorists always do,' said Eva and headed out towards the car.

'Just a minute, Eva,' Rose called after her. 'Before we go I'd like to leave a forwarding address and number just in case anybody tries to contact me here.'

'We haven't got one,' said Eva. 'The owner of our usual pension died – of a cancer that started in the bones of his feet and spread up in the matter of a month to his brain.'

'We think it was the water, seeping up through his body, that rotted him,' said Otto, who had appeared in the doorway. 'Like the wooden pillars that the city is built on, he decayed from the feet upwards.'

'Then we don't really know where we're going,' said Rose, still clutching the piece of paper on which she had planned to write her Venice address and a small note for Leo.

'Just say Venice,' cried Otto and disappeared after his sister into the snowy street.

Rose wrote Venice and a question mark in large letters across the envelope under Leo's name.

'If this person calls, that's where I am,' she said to the receptionist. Otto was outside the glass door waving soundlessly to her to get a move on. She shrugged and turned towards the door.

'Venice is a big place,' said the receptionist. 'A big dead place.'

Chapter Twenty-Three

Leo woke early the next day and decided to drive north to Bellagio. Because he intended to return to Milan that evening he took nothing but his wallet and car keys. As he made his way towards the Mercedes he realized that he had no idea why he wanted to spend the day in his lakeside home.

At a traffic light on the outskirts of Milan, he felt in his pocket and found the piece of paper with the hotel name and phone number. He memorized the number. He would call Rose at a respectable hour. From the early years of his career, he knew the kind of walls and ceiling and doors that enclosed her sleeping body at that moment. His imagination drew an accurate picture of a small cramped single bed in a narrow room that looked out onto a bleak courtyard.

The light changed. Leo sat in his car enjoying the warm wave of pleasure that washed over him as he pictured the softly rounded body on its back beneath the white sheets. A horn honked behind him. He sped away, driving too fast as usual and within a short while was on the road that ran alongside the lake. For the second time in a week, he paused to marvel at the frozen winter splendour. As he had gazed at the snow-flakes on the glass wall of the departure lounge in Heathrow, now he gazed at the snow-wrapped pines and at a thick cushion of white on a chapel bell. Now he knew why the sense of wonder so long lost to him had returned. He hummed a few bars of his new role as he drove into Bellagio, skidding on the icy cobble-stones in front of the Casa Lillia where Cosima Wagner was born.

Leo glanced at the house as he accelerated. Until this

morning he had forgotten the little town's link with the German composer. Plain, severe, devoted Cosima, champion of all things Aryan, had come into the world in this languorous, sensuous Italian lakeside town. He fingered the card in his pocket again.

With the energy of genius old man Wagner had started a new life, fathering children with this younger married woman at well past fifty. Whereas his former and fading hero, Verdi, had lost his offspring to typhus, never to embark on fatherhood again. Bereaved father Verdi, creator of so many operatic fathers, had been a source of consolation to Leo until this morning. Now as he sped around the corner towards the great wrought-iron gate of his villa, he decided that it was not by chance that he was driving north, the plains of Verdi's Emilia Romagna hundreds of miles behind him. It was not by chance that the Breva wind was blowing him northwards. Leo tucked the card deep into his pocket as he drove towards his silent house.

The wrought-iron gate was open. Leo had been reaching for the remote control in the glove compartment when he saw that the gate was already ajar. His sharp eye saw also that a night's snow had built up in the opening. Because the efficient electronic mechanism could not function and swing the gate wide open for the Mercedes, he had to get out and push the heavy black iron through the snow. As he was climbing back into the car he heard the voices coming from the house. Leo's ear, even sharper than his eyes, distinguished a man speaking in Italian. For a wild, irrational moment he thought, She has a lover, has had him for years. My guilt is cancelled out by hers. I am free.

He skidded up the driveway, parked within an inch of the front steps and burst through the door of the big house. The Pekinese raced to meet him, fully recovered from its earlier trauma and, apparently, bearing the bass singer no grudge. Leo, in a hurry to play the wronged husband, none the less took the time to bend down and scoop the dog gently into his hand. He tucked it under one arm and strode towards the staircase. His ears had already registered that the Italian voices droned on, indifferent to his entrance. He knew now that the Italian lover existed only on a piece of tape miles away in a TV studio. Leo's disappointment was immense as he walked towards the library and turned off the set. Then he stood and gazed around the dishevelled room. His gaze took in the empty wine bottle and the one wineglass.

Now that the possibility of a secret love had vanished, he realized that he had no idea what to do about Kay. The old guilt washed over him. His Protestant mother would have said that he had already gained more success and glory than he deserved. Someone in the heavens kept accounts, she had believed, and Leo's balance sheet could not ever include an abiding love.

The Pekinese stirred. Leo stroked its muzzle, knowing instinctively that it was hungry. Kay must have gone out. He carried the dog into the kitchen, found some food in a cupboard under the sink and stood gazing at the mountains beyond the lake while the little dog snorted and grunted and emptied the bowl. Again Leo's gaze was carried by the Breva wind towards the north, land of that austere long-dead mother. Thanks to her language and discipline he would soon scale another summit. Glory and success had always been unnervingly accessible to Leo. But always they carried loneliness along with them. He banished Rose's face from his memory and decided to go up to the music-room and play through some of his Wotan monologue.

Not bothering to remove his coat he made his way up the stairs and along the corridor. If there was nothing else there was music, he told himself, as he walked towards his private room. Again a door swung open in the wind. The previous evening, Leo had been too lost in his thoughts of time passing to see the opening and closing of the restaurant door. But an hour earlier as he had driven along the lake, he had dared to believe that a door had opened in his life. Now the gates and doors of his own silent home seemed to confirm his conviction.

He saw the shattered statue immediately. Leo had never felt affection for the composer whose marble features were scattered across the floor. He had never patted the back of the stone head as he occasionally did with Verdi or Mozart. But this morning he had dared for a few seconds to compare his destiny with that of the opportunistic, egocentric genius.

But I am only a channel for that genius, he remembered, and cannot expect— Leo paused. Cannot expect what? To thumb my nose at heaven's accountants as Wagner did? But what a hefty return he had offered for his arrogance.

Cannot expect what? Leo supported himself on the piano as he surveyed the shattered marble. Outside the window the snow clouds huddled against the brooding grey mountains. Leo knew again that the answer was love. He was so desperately lonely and for a brief evening had dreamed that kind and clever Rose could rescue him. Rose, softly rounded and imperfectly lovely, had come to La Scala in a wet wedding dress and given him hope. To Rose he would tell everything, everything, and she would understand and forgive him. Rose would redeem him.

Kay was standing in the doorway, wet and naked. Kay. But of course, Kay. He looked down at the shattered marble bust on the floor and he looked for the first time with no pity at the slender naked woman before him.

'The Breva did this?' He reached down and scooped a handful of crumbled marble into his hand.

'I doubt it,' said Kay.

Leo removed his coat and threw it at her. 'Cover yourself.' He had decided not to question her nakedness. He had dared to believe that she was in a lover's arms but now he knew that she'd come from the cold grey caress of the lake.

226

'I can't go on being guilty any more. I have just so many years left to me. I have tried. It is finished. I no longer wish to try.'

'You can't undo things, Leo. What you did remains done for ever. No amount of guilt will remove it.'

Leo stayed where he was crouching on the floor, letting the pieces of marble run through his fingers.

'It is finished,' he said and walked past her to the bedroom where he grabbed a random armful of clothes and took them down to the car. Only when he was turning the key in the ignition did he remember that he had left his coat on Kay. He was cold, very cold, and hadn't selected any clothes that would warm him as could his beloved old cashmere coat. But far worse than the cold that gripped his shoulders was the realization that the coat contained the paper with Rose's hotel name and number written on it.

He had memorized the number, didn't need the card, but he missed the feel of the paper in his pocket, softened and familiar from his earlier caresses. He was tempted to turn around but, 'It is finished,' he announced to the wrought-iron gate as it crashed closed behind him.

He had spent less than an hour in his home – and in those brief moments it had ceased to be his home. The Breva had blown, doors and gates had slammed, the house had heaved and flung him out. He stopped the car on a bend overlooking the jetty and stared out at the lake. The cold, silent villa was behind him for ever and he was glad. Oh, there were practicalities to be dealt with. He wanted his piano, his music, his books, his statues, but anonymous hands would come one day and gather them up for him. Anonymous feet would walk across that marble floor, a calloused hand would give Kay a piece of paper to sign, and all that had ever mattered to him would be packaged up and delivered to wherever he had come to land. He didn't even need to think about that for the moment. In days to come, a decision would be made, an apartment rented, a house bought, but as he sat staring for the last time at the lake, Leo wanted only to savour the solitude and the terrifying freedom that had fallen like the shattered statue at his feet.

Again he felt for the paper in his jacket pocket and again the emptiness felt like a desertion, as if Rose had already left him. But of course she hadn't. He glanced at his watch. Twelve o'clock. The late hour unsettled him. He could no longer imagine her sleeping alone in that narrow bed. He could not know where she was. In his youth he had read a Camus novel where a character, separated from his mistress, described the comfortable pleasure of thinking of her at 4 a.m. when any perfidious love-making would be over and his woman would be isolated in sleep. The young Leo had read the passage and failed to understand. The weary older man gazed out at the lake and longed for the silent pre-dawn hour. For he could think of Rose and long for her but he could not call her – not now. Had the encounter with Kay consisted of nothing more than a cup of coffee and a neutral chat about the *première* and the Pekinese, he would perhaps have pulled into a restaurant or gas station on the way back into Milan and called Rose as he had called a dozen other mistresses in his past. Now to reach out to this stranger would be an act of desperation and Leo knew too well the folly of a desperate act.

PART III
The Phoenix

Chapter Twenty-Four

'Snow in Venice,' said Otto. They were on the causeway that joined Venice to the mainland. Ahead of them a lorry had skidded on the ice. They had been stuck in the resulting traffic jam for half an hour. 'Snow in Venice. Can you imagine anything more beautiful?'

'How can you see it if there's water everywhere?' said Eva.

'*Airone*!' said Stella, nudging her husband and pointing out of the window.

'A heron,' said Otto, pointing to the solitary, spiky grey bird on a buoy near the bridge.

'When we retired,' said Alberto, 'we joined LIPU.'

'That's the league for the protection of birds,' Otto explained.

'Now we don't work late at night,' said Alberto, 'we get up in the morning and watch the birds through our opera-glasses while we eat our breakfast. Here in Italy the fools eat goldfinches for dinner. And we singers, we are like birds in so many ways – moving around the globe—'

'That's bollocks!' said Eva. 'You never moved around the globe. Chorists are like civil servants. Don't you even punch in and out at La Scala?'

'Don't underestimate the chorus,' said Alberto.

'All opera depends on the chorus,' declared Stella.

'Except opera where there is no chorus,' said Otto.

'Anyway,' said Alberto, 'maybe if you'd sung in a chorus you might have had more fun, Otto. All this "Gotta be a star or nothing." Look how you wasted your life.'

'I don't think my life has been wasted,' said Otto. He

was sitting alongside Rose and had not once turned around during the conversation.

'Oh, I didn't mean that,' said Alberto. 'What I meant was that you have a beautiful voice and maybe you should have given the world a chance to hear it instead of giving up so easy.'

'I ran out of money,' said Otto.

'And faith,' said Alberto. 'You never had enough of that.'

'Sing for us now, Otto,' said Stella, leaning forward and stroking the back of his blushing neck.

'Oh, no,' said Otto.

'Then we'll all sing together,' said Alberto. 'Quartet from *Rigoletto*?' He raised an eyebrow in his wife's direction.

'With only three of us?'

'We can do without the mezzo. Do you know this piece, *signorina*?' He leaned forward. Rose smelled her perfume on the handkerchief in his pocket. 'I'm going to be Rigoletto, the father, and I'm trying to tell Stella here, my daughter, that he,' and he pointed to Otto, 'the Duke of Mantua is no good.'

'Oh, no,' said Otto. 'I haven't sung in years. I couldn't – I just couldn't.'

'This man,' said Alberto, 'sang the last act of *Lucia* with Kay Lindstrom. You know who she is now? Kay dalla Vigna – the beautiful blonde wife of the great Leo. This man sang duets with her and now he can't even sing in a car for us.'

'You sang with Leo's wife?' said Rose.

'Just once, in that one brief summer that I spent in Siena,' said Otto. 'I haven't sung since.'

'And I don't think you should start now,' said Eva.

'Singing is joy!' said Alberto. 'That's what I was saying about the birds. All this stuff about territory. Now I say, when a – a ... *Come si chiama 'un allodola*?'

'A lark,' muttered Otto.

'That's right, when a lark rises up towards the

232

heavens, I think it's singing for joy. Singing is about joy and sex,' concluded the fat chorist.

'Sex?' said Rose.

'Oh yeah. Singing is very sexy. Singers are very highly sexed. Didn't you know that? It's the good breathing or something, I guess. And I know what you're thinking, *signorina* – I see everybody think it about Stella and me so I'll tell you something. You lot don't know nothing about sexy. If you think skinny womens in magazines is sexy you haven't understood nothing.'

'And you sang with Leo's wife?' Rose switched off the car engine and scrutinized Otto's profile.

'Years ago I tell you, years and years ago – just once for about fifteen minutes.'

'Come on, Otto,' said Alberto. 'Sing with us. We're all friends here. For the joy of it, sing. Come on . . . *Bella figlia dell'amore.*'

'Don't, Otto,' said Eva. 'Don't sing.'

'Come on, *caro*,' said Stella. '*Bella figlia dell'amore.*' She and Alberto hummed the opening bars of the great quartet over and over again. Otto continued to stare ahead at the back end of a Milanese removal lorry.

'Don't, Otto,' said Eva. The chorists hummed on.

'*Bella figlia dell'amore*,' Otto whispered.

'Louder, Otto, louder,' said Alberto.

'No, no, I can't. I mustn't.'

Rose reached over and stroked Otto's slender hand.

'Go on, Otto, I'm sure you can.'

'What the hell do you know?' said Eva's voice from the back of the car. 'Don't. Don't try to sing.'

'Please,' said Rose. The chorists hummed on.

Otto coughed, undid the seat-belt and sat up straight in his seat. He folded his hands, closed his eyes; the chorists stopped humming.

'*Bella figlia dell'amore.*' This time his voice filled the car. Rose had recognized the quartet and her ear rushed to follow the sounds that issued from the seat next to her. But Otto's voice quavered, wobbled, chuddered up above the written note or tumbled too far below it. He ran out of breath, forgot his words,

233

muttered, 'Sorry, sorry,' and tried to start again. He sang even louder but the sound was reedy and thin. Stella had rushed in to sing her soprano line and soon both she and Alberto were filling the car with their own rich, resonant sounds. For a few bars Otto's quivering falsetto hooted along with them – then he stopped. The chorists stopped a few bars later. The car was silent again.

'The joy of singing,' muttered Eva from her cramped seat in the back.

'You a little rusty – is all,' said Alberto. 'We try it again later – maybe something easier – a nice Tosti Napoli song.'

Stella nudged him and shook her head.

'No, no more,' she tried to whisper but her habitually loud voice echoed through the car.

The traffic started to move up ahead. Rose hadn't dared to look at Otto once he stopped singing. Now she heard him click his seat-belt back on.

'We should be in Venice within the hour,' she turned towards her neighbour. Otto was staring out at the Milanese removal van. He didn't reply.

'Too late for lunch,' said Eva. 'And if we're going to the theatre it means we won't have dinner. That's something I've always hated about opera-going – you eat all the wrong food at the wrong bloody times.'

'More herons,' said Stella, pointing out of the window. 'And a flock of *ciuffolotti* – I don't know that in English.'

'Bullfinches,' said Otto.

Nobody said another word until they arrived in the car-park and then Eva issued a few orders about locking doors and removing the radio-cassette, and Alberto scuttled around, surprisingly nimble for such a big man, and offered to carry everyone's bags.

Nobody bothered to point out to Eva how wrong she had been about Venice in the snow. It curved around the domes, clung to the bridges, draped the statues, caressed the grim black prow of the gondolas and only succumbed to the grey blue sweep of the canal.

234

'Where are we going?' said Rose, as they struggled over the bridge with their bags.

'To the vaporetto stop,' said Eva.

'Yes, but where after that?'

'To the Fenice to get our tickets.'

'But where are we sleeping?'

'Probably in the *pensione* next door. We'll worry about that once we've got our tickets,' said Eva.

The Number 1 vaporetto, the slow boat that weaves its way all along the Grand Canal, was empty that winter afternoon. The little group scattered once they were on board. Eva took a seat in the only corner of the boat that offered no view. She removed her coat, fanned herself with a newspaper and stared at the chipped, blue-painted doors that led out of the cabin. The fat chorists went straight outside into the icy afternoon air. Alberto put his arm around Stella and with his free hand pointed out familiar landmarks along the canal. Rose was filled with a sudden sadness as she watched their broad, ungainly but deeply united forms leaning over the rail as the vaporetto sailed towards the stop at the municipal casino – formerly the Palazzo Vendramin.

Otto had remained alone at the boarding point of the boat, his hands hanging at his sides, his gaze fixed on the domes and crosses, spearbearers and winged lions of the Venetian skyline. Now Rose sensed that he had come to stand next to her.

'Vendramin,' he said. 'Wagner died here on the 13 February 1883. Cosima held her dead husband in her— Oh, who gives a fuck?'

'In her arms for twenty-four hours – think about that.' Rose finished his sentence for him.

'Disgusting thing to do when you *really* think about it,' said Otto and started to walk away.

'Tell me about Kay, Kay— What was her name?' Rose called after him.

'Leo's wife?'

'Yes, but she must have a name.'

'She was the most beautiful woman I have ever seen in my life,' said Otto.

235

'Oh,' said Rose. The vaporetto had banged up against the mooring post. Nobody got on. Nobody got off. On a freezing winter's afternoon there were no customers for the municipal casino and no curious music lovers wanting to gaze at the room where Wagner had died – and Cosima had held him.

'And she had the most crystalline, perfect coloratura soprano I have ever heard in my life.'

'So why didn't she have a better career?'

'Oh, she could have but there was that business of losing the child – that was all kept very private and it was years ago. I suspect she chose to dedicate her life and energies to Leo after that. If you had such an extraordinary man for a husband, wouldn't you?'

'That's not something I've ever had to think about.'

'Well, it seems obvious to me that someone would have to make a sacrifice in such a partnership. And it was probably easy for her to settle for the rewards of being married to a great, great artist.'

'Isn't that a rather naïve conclusion?'

'Oh, but I am naïve about relationships,' sighed Otto. 'What can you expect from me?' And he wandered off towards his original place at the entrance to the vaporetto. Rose followed him.

'Beautiful is a very vague word, really,' she said. 'How was she beautiful?'

'What a stupid question,' said Otto. 'Beautiful is beautiful. Everyone knows beauty when they see it . . . or hear it. This is beautiful,' and he held a hand out towards the sweep of the canal as it curved under the Rialto bridge. A light snow had started to fall. The flakes settled rapidly on Alberto and Stella but they remained where they were, their two plump profiles turned towards the Rialto and the curve of the canal beyond. Within seconds the snow thickened, the sky darkened and they became two dark round shadows at the prow.

'I don't think beauty is such a unanimous thing,' said Rose. 'Not everyone finds the same things beautiful—'

'Well everyone finds Kay beautiful,' snapped Otto.

236

'That's all there is to it and there's no use chewing it over and trying to twist the truth around just because you fancy her husband!'

'I never said I fancied him.'

'But you do – you and thousands of others. They wait at the stage doors in Munich and Vienna, go to corny Friends of the Opera receptions at the Met or Covent Garden, make out they want to talk about The Voice or Verdi when all they really want is to have the shit screwed out of them by *that* voice, by big old Leo. But it's not even big old Leo that they want – they want somehow, impossibly, to be fucked by his voice. You see, you're not very original, Rose. Bored, sex-starved women the world over have always done it. They did it for the castrati in the seventeenth century. It's a frustrated woman's sexual fantasy – nothing to do with music.' He paused and turned away from her towards a lamp that had just lit up on the Rialto. When he turned to speak again, the sly triumphant smile on his face was lit by a stream of lamp lights that had suddenly been illuminated along the canal. 'And it certainly has nothing to do with love.'

'But I thought we had just established that you know nothing about love,' said Rose, surprised at the rapidity of her response.

'And *you* think *you* do?'

But Rose had turned away from Otto. She was rummaging in her handbag, pushing her hand deep to the bottom to hide its shaking. She took out the keys to the Escort.

'That's it, Otto. I don't have to put up with this. We go no further together – I'll make my own way from now on. You and Eva can drive yourselves for the rest of your trip.'

Otto took the keys and slipped them into his pocket. Again his fine profile was lit by the lamps on the jetty.

'As you wish,' he said.

The vaporetto sailed on through the winter twilight. Rose hadn't dared to turn around and see whether Eva had witnessed her desertion. But as she walked to stand in the falling snow a few feet from Alberto and Stella, she glimpsed the older woman and saw that neither her expression nor her position had changed since they had boarded the boat. She would have to learn of the new order of things from her brother.

Rose lingered near the chorists, hoping that they would draw her into conversation but they were too absorbed in each other and Venice, and soon she decided to go back inside, avoiding Otto's hunched figure as she headed for a warm seat in the steamy, enclosed back cabin of the boat.

They had just sailed under the Accademia bridge and Rose had just noticed that the normally wide, dark wooden span had turned white in the winter storm, when Eva appeared in the cabin.

'This is where we get off!' she cried, bundling the pile of bags towards the exit. 'Stop Number 13.'

'It would be,' murmured Rose. She walked slowly from her seat towards the rest of the group, as they all stood and watched the vaporetto man deftly tying the mooring rope into place. Rose reached down and took her small bag from the pile that Eva had placed near the exit.

'I won't be coming with you, Eva,' she said.

'What do you mean you won't be coming with me?'

'Not just you, all of you. I – I want to be alone for a while,' she stammered. Otto had appeared alongside Eva.

'She's just pissed off because I told her not to expect anything from Leo,' he sniffed.

'I thought you were the only over-sensitive prima donna around here. For Christ's sakes, Rose, where do you think you are going to go in Venice in winter? Just ignore him.'

'No,' said Rose. 'No, I won't. Otto's childlike lack of tact has suddenly worn very thin, Eva, I'm afraid. And I can cope with being on my own here. I might not even bother to stay – I haven't decided yet.'

'Don't be such an arse-hole, Rose,' said Eva. She was shifting the pieces of luggage on to the quay as she spoke. Nimble Alberto was receiving them. He smiled over at Rose.

'You gotta come to *Don Giovanni*,' he said. 'You gotta see Raimondi.'

'No.' Rose smiled back at him, stepping over the pile of luggage and landing soundlessly in the newly fallen snow on the quay. 'Actually, I don't gotta do anything. You'll fight for tickets, they'll sing, you'll cry "bravo", they will bow, hold their hands on their hearts and it will all go on quite smoothly without me.'

Alberto shrugged.

'Shame to miss it,' said Stella.

'Oh, sod her,' said Otto. 'The Fenice box-office has already been open for half an hour. If we stand around here we'll miss any chance of a ticket tonight.'

Rose started to walk away, slowly at first, expecting one of the group to call her back or come after her, but when no-one did she increased her pace until she was around a corner, where she put her bag down and rested her back against the damp, freezing Venetian stone. She was standing in a small deserted *campo* – there was not a light on in any of the windows. She was thinking that she had never experienced such darkness, such stillness, when she heard soft footsteps padding along the small alleyway. Even in the freezing night, she caught a whiff of her own perfume as Alberto's plump head appeared around the corner.

'Eva told us we didn't know the way,' he said, as if this explained his sudden appearance. 'We not know the way to La Fenice! So they gone one way and Stella and me gone the right way. Stella wants me to tell you a good hotel down this way – a good *warm* hotel.' He handed her a piece of paper with the name of a hotel and a small diagram showing its location. 'I shouldn't have told him to sing,' shrugged the big man. 'And you come along tonight if you want – fuck him.'

'Thanks,' smiled Rose. 'But I don't think I'll bother.'

The snow kept on falling between them. Rose held her hand out and watched as the arm of her jacket was rapidly coated in white. 'Oh, when will it ever stop snowing?' she said to the dark, pelting heavens above their heads.

'I got to go,' smiled Alberto. And his bulky form padded softly away down the empty alley.

Rose picked up her bag, studied the diagram under the one light in the *campo*, decided that Alberto's hotel was as good a destination as any and set out. The little map led her up and down stairways, across bridges, under damp arcades where the black water lapped silent against the crumbling stone. Venice that winter's night was full of shadows and snow and silence. Each *campo* that she crossed was as empty as the one before – the only sound her muffled step on the freezing cobbles. She hadn't expected tourists to throng through the city, not in the dead of winter, but where were the people of Venice? Rose imagined them gathered around dinner-tables, making love in ornate chambers or thronging to the opera house. As she made her solitary way, Rose concluded that in all the old European cities the opera house, as much as any cathedral, invariably stood solid and immense at the beating heart of the town. And those beating hearts depended on the likes of Leo, who was surely at this moment in that other great house surrounded by admirers and friends and love, while she, Rose, made her way through the stinging snow to nothing more than a warm room for the night.

And as she walked through the silence away from the Fenice, Rose felt the flimsy foundations of *her* life crumbling beneath her. That same morning, less than twelve hours earlier, she had hung up on sensible Daphne to follow a group of ageing fanatics in pursuit of music. That was the foundation of their wretched lives and Rose had aligned herself with them – and pursued music that you can't see or hold. And invisible, intangible music had led her to these freezing, dark alleyways and to this lonely silence. But even Leo sometimes walks alone through the dark, she recalled, and the memory of Leo walking through the silent Milan streets comforted her.

She had come to the hotel. In the entrance was a small Christmas tree spangled with green and red lights. The foyer was warm. Her room was pleasant. Once she had closed its door behind her, Rose took off her damp shoes, lay on the bed and traced the shape of an invisible head on the pillow alongside her. Music was invisible but you could see and hold Leo.

You just want to fuck his voice. She recalled Otto's accusation and suddenly the haven seemed to fill with all the thousands of women and some men who waited for Leo at stage doors throughout the world. The well-spring of tenderness that had run from her to the singer since that first evening in London had been staunched by those bitter words. Now both the evening and frigid, silent Venice stretched out empty ahead of her. It was just six-thirty. She wanted company. She would go to the small bar downstairs, order a warming drink and decide what to do next. There was still time to call Daphne and say that she had seen the folly of her ways and would come home.

But she had left Leo a message that said Venice. Just Venice. How absurd to imagine that he would find her in this dark stone web of silence and shadows. How arrogant and vain to think that he would even want to.

Rose walked to the window and looked out at the Christmas tree and the darkness beyond and decided that she would wait here in this warm, safe place until Leo came.

Chapter Twenty-Five

'Can you find me an apartment? Furnished, near the theatre.' Leo was sitting on the bed in his hotel room. While he spoke to his agent, he studied a small map of Milan.

'I told you years ago you and Kay should buy a decent apartment down here. Wait until the winter is over and the real-estate market picks up and you can probably get a bargain.'

'I want it now,' said Leo. 'And I don't want to buy, I want to rent. I just want to walk in, put down my suitcase and have the basics – a bed, a table, a piano, somewhere to wash and somewhere to make a cup of coffee.'

'What does Kay think of this?'

'It's not for Kay – it's for me – a *pied-à-terre* when I'm in Milan.'

'Sounds sensible enough to me. Hey, I do know a retired violinist who lets out his place in the winter when he's off in California. Oh, Kay would love that apartment, Leo – that man has some of the most beautiful pieces of antique furniture – and you should see the paintings. Of course, he takes a huge deposit and he's fussy about who rents it but if he knew it was you—'

'Where is it?' said Leo.

'Two minutes walk from the theatre.'

'I'll take it,' said Leo.

'Don't you want to see it first?'

'No – in fact I want all the stuff taken out. I don't want paintings or vases or porcelain tea-sets. I want a bed, a table, a piano and somewhere to wash—'

'But the whole point of that place is the beautiful

242

objects. He's been making a fortune over the years renting it out to wealthy Americans and Japanese. He was featured in *Architectural Review*.'

'Tell him I'll take it if he stores his stuff,' said Leo. 'Oh, and I don't want a view either.'

'What kind of view do you think you're going to get in the heart of Milan?' said his agent.

'I don't know,' sighed Leo. 'But if it's the roof of the Duomo, well, you can tell him to put that in storage too.'

'Oh, Kay is going to love this,' said Roberto.

'Kay isn't going to live there,' said Leo. 'Look, I have to go to the theatre – call me and let me know when I can move in. Oh, and Roberto, there's one other thing – have you found out any more about the Munich *Walküre*?'

'I would have told you if I had.'

After Leo hung up, he saw that on the note-pad next to the phone he had scrawled the name and number of the Hotel Leonardo at least half a dozen times. But of course, there was no reason for Rose to remain there. For years he had seen the ageing twins at stage doors throughout Europe and he knew that once the performance was over, they always moved on to Vienna or Paris to the next *Traviata* or *Tristan*. He had never stopped to imagine those strange lives before but now that Rose was enmeshed with them, he tried to picture what they did when they weren't waiting for him.

It was only two o'clock. In the space of one morning, he had ended his marriage and left his home. Now he sat in the comfortable limbo of a neutral hotel room, free of the Sèvres vases, the tester beds, the sickly Pekinese; free of the sullen grey lake and the echoing marble floors; free of the scarred breast and the dead child. No, not completely free. He would be free when he had told somebody about that afternoon in the cemetery on the hill all those years ago. For now he would content himself with leaving Rose a note at her hotel.

'Don't disappear – leave your home phone number at the stage door. I will call you.' At first he didn't sign it; years of casual infidelities had made Leo prudent. In an era of flourishing scandal magazines and paparazzi, famous men knew better than to sign their billets-doux – but he wanted to mark the difference between Rose and the big-breasted Countess or Natalia the ardent Slav who sat with her legs apart while she told him the latest gossip. He took the note back out of its envelope and signed it: 'Leo.'

When he was about to leave the hotel room, five minutes later, he realized that he had no coat. The absurdity of his situation made Leo roar with laughter. He had lost his home and his marriage, was separated from his beloved books, piano and musical scores, yet nothing had hit like the lack of the coat. What would the legions of admirers make of the great bass who was now marooned in his hotel room, mortally afraid of catching a cold, a prisoner of the freezing winds and snows? When he did leave his room, clad in the tweed jacket, it was to hail a taxi and purchase an almost identical navy blue replacement. With the coat comfortably on his back, he settled into the seat and found that his hand instinctively felt for the crumpled card saying 'Hotel Leonardo' in the new pocket.

'Hotel Leonardo,' he said to the driver.

When he walked towards the reception area, he saw that the elderly clerk recognized him.

'To what do we owe this honour, maestro?' The old man gave Leo a stiff little bow.

'I wanted to leave a message for Signora Lorenzo.'

'Sorry, maestro, she left hours ago.'

'Oh,' said Leo, aware that his evident disappointment would provide a topic of dinner time conversation in the old man's assuredly large family.

'My sons and I saw you in Verona, maestro.' The clerk patted Leo's wrist. 'Never do I weep so much. I who saw Gobbi's Rigoletto! But this terrible King, so cruel, so ruthless and so lonely, I even feared you when you took your curtain call!'

'What a compliment,' said Leo. 'Tell me, did Signora Lorenzo leave any message?'

'No message,' replied the old man. He squeezed the cuff of the singer's new coat. 'Tell me, this story about you dropping your Italian roles for Wagner – it cannot be true?' He tightened his grip on Leo's sleeve. 'Wagner kills voices.'

'Not if he's sung properly,' said Leo.

'And it's filthy fascist bullshit. You're an Italian, signor. You must serve the Italian repertoire.'

'Must I?' said Leo. 'Look, are you sure there are no messages for me?' He leaned over and studied the cubby holes in the reception desk. The old man sensed the coldness in the singer's response and took one of the wads of paper, shuffling through them in an attempt to ingratiate himself.

'There!' said Leo, snatching a small envelope that bore his name. He tore it open but there was nothing inside, and only as he shook it in exasperation did he notice the scrawled word under his name.

'Venezia?' he said out loud to himself. 'Venezia!' And forgetting to bid the old man farewell, he walked from the hotel and hailed a taxi.

Chapter Twenty-Six

When Rose walked into the small bar next to the reception she saw the man with the three hoops in his ear and petulant blond Marco.

'Same old faces,' said Three Hoops. 'I suppose you've come up here for the *Giovanni* too.'

'Can we buy you a drink?' Marco held out his hand to Rose and ordered champagne from the barman.

'Feeling better, are you?' Rose couldn't help saying.

'Was I sick?'

'You were deeply troubled by the wind in the rafters, as I recall,' smiled Rose, wondering just what they were celebrating.

'Oh yeah,' Marco grinned. 'Well, you see, Madam Rose—' He makes me sound like a clairvoyant on Brighton pier, thought Rose, and found herself longing for a flamboyant gypsy to materialize before them and tell her the future. '—I also have perfect pitch. I hear decay setting in to the great voices long before the average man or woman. It is for me a source of physical pain.'

'Marco, here, is in fact Dottore Marco Bellocchio from Bologna University,' said Three Hoops, waiting until the barman's back was turned to put his arm around the younger man.

'Are we celebrating something in particular?' As Rose sipped her champagne, she thought of Otto and Eva who were probably eating a dried-up sandwich in yet another cramped hotel room. She missed them both but she also knew that she could not have Otto hovering above her and Leo like a wounded bird of prey.

'Five years since we met at La Fenice,' smiled Three Hoops.

'Do you know what a fenice is?' said Marco.

Rose shook her head.

'A phoenix,' said Three Hoops. 'The mythical bird that rises out of its own ashes.'

'A garden, a staircase and a phoenix,' said Rose.

'Covent Garden, La Scala and La Fenice,' said Marco but Rose wasn't listening. She was too busy trying to trace her own strange journey from a garden up a staircase to a bird rising out of its own ashes. Oh yes, she would wait in Venice for Leo.

'Are you here for Raimondi?' said Three Hoops, his tone more urgent. 'Can you pull some strings for us to meet him?'

'For who?' Rose hadn't been listening.

'Raimondi! Can you introduce us?'

'Oh no, no. I'm not here for the opera. I'm just, well – here. I'm waiting for someone.'

'Oh, and when is he going to get here?' said Marco.

'It might be a she—' Three Hoops nudged him.

'I don't know when he's due,' said Rose. 'I'll know when he's here, if you see what I mean.'

'Then you should come to La Fenice this evening,' said Marco. 'Have you never been inside the theatre? It is like stepping into a jewel box. A blue-and-gold jewel box. In itself it is a gem, the perfect size for a Mozart opera.'

Given the choice between a phoenix, a jewel box and a night alone in the quiet little hotel, Rose hesitated for only a second. Within an hour she was walking back across the wide stone web of streets that was December Venice. Like the rest of the marching army of opera fanatics, Marco and Three Hoops seemed unconcerned about her lack of a ticket. Like Alberto and Stella and Otto and Eva they knew someone – and if that didn't work they had a firm belief in an afford-able ticket appearing out of the air, and as soon as they arrived in the small piazza in front of the theatre a young blonde Venetian woman offered them a ticket in the second gallery.

'It's up in the gods, where we are,' said Three Hoops. 'But it's better than nothing.'

And as in the London garden and on the Italian staircase, Rose entered the Venetian phoenix as all the bells rang. She was relieved to see the chandeliers dim as they took their seats. Otto and Eva were thus safely locked into the darkness. She waited for the orchestra conductor but there was no sudden change in the energy level coming from the pit. The players tuned their instruments. And a man appeared in front of the curtain in a dinner-jacket. Lost in her own thoughts she only vaguely registered that the great singer for whom they had all come had been taken ill and had not himself arrived. She heard a long, slow hiss like a burst bicycle tyre issue from Marco's seat.

The replacement was the dumpy Bulgarian Dimitri Dimov. As Don Giovanni he was kept busy during the first act of the opera. He was called upon to seduce one woman and murder her father, deceive a strong-minded noblewoman and whisk a peasant girl from the arms of her betrothed on her wedding day. The Bulgarian couldn't keep up the pace. Rose noticed how his thighs banged together as he fought a duel and felt deep foreboding for the rest of the evening. And during the rapid-fire champagne aria when vocal agility and quick wit are all, the poor Bulgarian beached himself like a whale. Wrong note succeeded wrong note, his breathing went awry; he took the musical high road, the orchestra took the low road. They did not meet again.

'*A casa!*' came the cry from Marco's seat, followed by another bicycle-tyre hiss.

'Go back to Bulgaria! I'll pay your fare!' yelled Three Hoops.

'Give the man a chance!' Rose recognized Otto's voice coming from only yards away in the dark.

'Why should I? I paid my money!' Marco yelled back.

'He's stepping in for someone else!' yelled Otto. All around the small jewel box of an auditorium, there were murmurs of '*Vergogna*'. The singer had made a desperate motion to the conductor to start the aria again but his performance was no better second time around.

'Somebody shoot him and put him out of his misery,' cried Marco. A well-aimed programme hit Marco in the back of the neck. He leapt to his feet, turned in the direction from which the missile had come and lunged in the darkness towards Otto.

'Who hit me? Have the courage to show yourself!'

Otto rose to his feet. Rose could see his tall, pale figure reflected now in the lights from the stage.

'I threw it. And if you don't shut up and give the man a chance, I'll throw you.'

Before Marco could reply, another programme was lobbed at him from the side of the second gallery.

'Yes, siddown and shut up!' cried a Venetian. But while Marco reeled from this second blow, this new assailant was himself punched on the nose by the man directly in front of him.

'That programme you threw hit my wife's ear!' cried the latest participant; his words were accompanied by a woman's wailing.

'Who hit my Marco?' yelled Three Hoops, taking off his money-belt and swinging it wildly around in front of him.

'I told you I did!' yelled an exasperated Otto, but Three Hoops was apparently enjoying the dashing cowboy allure that the swinging belt gave him, and ignored this admission.

'Who hit my Marco?' he cried again, swinging harder and louder. At this point he himself hit his Marco who was knocked to the floor. The belt continued on its way and knocked out a retired schoolmistress from Padua who had been sitting in front of them. When the first-aid workers came to get her a few minutes later they had to fight their way through a shower of programmes, newspapers and a bunch of radishes.

249

Now why would anyone go to an opera with a bunch of radishes? thought Rose, who had decided to get out before things got any worse. The orchestra had stopped playing; the Bulgarian was shaking his fist at the audience and the curtain had been wound down but there was so much noise in the auditorium that nobody seemed to have noticed. Small, intimate fights had broken out in both galleries and the orchestra stalls. As far as Rose could make out, half of them involved long-held grudges and long-brewing conflicts that had nothing to do with the poor Bulgarian. As she ducked and wove her way to the door at the top of the stairs, she glimpsed Alberto and Stella, nimble and united as ever, arms locked around each other making their escape through a fire-exit. Back behind her, looking like a faintly deranged chicken, Otto was declaring, 'Why can't you all show some fair play and give a struggling second-best a chance? Why do you all blindly give your allegiance to the big names?'

Rose paused to look back at him. His long chin was quivering but he repeated his phrase about fair play. To Rose's linguist's ears the words sounded absurdly Anglo-Saxon amidst the Italian obscenities that flew, with the radishes and programmes, through the air. She knew Otto well enough to know that he considered this his moment of glory. She also knew him well enough to know that had he not suffered his own devastating humiliation that morning, he would have been booing and hissing along with Marco.

When she arrived at the bottom of the long cold flight of stairs Rose found herself in a small alley. To the left was the stage door and beyond that the path seemed to run off into blackness and what she suspected was a canal. To the right a few yards up, she could see the Taverna la Fenice. She turned towards its welcoming lights, but one glimpse through the window at the white linen and the poised waiters and Rose knew that this was beyond the means of a woman destined to wait in Venice for a man. She walked on alongside the blank, stone wall of the theatre. A few yards past the Taverna was a stand-up bar serving sandwiches and drinks.

Rose suddenly remembered that she hadn't eaten lunch or dinner. She went inside. Between acts the place was quiet. A couple of elderly Americans were laboriously choosing ice-cream flavours at the window. The man at the counter was stuffing pockets of pitta with slices of aubergine and paper-thin ham. A lone customer sat in a corner behind a copy of *Il Corriere Della Sera*.

When Rose ordered a sandwich, the man at the counter looked at the programme that she was clutching and consulted his watch.

'Out already?' he said.

Rose had been aching to tell somebody what was happening only yards away and she was relieved that the man had addressed her in English.

'There's a riot going on inside the theatre.' She had to raise her voice as a coffee-machine was switched on. The *Corriere Della Sera* in the corner was lowered a few inches. 'I ran out before it got any worse. There was no sign of the management. Perhaps someone should call the police.'

'Who was singing?' asked the waiter as he served up her sandwich.

'Some replacement. The big singer was ill or something and couldn't come.'

The waiter shrugged. 'It's political.'

'What does that mean?'

'In Italian theatres, it's always political,' said the waiter. 'Anyway, maybe I'd be mad if I paid my money and some old dog sings instead of the guy I'd come for.'

'He was in difficulty but nobody really gave him a chance. They threw radishes! Why would anyone go to the theatre with a bunch of radishes in the first place?' But the waiter had moved off to serve the Americans.

'It is a display of displeasure,' said a resonant voice from behind the *Corriere*.

'Leo!' cried Rose before she had even turned to look at the lone customer in the corner.

'As for riots, in Paris they once had a fight over Callas's Norma – even Yves St Laurent joined in and kicked people on the shins . . .'

'Leo,' Rose whispered, for she was now standing in front of him. He put his paper aside and kissed Rose on the top of her head.

Chapter Twenty-Seven

When Leo had read the word 'Venice' on the envelope, his singer's mind had immediately thought of La Fenice. And, hardly conscious of what he was doing, he had walked out of the small hotel, hailed a taxi and said the name of that theatre to an astonished cab-driver. The man had recognized him and soon they had agreed on a rate and were driving westwards out of Milan. Leo sat back and reflected on all that had happened in one day. He had taken a cab and not walked the half-mile to his parked Mercedes and driven himself because he needed time to sit with his eyes closed, absorbing the shocks of the long, cold day. He remembered the dramatic rule of unities and wondered if his life, like some perfect piece of theatre, was about to resolve itself in twenty-four hours. What hope these last hours had contained. And how life-transforming hope, and love, were, he reflected, as the cab roared off along the autostrada. At any other time, the discovery of the shattered marble statue would have filled him with superstitious panic but when he had uttered those words 'It is finished,' the deep sorrow they carried was entwined with hope.

Now fatigue came to wrap itself like some life-sucking bindweed around the hope and sorrow. He closed his eyes, started to doze, but slender naked Kay in the doorway surfaced in his mind. Scars and shat-tered marble would fill his sleep that night too, he knew, but between now and the night there would be Rose.

Leo did not see anything strange in riding 250 kilometres in a taxi on a winter's afternoon to meet up with a woman who had left nothing more than 'Venice' as a forwarding address. He had spent the better part of his adult life moving from city to city, and to ride from La Scala to La Fenice seemed a normal way to finish the day. Somewhere around Verona he remembered that he had intended to go over some work with a *répétiteur* that afternoon. Still, as the taxi carried him forward he remained convinced that he must go to Venice. It would do both Wotan and Wagner good to be ignored by him for a day or two.

The taxi had taken him as far as a motor vehicle could go. Leo sent the man off to have dinner in a decent restaurant, telling him to be waiting at midnight. Then he hailed a water-taxi and, giving very specific directions as to the route, told its pilot to take him to La Fenice. As they roared along the Grand Canal Leo was suddenly euphoric to be in Venice. He stood at the front of the motor-boat, pulled his scarf up over his throat and watched the canal whisk past him. Always in Venice he would instinctively watch for the Palazzo Vendramin as his first landmark. Now as its unlit stone mass came into view, he realized that he had begun and ended his day with Cosima. Funny-looking Cosima with her blind, ugly prejudices was not a woman with whom he would have cared to spend that much time. And yet when he read accounts of her marriage to Wagner he felt an absurd twinge of envy. As Vendramin disappeared into the dark behind him he realized that it was the unconditional nature of her love for the German composer that he coveted. Surely we would all wish to be loved unconditionally? Or would it be stifling, smothering, such all-embracing love? Leo wondered, as the taxi sailed through a smaller canal and past the abandoned mooring stage that had once been the entrance to La Fenice. The boat stopped at some steps so rarely used that the moss that covered them glowed green in the lights from the opera house. Leo paid the pilot and leapt from the boat into the alleyway.

Venezia. La Fenice, Here he was. What now? He needed a glass of wine and a plate of pasta. Then he would think. He paused for just a few seconds to decide where he would eat. But instead of restaurant names and familiar dishes, he found himself thinking that perhaps unconditional love is the one thing an adult should flee if he is to be an adult. And that only a genius has the right to such love because he must always remain in part a child. As he had made his way down the alley, he heard his fellow singers warming up in the dressing-rooms that he knew were situated just above his head. He wondered idly who was singing and even thought one of the voices sounded familiar but he didn't linger. He was relieved that the performance had started and that anyone who might recognize him was now safely locked inside the theatre.

He did see a critic settling a restaurant bill and scuttling off towards the opera house. Leo decided to have his drink in a corner bar, where he could spread out his paper and be sure of anonymity. And then Rose had walked in. She looked weary and pale. He bent down to kiss the top of her head.

'You got my note?'

'Yes.'

'And you came to Venice?'

'Yes.'

'Oh.' She sank down onto the stool next to him. 'Oh my. All the way to Venice?'

'It is nothing for me – a taxi ride.'

'You came in a taxi?'

'I've had a busy day – I didn't want to drive.'

'All the way in a taxi,' Rose murmured. She did not dare to ask him whether he had made the journey just for her. His life seemed to Rose to be full of sweeping gestures: angry departures, grand arrivals, just as the man himself was part of the great extravagant houses that dominated the cities of old Europe. All such large, rich, rock-solid living it was, compared to her paltry existence. This will divide us, this will divide us, she thought.

'I came to tell you that we should not lose touch,'

said Leo. 'That you can always reach me at the theatre
– no matter where I'm singing.'

'At the theatre?' said Rose.

'Yes, for the time being, at the theatre.'

'Of course,' said Rose.

'I had to imagine the lives of people like the old
twins when I first came to look for you,' Leo was
saying. 'To my shame, I'd never imagined them
anywhere else but at the stage door. You don't seem
part of that, Rose.'

'I'm not any more.'

'Are they still inside?'

'Oh yes,' said Rose, and told Leo of Otto's lone
defence of the singer.

'I always did like that man,' he said, when she'd
finished the story. 'But tell me who was the baritone?'

'I can't pronounce his name,' said Rose. 'I can't even
remember it. Dumoff? Timoff?'

'Dimov?' said Leo. 'And they booed him off the
stage?'

'Well, not quite. When I last saw him, he was
shaking his fist at the audience.'

'But I just worked with him in London,' said Leo,
pulling his coat on. 'I must go round and see him.'

And within minutes Rose found herself going back
into La Fenice but this time she entered through the
stage door. She just had time to notice a punch clock
and the cheap panelling on the walls and think, as she
had thought at La Scala, that it was wiser and safer to
stay on the other side of the proscenium arch, before
Leo led her up two flights of stairs to the Bulgarian's
dressing-room.

'He doesn't want to see anybody,' said a gloomy
Italian standing by the door.

'Except the guys from the restaurant across the
alley,' said his companion.

Leo ignored them, knocked once and walked in. The
baritone was sitting at a small, cluttered dressing-table.
He was eating a large plate of spaghetti and weeping.
With one hand he shovelled the pasta into his mouth

and with the other he wiped his nose on his sleeve. He didn't look surprised to see Leo. He didn't get up, but went on eating and looked hard at Rose.

'Beautiful woman,' he said to Leo. 'Were you in tonight?'

'No,' said Leo. 'What happened?'

'It was the costume,' said the Bulgarian. 'I know my legs are fat. They've always been fat — it runs in the family. I told the director this costume was ridiculous. Do they think we don't look in the mirror? That we don't see ourselves?'

'So vocally you were OK?' said Leo.

'Sure . . . if I hadn't had to run around the stage in tights,' sniffed the baritone.

'Aren't you supposed to be in Hamburg now?' asked Leo.

'Yes, but I got a chance to fill in here so I flew down this afternoon.'

'Perhaps you're taking on too much,' said Leo gently. 'It's better to build a career slowly and solidly.'

'Better to sing everything while I'm young and healthy and can enjoy the money I'll make,' said the baritone. 'With this fee and the Munich Wotan, I can buy—'

'I don't think you would be wise to take on Wotan at this point,' said Leo.

'Of course I should. A short life and a glorious one, I say.' He sucked up the last noodle.

'But was this evening glorious?' said Rose.

'Maybe next month will be, *signorina*,' the baritone winked at her.

'I think you should wait,' said Leo.

When they left the theatre a half-hour later, they walked for a while in silence.

'Opera has certainly conformed to its image today,' said Rose. 'Fat people and sweat and tears. What a strange world you inhabit, Signor Leo — at the same time absurd and tragic, ludicrous and sublime. The reasonable part of me wants to look with contempt upon all these overblown people and yet when it all

257

comes together and works well, I feel as though I have somehow been made better, improved upon. But you've heard all this many times before, haven't you?'

'Yes,' said Leo. He was walking a good yard away from her, frowning at the snow-covered ground in front of him, his hands plunged deep in his pockets. Occasionally he would hold out an arm to steer her away from an exposed stretch of canal. But then his hands would return to his pockets.

'Wagner died in Venice,' said Leo.

'People keep telling me that,' said Rose. 'And Cosima held him in her arms for twenty-four hours.'

'I've always wondered if that was true. And if it is – is it beautiful or sick? It seems that such obsessive love, people holding on to corpses, unable to let go, was very much a nineteenth-century thing. There was that stormy Yorkshire book—'

'*Wuthering Heights*?' said Rose. 'But there was also Dante Gabriel Rossetti burying his poems in his loved one's coffin. Then changing his mind and having the thing dug up,' said Rose. 'It was a very pragmatic century in the end.'

'Ha! I like that story,' said Leo. 'But back to Wagner – always back to Wagner – I think it would have been very difficult to have been a singer when he was alive, to know that he was such an obnoxious man and yet to want to be part of that extraordinary music. It's easier now that he is dust.'

'It certainly doesn't seem very difficult for our baritone friend back there,' said Rose.

'How wonderful it must be to be so uncomplicated,' said Leo. They had come to a dead end. A small trattoria was open on the right side of the little street. Leo looked at it, remembered that he was hungry but decided against dinner with Rose. For he also remembered his decision of the morning as he had sat all those miles away in the Mercedes looking out on the frigid lake. He had decided that he would not be subject to the folly of a desperate act, and only hours later, he had taken a taxi to Venice. This was not the moment for an intimate dinner. Leo knew only that he would be singing at La Scala in two days and that he was moving, sight unseen, into a blank, neutral apartment. Everything else hung in the air. He was not a young man; he was not going to make some rash declaration of feeling to Rose. He had come to Venice he now knew to reassure himself that she existed, that somewhere on this planet which he circuited without cease, there was someone to whom he could talk. Rose, to whom people told things – and she understood. Rose, a hybrid like himself, belonging neither to one place or another and struggling to encompass it all.

They walked on over bridges, through alleyways, along the cold stone walls of churches. Water lapped, frost glistened in lamplight, they talked and talked of their childhoods, their travels, the books they had read and the paintings they had seen. Leo had to pick his way through the minefield of his own past, avoiding his wife, mistresses and long-dead daughter.

'I think I may go home.' Rose's voice broke into Leo's thoughts.

'London? But I don't sing at Covent Garden again for three years,' said Leo.

'A garden, a staircase and a phoenix. What strange landmarks fill your horizons, dear Leo,' said Rose, who could not say that she had intended to wait in Venice until Leo came. For now that he had come and seemed about to leave, her own horizons were suddenly blank and terrifying.

'I travelled here to tell you not to disappear,' said Leo. He looked around at the deserted street in which they stood. A hesitant snow fell. 'And yet I can't ask you to wait around here. Give me your phone number in London.'

'I haven't got one,' said Rose. 'Otto had a fight—' But she was suddenly too tired to talk of Otto.

'Then write to me, Rose,' said Leo. Bells throughout the city chimed midnight. 'You have words – hundreds of thousands of them from three languages. I only have notes, sounds – write to me.' He flagged down a passing water-taxi. 'I must go back to Milano. A cab-driver is waiting for me back at the car-park – he must be getting impatient. Goodbye, Rose.' He held her to him for just a second, stroked the back of her hair and kissed her on the forehead. He leapt into the taxi and was gone.

Chapter Twenty-Eight

Rose awoke the next morning at 5 a.m. At almost forty Rose was in love, and it was the first joy of love that stole Rose from sleep. She padded across the warm pleasant room and opened the window. The air was frigid in the dark pre-dawn hour but Rose didn't feel the cold. She had to crane her neck to see the Grand Canal but Rose didn't feel the discomfort. She didn't feel the passage of time; didn't bother to count the bells as they tolled the hour. She just knew that bells tolled and boats glided along the water, that the roofs were white and the frost gleamed in the moonlight.

Of course, Rose also knew better than to place her faith in the love that had alighted upon her. Older love can rarely be as bottomless and limitless as young passions, for older lovers know that they are mortal. Rose knew that endings come too soon and that everything will end. She knew that men ride away on Lambrettas and keep beautiful wives safely in big houses. Taxi rides across the peninsula, a supremely beautiful wife in a great villa by a lake, colonnaded opera houses, celebrity and admirers, and always the same thought: The rift is too wide – this will divide us – this will divide us.

But still she sat by the window, filled with absurd childlike rapture as she craned her neck to see the Grand Canal in the frozen dawn. From a garden up a staircase to a phoenix, but just who had been reborn in the flames?

She did not hear the knock on the door. She sat on in the pink light, her stomach churning with hope and terror. There was another much louder knock. Rose heard it this time and walked across the Italian tile, noticing for the first time how cold it was on her feet. When she opened the door, she was confronted with an enormous bunch of blood-red roses. She backed away from the glorious bouquet. This was the act of a seducer; she had neither wanted nor expected this from Leo. It was too sleek, too easy, too calculated. Leo had a rawness that would, she had thought, send him striding past any florists, his brow furrowed, his eyes on the ground, his mind on his music. Then she looked below the bouquet, saw the small battered snow-boots and the darned woollen tights and realized that Eva was the bearer of this gift.

'At least have the manners to let me in.' The bouquet advanced into the room. Eva put it on the bed and sat down. 'Otto sends his apologies,' she said, shaking the slush from her boots.

'Then Otto can come and say so himself,' said Rose, but with little conviction for love and the terror that love carries with it left no room in Rose for anger.

'Of course he can't,' said Eva. 'He wants to take us for hot chocolate at Florian. He was up at dawn counting his money. And that's what he wants to do.'

An hour later when the clock on St Mark's Square struck ten, Rose sat down opposite Otto on a narrow red velvet bench in a small salon with a smoky, tarnished mirror that reflected her weary face. Otto reached over and tried rather clumsily to kiss her on the cheek.

'I was bitter yesterday, Rose. And you know why,' he said, sitting back down. 'But the fight must always be against bitterness.'

'Always,' said Rose, gazing beyond him at the frozen piazza. Some of the shops had wound foil and tinsel garlands around their windows and the stone columns of the arcades, but there were few tourists. The orchestras, the photographers, even the pigeons were absent from that frigid winter morning. Rose imagined the winged lion on his column breathing gusts of icy breath across the lagoon. They sat in silence. Eva took out her map.

'North,' said Otto. 'North to the Wagnerian summits, to ecstasies and passions that our beloved Italians can't even begin to imagine. We leave the pragmatic Verdi behind, ordering up his farm machinery and carefully checking the bill, and we go to the frenzied transports of his great rival to the north. Wagner just never bothered paying his bills – a far simpler solution.' He paused, rubbed his fingers under his eyelids and said, 'Is it me or has this journey lost its heart?'

I think it just found it, thought Rose. But it was Eva who spoke.

'What difference does that make?' she said. 'We go on until we come to the end.'

And in that dark, dying city on the lagoon Leo had found Rose. And with Rose he had found the faith that would carry him through the next days to the blank, neutral apartment that was to be his home. The violinist had done an efficient job and removed everything that could be considered personal or ornamental. Only the grand piano remained, bearing a handwritten note of welcome and a bunch of flowers that Leo immediately gave to the cleaning lady. But this austerity was not born of guilt and loneliness as he had imagined when he had requested such emptiness. Superstitious Leo had sailed away down the Grand Canal that midnight with no doubt as to the identity of the phoenix who spread its wings above the entrance to his beloved theatre. Somewhere within Leo lurked the same terror that had visited Rose. Somewhere within Leo was the same knowledge that everything must end and will end. But when he encountered such misgivings, he did what he had done all his life in times of fear and uncertainty – he sang at them. He sang in the Mercedes as he drove it into the grim underground parking-lot below his new home. He sang in the La Scala corridors on the way to work with a German *répétiteur*. He sang so loud that foreboding and even guilt fled and he was left with this strange new companion – hope.

*　　*　　*

263

In the villa up on Lake Como, Kay took a dustpan and brush and swept away the shattered pieces of marble. She opened a window and threw the fragments of German composer into the snow below. She took Leo's coat, locked it into a cupboard, gathered all the keys together and threw them out of the window too. She did everything as quickly as possible. She had once vowed never to come into the room and now that circumstances had forced her in she did not intend to linger. When she had seen the keys disappear into the thick white, she walked out, scooped up the dog and drove to Brescia where there was to be an auction of eighteenth century French porcelain that afternoon.

Lake Como grew blacker and more agitated as each winter day shortened into long winter night. The local people said to each other as they struggled with chains for the car tyres and salt for the frozen cobbles, that they had never seen a winter like it. The lake spiked and shuddered beneath their gaze. Leo would have said that his opulent, sensuous Italy had been embraced by the wild turbulent north, but Leo did not intend ever to see Lake Como again.

Chapter Twenty-Nine

Otto said very little on the drive north. Rose had expected him to regale her with tales of Ludwig for whom the ugliness of the real world was unbearable. Rose had assumed that he would be one of her companion's heroes but he didn't mention the mad king. If for Rose, the heart still remained in the strange winter quest that the journey had become, the heart had most surely gone out for Otto. He was silent, distant, and sat in the back with his brow furrowed, his thumb and finger gripping the bridge of his nose. If I didn't know better, I would be thinking he was plotting something, thought Rose, glancing at him in the rear-view mirror, but what could Otto possibly plot?

Eva was more talkative than she had ever been. She sat alongside Rose, handing her sandwiches, apples, and pouring cups of tea from a Thermos in a bag at her feet. As the twin sister talked, Rose realized that she had been working on her cultural and operatic tour programme all along. She had calculated every penny that names like Verdi and Wagner could bring to her own bank account. She had decided that their first stop in Germany would be in the old town of Füssen just a few miles from the castles of King Ludwig. She had noted down prices on menus and even quietly nego-tiated group rates with hoteliers along the way. She had a definite role for Otto in her programme. 'In the evenings Otto can give them one of his Wagner talks, over pre-dinner drinks at the bar. It won't matter which one – after a glass or two of schnapps they won't know the difference.'

In the back of the car Otto said nothing.

He said nothing over the drinks that Rose bought them in the bar at the hotel in Füssen that evening. She waited until Eva had gone to discuss group rates with the manager.

'Are you all right, Otto?'

'You tell me,' he sighed. 'Oh, Rose, I know I'm ridiculous, an absurdity, but I don't know what to do to live a flesh and blood life like other people.'

'Oh, I don't think other people have much idea, really,' said Rose. 'Most of them just muddle along, drift into things – you're too intense for that so I suppose you've really got the life that suits you.' Rose could afford to relax and philosophize. She had written her first timid letter to Leo and now it was in the limbo between her and him. He could not have received it and could not, therefore, act upon it. For this one evening she was free of anticipation and longing. She gazed up at a petulant portrait of young Ludwig above a vast fireplace in the lounge. 'I would have thought you would be delighted with King Ludwig.'

'He scares the wits out of me,' said Otto.

'Oh, I don't think he looks very prepossessing.'

'What he became – how easy it would be to slide into that kind of insanity because you can't bear the ugliness of the world.'

Eva reappeared from around the corner.

'Munich is closed,' she said. 'I just found out from reception that they've been having trouble with their curtain.'

'It can't be closed because of a curtain!' cried Otto. 'Why can't they just do without it?'

'Because it's computer-operated and has been behaving unpredictably, opening and closing whenever it has a fancy to. Right in the middle of arias sometimes, apparently.'

'Perhaps it's just a very astute critic,' said Rose.

'So what happens to our Ring?' said Otto.

'Cancelled. They have to wait for some Japanese technicians to fly in and see if they can fix it. It will take at least ten days—'

'Ten days!' cried Otto. 'Then I suppose we have to go home. There's nothing to wait around for—'

'Not quite. They might manage to put on a *Walküre* – not the whole Ring but at least the first day—'

'The most beautiful,' said Otto. 'But I can't bear *Walküre*—'

'If it's the most beautiful, why can't you bear it?' asked Rose.

'Because I always think, oh shit! Now she's just a rotten fallible mortal like the rest of us. She was a goddess, beautiful and invulnerable and now—'

'Who? Who are you talking about?'

'Brünnhilde, of course,' said Otto.

'Oh yes!' said Rose. 'The big lass with the breast-plates.'

'I'm going for a walk,' said Otto, and before either of them could point out that there were blizzard conditions outside the carved wooden doors of the Hotel Alpenhof, he was gone.

'How can you stand him?' Rose asked Eva.

'A lot of the time I can't, but he's all I've got.'

'I suppose if he can't bear *Walküre*, that means we head home,' said Rose, aware that Otto's whims and desires would ultimately dictate their destinations.

'Oh, he'll want to see it,' said Eva.

'But it will cost a fortune to wait around here, paying hotel bills,' said Rose.

'We can string it out for ten days or so. Because Otto works in a travel agency, they've given us a special cheap rate. You see he isn't as useless as he seems to think. Anyway, I'll be glad to stay in one place and do some prospecting. Do you want to come to the – just a minute—' Eva studied one of her papers. 'To the Wiener Bierstüberl for supper? Sample some local cuisine?'

Rose refused Eva's invitation. She was too tired to eat and wanted nothing more than a bath and a warm bed and time alone to think about Leo. Now that they had crossed the Alps and changed language and landscape, the encounter of the previous evening seemed to have slipped into the Venetian mists. She couldn't even remember Leo's face. Oh she could conjure up broad cheek-bones, wide sensuous nostrils on a noble Roman nose, she could picture brown eyes and the stern frown lines above them but when she tried to assemble the parts the result was like a police identikit photo for a sinister stranger, and Leo himself slipped out of memory's grasp.

They waited in Füssen as Christmas loomed. The Bavarians decorated the shops, the streets and the houses. Eva rose early every day and went into town and talked to railway clerks or travel agents.

Otto made a daily call to the theatre in Munich to enquire about the progress of the Japanese technicians. He went for long silent walks through the mediaeval streets of Füssen. In the evenings he complained of migraines brought about by the glare of the snow, and took his dinner in his room.

'We can't surely be waiting for one opera performance?' said Rose to the portrait of the young King Ludwig above the roaring log fire in the lounge. The King's plump, petulant face gazed down at her. 'Oh, but you would, wouldn't you?' For Rose had read her way through the empty evenings and knew that the king had arranged for whole operas to be put on for his solitary person. She had learnt that this isolated, sexually ambiguous young monarch had virtually bankrupted the state of Bavaria to finance his hero Wagner's work. Somewhere not far from Füssen was a castle with a man-made grotto where poor lonely Ludwig had sailed in his swan boat. But Otto never suggested that they visit it, just as he never looked up at the portrait of the king.

She knew why she waited. And Leo didn't call or acknowledge her letter. She too walked through the snow-caked mediaeval streets but never for long, just in case the phone in her room should ring.

Clara pushed past a doorman at the Munich opera house and made her way into the ticket-office. The woman behind the desk smiled politely and started to say that they were closed for the day.

'I want my ticket for tomorrow night—' said Clara.

'Tomorrow's performance is cancelled.' The clerk handed her a typewritten notice explaining in four languages that the curtain had decided to live a life of its own. The bulletin was written with a wit not usually expected from German organizations, and throughout the day the box-office clerk had watched as the customers' disappointment changed to wry amusement. Clara did not smile. She read the notice and reread it. She had come to Munich intending to dizzy herself with Otello's downfall, and Butterfly's desolation. Now there was nothing but an empty stage and a stuck curtain.

She had been too busy travelling to notice the Christmas trees and lights that filled the streets. Now that Munich had failed her she had little choice but to return to England and the kindness of her boring stepmother and all her ordinary, well-meaning friends in Hampshire. Clara wanted champagne receptions and galas; she wanted to be among men of power and talent; she wanted to be surrounded by talk of which conductor would take over which orchestra, who was to sing at La Scala, who was to direct at Bayreuth. She had neither the energy nor the inclination to achieve anything herself but she was determined to wallow in the wake of all those glories that flowed from the singing houses of Europe.

And as Clara walked towards the stage door, she saw what she considered a rather faded glory coming towards her. Annaliese Hartman and her husband Fritz Schreier were trying to hail a taxi. Fritz saw Clara and looked to each side of him for a quick escape route. But Clara rushed towards them. Fritz turned and guided his wife in the opposite direction. Clara caught up with them. Annaliese Hartman, a matronly-looking woman who was five years his senior, stopped and held out her hand to Clara.

'What are you doing out in this terrible blizzard,

Clara? There are no performances at the theatre, you know.' The soprano studied Clara's spindly frame and shuddered as an east wind blew around the three of them.

'Sorry, Clara, but we have to get a taxi,' Fritz scowled at his wife. 'We are already late for an appointment.'

'Nice to see you, Clara,' said Annaliese, slipping her arm through her husband's as he stared off into the distance. 'But do go on inside. It is ten degrees below freezing, you know.' Fritz and Annaliese crossed the road, heading in the direction of Max Josef Platz.

'I told you we should have taken the car,' Annaliese sighed, as the only cab to appear sailed by filled with four Japanese men.

'I hate driving in snow—' Fritz started to say but was interrupted by the sound of frantic panting just behind him.

'Isn't it amazing that a curtain can cause so much trouble?' Clara came crunching through the snow to walk alongside them.

'Amazing,' said Fritz.

'You'd think there would be something they could do, wouldn't you?' said Clara, looking up into his handsome blond face.

'Well, it's all so sophisticated now – computer-run, apparently,' said Annaliese. 'I never understood it myself.'

'Come on, Annaliese.' The conductor addressed his wife in rapid German. 'Don't encourage her.'

But Clara kept up with the conductor's rapid pace.

'If there are no performances what were you doing in the theatre?'

'Well, they may try to do at least one—' Annaliese started to say.

'Taxi!' cried Fritz and, to his relief, the cab stopped.

'Excuse us, Clara, but goodbye,' he smiled, and helped his wife into the car. But as he tried to close the door, it encountered an obstacle. Clara had thrust her left foot into the cab and was trying to squeeze inside.

'You won't mind my sharing your cab on a day like this?' she said. 'My hotel isn't far.'

'Where is it?' said Annaliese.

'By the station.' Clara still hadn't succeeded in climbing inside. Fritz's strong right arm had not released its grip on the cab door.

'Wrong way, I'm afraid,' said Fritz and started to pull the door shut. He announced his destination to the driver. Clara pulled the door back open.

'You must let me in. I'll catch my death out here.' But the cab had started to accelerate. Clara wedged her foot back inside. Annaliese called to the driver to slow down but it was too late. They all heard the crack as Clara's thin ankle snapped and she fell like a wounded black crow into the thick snow covering the Max Josef Platz.

That evening Clara sat propped up on a Recamier sofa in the opulent guest bedroom of the Schreiers' Munich apartment. Fritz had spent the hour since their return from the hospital calling friends in England to see if someone could meet the now immobile Clara once he had arranged her flight back to England. But with the Christmas holidays approaching Fritz found most of his British friends absent or, at the mention of Clara's name, unwilling to help.

'Then she'll just have to stay here,' said his wife, as he closed his address book.

'No, not here. I'll pay for a private clinic if necessary but I won't have her here.'

'She cried when I mentioned a private clinic,' said Annaliese. ' "Christmas all alone in a clinic," she kept saying.'

'Where're her friends and family?' said Fritz, exasperated. 'Why can't they take her?'

'You know her father is dead. She was an only child. You remember what a funny lonely little adolescent she was. And she says her stepmother has never wanted anything to do with her. Apparently she has always been jealous of Clara.'

'I can't think why,' scowled Fritz. 'Anyway – we

can't have her here. Not with all the people who will be coming through over the holidays. I can't have her staring in their faces, asking them her nosy questions.'

'We don't have to include her in our lives,' said Annaliese. 'She is immobile. She can stay up in the guest-suite. Besides, if you hadn't been so rude to her this would never have happened.'

'You're too sweet-natured, Annaliese dear. You don't have any rudeness or hardness in you,' sighed Fritz. 'You might have had a better—'

'I might have had a better career if I'd been a little meaner? You say that at least once a week, Fritz.'

'Perhaps, but believe me you're going to have to harden up if Miss Clara is going to be around.'

Up in the guest-suite, Clara studied the plaster around her ankle. Fresh and white as the snow on the Max Josef Platz, it was not due to come off for at least six weeks – it was as if a piece of the Munich winter had wrapped itself around her bony limb and would keep her there until the snow melted.

Chapter Thirty

'Will it ever stop snowing?' Leo said to the woman at the check-in counter at Linate Airport.

'The forecast says that there will be intermittent snowfalls until at least this afternoon,' she replied, handing him his boarding pass for Munich.

'I didn't just mean today, *signora* – I meant ever – ever. Sometimes these past few weeks I have believed that it is possible that this snow will go on for ever – that we will all have to move up to the second floors of our homes – and evolve very long, narrow feet like skis.'

'But in six months it will be summer.' The young woman frowned. 'You can't have snow in summer.'

'No, no, of course not,' said Leo, but his buoyant, talkative mood continued into the departure lounge where he sat down next to an elderly dentist from Verona. The old man introduced himself, expressed his admiration, then lapsed into silence. Leo reached for his *Walküre* score.

'Why do you never sing at the Arena?' said the man as soon as Leo had managed to concentrate on the music in front of him.

'Oh, I have done, twice in *Don Carlos* and once in *Attila*,' smiled Leo and named the years.

'But I was visiting my granddaughter in Bari in those years,' snorted the dentist.

'If only I'd known,' smiled Leo, abandoning his attempt to work.

'You were never as good as Pinza in any of your roles,' sniffed the dentist.

'Oh, I'm sure I wasn't but then he's dead, isn't he?' smiled Leo. 'The greatest voices always have the good grace to be conveniently and eternally silent when it comes to comparing them with present singers.'

'And you're too tall,' said the dentist, standing up to board the flight. 'Italian singers shouldn't be that tall – it's not right.'

Leo couldn't think of anything to say to that and remained where he was until the dentist and the dozen other passengers were on board. He waited until the stewardess was about to close the door, then slipped in and took a seat at the front of the cabin.

'Will it ever stop snowing?' he said to the stewardess when she served him a glass of warm Asti Spumante.

'What if it didn't, Signor dalla Vigna? Have you wondered that too?' She smiled down at him.

'That perhaps we have entered some sort of strange and wonderful Winterland? Yes, yes I have. I think it's beautiful.'

'So do I,' said the girl and continued down the aisle.

Leo had not yet been given his coveted Wagnerian role. The Japanese technicians who were working so assiduously in Munich still considered the wayward curtain liable to bring itself down upon Valhalla and its erring gods and miserable mortals long before the sixteen hours that Wagner had allowed for the task. Besides, the Bulgarian had also made the journey from Venice to Munich and was at that very moment eating a breakfast of sausage and four eggs in the Vierjahreszeiten – the Four Seasons Hotel.

Leo's agent had, however, called the previous evening to say that the Munich intendant would like to have lunch with him the next day – if the singer could possibly be free at such short notice. Leo guessed that the Bavarian had calculated that he was sure to have a previous engagement – thus the intendant relieved himself of the tantalizing but dangerous possibility of handing the role over to Leo.

'I'll be there,' Leo had said. And after he put the phone down, he had sat at the piano in the big, bare apartment and sung through the whole role. Then he slept just three hours, and now he sat, still nursing the warm glass of wine, with what seemed to be a boundless supply of energy. In the pocket of his new cashmere coat was a much-fingered letter from the Hotel Alpenhof in Füssen.

'Ladies and gentlemen, on the left-hand side of the aircraft you can see Lake Como,' announced the stewardess. Leo did not look out but he did look at his watch and note that it was at just this time that Kay went for her lunatic swim. He had a sudden lurching fear that if he were just to glance through the aircraft window, he and all the other passengers would see her diving blonde and naked through the pristine morning air. The passengers on the left-hand side of the aircraft who did gaze down at the lake saw no blonde water-nymph, just the ferry chugging its way from Lecco to Como – and a police boat on a routine morning patrol.

On that day of the winter solstice as Leo's plane flew overhead, Kay had finished her swim and was busy polishing the tester bed. The phone rang as she rubbed away at one of the wooden feet. The phone often rang and the villa by the lake would echo with the disembodied voices of friends and business associates leaving their message on the machine. Kay rarely stopped what she was doing. Leo himself had telephoned just once but when the machine had come on, mechanical and indifferent, he had hung up. After that his lawyer had called. Now his lawyer communicated through the post, sending Kay large buff envelopes containing legal documents that she had to sign for but then placed unopened on a table in the hall.

Closing the door on the postman one morning she had noticed a pair of snow-boots to the left of the front door. Kay saw at once that they were too small for Leo. She shook the snow out and stared at them, realizing that poor John Tillson had not even dared to reclaim his boots. She imagined colds, pneumonia, that tawny blond face growing wan and feverish. She consulted her address book and started to dial his number in Como. She would think of something to say when he answered. The phone rang and rang. Kay was more disappointed than she had expected. But of course, John had said he was going home for Christmas. He wouldn't need his snow-boots there. He would hardly have time for his music. He would be going to parties with beautiful, flawless southern girls and would have forgotten her. Perhaps he would never return to Italy. But as she gazed at a small Indian miniature on the wall, Kay realized that being forgotten didn't trouble her. The true pain came from the thought of never seeing his superb young body again. Not for the first time, Kay wished to be timeless and invisible, to be able to fly and hover over all the beautiful things of the world – the temples, jewels, brocades and porcelains unseen and unheard, immune to passing time.

'Merry Christmas!' cried a disembodied voice on the answering machine in the hallway. It was the count from Como calling from England. Kay let him talk to the tape and put the boots next to the stove to dry.

Severe turbulence hit Leo's aircraft as they flew over the Alps. The plane jolted, shuddered, dived then righted itself and flew smoothly, but within seconds the pilot's voice announced that the cabin crew should sit down and fasten their seat-belts immediately. The plane lurched downward again. Hearts and stomachs followed seconds later. Slippery hands gripped the seat-rests. Leo tried to concentrate on his libretto but it fell from his grip. When he picked it back up, he let the pages fall open where they would, as so many desperate souls had done throughout the centuries with the Bible, hoping to find guidance in a random phrase. Leo wasn't desperate. His mood, in spite of the turbulence, was still buoyant and he wasn't seeking guidance. He knew where he was going. Still, it was with intense interest that he tried to focus on the leather-bound book on his knees. It had fallen open on Act Two. A despairing Wotan, bound by the rules he has created, is weary, unable to save his own son from death. And he utters his ultimate desire in the words that now loomed up at Leo.

'*Das Ende, Das Ende.*' Leo gazed expressionless at the words on the page: '*Das Ende, Das Ende.*' Then the plane swooped and shuddered; the floor seemed to lurch away from his feet. The stewardess who hadn't had time to get to her seat, was flung to the aisle alongside him. Leo reached out and put his broad hand around her slender waist, pinning her securely to the floor, as coats and cushions flew through the air and a tray of drinks crashed onto the carpet.

'*Grazie, signore,*' said the young woman, and closed her eyes and wrapped her arms around the base of his seat. Her skin was damp and white. She shifted slightly and rested her cheek against Leo's calf. With his other free hand, Leo felt in the pocket of his new coat and caressed the letter from the Hotel Alpenhof. Still he gazed at the words before him: *Das Ende, Das Ende.* And he held that flimsy airmail paper like a talisman. This could not be the end.

For a few seconds the plane entered smoother air currents. Leo was about to relax his grip on the young woman's waist when the aircraft plunged downwards. A woman behind him screamed as the plane seemed to plummet out of control. A loud hammering pummelled against the fuselage.

'Machine-gun fire!' he heard the Verona dentist yell at the back of the cabin. 'We're being shot down! We're all going to die!'

'Hailstones!' yelled Leo, who could out-shout anyone on that plane. 'It's just a hailstorm!'

'The *signore* is right,' sighed the stewardess at his knee. 'It's a hailstorm.'

In the back of the cabin, the old dentist set up a low moaning. Other passengers joined in – some whined, some groaned, some said Hail Marys. Leo could not stand these sounds and he closed his eyes and hummed to himself to block them out. At first he hummed wordlessly, almost silently. But as the plane struggled on, seeming destined to hurtle eternally through the raging currents outside, he added words and volume. His voice surged up through his chest and head, pushing out doubt, fear, and *Das Ende.* As always, his voice, the air from within him, wove him into harmony with the whirling air in the world outside. Unbeknown to Leo who, eyes closed, was lost in his own private rapture, his voice had also filled the cabin and wrapped itself like a muffler around the fear and desperation of the other passengers. Even the dentist from Verona was listening, head cocked to one side.

'Siepi wouldn't have shown off like that,' he muttered but he had released his grip on the armrest and relinquished all thoughts of approaching death.

The plane entered calmer air currents. Leo could release his grip on the stewardess. She bent down and kissed him hard on the cheek. He hugged her to him, enjoying the feel of warm female flesh, that even he had feared he might never touch again. And as he smelt her perfume and her warmth, he concluded that *Das Ende* had not meant the end of life but the end of a chapter in his life – the end of superstition and the end of guilt. He had come through the tumult. The storm had marked a crossing-over from the earthy, easygoing land of his father to his mother's wild, severe northern home, from Verdi to Wagner, from Kay to Rose . . .

When he stepped onto the hard, unmoving floor of the air terminal he walked straight to a phone and dialled the number of the Hotel Alpenhof. When he had burst into song in the tumbling aircraft, he was singing not just to banish fear but because he was on his way to Rose. He hadn't told her that he was flying to Munich for she was not the official purpose of his trip. He had even convinced himself that he should wait until the role was his and sung and succeeded in, before he even made any contact with her. Now he wanted Rose.

Rose was walking through the old town of Füssen as he dialled the hotel number. Otto was walking with her. She had bumped into him outside a florists in a side-street.

'I have just calculated that I have sent enough bouquets to divas to fill this shop twice over,' he had said to her, his eyes on an opulent spray of imported orchids. 'I can remember every one of them – what I sent and to whom. A whole adult life based on adulation – pathetic, isn't it?'

'I think there are far worse ways of spending a life,' said Rose.

And Otto linked his arm in hers and said, 'I do love you, Rose.'

'Any news on the curtain?' she asked as they walked back towards the hotel.

'It is fixed – rehearsals for *Walküre* are going ahead.'

'And you want to see it? I thought this was the one you couldn't bear.'

'It's better than going home. And it is some of the most glorious music ever written.'

'Well, I'll be glad to go home,' said Rose as they arrived at the hotel. 'I'll be glad to get my finances straightened out, knuckle down to ordinary life.'

'Appalling prospect,' sighed Otto.

'Not really. I think it's called living in reality,' said Rose. 'Isn't that what you've been brooding on?'

'I thought you just said there were worse ways to live,' said Otto.

'Oh there are! There are! And there is something magical and pure about you and your passions, Otto. I just thought that you yourself had expressed a desire to – oh, I don't know— Wait a minute, is that my phone?'

They had arrived in the long corridor that led to their rooms. Rose left Otto and ran past the painted Bavarian cupboards, the hunting horns and stuffed birds that lined the walls. The phone could be ringing in any one of the rooms and as she ran, her relief grew as the sound grew louder. She prayed that an invisible hand behind a door would not pick up an invisible receiver and condemn her to a silence that she feared would last for ever. But the phone rang on. It rang as she felt for her key, it rang as she fumbled with the door

279

handle, flung her handbag on the bed and grabbed the receiver.

'Leo!'

Otto, who had followed her along the corridor, paused now and waited just out of sight, leaning against the wall next to the open door.

'I've been calling you for half an hour,' said Leo.

'Just half an hour?' said Rose.

'It doesn't matter – you're here now. Can you have dinner this evening?'

'This evening – where are you?'

'Munich – I have a business lunch up here but afterwards I thought I'd rent a car, drive down and take you for dinner. I have to be back in Milan this evening but the Germans dine early. Is there somewhere decent in Füssen?'

'I don't know – I don't really like German food so I've been living off sandwiches from the local deli—'

'Then you need a good dinner. Oh, Rose, I am so happy to hear your voice. I had such a flight to get here. We hit the most extraordinary storm. I thought for just a second that I was going to die. It is one of the great delusions of our modern world, this travel business, don't you think?'

'What do you mean?'

'Well, a man like me or any businessman in any city in the western world says, "I'm going for a business lunch in Munich or Paris or Vienna." We convince ourselves that it is so easy – like going to the end of the road to post a letter – but between Milan and Munich, no matter how fine the technology, out there above the Alps, the elements await – invisible winds, swirling tempests to spin us around and make us sweat into our suits and clasp our hands in prayer underneath the leather attaché case. Oh, Rose, I thought it was the end. And never have I wanted so much to live.'

'I had just convinced myself that I should go home,' said Rose.

'You are lucky to have a home to go to,' said Leo.

'It's just a room – what I meant was that I should

280

go back to a more sensible life – anyway, you have more of a home than I could ever dream of, Leo. Otto told me about it – the priceless paintings, the Sèvres vases—'

'You can't live in a Sèvres vase, Rose,' said Leo. 'Unless you are some kind of genie. Look, don't go back to your sensible life yet, not this afternoon – I'll drive down earlier – we can visit some of the countryside.'

'It is such short notice,' said Rose. 'You really do go in for these grand, impetuous gestures—'

'Listen to me, Rose.' All the buoyancy, all the joy was gone from Leo's tone. He was stern and irritated. 'My life is signed away for the next four years. Can you tell me what you will be doing on 18 November three years from now? Of course not, but I can tell you right now that I will be singing in *Faust* in Hamburg. For me it is the ultimate luxury to call somebody and say, "Let us do something within the next few hours".'

'I can understand that,' said Rose. 'Did you get my letter?'

'I have it here but I waited to call you because I too was trying to live a sensible life.'

'You were?'

'I can come earlier,' Leo was saying. 'Then we can have part of the afternoon. It is the shortest day of the year today, Rose. Did you know that? The winter solstice. We must grab all the light that we can.'

'There was vague talk of my going to Ludwig's castle with Eva this afternoon.'

'We'll go to the castle together,' said Leo. 'They have Wagner's piano in a room overlooking the Schwann See, the swan lake.'

'Then you've already been.'

'Twenty years ago. We'll take tea in the village below the castle, Rose. That should appeal to your English half. I vaguely remember a coaching inn just below the royal family residence and looking out on Ludwig's dream castle.'

Dream castles, swan lakes, Wagner's piano, a mad

281

king, a winter solstice and Leo. Rose lay with her eyes closed, resting her cheek against the receiver and thought that human beings are not equipped to cope with so much joy.

'I'll be waiting outside at four-thirty,' Leo was saying. 'In a Mercedes like half of Germany, but I'll see you, Rose.' And he was gone. Still clutching the receiver, Rose didn't see Otto tiptoe past her door to his room.

Chapter Thirty-One

'It wouldn't seem right – you stepping in for an inferior performer – and at the last minute.' The intendant of the Bavarian State Opera stirred three lumps of sugar into his coffee. The lunch was finished and he and Leo and Fritz Schreier were sitting full and comfortable in a corner of the Schwarzwald restaurant. 'No,' said the intendant slowly. 'If you make such a surprising change in your repertoire—'

'*When* I make the change,' smiled Leo.

'*If* you make the change,' repeated Dieter, 'well, it should be an event, announced to the Press months in advance—'

'So that the critics can say he'll fall flat on his arse this time?' said Fritz. 'And all the fans can fight for tickets to see him do it? And you can put your prices up, right?'

'Why not? But you do see my point. There's something a bit scrappy about Leo just filling in at a time when the house has had so many problems and we're just about managing to get a performance together. Anyway, Dimov is under contract.'

'He is twenty-eight. Twenty-eight,' said Leo. 'He has been singing in the big houses for less than three years. Have you all gone mad?'

'He can sing it,' replied the intendant.

'Perhaps, but only just, and where will he be in ten years?'

'Of course, that's why our Leo flew up here today,' smiled Fritz. 'Deep concern for Dimov's career.'

'He is under contract,' repeated Dieter.

'Our manager will take care of that,' said Leo. He looked at his watch. 'Look, if I don't care, why should

283

you? I've even said I'm willing to accept the same fee as Dimov.'

'Would you consider doing a Basilio for us in the festival next year?'

'I've dropped Basilio,' sighed Leo.

'Then let me think,' said the intendant.

'Twenty-four hours?' said Leo. 'Look, I have to go. I have an another appointment. Roberto will call you tomorrow.'

'He should have been here today,' sighed Dieter. 'Or does he think all this is as ill-advised as I do?'

'He'll call you tomorrow,' said Leo, and with a brisk shake of Dieter's hand, collected his coat and walked out of the restaurant. Fritz followed him.

'That was good gamesmanship, that bit about another appointment.'

'Oh, but I do have another engagement,' said Leo.

'Who with?' said the conductor.

'Ha!' said Leo, and putting his arms around the baffled conductor's bulkily clad form, hugged him tight. 'Must go, Fritz. I'm taking tea in a coaching inn in the country.'

'Oh, a woman!' said Fritz. 'Which one?'

'That's a question I should ask you,' said Leo and started to walk briskly down the street. Fritz walked with him.

'Well, in a way that does rather help Annaliese and me out because we did want to have you to dinner—'

'Can't make dinner,' said Leo.

'Thank God for that,' muttered Fritz. 'You see we have this unexpected guest, Leo. I wanted to tell you about it—'

'We'll talk tomorrow,' said Leo, squeezing Fritz's shoulder and pausing at the door to a car-rental office. 'I'll call you from Milan.'

'I don't suppose it would be appropriate to say "Give my love to Kay" at this point in time?' said Fritz.

'Don't be sanctimonious, Fritz – it doesn't sit well on a man who has had three wives to my one. Wish me luck—' And he hugged the conductor again.

'I don't mind you doing that after a performance but not in a Munich street,' said Fritz, untangling himself from Leo's grasp. 'And what exactly am I wishing you luck for?'

'Whatever you want,' laughed Leo. 'Do you know I almost died this morning, Fritz? Or at least I thought I was going to die in a storm on the flight here. And as we plummeted through the heavens my *Walküre* score came open on *Das Ende, Das Ende,* but it wasn't the end. Here I stand. So you see I don't need your luck.' And kissing the conductor hard on the cheek, he disappeared into the rental office.

Rose had no appetite for lunch. She had nibbled a sandwich in her room and gazed in despair at her wardrobe. She was ironing a three-year-old skirt when Eva knocked at the door.

'Have you seen Otto?' she said.

'I saw him this morning,' said Rose. 'But not since.'

'That's funny. He said he'd have lunch with me out at Hopfen. The manager of a resort hotel out there offered me a trial day with lunch and dinner and skating thrown in.'

'Skating?'

'Optional, of course, but Otto said he quite fancied a skate and now I can't find him.'

'Probably gone for one of his walks,' said Rose. 'Look, Eva – about the trip to the castle, I'm afraid—'

'Oh, I haven't got time for that now,' said Eva. 'Where does that fool brother of mine usually go for his walks?'

'Around the old town,' said Rose. 'He says it looks like a set from *Meistersinger.*'

After Eva went to look for Otto, time suddenly started to move very quickly for Rose. She tried to imagine Leo in a Mercedes driving down an autobahn but decided that this was unlucky and that she would not even think of his face until she saw it before her on the street outside the hotel. On that freezing day of the winter solstice she was sweating so hard that she had to change clothes twice. At four-fifteen she had a bout of diarrhoea. 'Oh, why do our bodies get in the way?' she said to her clammy reflection in the mirror, and knew immediately that our bodies also bring us the greatest joys.

She took a deep breath, opened the window and leaned as far out as possible. The hotel overlooked a few stocky, dull suburban German houses but even these had gained grace in the snow. Rose looked past the chimney-pots and the TV aerials to the smoke-pink sky over the nearby mountains and tried, in spite of her earlier superstition, to calculate which way lay the north – the north that now contained Leo. Off in the distance, she saw a lone swan – its vast wings silently carrying it towards the distant pine forests.

Where do swans go in winter? she wondered. When the lakes and rivers freeze, where can a swan go? It can't stay suspended for ever in the cold air or roam through the woods. The swan was gone and her watch said three-thirty. Rose went downstairs.

The Mercedes was parked in front of the entrance.

'Already the light is going,' said Leo as she sat down alongside him. 'We must hurry.' He leaned forward, hugged her to him for just a second, did not kiss her but turned back to the steering wheel and drove away.

'It's only about five minutes away by car,' said Rose. 'The one at Hohenschwangau, I mean. You didn't say which castle you meant.'

'I'm not sure I really cared,' said Leo.

'Well, there's the one that has the grotto and the swan boat, and there is the one that is like the ones at Disneyland, or rather, they are like it ... you know what I mean.'

'Disneyland. I meant that one.'

'Good, because that's the one that is five minutes from here.'

'Good,' said Leo.

'Good,' said Rose and couldn't think of another word to say.

They drove out of the town in silence. Leo drove

very fast, she noticed, as if he really were trying to outpace the fading light. The car left Füssen behind but the countryside remained disappointingly suburban. A gymnasium, a library and a petrol station marked their route to the mad king's castle. Within minutes they were at the foot of the snow-enfolded pine forests that swept across the mountains. On the ground the feeling of suburban safeness and predictability continued. There were fewer houses and they were in the Bavarian style, but the BMWs in the driveways and the uniform rectangular gardens gave a banality to the landscape that was strangely at odds with the dense, secretive pine forests that loomed above.

'There!' cried Leo.

'What? Where?'

'There! On the edge of that cliff. You can hardly see it – it's lost in the white.' Leo had stopped the car. They both gazed up at the castle that clung to the cliffs above.

'Do you want to visit it?' said Leo.

'Of course, but perhaps you don't – if you've seen it before.'

'Years ago – I came here more than a quarter of a century ago. A quarter of a century ago! And yet today I don't feel that I've lived that long – today I feel sixteen,' said Leo and drove the car up the small hill that led to the hamlet of Hohenschwangau.

In the depths of the Bavarian winter most of the shops and all but one of the hotels were closed. Leo's coaching inn was open. They left the Mercedes in the car-park and stood in the silent single street that was Hohenschwangau. To their left, way up above the pine forests and disappearing from time to time into the clouds, was Neuschwanstein, the king's dream castle. To their right was a much lower, warmer, homelier building – the royal residence of Ludwig's family.

'And if you walk down to the end of the road you will come to a lake – I do remember that,' said Leo. 'Shall we walk down there?' He held out his arm to Rose. She slipped her arm through his, touching the familiar cashmere coat for the first time since that day in Milan. But the material felt different, stiffer and colder. It must be my nerves, my stiffness, that is changing things, thought Rose, and drew closer to Leo, hoping to draw on some of his warmth and solidity. They walked the couple of hundred yards to the edge of the frozen lake.

'So silent, so brittle and frozen,' said Rose.

'Oh, there are tourists,' said Leo. 'I saw their heads bent over their meals in the hotel where we left the car.'

Rose had noticed nothing but Leo. Now she stood alongside him and looked for swans. The lake looked as solid as marble in the early twilight. With Leo's tourists behind them in the village, there was no sign of life. No duck waddled through the frozen undergrowth – no white swan winged its way home here. Where do swans go in winter? she wondered again.

'Shall we start with the family residence? And leave the dream place till last?' said Leo. 'It's just a short walk up that hill and that's where the Wagner piano is – a beautiful, light-coloured instrument – made of maple, I think.'

But when they got to the castle entrance, an apologetic woman in the ticket-office explained that only guided tours were available and that if they took the last one of the day in twenty minutes, they would not be able to visit the other castle.

'So our choice comes down to a solid family home or a dream perched high on a cliff,' said Rose as they walked away from a group of Japanese tourists who had tried to line up behind them.

'I want to see the piano again,' said Leo. 'But I'm not patient today – I'm not sure that I want to wait.' They had stopped at the bottom of a flight of deep stone steps. A stream picked its way through the snow just yards from their feet. Below them, horse-drawn carriages picked up tourists and started their slow, winding ascent to the other castle on the opposite mountain.

'Can't they give you a private visit? You being a big opera singer and all that?' said Rose.

Leo rounded on her.

'Don't say things like that, Rose. Not you, not you.' He pulled her to the ramparts out of sight of the Japanese. The force of his grip lifted her feet from the ground. He swung her round to face him. The land of the lonely king whirled before her. All he must have seen she now saw from his first castle in the pines – all white, white everywhere. Where do the swans go? she wondered frantically, absurdly, as Leo stared down at her with that same puzzled, anxious expression that she had first seen in London. She pulled away from him and went to lean against the ramparts.

'I didn't mean that you should demand some sort of special privilege – at least I don't think I did. I can't seem to say anything I truly think or feel today.'

'Neither can I,' she heard his voice behind her.

'Oh, I'm not sure you understand. It's just that you are so big, Leo – I don't just mean physically, I mean as a being – you are overwhelming. I hardly know you – we've not spoken that much. And you keep doing these wonderful, terrifying things like sweeping into Venice, and whisking me off here. And I have to keep separating the myth from the man. The myth is thrilling, of course, but I think I like the man more. And yet how can I expect you to be yourself if I can't even be myself?'

Leo had slipped his hand under the collar of her old coat and was caressing her bare neck.

'I'm the one who should be sorry, Rose. I came up here in such an aggressive, conquering mood and I can't seem to shut it off. There is so much I want to tell you about today – it has been an extraordinary day – an extraordinary few weeks, but what happened today is linked to other days, other years. That is what is so difficult about forming any kind of relationship after a certain age, don't you think? There is so much of the past to explain . . . to justify . . . When you're twenty-one and you meet a girl, you're hardly made, hardly formed—'

'But when you're a married man of – how old are you?'

'Forty-eight,' said Leo. 'How old are you?'

'Thirty-nine.'

'That's what I guessed.'

'At this point I should say, "Why is a married man trying to form a relationship at forty-eight years of age?" but I don't want to—'

Leo put his arm around her shoulder.

'Shall we walk some more?'

'Where to?'

'Well, as you said earlier we have a choice. We can either tour this rather lived-in, family home or ride in one of those carriages to the dream on the mountainside.'

'I've never ridden in a carriage,' said Rose. 'In the snow under the pines.'

'It would be highly romantic,' said Leo. 'I would hold you in my arms, perhaps kiss you. We would be doing what lovers are supposed to do. But we are not lovers – yet – perhaps we never will be. And in all honesty, Rose, I would be deeply uncomfortable.'

'So would I,' said Rose. 'Anyway, you did say you wanted to see Wagner's piano.'

They joined the guided tour with a party of two dozen Japanese. They walked from room to room of the twelfth-century 'jewel of German Romanticism' as the guide put it, listening politely to his explanations, and only touching each other when Leo brushed against Rose to usher her through a door or up a staircase. He was so much taller than the Japanese that the Bavarian guide addressed all his little speeches to him. Leo found himself obliged to smile and nod at the appropriate moments. The Japanese watched and smiled and nodded with him. Rose slipped away at each window and gazed out at the frozen lake. Should we have gone to the other castle? she wondered. Should we have ridden up the mountain in a horse-drawn carriage in pursuit of Ludwig's dream? Such a cold dream it seems from here – full of heroes and myth, perhaps, but devoid of human warmth – and why am I fretting about our choice of castles when Leo has come to me again out of some turbulent mountain sky? She looked over at his calm, stern, absorbed face and thought, as she had thought in London, I have always known this man.

Only when they came to Wagner's piano did Leo show any irritation. He watched and waited as the Japanese took their photos.

'I can't imagine anything with them here,' he whispered to Rose. 'I wanted to stand here and see him and hear the sounds that would have echoed through these rooms but I can't.'

They both stood and waited until the Japanese were gone but the Bavarian guide stood and waited for them. Leo turned his back on him and addressed Rose. 'In one of Beethoven's many homes in Vienna, they have not covered the piano keys as they have here. I touched the keys that his fingers touched – can you imagine that? But I didn't sense him, his presence, until I saw a lock of his hair in a glass cabinet – paler than you would imagine – so pathetic that lock of hair.'

The guide came up to them and motioned to them to go on into the next room.

'Oh, to hell with it,' sighed Leo. 'Come on, let's go and have that tea I promised you.' And he nodded a farewell to the guide and the Japanese and led Rose out of the residence.

'I suppose we go to your coaching inn place,' said Rose as they walked back down Hohenschwangau's only street.

'I wish it was a coaching inn,' said Leo. 'That's what my imagination made it. I think it's just a rather expensive German hotel.'

'But I like the bay windows that look out on the other castle,' said Rose as they walked through the door. 'And the carved wood – I love the warmth of all this light carved wood they have here – the warmth and the curves – my God, this place is packed!'

They had entered a dining-room, with the tacit

understanding that they would sit in the big bay window that looked out on the dream castle. The table at the bay window was occupied by a dozen Japanese, as was every table in the room. Like an enormous flock of chattering starlings, they had alighted upon the room, dozens of them, their sleek black heads shining in the lamp lights. Leo reached down and picked up some chopsticks and a bottle of soy sauce.

'I don't understand,' he said to Rose. He shook his head and examined the chopsticks.

'I don't understand,' he said to a passing waiter. The waiter stopped, put down a plate of noodles and said, '*Ma è Leo dalla Vigna!*' Rose listened to the brief exchange between Leo and the waiter and listened again when Leo came to translate it to her.

'He says it's the standard winter business around here. Coachloads of Japanese. No-one else much comes in the cold, and they are a guaranteed income and not too fussy about food.' He put the chopsticks and the soy sauce back in their place. 'Let's go, Rose.'

'I have nothing against the Japanese,' said Leo as they sat in the car, 'but it doesn't feel like Bavaria.' He tuned the radio to a station that was playing a string quintet. 'I don't seem to be able to live in my time.' He increased the volume. 'Listen to that, Rose. How did Schubert know that by putting that note in front of that one he would eventually sweep us along to that?' He listened intently. 'How could he know? I will tell you something that I've never told anyone else. Because he is dead – and Mozart and Wagner and Verdi – because they are dust, in a way I will always be lonely. They went ahead and now all I can do is follow behind, gathering up the scores that they left and look and study and wonder: Would he have wanted this like this? How would he have heard that? But they can never answer. They who have created the most beautiful sounds only answer with silence. They will never come back. The dead can never, never come back.'

And Leo kissed Rose. In the darkened Mercedes, with Schubert on a fuzzy car radio and the scores of sleek-headed Japanese drinking tea behind the bay windows, and the castle standing stone cold in the black night of a winter solstice, he leaned forward and took her in his arms and kissed her on the mouth. Rose felt once more the surprising stiffness of the cashmere coat, the roughness of his beard as his cheek brushed against her and the wonderful warmth of his lips and tongue.

Chapter Thirty-Two

'All the light has gone,' said Leo.

Rose lay across the front seat of the Mercedes, resting her head on his chest. She could hear his heart beating through the thick layers of winter clothing. It was such a vulnerable sound. She couldn't bear to listen for too long for fear that it would stop, there in the parking-lot of the hotel, while behind the bay windows the Japanese sprinkled soy sauce on their rice.

'This is a new coat,' she said suddenly. 'This isn't the coat you were wearing in London.'

'I bought it in Milan two weeks ago,' said Leo.

'Oh, but why? I mean I knew the feel of the other one – it was part of you. This is so new and cold—'

'I lost the other one,' said Leo.

'How strange to lose a coat in winter,' said Rose. She shifted her position until her cheek was rubbing against Leo's beard and her ear was resting on his shoulder far from the frightening sound of his beating heart.

'Look how suddenly all the light went,' said Leo. 'The mountains, the pine forests, the shuttered guesthouses and cafés, they have all been sucked up into the night.'

'Your command of English is amazing,' said Rose.

'My wife is American.'

'A perfect natural blonde – a beauty,' said Rose.

'That little Otto man told you that, I suppose,' said Leo.

'He's not little,' said Rose.

'Thin, he's thin. Otto – Otto – *mamma mia*! That's where I got the dog's name!'

'You have a dog?' said Rose.

'My wife has a dog.'

'But no children.'

'We had a daughter,' said Leo. 'She died when she was just eight months old.'

'How?'

'Edward's syndrome. It's a severe birth defect – happens to about one in five thousand children and it happened to ours. She was born all misshapen – you could see she had no chance the minute you saw her. Her head was too small – her ears were very low-set and not quite developed. Can you imagine that for an opera singer's child? To perhaps never hear? But it wasn't just that – she was all wrong, Rose – I don't want to describe the way she looked – it seems disloyal somehow. The doctors at the clinic said she wouldn't make it to a year old. And then Kay, that's my wife, got this kind of American fervour that if she fought enough and worked enough the child would live and become whole.'

'And you didn't agree?'

'I was just starting out on my career. I didn't even have a manager at the time. I was fending for myself. And when I looked at that baby I was overwhelmed with pity and hopelessness. I'm not an American, Rose. I don't have that boundless capacity to believe that things will work out. All around us every day is the proof that they don't.'

'So you wanted to let the child die?'

'I wanted to let nature follow its course but Kay was like a fury. She took the poor little thing to the States, consulted specialists in New York and California—'

'And all the time Kay was doing all this, you were busy building your career?' Rose had shifted to look into Leo's eyes. He had been right about the disappearing light. The dark of the winter solstice had filled the car but she wanted to see his eyes. She drew closer to him, so close that she could feel his breath warm on her cold face as he spoke.

'I had to. There are thousands of fine voices out

there, Rose – just waiting for their chance to come along—'

'Ah, but Otto says that with you it's more than just a voice, it's a presence, a kind of white hot— Oh, you know what they all say – I'm not going to start reciting it to you now.'

'I do know. I also know that people need myths – and that they are ready to settle on whatever talented person takes their fancy and cloak them with all the magical qualities they need to find in them. If it hadn't been me, there would have been another. There were some extraordinary voices around at that time. I remember sitting in at a singing competition and being amazed at how many wonderful singers there were—'

'But you still won the competition?'

'Oh, I didn't enter. I never did. I didn't believe in competitions – how can you judge a soprano over a tenor or a bass? And is music about competing?'

'So how did you make a name for yourself?'

Leo turned away from her to stare out at the coaches in the parking-lot. The moon had come out and the tops of the pines glowed white in the night.

'I worked like a Trojan. I learnt all the big roles at lightning speed, studied Russian, did *Boris* when an old fellow in a provincial company fell ill. Oh, I was ready to go anywhere, take on the most demanding parts.'

'You're lucky your hard work did pay off,' said Rose. 'That's not always the way of things.'

'And what is the way of things?' said Leo, his back against the cold, hard door of the Mercedes.

'Oh, come now, Leo, I don't have to tell you. People get on because they know people or they work some kind of fiddle or step on someone else. Of course, in your business I suppose that's impossible because you can't fake it, can you, when you're out there on your own. No microphone, no sound-engineers to pretty things up. I suppose that's one of the things I like about your world – there's no room for fraudulence.'

'So you like my world?' said Leo. He had turned to face ahead of him and was switching on the ignition.

'Yes, yes I do – what I know of it. I told you in Venice, it is endlessly absurd and wonderful all at the same time. And I suppose I like it because it contains you.'

'That is the nicest thing I've heard in months, years,' said Leo and leaned forward to kiss Rose again. But she drew away.

'And that rift between you and your wife about the child – has it been there all these years? With no attempt made to heal it?'

'Of course not. Marriages go through different phases, I think. At first we tried and tried to have another child—'

'What a strange way of putting things that is, I always think – tried to have another child, people say they are trying for a baby. I can never quite reconcile the rapture of sex with that mundane verb.'

'But sex isn't always rapturous,' said Leo. 'It can become a very routine banging away at each other. You should know that.'

'I do but I wanted to hear you say it because I was so jealous of the thought of you trying over and over again to make a child with her – this perfect natural blonde beauty in your wonderful villa by the lake.'

'I left Kay thirteen days ago,' said Leo.

They drove out of Hohenschwangau. Ludwig's castle hung above them, suspended and floodlit in the long winter night. Neither of them looked up at it.

They were almost in Füssen when Rose spoke.

'I wish you hadn't told me that,' she said.

'But I had to,' said Leo.

'It fills me with hope.'

'What's wrong with hope?'

'I'm thirty-nine, Leo. I have lower expectations than some twenty-year-old. I'm not good on quotations but what was that Balzac line? *Il faut que le coeur se bronze ou se brise* – something about the heart having to bronze over in order not to break. When I hope, I am filled with terror. The two feelings run alongside each other. They come as a kind of package.'

'Not for me they don't, and I'm a decade older than you. I've been filled with hope these past couple of weeks.'

'For what? Hope for what?'

'Ah. Now I'm a superstitious old opera singer so I'm not going to put it into words. Let's say I have a belief in renewal – redemption even.'

'Now there's a big, operatic word,' sighed Rose. They had arrived at the hotel. 'Bigness again, you see, Leo. Vastness, immensities. My life was set to be small and neat and well-ordered and you keep sweeping into it and leading me off to gaze over the precipice.'

'Ah no, Rosalinda,' Leo motioned to the piles of ploughed snow around the pink hotel. 'No precipices here – it is all quite flat and safe. Nothing more threatening than a Bavarian supper lies before us tonight.'

'I couldn't eat dinner,' said Rose.

'You didn't have tea.'

'My stomach has locked shut. It would be thirteen, wouldn't it?'

'What?'

'Thirteen days. You said you left your wife thirteen days ago.'

'In a few hours' time it will be fourteen.' Leo shrugged and took Rose in his arms. Again she felt his heart beat, again she felt the warmth of his lips and tongue. This time she put her arms inside the new coat, up underneath his sweater and felt the warm, solid bulk of his chest through his cotton shirt.

'I should be heading back to Milan.' Leo relaxed his hold on her and looked at his watch.

'So we couldn't have had dinner anyway?'

'I was probably being over-ambitious – the last flight goes at eight o'clock.'

'And away you go again,' said Rose, 'flying out of my life and over the stormy mountains. It sounds like something one of your characters would do.'

'Wotan,' smiled Leo.

'Oh, I've heard of that one,' said Rose. 'But he was a god, even I know that.'

'And he didn't have to rely on Lufthansa schedules,' smiled Leo. 'Oh, Rose, I must go, and there's so much I thought I'd say today—'

'Where do you live these days if you don't live in that villa?' Rose had felt the shift in Leo's attention, had sensed that airline schedules and other unknown obligations were already pulling him away down the autobahn. Fearful of appearing to want to linger, she opened the door of the Mercedes and put her right foot on the ground. 'I want to be able to imagine you somewhere. When I thought you lived in that place on the lake, I couldn't bear to think of you there—'

'I don't have a home any more – I have a perch – a big, empty, neutral apartment in Milan—'

'What colour are the walls? What do you look out on when you eat your breakfast?'

'I don't know. I don't know. I've paid no attention to the place. There's a piano, a Steinway grand – in a corner with a pale space on the wall where a painting once hung. Now there's something I have noticed – this apartment is full of pale spaces where pictures once were. I like that – it gives me a feeling of infinite possibilities.'

'Then I'll imagine that.' Rose had both feet on the ground and was about to step out of the car but she paused and turned to face Leo. 'Don't you want to know where I'll be?'

'Why, you'll be here,' said Leo. 'I can imagine a hotel room with no difficulty.'

'It's that simple for you?' said Rose.

'But you'd tell me if you were moving on,' said Leo. 'And if all goes well, I'll be in Munich for the next few weeks myself.'

'Why? Doing what? Otto and Eva never mentioned that.'

'I can't tell you yet, Rose – give me twenty-four hours. I'll call you.'

299

He had turned on the ignition. Rose looked at his broad hands on the steering wheel and decided against leaning back into the car for a last kiss. Leo turned to her and smiled a smile of the purest, almost childlike trust. For the third time that day she felt overwhelmed by some unnameable enormity.

'Go on, go away again,' she whispered to the revolving door of the hotel. 'Back to your perch across the Alps. You may speak perfect English, Leo dear, but perch was the wrong choice of word.' Leo couldn't hear. He had closed the passenger window and was about to drive away. The smile was gone and he was frowning at the dark night road ahead. A perch, Rose wanted to say, implies lightness, a readiness to be carried by the winds. The Leo that had whirled her round to face him on the frozen ramparts up above the lands of lonely Ludwig had seemed massive and sombre to Rose, and to drive the winds before him. And yet only minutes ago, the naïvety of the same man's smile had made her feel protective and filled her with foreboding.

Leo sounded the horn on the Mercedes. He winked, mouthed the words *Ciao, bellissima* and waited for Rose to wave back, but she was frowning now, concentrating on that absurd word: perch. A perch.

'I know!' she cried to the departing Leo. 'There is something you should have told me. Why did you give Clara a parrot?'

Leo scowled, put a hand to his ear and shrugged. With a last smile he drove off into the night.

300

Chapter Thirty-Three

Alone in the villa Kay tried to ignore the festivities, but cards addressed to the two of them poured in from around the world. An antique-dealer friend even attempted to cheer and surprise her by pinning an American wreath of holly on the front door but Kay mistook it for a funeral wreath and a bad practical joke, and flung it into the lake. She ignored Leo's offer of a trip home.

Only Clara relished the prospect of Christmas. Her breakfast was brought to her that December twenty-third morning, as every morning, on delicate green and white Herend china. She limped to the door, greeted the maid with an agonized expression and hobbled breathless back to the Recamier sofa by the window.

'No marmalade?' she said to the maid.

'*Ja*, marmalade.' The girl pointed to the jam in a porcelain pot.

'No, no, stupid. That's not marmalade, it's jam. Jam! I've told you that every morning since I've been here. I want marmalade. *Ich will* marmalade.'

'The German for jam is "marmalade",' said Fritz who had appeared in the doorway behind them. 'Brigitte has been giving you exactly what you ordered.'

'Oh, Maestro! So you do actually live in this apartment. I was beginning to wonder.'

'I'm a busy man, Fräulein.'

'So what brought you here today?'

'I came to see how the ankle is progressing. You must be in a hurry to get back to England?'

'I'd love to if I could but it's a complex fracture, the

301

doctor tells me. You can't rush the healing process.'

'I'll send the doctor around this afternoon,' said Fritz. 'If he gives you the all-clear I'll have my secretary book you on a flight tomorrow morning – that way you'll get Christmas with your family.'

'Speaking of family, how's that young soprano getting along? Your little London protégée? Is Annaliese as impressed as you by her talents?' Clara had lowered herself onto the sofa and was intent on buttering a slice of toast.

'Annaliese knows that I have to work with any number of young women,' said Fritz.

'And rehearse them in Manor House hotels up in the Cotswolds?' said Clara. 'Still I expect they had a better piano there.'

'I'll send you the doctor this afternoon,' said Fritz.

'Oh, I don't think that would be a very good idea,' said Clara. 'Of course, I can always talk to Annaliese about things. Ankles, I mean. Broken ones.'

'I'll send you the doctor,' said Fritz and walked out, slamming the door behind him.

'No you won't,' said Clara to the closed door. She surveyed the snowy-white cast around her ankle. Then she went into the bathroom and opened the window. By propping herself on her good leg she could lean out and listen to the sounds that issued from the room below. Sometimes someone played the piano or Annaliese sang. She longed to be invited down to sit with the people in that room and she believed that if she stayed long enough and pushed Annaliese and Fritz hard enough they would eventually accept her. The previous evening Clara had heard talk of a Christmas Eve dinner and had almost fallen into the courtyard in her excitement at hearing the guests' names. She intended to hobble down for the dinner and had spent the hour before her late breakfast ordering gifts for the illustrious guests from the biggest Munich department store and charging them to her stepmother's credit card.

*　　　*　　　*

302

At seven-thirty in the Bierstüberl of the Hotel Alpenhof, Otto, Eva and Rose sat down to dinner.

'Well, here we all are together for Christmas,' said Eva. She put an envelope in front of each of the others.

'What has got into you?' said Otto. 'It's not like you to go all sentimental over something like Christmas. If you must know, I find all this a bit embarrassing. Anyway, it's not Christmas – Christmas Eve is tomorrow.'

'Tomorrow there's a big party booking in here,' said Eva. 'And if Christmas means nothing to you, you shouldn't care what day we do things.'

'I hate this kind of thing,' muttered Otto. 'why do we have to suddenly start changing our behaviour towards each other just because of the day on the calendar?'

'Open your envelope, Otto, and you, Rose,' said Eva. Rose was staring out of the dining-room window at the dark in the distance, where the mountains of Ludwig's castle would be.

'If we celebrate Christmas today then what will we do for the actual holiday? I mean won't everyone in the hotel go home to their families? What will we do?'

'*He* certainly won't call, if that's what you're hoping,' said Otto. 'Married men always scuttle off to their comfortable homes for the holidays.'

'Mind your own business, Otto,' said Eva.

'He lives in a—' Rose started to say but stopped.

'In a fabulous villa on Lake Como,' said Otto. 'I've seen it in magazines. I can show you pictures of it—'

'No he doesn't.'

'There's even one photo of him. It's an old one – he didn't know it was being taken – he wouldn't have let them. He's walking on a terrace in springtime with these glorious azaleas in the background—'

'He doesn't live there any more,' said Rose.

'Is that what he told you?' Otto smiled across at her.

'He's left his wife, Otto. That's what he said and I believe him, but if you keep making snide remarks—'

'If you don't want him to make his snide remarks, don't tell him things,' said Eva. 'I learnt that long ago.'

Otto sat hunched over the unopened envelope.

'I say these things because I don't want you to lose sight of reality the way I did,' he said.

'Your motives are that noble?' said Rose.

Otto reached over and grabbed her wrist.

'Look, Rose, don't get what our mother would have called ideas above your station. That man is an immense artist, a legend. Beautiful women wait for him in dressing-rooms all over the world. He can have his pick of any of them—'

'So what would he want with a fading flower like our Rose? Is that what you're trying to say, Otto?' She wrested her hand from his grip.

'You have to live in reality, Rose. If you don't, you'll be lost for ever. Our place is in the audience, or the queue at the stage door. We can admire from a distance but you can't have a relationship with people like that. They're different.'

'He's right,' said Eva. 'He's too bloody spiteful in the way he says it, but he is right, Rose — they are different.'

'Different in what way? He's a human being, isn't he? He eats, sleeps, shits and pisses like the rest of us, doesn't he?'

'They are different,' said Otto. 'Leave him on his pedestal, Rose. You'll be happier. And so will he.'

'And where, pray, do these legends of yours find love and warmth in this world? A pedestal has always seemed like a rather cold, uncomfortable place to spend one's days.'

'With people like themselves,' said Otto.

'Even the gods on Olympus gallivanted with the odd mortal woman, you know, Otto.'

'And that never turned out very happily,' sniffed Otto.

'And if you're trying to tell me that Leo can only belong to that perfect natural blonde in the villa by the lake, I told you five minutes ago that he's left her.'

'Oh, they all say that,' said Otto.

'He's right,' said Eva. 'They do.'

'What the hell do either of you know about "Them"?' cried Rose, ashamed of herself for having exposed Leo to their cynicism. She was scared now of the long Christmas days that lay ahead and of the dark silence that seemed to stretch to infinity over Ludwig's mountains. 'What do either of you know about life? You've spent most of yours sitting in theatre seats watching other people pretend to live on a lighted stage in front of you. It's all very safe, isn't it? It lets you think you're alive without any of the risks of really living. What can either of you know about loving someone?'

'Fräulein Lorenzo?' The man from the reception desk had appeared at Rose's elbow. 'There is a phone call for you at the front desk.'

Within hours of the lunch in Munich, Leo was given his part in *Die Walküre*.

The producer had been quite happy to work with the Bulgarian baritone. 'He's a bit of a lump,' he'd confessed to the intendant, 'but I think I can mould all that soft clay into something.' Leo, however, was a different proposition. 'He'll upset the balance,' the producer moaned to Dieter and Fritz. 'These immense stars always do. He'll swan in late in a fur coat and expect me to adapt to him.'

'Leo wouldn't wear a fur coat,' said Fritz. 'And he won't be late because he came to Munich as soon as he knew the part was his. He's been in his suite at the Four Seasons for the past twenty-four hours. Besides, it's only a revival and a couple of performances. Play along with him – let him get this Wagnerian fancy out of his system—'

'From what I've heard he's too intense to be played along with—'

'He is intense but I would have thought that's what you'd want from a Wotan.'

'He'll upset the balance,' repeated the producer. 'Oh, how I hate working with these superstars.'

'And how you love earning the fees that working

with them brings,' smiled Fritz and disappeared into his office to phone his doctor. That morning's rehearsal belonged to the producer. Details of characterization and movement would be worked out in one of the rehearsal rooms. Fritz would not be needed and was free to make that call to the doctor to investigate the progress of Clara's ankle. He was about to pick up the phone when Leo walked into his office.

'I hope you haven't come to kiss me,' said Fritz as the bass walked towards him. 'I'm not very demonstrative in the mornings. How was your tea-party?'

'Very Japanese,' said Leo.

'Ah, an Oriental. I've never been able to decide whether I find Oriental women desirable or not—'

'I didn't say I was with a Japanese woman, but did you know that Bavaria is full of Japanese at this time of year? It's disconcerting.'

'Then you were with a Bavarian? I find that even more surprising. And how very civilized to take her to tea. I personally would find a rendezvous at four o'clock a little confusing. When do you make love? Before the scones and Earl Grey or after? With dinner the pattern has been established since time immemorial—'

'Is the producer here?' said Leo.

'Of course he's here.'

'Of course nothing,' said Leo. 'It's a revival so I was hoping a staff producer would take it and that he'd stay in Dresden or wherever he comes from.'

'You don't like him?'

'I don't know anything about *him*. I hate his work.'

'That's my Leo, ever moderate in his opinions.'

'I hate his work,' repeated Leo. 'I know I'm stuck with it if I want to sing this Wotan, so it's easier for me if he's not around.'

'And you can mould some poor little assistant to your wishes?'

'Not at all, but things can be, let's say, adjusted. How does this thing look?'

'Fairly traditional – no spaceships or nuclear power stations,' said Fritz, looking at his watch and impatient to talk to his doctor.

'Is it all fur and steps?'

'Mmm? Fur what?' Fritz's secretary had taken an early Christmas break and as Leo spoke he started to sort through his drawer for a phone book with the doctor's number.

'Fucking fur and steps!' declared Leo. 'I did an *Attila* with him in Paris. I can see the point of the fur there but all the Huns had to keep marching up and down steps. Up and down, up and down . . . Then I did a *Don Carlos* of his in Houston – more fur, more steps.'

Fritz had found the number. In the sorting he had also come across a list of Christmas flight cancellations into London and realized that if he didn't get Clara out of his home by tomorrow, she would be settled in on her sofa until after the holiday. And why was everyone talking about fur today?

'Look, Leo, I have an important phone call to make but I did want to ask you, or rather, Annaliese and I wanted to say that since you're in Munich why don't you come over for Christmas dinner tomorrow evening?'

'I'd forgotten it was Christmas.'

'Annaliese won't let me forget,' said Fritz. 'She'll probably get to work on you in the rehearsal room. Germans take Christmas very seriously, Leo, so if you want to run off with your Bavarian woman you'd better stay out of Brünnhilde's way.'

'How does she feel about working with this man?'

'She's too busy organizing dinner and decorating the tree to think about it, as far as I can make out – it's not the big deal to her that it is to you,' said Fritz, and with a movement towards the phone he dismissed Leo from his office.

'How many people in life do we kiss on the forehead?' said the producer to nine Walkyries, Wotan, and a *répétiteur* seated at a piano in the corner of the

307

rehearsal room. 'I know Wagner says eyes but I want Wotan to kiss his daughter his final farewell on the forehead.'

Leo was sitting on the floor, resting his back against the wall. Annaliese was lying at his feet, with her eyes closed. Two of the Walkyries were knitting, the *répétiteur* was reading *Paris Match*.

'How many people in life do we reserve the forehead for? He could kiss her on the lips – the school of thought that sees an incestuous attachment between the two might opt for lips. I'm not of that school. But the forehead – that wall between the world and all our thoughts – how many people do we kiss frankly and lovingly on the forehead?'

The producer repeated his question, this time looking at each Walkyrie in turn as if he expected them to give him a list of persons most recently kissed. His insistence worked on Leo. He found himself trying to remember a multitude of kisses. All those perfumed women in Milan, Vienna, Munich and Paris whose cheeks had brushed his or whose moist red lips had blown little bubbles of air at his chin and neck.

The producer addressed his question to the prone Brünnhilde but Annaliese's eyes were still closed. Did the absurd man actually want an answer? Leo wondered, and detached himself from the scene. He thought of other kisses, of the last time he had kissed Kay on the mouth; he remembered, with a sudden tingle of excitement, the red-headed countess and Natalia. And then he thought of Rose. He had kissed her on the lips too and been weak with desire, but before and after their lips and tongues had met, he had kissed Rose over and over again on the eyelids and the forehead, holding her face between his two hands and gazing down at her as if he had never before seen anything so precious and wonderful.

'And not just on the forehead but right here!' The German's leather dungarees creaked as he bent over and kissed an unsuspecting Annaliese on the forehead.

'We can't see where you're kissing her, Gottfried,'

said Leo. 'Your head is in the way. My head will be in the way on stage.'

'Even if it is, it really won't matter because if you get it right then all the sorrow and tenderness that the kiss conveys will be expressed in your body *and* your singing.'

Leo was not sure that he believed him. He often had doubts about the value of all this theatrical lore. Gottfried was motioning to him to move alongside him.

'Right there,' he said, pointing to a spot just between Annaliese's eyebrows. 'After the kiss, your right hand, which is turned towards the audience, must come up and in a gesture of immense tenderness sweep all that beautiful blonde hair back, and as the orchestra goes into the magic sleep music, you gaze at her face one last time.' He clambered back over Annaliese's body and motioned to Leo to take his place. 'If you would play that, Heinrich: "*So küsst er die Gottheit von dir*".'

Heinrich's piano picked out the magic sleep theme.

'Wotan's gaze, like the music, will be full of tenderness and regret. No, Leo! No! Nothing's happening. Do it again.' Leo and Annaliese and Heinrich did it again.

'Why so wooden, Leo? What are you holding back?'

'Nothing as far as I know.' Leo sat back on his heels.

'I'm all for stillness, my friend. Your stillness can convey more than a thousand singers flinging themselves around a stage, but here nothing is happening. Let's try it again.'

'*So küsst er*,' sang Leo and kissed Annaliese, noticing the lines on his fifty-five-year-old daughter's forehead as he moved his right hand up to stroke her hair.

'You're kissing your daughter farewell, Leo! Forget gods and godheads. Forget that Wotan is turning her into some kind of sleeping beauty behind her ring of fire. A father is bidding farewell to his daughter, as all we fathers must. It's one of the most poignant and universal of life's landmarks. We're all middle-aged in here.' He ignored the younger Walkyries. 'We all have children – we all know how this must feel.'

'Leo hasn't,' whispered Annaliese.

Two of the older Walkyries had blurted out the same words – 'Leo hasn't.' They too tried to whisper, but there in the opera rehearsal room the words echoed and bounced off the walls as if Wagner had written those two awful words for a trio of female voices: Leo hasn't. To be sung pianissimo.

Chapter Thirty-Four

Fifteen minutes later, Leo locked the door of his dressing-room, sat down on the only chair and wept. Twice somebody knocked on the door but Leo didn't respond. The third knock was accompanied by Annaliese's voice.

'Let me in, Leo.' He opened the door. Annaliese stepped quickly inside, closed the door behind her and took him in her arms.

'You poor old thing,' she said, stroking the hair back off his forehead in the gesture sought by Gottfried a half-hour earlier. 'I know what this is all about.' She paused, waiting for Leo to respond but he remained silent. He was holding her so tight that her chest hurt. 'Even without that, it must be hard to look at my battered face and see a daughter.' Annaliese studied her face in Leo's mirror. 'What was it some actress said? "I look like a burst paper bag."'

Leo laughed. 'I'm glad it's your face I look at. It's a wonderful face.' He released his grip and motioned to the chair but Annaliese stayed where she was, leaning up against the dressing-table. 'And I'm glad you know what this is all about, Annaliese, because I'm not sure that I do.'

'Oh, I think that in some part of you, you will mourn Antoinetta for ever,' said Annaliese.

'I haven't heard her called by her name in twenty-three years,' said Leo. 'I don't even think about her that much.'

'I'm sure you can't let yourself think about her—'

'It's not just the guilt. I don't know what to think. She was here so briefly. If I let myself wonder about the point of that life, I wonder about the point of all life—'

'God valued that short life as much as—'

'I'm sorry, Annaliese, but you know I don't share your beliefs. If either Kay or I had, perhaps things would have been different—'

'So it's ever onward and upward aye, Leo, with no time to look around, no time to think and wonder—'

'I've started to look around,' said Leo. 'For the first time in twenty-five years I've looked at life outside the theatre.'

'And?'

'I've left Kay.'

'You don't have to tell me this. You don't have to explain your private life to me,' said Annaliese.

'But I want to—'

'And what do you want me to say – that I'm shocked? How could you do it? Why *did* you do it? Why now – after so many miserable years?'

'You knew I was miserable?'

'You're a rotten actor when you're not on stage, Leo.'

'And Kay? Did Kay seem miserable?'

'I was never very close to Kay—' Annaliese started to say but Leo wasn't listening.

'We weren't always miserable!' he said in a voice too loud for the tiny room. 'Only a couple of weeks ago things seemed fine. She was even going to come down to Milan with me for *Attila*. She would have come down had it not been for—' He stopped. 'Oh, I don't know, Annaliese – I suppose I never took the time to admit to myself how awful things were. It would have been fairer on Kay if I'd done this years ago—'

'And on you,' said Annaliese. 'You deserve some happiness.'

'But not as much as Kay.'

'Why not?' said Annaliese. 'What kind of accounting system is this? Where did you come up with your figures? Why are all the credits on Kay's side?'

'Because they are. Because she lost the chil— Antoinetta more than I did. You know that, Annaliese. Because I love – loved my music more than any- thing. Because, because—' Again Leo stopped in mid-sentence. He moved to stand in front of Annaliese and look down at her plain, anxious face. 'You're not shocked that I've left her, are you? I thought with your religion and everything you would be scandalized.'

'No,' said Annaliese. 'I'm not shocked. In fact – I don't understand why you didn't do it sooner—'

'But I thought you liked Kay. The two of you always got on so well together.'

'That's rubbish, Leo, and you know it. We stopped seeing each other after Antoinetta died. Or didn't you notice that? It was my choice, Leo! I chose not to see Kay. When we did bump into each other in a dressing-room we'd exchange a few pleasantries and Fritz and I would go on our way. I thought you were aware of the rift—' Annaliese gripped his upper arm and stared up at him. 'You mean you never noticed? You've been so absorbed in your career that you didn't know that I've been avoiding your wife for the past twenty years?'

'I had no idea,' said Leo. He paced around the small room, stopping to press the palms of his hands against a wall, as if he were trying to make it expand enough to contain what he was about to hear. 'Why, Annaliese? What did Kay ever do to you? What did she ever do to anyone?'

'I hoped I'd never have to talk about it.' She turned the only chair away from the mirror and sat down.

'When I visited her in the clinic, the week after Antoinetta was born,' Leo closed his eyes at the sound of the name, 'and it was all so terrible, the child so doomed, I found her sitting up in bed, beautifully made-up, flawless, with the baby in the cot alongside her. I reached down and kissed the poor little thing – on the forehead! – and Kay said, "How can you do that?" At first I thought she meant that the child was too ill to be handled but then she added, "How can you bear to kiss it – it's so ugly. I'll never be able to do that."'

'Kay said that? Why didn't you tell me?'

'How could I?'

313

'But she worked so hard on the child, took her to doctors the world.over trying to—'

'Trying to make her look perfect. Oh, I know the first fight was to keep her alive, but all along Kay was talking as much about plastic surgeons to reshape her face—'

'But of course! These things matter in this life. They shouldn't but they do! You know that—'

'Did she ever kiss her? Did she ever show her any real physical affection when she was dragging her all over the world trying to get her rebuilt? Did she?'

'I don't know,' sighed Leo. 'I honestly don't know. I wasn't there enough—'

'There you go, making it all your fault again, all your responsibility,' said Annaliese.

'It *was* my responsibility,' said Leo, and before Annaliese could contradict him, he sat down on the edge of the dressing-table and placed his hands on her shoulders. 'Why did everyone wring their hands to me about beautiful Kay, wonderful Kay, poor martyred Kay?'

'Well, you just said it in a way – beautiful Kay. Any criticism by another woman is always taken as jealousy when someone is that lovely. And as for you, Leo, well, it's difficult to tell you anything. And it was impossible as most of us were scared of you.'

'Scared of me?'

'You were terrifying in your guilt – a guilt out of all proportion to what had happened, it seemed to me. It was safer to stay out of your way, or make things seem purer, more black and white than they were.'

'But look at the terrible cards Kay has been dealt – Antoinetta, the cancer—'

'I know, I know, but my belief is that the cancer was a lesson—'

'I hate that kind of talk! What kind of a lesson is a mutilated body? And for what? For not being up to loving an impossibly damaged child? Oh no, Annaliese, I can't live with Kay any more but I'm still on her side. What kind of a lesson did she more than anybody else have to learn?'

314

'To look beyond the surface of things. To value something other than beauty. I'm not saying she deserved to suffer any more than anybody else, Leo, but she might have suffered less if she had—'

'Don't say any more. We can never agree on this and I don't want to fight with you now.'

'All right,' sighed Annaliese and stood up to leave. She had opened the door and was about to step into the corridor when Leo came up behind her and took her in his arms.

'No, no. We mustn't part angry.' Again Annaliese found herself being squeezed too tight against his chest. She pulled away from him and kissed him on the cheek.

'I'm not angry, Leo – I really have to get going.'

'Not yet. Not yet. There is something else I must tell you. I've got no-one else in the world I can talk to. Isn't that strange? Isn't it wrong to be forty-eight years old and so isolated?'

'I think it comes with the job,' said Annaliese. She waited for Leo to speak but again he turned to the window and stared out. As he turned his back, Annaliese consulted her watch. In less than an hour the doctor would arrive at the apartment to examine Clara's ankle. Fritz was not free and had asked her to be present. She waited in silence while Leo sought his words.

'I love a woman, Annaliese. I am forty-eight years old and I am in love.' He walked back to the dressing-table and leaned on it, frowning as he glimpsed his face in the mirror. 'I think it's the most important thing that has ever happened to me. I thought that getting this part would be. I thought that nothing could ever matter more than my career, that nothing should matter, but this has swept them all away. And I want to come to it new and fresh but I can't because as the years go by we carry more and more of our past around with us.'

'We are our past,' said Annaliese.

'But not just our past! We have to be more than that.

We have to have some hope of renewal, rebirth, of another chance. After all, here we are in the opera house, Annaliese. What do we do here? We sing about love! Whole orchestras, choruses, producers, designers, stage-hands, scene-painters come together to convey the experience of love. Now I actually love a woman. Is that not more important?'

'Nobody said it wasn't,' smiled Annaliese.

'I know, I know – it's just that I can't believe I have the right to this.'

'Well, you must do because it has happened,' said Annaliese. 'Tell me about her.'

'I can't. I'm too superstitious. If I say her face is beautiful, and it is, then I'm suddenly convinced I'll never see it again. If I say that she is intelligent then I think that she'll have the wit to leave me and find herself someone more deserving, less complicated. You see, I don't know how to do this kind of thing any more, Annaliese. People like me, people like *us*, are so used to being automatically accepted with no effort that we stop knowing how to approach someone else. Almost every night of my life someone is hovering at a stage door or in a dressing-room waiting to tell me how much they admire me. And you, they do it for you too.'

'Not that much,' smiled Annaliese. 'Thank God. Never that much,' she murmured.

'But you do know what I mean. We are accepted without having to earn acceptance. We stop using that part of us that has to try to reach out to another human being. I certainly don't seem to know any more. She told me as much herself.'

'Oh really?'

'Oh, she said that I go in for too many big operatic gestures,' said Leo with a sweep of his hand. 'That I scare her, overwhelm her or something of the sort—'

'There are far worse offences,' laughed Annaliese. 'Look, why don't you bring her to our Christmas Eve dinner. That way I'll see her for myself. Is she here with you?'

'Of course not. That would be sordid at this point. She's in Füssen.'

'Then she's a Bavarian?'

'No, she's half-Spanish and half-English. A mixture of north and south like me, you see. She's driving a couple of elderly friends around Europe on a tour—'

'Füssen's not far. Bring her. Bring her, Leo. I'll tell Fritz, if that's all right?'

'Of course.'

Annaliese tried to consult her watch without being noticed. 'Look, Leo, I must go—'

'Oh, why? I was going to take you for coffee and a cake.'

'I'll have far more cake than I need over the holidays and I really must go, Leo. It's absurd but we have an unexpected house guest that Fritz wants to see on her way before the holidays start. And I must attend to that now.' She took Leo in her arms. '*I* think you deserve this, Leo. You are my most beloved colleague, you know. There's no-one I'd rather have for my father.'

The doctor was already with Clara when Annaliese arrived at the apartment.

'Almost done,' he said, as she entered the guest-bedroom. 'I think we will have this young lady home for an English Christmas.'

'Have you ever experienced an English Christmas?'

'Better weather than here,' said the doctor, closing up his bag. 'Annaliese, perhaps I can have a few minutes of your time outside?'

Once they were in the entrance hall with the door to the guest-room closed behind them, the doctor raised his eyebrows and whispered, 'She could have left right after the injury, really. All it needed was a little effort with her crutches but she claims she can't get on with them.'

'Well, perhaps she can't but how about now? Can she travel now with her ankle still in plaster?'

'Of course. The airlines have procedures to deal with

317

that sort of thing. She can ask for a wheelchair at each end—'

'But what about afterwards – what will she do afterwards?'

'That's not my domain, Annaliese dear. She must have friends or family. All I can do is reassure Fritz that she can go home before Christmas. Isn't that what he wanted?'

'I suppose it's what we both wanted but it doesn't seem to be in the spirit of Christmas to bundle her off if she's going to be alone,' sighed Annaliese.

'Oh, I wouldn't lose any sleep about that one,' said the doctor.

Clara was lying back down on the sofa by the window when Annaliese returned to her room.

'Isn't that good news?' The soprano addressed her in slow deliberate English. 'And I've contacted Lufthansa. They really are very organized – apparently they tell the computer that you need a wheelchair and the message goes to London and the flight crew, and you'll be taken care of all the way.'

Clara said nothing.

'And I'm sure you'll be glad to get home for Christmas. It is a time to be with family after all.'

'Haven't got any family,' said Clara.

'Friends then,' said Annaliese.

'Fritz has got a lot of friends, hasn't he?' said Clara. She had propped herself up on the palms of her hands and was turning very slowly to face Annaliese.

'Why yes, of course he has. He doesn't see them as much as he'd like but—'

'He sees them more than you think,' smiled Clara.

'I'm sorry. I don't quite see what you—'

'He's got one very good friend in London. I think he saw an awful lot of her—'

'Oh, he's got more than one friend in London,' said Annaliese with a little laugh. She had turned away from Clara's gaze and was rearranging some figurines on top of the chest of drawers. 'They say the English are reserved but in fact we've got so many friends there

318

that we don't have time to see them all when we go.'

'Oh, that must be why he took this friend to the Cotswolds for the weekend – so that he'd have time to see her.'

'And, of course, Fritz has a lot of business acquaintances too,' said Annaliese. 'They take up more time than we'd like. Young players wanting auditions and singers too. My husband has to audition any number of young, hopeful sopranos.'

'In Country House hotels in the Cotswolds?'

'My husband has to audition any number of young, hopeful sopranos,' repeated Annaliese. She turned her attention to an advent calendar that she herself had sent to Clara's room a week earlier. 'You haven't been opening your windows, Clara,' she said, fumbling with the cardboard flaps. Images of a family sitting at a table and a baker surrounded by cakes appeared before her.

'I hate fresh air,' sighed Clara and lay back on the sofa.

'No, no, I meant the windows on the calendar.'

'I'm not religious.'

'But it's fun anyway – it's like going back to childhood.'

'I had a miserable childhood. Why would I want to go back there?'

Annaliese didn't reply. She seemed to be absorbed in prizing open the cardboard flaps.

'There!' she said as she opened the second to last window and turned to hand it to Clara.

'I owe you an apology,' said Clara as Annaliese slipped the calendar between her fingers.

'What for?'

'You know what for. I've behaved appallingly. I do these things and I can see myself doing them and I can't seem to stop. And then the damage is done and people kick me out of their lives. I'm always being thrown out, you know. I get thrown out of dressing-rooms and hotels – even my cat moved out on me.'

'Have you got anyone to go back to in England?'

'No-one.'

'How did you get yourself into such a state, my poor girl? We all need friends. Can't you join a church or a club or something? What about a dating agency? I hear they are quite acceptable now. You might meet a nice man.'

'Brünnhilde suggests I join a dating agency,' sniffed Clara and started to cry.

'I left Brünnhilde behind in the dressing-room,' said Annaliese and patted her hand. 'You mustn't mix the two worlds up, you know. You can't live up on Wagnerian summits all the time. Not when there's the gas bill to be paid and the kitchen sink is blocked up.'

'When my kitchen sink got blocked up I just gave up using it,' sobbed Clara.

'Oh my dear, you are in a mess.' Annaliese paused, went to the door, looked out into the passage and closed it behind her. 'Look, you can stay here until the holiday is over – it seems unChristian to send you back to all that – but you must promise me that afterwards you'll go home and put your life in order. At least call in a plumber.'

'All right,' said Clara. 'But what will you tell the maestro?'

'I'll tell him that the doctor said to hold off travelling for a couple more days. You can stay until the twenty-sixth – then Fritz's sons will be arriving, I'm afraid, so the place will be a madhouse anyway. You'll be glad to get back to London.'

'Won't I be in the way over Christmas?'

'Well . . . I'm afraid we won't be able to entertain you – not tomorrow at least. Fritz has some business acquaintances coming over for dinner – all very boring stuff—'

'Oh, but I love that kind of talk. I wouldn't be bored.'

'I can't invite you, Clara. It's out of the question but look, I'll bring you up some of the dinner and keep you company for a while. *I* find opera house politics a little tedious even if you don't. We'll talk about what you can do to liven up your social life back in London, get you back into ordinary living. It's not that bad – you'll see.'

And with an embarrassed wave Annaliese left the room, closing the door gently behind her.

'I hate ordinary living,' said Clara, glaring at the baker and the family that gazed at her from the windows of the advent calendar. She threw it across the room.

Chapter Thirty-Five

'You're in Munich, Leo?' Rose had picked up the phone at the reception desk.

'Why yes – I'm rehearsing *Walküre*.'

'You're Wotan? That's what you were being all mysterious about.'

'Superstitious. I was being superstitious. I know I said I'd call yesterday but I was busy moving between Milan and here. Will you come to a Christmas dinner party tomorrow?'

'Whose party is it?'

'The maestro and his wife are having a few people in. Most of them musicians who got stranded by the snow and the Christmas holidays.'

Rose pulled the phone to the end of the desk and sat down in a leather armchair.

'I'm intimidated, Leo.'

'They're only people.'

'Wagnerian people. Will they all be standing around in helmets with horns as they sip on their cocktails?'

'I'll suggest it to Annaliese.'

'Who is Annaliese?'

'The maestro's wife. She's singing Brünnhilde. You may have seen her in London. I think she just did an Isolde—'

'I remember a photo of her. She looked kind.'

'She is. I told her about you, Rose, and she wants to meet you.'

'Will they talk shop? I'm quite opera-ignorant, you know. The Ring has always meant horns, helmets and Hitler to me. The *Walküre* is a lot of hooting women in breastplates.'

'That's because you've never seen it. I know the Ride

has become a cliché but the rest of the work contains some of the most sublime music ever written—'

'But so much of it! Otto says more books have been written about Wagner than anyone else in history apart from Christ and Shakespeare—'

'That one varies from country to country. In France they say Christ and Napoleon. I'll tell you what *Walküre* is, Rose – it's a farewell. A farewell to being a god – a farewell from a father to a daughter – a farewell to the loveless world of the gods and their invulner-ability and the beginning of—' Leo stopped himself in mid-sentence. 'Why am I going on about that? They won't talk that kind of shop. They might talk opera house politics, subsidies, who will get what post – if they do that, we can talk to each other. You will come?'

'Yes.'

When Rose put the phone down she saw that Eva was standing a few feet away at the reception desk.

'What did he want?' Eva nodded towards the phone again.

'To take me to a dinner tomorrow evening with some friends in Munich.'

'Well now, there's a turn-up for the books. I'm afraid my little gift is going to look a bit tame if you're running around with people like that.'

'Can I open it anyway?' Rose started to tear open the envelope. Inside was a ticket to *Die Walküre* at the Bavarian State Opera. A ticket to a farewell, thought Rose. She studied it for a long time. Eva had unwit-tingly brought back the myth that was Leo and placed it in her hands. She felt dark and plain and diminished. Had Eva intended to do that? But how could she have known that Leo would call? Rose looked up to thank her but Eva was gone.

Neither Eva nor Otto were anywhere to be found when Rose went downstairs to meet Leo the next evening.

'You're wearing your wedding dress,' said Leo as they stood in the elevator up to Fritz and Annaliese's apartment.

'It's all I've got,' said Rose. 'And you're wearing your new coat.'

'It's all I've got. The dress is beautiful – and I like it better dry.'

Less than fifty yards away, Clara was wrapping the gifts that she intended to distribute at the dinner party. They had been delivered the previous afternoon when Fritz and Annaliese had both been at the theatre. Clara had chosen a Hermès scarf for Annaliese whom she considered a hopeless frump, and a bottle of the rarest and finest Bordeaux for Fritz. Her gift for Leo had not come from the department store. She had carried that gift with her throughout this latest European journey and, with the jealous rage of Milan as far behind her as the city itself, she could now think of nothing but Leo's face when he saw what she had found. She wrapped the first two gifts with care, matching satin ribbons with coloured foil and scowling at scissors and Scotch tape as she struggled to put bows and labels in the right place.

Then she took Leo's gift from the bottom of her suitcase. It was a framed letter from Wagner to Liszt, written at the time of the composition of *Die Walküre*. The letter had belonged to her father. It had been passed on to the stepmother in Hampshire who had locked it in a safe. Clara had found the combination and removed it. Now she wrapped it, not in mass-produced foil and ribbons, but in silk. She intended to point out to Leo that since Wagner liked to wrap himself in the finest silk, it was only natural that his words should be similarly attired.

'I'm terrified,' said Rose and led Leo towards the emergency stairwell. He sat down on the stone step and pulled her down next to him.

'They are only people. You can talk to Fritz about homoeopathic cures for arthritis. That's one of his favourite topics. He's got arthritic knees and is terrified that it will spread to his upper body. He always gravitates towards people who talk with conviction about cures – I once saw him entranced by some

324

beautiful Indian woman who told him to piss on his knees. The infatuation wore off when he realized that it would be a more complicated undertaking to piss on his own shoulder-blades. As for Dieter, he is an old wiry German who has worked with some of the most legendary performers the musical world has ever known. He knew Richard Strauss! Toscanini! He'll talk to you about all of them as if he were reading a menu in a Chinese restaurant, but when it comes to money, grants, patronage, etc., his eyes light up with such passion – as if he were talking about the woman he loved.' Leo had been holding Rose's hand. Now he slipped his other arm underneath her and took her onto his knees. He wrapped both arms tight around her and rocked her back and forth in the cold, concrete stairwell.

'Nobody has done this to me since I was a child,' said Rose. 'Then it was my father—'

'Your Spanish father? Tell me about him.'

The door to the stairwell was being pushed open. Annaliese's homely face appeared. She had plaited her greying, blonde hair and woven pearls through the braids. Rose stared at them, trying to remember why they should seem so familiar and at the same time such a remote memory. She was so intent on the hair that she hadn't noticed that Annaliese was blushing. She started to greet Leo in German, glanced at Rose and changed to slow, careful English.

'I thought I hear voices – I know your voice anywhere, Leo, but why do you sit here in the cold? And this must be Rose.' Annaliese advanced towards them, her hand outstretched in greeting. Rose had to untangle her arms from Leo's embrace. She stood up to greet the German woman who shook her hand firmly and stared so intently into her face that Rose found herself backing into Leo. Like him, Annaliese seemed to be seeking something in Rose. Again the feeling of inadequacy submerged her. Annaliese was holding the door open. She had just seconds to stop everything and back away from this world that so surely wasn't hers. But she followed Annaliese out into the corridor and through the doorway of her apartment.

And there it was Christmas. The festivity that Leo and Rose and Otto and Kay had tried to ignore filled that Munich apartment. As she crossed the threshold Rose was aware of Christmas trees in several rooms, a glass of champagne being thrust into her hand, candle-light, firelight, all around her warmth and colour. In that most freezing winter of her life, in a country and culture that held no attraction for her, she was suddenly enveloped in immense warmth. And she had finally come inside from the white. Here were red-and-gold oriental rugs, and red-and-gold flames. Here the chandeliers shone yellow and the candles ivory. And in the entrance hall and in the dining-room next to the fireplace were the first green trees she'd seen in months. She just had time to glance at their loving and careful decoration, wonder who did it and guess correctly that it was Annaliese, when she felt Leo's hand on her shoulder. The handsome blond man who had handed her the champagne was leaning forward to kiss her cheek. She liked the smell of his cologne and his distinguished face. He too was looking hard at her but with the champagne inside her, she felt more confident and almost said to him: Whatever you are seeking in my face, you will find; I am equal to anything you ask of me because I love him.

And once those words were said, if only within herself, all feelings of inadequacy fell away. She could look at the distinguished maestro, for he it was, and his celebrated wife and the wiry old intendant and know that they belonged to Leo's external universe, to all that was tangible, to all that could move ahead and change – and fade away. But 'I love him' belonged to a silent, internal world – invisible and absolute.

'Leo tells me you are half-Spanish,' Fritz was saying. 'I hope that doesn't mean that you have kept their strange custom of eating at half-past midnight—'

'Not at all,' said Rose. 'I was brought up in England by an English mother.'

'Good, good,' said Fritz. 'Because unlike most people in my business I like to eat early. We'll be sitting down in a few minutes once the candles on the table are lit.' He turned to Leo, took his arm and whispered to them both, 'My wife is religious. I believe in nothing. But on this evening I always indulge her desire for candle-lighting and silent prayer. Are you religious, Rose? Catholic, I suppose?'

'My Spanish father was an atheist,' said Rose. 'And a month ago I would have said that I was too. Now I don't know what I think—'

'And what has brought about this change? I envy people who can experience such transformations beyond the imbecile credulity of youth—'

Before Rose could reply, the lights in the dining-room went out. Then one candle was lit and Anna-liese's face appeared in the oval of light above it. She said something in German and, in the half-lit room, Rose discerned a sudden bowing of heads and folding of hands. Leo was no longer at her side. He was standing near the door that led to the corridor. He had been frozen into position there when Annaliese's head had appeared above the single candle. Leo was familiar with this Christmas ritual but had never been comfortable with it. In the past he had slipped from the room and waited in the corridor during Annaliese's minute of prayer but the proximity of Rose had made him linger. He was stranded now in the dark by the door. He tried not to listen to Annaliese's words. They reminded him too much of his Protestant mother. She would never have approved of his escape into this love with Rose. And he too started to pray for the first time since adolescence, coming straight to the point in his prayer to a God in whom he did not believe. He prayed that Kay had accepted his offer of a ticket to her homeland and that jet-streams had carried her far from the frigid villa and the frozen lake and out into such warmth as he now knew.

Into the silence that followed both their prayers, came a distant tapping. Leo's keen ears traced it to the corridor beyond the dining-room. It was coming closer. He opened the door no more than an inch so that he could look out and not let the light into the warm, dark room.

He saw Clara immediately. She had donned a long black velvet dress for the occasion and this, combined with the crutches and the bag of gifts that she pushed along in front of her, hampered her progress along the corridor. Leo shut the door tight and walked over to Fritz.

'What the fuck is Clara doing here?' The guests were rushing to fill the uncomfortable silence after the prayer with small talk. Leo could push Fritz towards the kitchen and shut the door behind them without attracting anyone's attention but Rose's.

'She broke her ankle and Annaliese took pity on her. I was trying to tell you about it the other day – wait a minute – how do you know she's here? She's confined to the guest-room.'

'She's on her way up the corridor. I just saw her. Damn your wife's good heart, Fritz. I can't stay here.'

'I'll deal with her. I made it clear to Annaliese that she would have no part in the Christmas celebrations. I know what she's like.'

'Not well enough,' sighed Leo. 'Otherwise you'd have put bars on the guest-room. I can't stay, Fritz. You can make my excuses to Annaliese but I won't have Rose exposed to Clara.' He pointed to the kitchen door. 'Can we go out through here?'

'You're behaving like someone out of a thirties film, Leo. You can't go making a dramatic exit down the fire-escape. Anyone would think you were afraid of the silly tart.'

Rose put her head around the door.

'Come on in, Rose.' Leo went to the door and pulled her into the kitchen. 'I'm not afraid of her, Fritz, but she's a bad omen.' He turned to Rose. 'We've got to leave here. I'll explain later—' The maid came into the kitchen carrying an empty tray. Leo grabbed her elbow. 'Would you bring us our coats, young lady?'

'This is absurd!' Fritz stepped forward to stop the young woman but Leo urged her through the door. 'I'll send her back to her room. This is my house and she will do as I say.'

Leo opened the door a chink. He nodded in the direction of the far side of the dining-room. 'She's giving a gift to Dieter. He looks delighted with it. Now tell me that you're going to go in there and kick her out. A woman on crutches!'

The maid had returned with the coats. Fritz watched in silence as Leo wrapped Rose's coat around her shoulders. Then the conductor walked to a drawer and took out a set of keys.

'If you must go, go to the hunting-lodge. We had it set up in case we could get away – it's heated and the fridge is full.' He pressed the keys into Leo's hand. 'I'm sorry, Leo. I imagined myself to be more in control of my household than I am.' He turned to Rose and kissed her on each cheek. 'You look as baffled as I, young lady. But it is impossible to oppose Leo when he has an idea. Have you learned that yet? Will you able to stand it?' With a wave of his hand he dismissed the question. 'No, no, don't answer that. Go with him. Hurry – hurry before Annaliese comes back. I'll explain to her.' He put his right hand on her shoulder. 'The fire-escape will lead out into the courtyard. Goodbye. I was glad to meet you, Rose,' and before she could reply, Rose felt the door closing behind her as she was ejected from the warm, festive apartment back out into the freezing air.

'That was nice while it lasted,' she started to say but Leo was hustling her down the steps.

'I'll explain when we're in the car,' he said. But when they were both seated in the car and driving through the empty Munich streets Leo said nothing.

'Where are we going?' said Rose. 'Perhaps you should take me back to the hotel in Füssen.'

'I don't want to do that,' said Leo, accelerating as they passed a signpost for the autobahn.

'What happened, Leo? After all the persuading you

329

did to get me in there, why did you suddenly drag me back out? Did I do something or say something?'

'Of course not.'

'Then what? What happened? And where are we going now? I agreed to go with you to a dinner party. And to return to my hotel afterwards. Now you and Fritz are passing keys around in some sort of male conspiracy and muttering about hunting-lodges being heated and ready. Ready for what?'

'I'll explain when we get there.'

'No, Leo, that's not fair. I won't spend the night with you because the boys have arranged it behind my back.'

Leo turned the car into a side-street and switched off the ignition.

'If you want to go back to Füssen I'll take you, Rose,' he said, staring ahead at a Lufthansa sign flashing yellow and blue above a darkened office block.

'Just like that, without another word of explanation? And then what?'

Leo shrugged. 'And then perhaps it would be better for you to get on with your life back in England.'

'I don't believe I'm hearing this. You want to take me home and drop me? What has happened, Leo? What did I do?'

'Nothing, you did nothing.'

Rose sat in silence watching the snow falling. Only after a few long minutes had elapsed did she realize that she was breathing in small tight gasps and that her chest had locked tight.

'I want you to come to the lodge with me,' said Leo. Still he grasped the steering wheel, still he gazed at the airline sign. Rose longed for him to reach out and touch her or look at her but he sat, motionless, staring ahead.

'This isn't you, Leo. That's what I don't understand. You know you don't need to set up some sordid bargain to make me sleep with you—'

Leo roared with laughter. He released the steering wheel and before Rose realized what he was doing had

330

pulled her onto his knees for the second time that evening. Now the steering wheel dug into her aching ribs as he rocked her.

'My poor Rose! Oh, we haven't understood each other at all. I'm taking you to the lodge to talk to you! Remember, you're the interpreter – people tell you things and you understand them. I have so many things I have told no-one that I want to tell you. If I just wanted to sleep with you I wouldn't bother driving miles through the night. I'd take you back to my suite at the Four Seasons.'

'Why don't we go there to talk?'

'Because the lodge is miles from everything. There's no chance of bumping into a producer in the elevator or seeing a critic in the bar. The lodge has enough bedrooms for you to sleep fifty yards down the corridor and wake up on your own and look out at the pines. Or you can go back to Füssen and forget any of this ever happened.'

'Those are my only choices?'

Leo nodded.

'There is always something so desperate and urgent about you, Leo. And so all or nothing. Why not talk here? Why couldn't we stay with your charming friends in that lovely apartment? Why—'

'Because I'm afraid you might not like me very much when I've said what I have to say. But something happened tonight that made me realize that I have to tell you if we are to go any further . . .' He was still rocking her, more gently now, his hands stroking the back of her neck. From time to time he kissed her forehead. Then he stopped and looked past her to the Lufthansa sign.

'Oh, Rose, do you think we have infinite energy for such things as love? Or because I am almost fifty are my stocks worn down? Deteriorated?'

'Of course not. Life renews itself all the time if you'll let it.'

'Do you really believe that?'

'Yes,' said Rose, who had spoken without thinking.

Now she thought hard. 'Yes, yes I do.'

'But life can only renew itself if we are, how do you say, clean?'

'Clean?' Rose drew back and frowned her frown of professional concentration as she struggled to interpret just what Leo meant. 'Oh, you mean like in the expression "to wipe the slate clean" – to have a new start.'

'I think I meant what I said,' said Leo.

Chapter Thirty-Six

Although Rose thought that nobody had seen her climb into the Mercedes with Leo in Füssen, Otto had been watching from behind a Christmas tree in the hotel courtyard. When he saw them drive away, he picked up a small overnight bag that had been lying at his feet and made his way to the station. The timetable that he had collected in secret was carefully folded in his pocket. He had studied it for long hours in his hotel room. Otto had never before needed to read a railway schedule and he was terrified of making a mistake.

He didn't relax when he reached Munich's main station. There he was carried forward by the Christmas crowds. To Otto everybody else seemed so sure of where they were going; from time to time he imagined that he saw Eva's sturdy figure striding before him and would start to follow it, only to realize that he was making this journey on his own.

The crowd carried him to the platform where a train was waiting to board southbound passengers to Milan. He stood in a corridor for most of the long journey through the tunnels under the Alps. He changed trains in Milan, and travelled on to a small lakeside town called Varenna. There he carried his bag down to the jetty where he tried to board a ferry to carry him across the lake. But he had forgotten that it was Christmas Eve and that the last service had left hours earlier. He stood and stared across at the lights of inaccessible Bellagio until cold and hunger engulfed him. Then he booked into a two-star hotel by the jetty and ate a stale croissant which was the only food the bar had left.

In the morning he ordered a bottle of Chianti with his breakfast and told the baffled waiter to uncork it but to put the cork back in. He didn't drink any of the cheap wine, couldn't bring himself to even look at the bottle until he was back down at the ferry. Then his fear so overwhelmed him that he took a long swig straight from the straw bottle. When he saw the ticket-collector staring at him, he muttered something about Christmas spirit and took another swig as soon as the man was out of sight.

Once in Bellagio he had no idea where to go. He stood for a long time on the promenade, his hands hanging at his sides, his bag and Chianti bottle at his feet. He tried to think what Eva would do in his situation – or better still, Clara. But they both seemed so distant and so foreign; he could only think in terms of his own desires. He reached into his bag, took out his Mont Blanc pen and his autograph book. Wait in the shadows for a signature – that was all he felt himself capable of doing. It would not get him far today. He walked into the most exclusive hotel in the small lakeside town and sat down in the lounge. He took the old copy of *Architectural Review* from his bag and turned to the pages that featured Kay and her treasures. One very small photo showed a front view of the villa. The only solution was to ride around the tip of the headland until he found it. He would hire a taxi and tell the driver that he was an American. That would explain such lone, extravagant tourism on Christmas morning.

Inside the taxi, he bent down until his long chin was almost touching the floor and swigged some more wine. He was beginning to feel quite euphoric. The sun had come out and the snow was glistening and the lake was blue. He had the driver pause in front of the Casa Lillia where Liszt sojourned with Madame D'Agoult. Like John and Leo before him, he thought of Cosima Wagner. And he didn't think of Cosima as plain or obsessive. Wagner had loved her hair and at his death she had laid it in his coffin. Otto pondered this image while the cab-driver smoked a cigarette and looked at his watch.

Then the cab drove along the headland and Otto saw Kay's villa immediately. He stuffed a wad of notes into the driver's palm, drew himself up, said, '*Famiglia americana per natale,*' pointing to himself and headed towards the wrought-iron gate. It was locked.

He looked around for a bell. Instead he saw a camera perched alongside the top of the gate. Its glass eye was gazing down at him. Otto shrank from its view and walked further along the stone wall until he came to one of the privet hens. The weight of the snow had led its lower branches to sag. Otto was about to jump up and use them to lever himself onto the wall when he heard a car on the road behind him. It stopped outside the gate and Otto gasped out loud when he saw Kay step out of it. She was carrying a large flat package, wrapped in gold foil. He ducked behind the bush keeping Kay just in view so that he could gaze at her while he decided what to say. But he was so entranced by the sight of the blonde woman that he could not push his mind into action. Before he knew it his feet were carrying him forward. Kay was wearing high heels and obviously did not intend to linger any longer than it took to open the gate and walk up the driveway. A glance at the frozen approach to the house explained her reluctance to drive the last few yards. Otto felt a sudden pity for this woman, struggling with the elements while her husband drove around Bavaria with Rose. Rose! Leo should be here shovelling the driveway, thought Otto, then remembered the dangers of draughts and colds for a singer and changed his mind. He felt his own hands reaching for the autograph book. He lurched towards the car.

Kay didn't see or hear him. She was about to put the package down and open the wrought-iron gate when he came at her from around the frozen privet and shoved the autograph book and pen under her nose.

The package fell to the ground and shattered.

'What the—'

'Oh my God, it broke, didn't it?' said Otto, staring down at the package. 'What was it?'

'A mirror,' said Kay.

'Oh no – oh my God, a broken mirror!'

'Who the hell are you?' She stared up at him. She was as blonde and as flawless as ever. Otto had sung just one duet with her in a summer concert twenty-six years earlier but he remembered every square inch of that beautiful face.

'I'm – I'm so sorry about the mirror,' said Otto, unable to say who he was, not even sure at the moment what his identity could be in relation to this woman. I'm a singer – we studied together. But he wasn't a singer. If there was one thing he was now sure he wasn't, it was a singer. And so he just said, 'I'm sorry.'

'It doesn't matter – at least not in the way you mean – I'm not superstitious,' said Kay.

'But I am!' said Otto. Sorry and superstitious – he was gradually building an identity for himself. He bent down on the ground and tried to gather up the shattered pieces from within the foil wrapper. 'Seven years of bad luck,' he sighed.

'Don't talk rubbish,' said Kay. 'That kind of dumb superstition is for theatrical folk. Who are you?'

'Don't you remember me?'

'Should I?'

'Siena – twenty-six years ago. We did the duet from Act One of *Lucia* in a summer concert in the town hall.'

'I sang in a lot of concerts,' said Kay.

'But it was a duet – we rehearsed together for two weeks that summer. We used to all go to dinner in a trattoria behind the piazza.'

Otto had sat back on his haunches alongside the shattered package on the snow. Kay stared down at the pale blond man. Twenty-six years had not left their trace on his long, mournful face. Had he not told her of their previous encounter she would have assumed that he was yet another music student come to look for a part-time job.

'I must have eaten in every trattoria in Siena,' she said. 'I'm sorry I don't remember you.'

'I suppose I couldn't expect you to,' said Otto, rising to his feet in one agile movement.

'Are you on holiday around here? I mean, was there something specific that you dropped by for?'

Otto stared at her. The direct question almost shocked him into a direct response but he couldn't form a sentence that would say that he had come to try to live in the real world, that he had travelled alone on trains, boats and taxis to try to break out of the shell of his failure and of the other protective shell that Eva had built to cushion him from facing his own inadequacy. He knew but could not say that he wanted to reach past the operatic characters, the dead composers, the intangible beauty of music and touch female flesh. Kay's image had come to him from that time when he still had faith in the future and in his own abilities. And, without giving his action any conscious thought, it was towards that image that he had automatically returned.

'Is there a specific reason for your visit?' Kay repeated.

'I – I came to wish you a Merry Christmas,' said Otto.

'Well thank you, and a Merry Christmas to you,' said Kay, turning to walk away.

'But the mirror,' said Otto.

'It doesn't matter,' said Kay. 'I was given it as a Christmas present by an antique dealer down in Como but I didn't like it. That frame is very vulgar, don't you agree?'

'I wouldn't know,' said Otto. 'I never know things like that.'

'But look! It's a cheap paint job.' She extended a long nail and scratched the gold away. 'You've done me a favour by smashing it.'

'Oh no – I don't think so. What about the poor person who gave it to you? What will they say?'

'They should have had better taste,' laughed Kay. When Otto didn't laugh she added, 'Anyway, they gave me two glasses of champagne when I dropped in there this morning so I was probably a little tipsy. Let's blame the champagne for the broken glass, shall we?'

'I can't drink champagne,' sighed Otto, remembering that he had left the Chianti bottle behind the privet. 'It sends me to sleep.' He stood between Kay and the wrought-iron gate. He was unable to move.

'I suppose you'd better come inside and have some coffee before you go on your way,' sighed Kay.

'And we can talk about the old days in Siena,' said Otto, following her up the slippery path to the front door.

'Let's not,' said Kay and added, 'You must have noticed how bad my memory is.'

'Oh,' said Otto, wondering just what he could contribute to any other topic.

Kay was fumbling with the key to the front door. When she did open it, she stepped inside and waited for Otto to utter the cry of pleasure that issued from all visitors upon first glimpsing the entrance hall. But he walked straight in with hardly a glance at the bold sweep of the staircase or the rare Persian rug that bore their feet towards the kitchen.

'I've followed every episode in your life since you gave up singing,' he said. 'I buy all the Italian magazines – I even have a whole colour spread on you in *Architectural Review*. That's how I found the house.'

'Now that was a good article,' said Kay. 'Though I did think the colours were a bit pallid on some of the interior shots.'

'Oh, I wouldn't know that,' said Otto.

'Of course you wouldn't if you've never seen the real thing.'

'I wouldn't know even if I had. I was surprised they didn't put a photo of you along with it – they usually do.'

'I didn't want them to. The house was the whole point of the article. How would you like your coffee?'

'Anyhow. I mean, however you think.' Otto came to stand alongside Kay while she filled the percolator. 'I know why you gave up singing, and I do understand.

At least I think I do even though I've never had a child—'

'I don't want to talk about that,' said Kay, holding up a hand in warning.

'Oh, I wasn't going to. I was going to ask you if you still sing ever? For your own pleasure?'

'Never,' said Kay.

'Neither do I,' said Otto.

'Well, why on earth would you?'

'Well, just because I didn't pursue a professional career—'

'A professional career? Oh, that's right, you sang too. I'd forgotten already – it must be the champagne.'

Otto stepped back from Kay and scowled at her. He was listening to the silence and thinking of his own slightly shabby house full of song and invisible orchestras back in London.

'I suppose the fact that we both gave up singing links us in a way,' he said.

'Oh, I don't think so,' said Kay. 'If it did we would be linked to hundreds of failures from *conservatoires* the world over.' She looked up from the percolator but not at Otto. She was staring out at the lake which was shining saucer-blue for the first time in months. She forgot Otto until the percolator bubbled, and she filled his coffee-cup and turned to give it to him. He had gone to sit at the kitchen table. He had unwittingly chosen Leo's seat. When she set the coffee-cup down in front of him, she saw that he had taken out a handkerchief and was wiping his eyes.

'Why, what is the matter?'

'Oh, don't take any notice of me,' he said. 'It's the cheap Chianti I drank to get the courage to come over here. And it's being called a failure. Nobody wants to hear that, you know, especially not on Christmas morning. I failed and you gave up. I would have given the earth to have what you had—'

'What I had? How can you know what I had? What do you know about my life?'

'I told you I read all the Italian magazines. I

subscribe to magazines about music from five European countries—'

'And that gives you the right to talk to me about my private life?'

'Probably not. My sister says I always say the wrong things anyway, but she's not here. And I mean it. I would have given the earth to have what you had. Not the dead child – of course that's terrible, dreadful, but wouldn't music have helped to heal it? Beethoven thought so. He once played all afternoon for a woman who had lost her child. Perhaps it helped. And as for the breasts, so you've got one less than most women – but you survived – you're alive – it didn't hurt your voice—'

'How dare you!' Kay could not move from where she stood in front of Leo's seat at the table. 'Stop it!' she cried. 'Stop it!'

'I can't. Once I get going I can't stop. And I've been thinking about all this for years, and travelled on the train all night without telling Eva. You see, I think you're the loveliest woman I ever saw and I don't see how your scar can detract from that – not one flaw. I'm flawed but you can't see my flaw. I'm stuck with this little-boy face that looks as though I don't shave, and my flaw is hidden in here.' He pointed to his throat. Then to Kay's amazement he started singing. He sang the male part in the duo from *Lucia* – only a few phrases. She was glad when he stopped. His voice was shaky and reedy. Most of the notes were wrong. When he stopped he was blushing. Kay poured herself a whisky and drank it down in one gulp. She poured herself another.

'Can I see your scar?' said Otto.

'What did you say?'

'Can I see your scar?' He was looking right into her eyes. If she did not make the physical effort to turn away she realized that his eyes would not leave hers. She stood clutching the whisky glass, mesmerized by those blue eyes. 'You were always so perfect you were terrifying.' He gazed up at her, lifting one hand towards her waist and on upwards. Kay breathed in and held the breath. The long hand that extended towards her was beautiful; slender and white it hung suspended in the warm air that filled the kitchen. 'And I could never cope with sex,' she heard his voice in the warmth somewhere below her, could still feel herself fixed in the blue of his eyes. 'Was always intimidated by bodily bits and the like so I don't see a woman's body the way some men do.' The beautiful white hand was just inches from her lower belly. Kay parted her legs slightly as his hand hovered in the air less than an inch from her flesh. 'And yet I think I feel desire. Please let me look at you.'

'Why?' Kay closed her eyes to shut out the hypnotic regard.

'You'll see,' said Otto and the confidence in his voice forced Kay to open her eyes and look down at him. 'You'll see,' he said again, and the slender fingers reached for the button on her blouse. Kay stepped back in one last hesitant attempt to resist. She leaned against the kitchen wall, never once taking her eyes off Otto's. She could feel the fingers releasing button after button. She watched like some remote spectator as her own white flesh was revealed. She wore no bra, and within seconds her chest was exposed to those blue eyes. He said nothing, just gazed at the smooth expanse of skin where the scar had long since faded.

'Such beautiful flesh,' he said, and suddenly the link with his blue eyes was broken and Kay saw nothing but his blond head as he bent forward and kissed the pale white patch of skin.

Kay shut her eyes, felt Otto's lips move to caress her one true breast and then return and brush the empty space again. She felt the warmth of his tongue, his hands resting on the top of her hips. She thought, as she so often did, of her beloved lake. But still Otto's blue eyes filled her vision. They are pieces of the lake, she thought to herself. He is a wonderful water creature who has swum into me.

Then she wanted him to leave. She almost said, 'Go

back to the lake,' and half expected him to slide silently across the floor and disappear into the water. She walked past him, out of the kitchen and through the library onto the deck. She intended to wait there until he disappeared. She was barefoot and the snow was starting to sting her feet. She turned away from the figure in the kitchen and stared out at the lake. She wanted the cleansing cold water so much that she soon forgot the solitary creature with the wonderful white fingers, and started to remove her clothes. Within seconds she was naked and diving into the freezing blue below – diving into the lake creature's eyes, she thought, but forgot him as soon as she plummeted below the surface and opened her own eyes and saw the familiar underwater world.

But when she came up for air the familiar sight of the mountain, the smooth lake and the empty deck were gone. A police boat was sailing towards her. They never came up this far, Kay knew. Nothing came up this far. She turned to swim towards the deck and saw that Otto was standing there watching her.

'Oh shit! Shit!' she cried to herself and dived back under. When she came back up the police boat had turned in a semi-circle and was sailing away, but Otto remained where he was.

'You shouldn't swim in this cold,' he cried.

'I'll swim when I want,' said Kay.

'You'll catch pneumonia,' said Otto.

Kay swam away from him, not once looking back, until he was just a speck on the deck. When she was sure that he would be gone, Kay climbed out of the lake, gathered up her clothes and walked inside.

'I suppose I must go.' Otto was sitting on the green baize seat that had once been a sedan-chair.

'Yes,' said Kay.

'Won't you be lonely here in this big empty house on Christmas Day?'

'Oh but I won't be here all day. I'm driving into Como for dinner with friends.'

'But I'd imagined—'

'Far better to imagine,' said Kay, and walked with Otto towards the door.

'No it's not,' sighed Otto. He reached out and took Kay's hand. In spite of her hurry to see him through her door, she did not resist his touch. 'Something has come to an end for ever,' he said. 'I couldn't say what, can't grasp it firmly enough in my mind to put it into words, but something has gone.'

'What a complicated creature you are,' said Kay, removing her hand. 'It's a good thing you didn't become a singer. They need to be much more straight-forward.'

'Do you think so? All of them? Even—'

'Perhaps not him,' said Kay. She opened the door.

Otto drew himself up, looked out at the stark white mountains and said, 'The fight must always be against bitterness.'

'I don't know what you mean,' said Kay, looking into the blue eyes and wondering again why this strange creature wasn't walking towards the lake. She had to make an effort to remember that he was a man – a man who had travelled to her from out of the past. But not the past that hung silent over her sumptuous house. That dark, resentful quarter-century had hidden this other brief hopeful time behind it. This man had come, not from the lake, but from that long-forgotten summer of song.

'Will you be all right on your journey back? Where do you have to go to?'

'Munich,' said Otto.

'So far!' said Kay. 'Just a minute.' And she dis-appeared into the kitchen. When she came back she was carrying a plastic bag. 'I've put some Christmas cake in there. Something to eat on the journey.' She shrugged and looked hard into those blue eyes won-dering just how old this solitary traveller was.

'Thank you,' said Otto. He turned to leave but Kay had taken one of his hands in hers. She raised it up to her lips and kissed it.

'Thank you,' she said.

When the door was closed behind him and Otto was halfway down the treacherous front path, he was suddenly overcome with a gnawing, animal hunger. He looked at his watch – he hadn't eaten anything more than a roll in twenty-four hours. He opened the bag. Inside was the Fortnum's Christmas pudding and brandy butter that Leo had brought from London. His first thought was: She must have known this is in an inedible state. She knew and is mocking me. But these were hurts and humiliations that belonged to an Otto who had ceased to exist when he had placed his lips on her smooth white flesh. He ripped open the packet of uncooked pudding and clawed at its surface until enough suet and raisins came away for him to eat.

Chapter Thirty-Seven

An hour out of Munich, Rose and Leo left the autobahn and took a narrow country road that led to the lodge. The road cut through a dense pine forest and had been cleared that morning but the trees were now heavy with newly falling snow that the Mercedes ploughed uphill, pitching piles of white up into the headlights and onto the high frozen verge. At the top of the first hill they reached a plateau where the forest ceased and the night fields stretched away, black behind miles of frozen barbed wire.

'I'm exhausted,' said Leo. 'My eyes can't focus. All of a sudden, something has collapsed inside me.'

'Do you want me to drive?' said Rose.

'Are you used to driving in such conditions?'

'That's all I've done for the past few weeks.'

'Of course. Then, yes please, drive or I'll have us over a precipice.' He stepped out of the car and walked round to the passenger door. Rose shifted over into the warmth of his place at the driver's seat. As soon as she drove away she became aware of the deep silence in the seat next to her and knew that Leo was sleeping.

Through the windscreen she could see from the angle of the frozen barbed wire that the hill continued to climb steeply. Rose ploughed on. At some point she must have rounded a bend or the wind changed for suddenly the fat white flakes were coming at the car full pelt. The wipers couldn't keep up with them. She tried to remember a time when the world was not white, when snow hadn't fallen every morning or evening, covering and blotting out any trace of human energy or activity. But Leo had been borne in on the snow. A freak snow had blown across that house in

London, carrying this man in its wake and burying her old life for ever. Still, she knew that one day the green would return, one day lilac would hang fragrant on branches brushed by warm air, and where would she and Leo be then? For now they had passed the barbed wire and were on flat ground, driving through more dense pine forest. Rose wanted to look at Leo. She wanted to stop the car in the midst of this terrifying frozen black forest and look at his face as he slept. Rose feared the dark and at any other time she would have pushed the car through the snow towards lights and life. But in this dark wood, Leo slept alongside her. She stopped at the side of the road and switched off the ignition.

Dark flooded into the car. Outside, the wind shrieked and goaded the blizzard forward. She moved towards the sound of Leo's deep, regular breathing. After a few seconds her eyes adjusted to the blackness and she could look and look at the weary middle-aged man who slept beside her. She looked at the few grey streaks in his beard, at the lines around his eyes that didn't go in repose, at the broad high forehead, the stern Roman nose and the thick neck. Never was a man's face looked upon with so much love, Rose was sure. Only as he slept could she look at him in this way. For fearful, cautious, thirty-nine-year-old Rose knew that no human being should ever see so much love on the face of another. She knew that in some more arid moment in the future to love so much must be used against her – even by Leo himself – most of all by Leo himself. With no fear of the dark she sat on in that Christmas blizzard and looked, as she feared she might never look again, at this man whom she now knew was the snow's gift to her. Again she wondered: Where do swans go in winter when the lakes freeze over? Where will I go when they thaw and the world grows green again? Where will I go after knowing this man?

She heard the car on the road at the very same moment that she saw the headlights. It stopped behind them and she knew that it was a police car. She had been about to lay her head very gingerly on Leo's shoulder. Now she withdrew and waited as the policemen walked towards her. At some point they had crossed a border. She no longer knew if they were in Germany or Austria. She didn't know if it was Christmas Eve or Christmas Day.

A smiling blond officer looked through the window and said something in German. As Rose fumbled to find the button that lowered the window she saw that his partner had looked past her and was staring at Leo. Unable to lower the glass barrier between them Rose shrugged and smiled. The second man had recognized Leo, Rose realized, and was telling the first man. Leo stirred, looked to Rose, and with a start saw the uniformed men behind her. He immediately found the button and lowered the window.

'Have you broken down?' said the first policeman.

'No, I was just too tired to drive on,' said Leo.

'Ah good, yes, good.' The second man's head was almost in the car. 'It is never a good idea to drive when you're tired, Herr Maestro – I mean, Maestro. Er . . . Hmmm . . . Would you mind?' He thrust a note-pad and pen towards Leo. 'You were a wonderful King Philip, Herr Leo. I've seen you six times—'

Leo was barely awake. Rose watched his unguarded, vulnerable face as he took the sodden note-pad and tried to write his name over the snowflakes.

'Will you be coming to *Die Walküre*?' he said as he handed the pad back to the man.

'I wouldn't miss it. I think you will be a great Wotan.'

'Why thank you. You're one of the first people to say that.' And Rose saw on Leo's face that smile of perfect faith and naïvety that she had glimpsed outside the hotel in Füssen.

'I think it is an honour for the German people to have a great Italian singer take on the Wagner repertoire,' said the stiff, shy policeman. And he gave a little salute. His colleague leaned into the car.

'Where are you headed, *mein Herr*?'

Leo named the hunting-lodge.

'Where the conductor lives!' said the second policeman.

'But there has been an avalanche up that way,' said his colleague.

'Are you sure it's on the road to the lodge?' said Leo.

'I couldn't be sure,' said the policeman. 'The last part of the journey up there is always difficult.' The policemen and Leo discussed the impossibility of alternative routes; Rose stared off into the night and sensed that the dream of the hunting-lodge had, like Ludwig's castle, faded away into the mist.

'Oh why are we wasting time talking!' Leo had raised his voice and was climbing out of the car. He motioned to Rose to move back into the passenger seat. 'If this thing doesn't get any worse and the avalanche is not on that road, I'm sure I can get through.' He sat in the driver's seat and turned on the ignition. Both policemen stared after the car as Leo thanked them and drove away. They ploughed on for another ten miles. It took them an hour.

'What was I thinking of when I went blasting off into the night like that?' said Leo, stopping the car in front of a farmhouse and reaching for the map. 'I don't even like driving. What did I imagine?'

'That you really were Wotan and could drive the blizzard away,' said Rose.

'But I left my spear in the dressing-room,' sighed Leo.

'So here we sit in the middle of nowhere. Do you know where we are, Leo?'

'Still twenty miles from the lodge. I think we'll have to give up on that idea unless you want to drive like this all night.'

'What time is it?'

'Just ten o'clock. Aren't you hungry?'

'Starving, but I don't seem destined to eat many meals with you—'

'There's a village just a mile from here. Shall we see if they have a guest-house?'

'Room at the inn?' said Rose.

The village consisted of nothing but a half-dozen houses, an onion-domed chapel with paintings of the crucifixion and the Gasthof Post.

'It's open,' said Leo. 'There's a light in the restaurant. Wait here and I'll ask about rooms.' He raised his collar up around his neck and pulled his hat down low over his forehead to keep the pelting snow from his face.

'You look like a gangster,' said Rose to his departing figure. 'I wouldn't let you into my guest-house.' She watched as he ran towards the door. As his figure disappeared inside, Rose studied the mural that enclosed the centre window above the door. Two hunters, Bavarian down to their feather caps and hunting-horns, drank a toast to each other from their posts on either side of the window.

Almost a hunting-lodge and miles from most worlds, thought Rose. And here while the hunters drink their endless toast, you will tell me something and I will perhaps cease to love you. It seemed a big responsibility to confer on this small, inviting Bavarian inn. She waited for Leo to reappear through the big wooden door and wondered if there was a way to say: Don't tell me. I don't need to know. For me you were born the day I met you. And then the Gasthof Post would become the place where on this Christmas night she would make love to Leo.

A chamois darted through the pines. It ventured out and stood in the teeming snow next to the onion-domed chapel. It gazed for a moment in the direction of the inn and then the door opened and Leo appeared and the wild creature darted back into the woods.

Leo walked slowly back to the car. Above his head she could make out the first two figures of a carved date: 16— As they had tried, and failed, to imagine kings and composers in Hohenschwangau, now she tried to imagine carriage wheels where the Mercedes tyres had passed. Had Wagner passed this way in a carriage? She would ask Leo and keep his mind and their conversation on the glorious, sensual music that he was about to sing. Leo had paused on the bottom step and was kicking layers of ice from his shoes. Rose recalled Otto's tales of Wagner. She remembered that the composer liked to travel first-class on trains even when he was penniless. But her mind couldn't fix on the dead distant figure and she found herself thinking of Otto himself and feeling sorry that she hadn't said goodbye to him. Of course, she hadn't known then that the evening would stretch and fill with sudden departures and avalanches, policemen, chamois and coaching inns.

'There's nothing but room – about a dozen of them. The only trouble is Wednesday is always their "*Ruhetag*".'

'Day off?'

'That's right. I've come across it before in Germany. Hotels will let you in on a *Ruhetag* but they won't feed you, and some, like this one, close up their reception area and make you take your keys. I had to get them out of their private quarters. I think they thought I was mad to be roaming around on Christmas Eve.'

'What about food? What shall we do?'

'Oh, I gave the woman some money and she is going to make up a couple of plates of cold cuts. Merry Christmas, Rose.'

When they walked into the entrance hall Rose saw that two polythene-wrapped plates lay alongside two keys.

'You booked two rooms?'

'Yes – alongside each other.'

'That was sweet. And I suppose this means that we are to take our Christmas dinner to eat upstairs and not disturb their "*Ruhe*".' She pulled back the polythene. 'Oh my, they really meant cold cuts, didn't they?' She examined the plate and saw that it contained thick spongy slices of tongue, fat-filled slices of Mortadella and a grey gristly sausage.

'I hate everything on that plate,' said Rose.

'It's the best I could do,' said Leo. 'Look, let me at least try to get you some bread and cheese.' And he disappeared down a corridor. When he came back he was carrying a bottle of wine along with a loaf of pumpernickel and a packet of cheese slices. He shrugged and led the way upstairs. The lights were on a timer and Leo, whose hands were full, had to pause at each bend and landing while Rose searched for the light switch.

'We must be the only people in this place,' she said.

'But they were expecting us, or you, at least,' replied Leo nodding towards the door to a room. On all the doors in the corridor, a rose was painted; the rose motif was continued on a green painted cupboard and a chest of drawers.

'You are everywhere,' said Leo.

'Ten years ago I would have been convinced that it was a sign,' said Rose.

'But not any more?'

'I think I've outgrown all that.'

'But it was a form of hope,' said Leo. 'We must never outgrow hope. What would all those roses have meant tonight?'

Before Rose could reply, the automatic timer extinguished the lights in the corridor.

'Damn!' said Leo.

'And what does this mean?' Rose's voice came to him through the dark. 'You see, Leo, once you start with signs and portents, it never ends.' For the second time that evening, she moved towards Leo's body in the dark. At first she encountered the cold, hard glass of the winebottle. She stretched out her hand and ran it beyond the glass until it reached the fabric of Leo's coat. She slipped her hand between the opening of the coat and let it rest on the solid curve of his warm belly. Her lips brushed the roughness of his beard. Her fingers stroked the smooth cotton of his shirt. They found the indentation of his navel, circled around it and slid downwards.

'Not yet,' murmured Leo.

'Better to at least find our rooms?' said Rose. Her fingers had lifted the warm cotton and were brushing a light covering of hair.

'Not yet,' said Leo, and gently detached himself from her fingers. 'Let me find that light switch.'

'I'll find it,' sighed Rose, and within seconds the small hallway was filled with light.

'Our rooms were right behind us,' said Leo. 'Ten and twelve.' Rose opened the door to Number 10. They walked in and deposited their only baggage, the bread, cheese and wine on top of a chest of drawers by the door.

'I think I will go down and get the plates of cold cuts,' said Leo, throwing his coat and hat across a chair. 'I'm starving and there might be something on them that I can eat.'

'Mmm,' sighed Rose, mute with humiliation and spurned longing. After he left the room, she turned on the two bedside lamps and turned off the harsh overhead light. The little room was simply furnished but the warmth of its painted wooden furniture and the plump, pure white duvet and apricot walls made it the most welcoming room of her travels. The low eaves would make it impossible for Leo to stand up, she calculated. Then he will lie down, she whispered to the lovely room. Kneel down, more likely, said another voice within her and she knew then that whatever she did, no matter how much she stroked and caressed and cajoled, Leo intended to make this room a confessional.

When he came back he put the two plates of meat on the chest of drawers and removed the polythene.

'Oh, they are hideous,' said Rose, pushing them away towards the wall. Leo was occupied in opening the wine.

'I had to interrupt them again for a corkscrew,' he said. 'I think they hate us by now.' He poured the wine into two glass tooth-mugs above the sink. 'Here, Rose. *Saluté.*' He clinked his glass against hers and leaned forward to kiss her on the forehead. Rose kissed him on the lips, running one finger along his eyebrow and pushing her tongue between his teeth. Leo started to respond; his tongue met hers, his free hand caressed the back of her neck. Then it pulled her gently away.

'Come and sit by the window. Bring the food over here and we'll eat looking out at the storm. We even have a window-seat.'

'You have such self-discipline,' said Rose. 'It makes me feel sleazy and self-indulgent.'

'My Protestant mother,' said Leo.

'Tell me about her,' said Rose.

'Not now,' said Leo, and stood up and poured himself another glass of wine.

'Then tell me about Wotan! Tell me this whole story of the Ring. I believe you when you say that it is like walking into a treasure house of glorious sound—'

'You have to listen to it many times – get the music inside your ear, have your mind and your heart organize the sounds, and then I promise you that once you do, it will be as though you have taken – oh, I don't know – the David of Michelangelo or all of Shakespeare within yourself, that you contain them for ever and are changed as a result.' Leo was animated now, pacing from the window-seat to the bed, his eyes moving from the snow outside to Rose's green eyes.

'But I have to start by knowing the story – you can tell me that now.'

'Not now, Rose,' said Leo.

'Please, Leo, please don't. I don't need to know any more about you than I do already. You were born the day I met you—'

'A lovely idea, Rose – and full of poetry, but alas not true.' He sat down at the end of the half-circle window-seat. 'Remember what you said in Venice about opera being a mixture of the absurd and the tragic? The grotesque and the sublime?'

'Yes?'

'And you don't mind that? It doesn't repel you as it does many people?'

'I love it.'

'Then come and sit next to me, Rose.' She shifted along the seat. A ripple of wind pitched a sheet of snow past the window, making the room suddenly darker. 'Closer,' said Leo. But when he was satisfied that Rose was close enough, he leaned against the window-frame and stared ahead. With his right hand he reached over and pushed the bread and cheese towards her. 'Eat, *cara*, eat. It has been a long evening.'

'I can't. My stomach has locked shut.'

'Mine does that before a performance,' said Leo. 'Remember when I told you that I didn't enter singing competitions but that some extraordinary voices did?'

'Yes.'

'And that I had sat through some of the performances and had been amazed at the talent? Do you know what happened to the four winners that year?'

'How could I?'

'One is selling cheese back in his home village. And the other two are singing teachers.'

'And the fourth?'

'Oh, I don't know. I don't remember him – but he probably didn't come to anything.'

'What year was this?'

Before Leo said the year and the name of the contest, Rose knew both answers and she knew who the forgotten fourth contestant had been.

'None of that is relevant, Rose – what I'm trying to say is that the first two winners, the ones I remember, were deeply talented—'

'That's life, Leo – they didn't live up to their promise.'

'Or they didn't get the right manager and I did. A pianist, for example, can't go to the Carnegie Hall and say "Look, I'm a great player and free on Friday so fix me up with a concert." You can have all the talent in the world but unless some business-minded person decides to package it and sell it you may as well sit at home and sing in a closet. When I started singing there were two or three impresarios who carried the key to the world that we musicians didn't understand – the world of contracts and engagements and fees. One of them was Clara's father.'

'I knew she came into this somewhere.'

'He had agencies in Milan and London and came to hear me sing in a concert in Bergamo. He brought her with him. After the concert he came back and said he was impressed. But I knew that he traditionally signed the four competition winners. And for all his good impressions he made no mention of signing me. But he came again when I was singing Mephisto in *Faust* a couple of months later. Clara came too. Again he heaped praise on me and went away. But she didn't. She came to every performance of that *Faust* and when I did a Basilio in Stresa she came to that. At first, she would wait outside for my autograph. And, of course, when other people at the stage door saw her do that, they did the same. Such sheep, people are, but I blessed them. It flatters an insecure twenty-three-year-old, you know.

'But then she seemed to think she had some kind of priority over the others and would come to my dressing-room and sit down and talk. She was knowledgeable. She knew almost more than I did at that time. She could talk about all sorts of singers who had been in her father's stable. I wanted her to talk about her father. But she was evasive, said that he was ill and tired and reluctant to take on new people. And all the time all this was happening, my wife, Kay, was pregnant. And then she gave birth and they said that the child was doomed from the outset and, well – you know the rest.

'I did a *Giovanni* in Bari. I stood in for someone else. I was far too young to be singing it but I was sick with ambition and didn't do a bad job. When I got back to my dressing-room, she was already inside. I was furious. She seemed to think we were going to have dinner together. I tried to send her away. She wouldn't go. I had to get hold of her and push her out of the door. I heard her stamping away down the corridor, slamming the fire-doors behind her as she went. And I sat down and thought, Well, that's it. All I've worked for come to nothing. Five minutes later the stage doorkeeper called me to the phone and I learned that my daughter had died.

'And then there was the return to the villa which we had only rented at the time – it was very pretentious for a young couple – and in that villa was Kay. She seemed mad with grief and anger and I couldn't comfort her.'

Leo got up and walked away from Rose and the window-seat. He went to the door, opened it and looked out into the dark corridor.

'We are the only guests in this place,' he said. 'Do you realize that nobody in the world knows where we are? Maybe we'll stay here for ever, eat simple meals, walk in the snow and never see another theatre or intendant or manager—'

'But you want to sing your Wotan.'

'Do I? Yes, I suppose I do.'

'And the snow will melt.'

'It was melting on the day we buried my daughter,' said Leo. 'There was the most God-awful wind blowing. I remember standing there and wondering where it came from and why it had to blow so bitter and cruel on that day. Afterwards, long afterwards, I decided it must be the Föhn – the wind that blows across Munich and the Alps. They say it makes people crazy. And that's why I wanted it to be that wind, my wind. But the Föhn is warm and blows too far north. Still, something fierce and twisted was in the air that day. The snow was dirty and patchy and from beneath it the trapped dead leaves of last autumn got blown around, sticking to people's legs and feet – one even blew into Kay's sister's face, blotting out her nose and mouth and making her look as though she wore a Venetian carnival mask. I remember thinking, Why are those buried leaves returning from a long-lost autumn when my daughter is just gone and can never return? Kay took hold of my arm as we stood around the grave. I was so glad of that. For a second I turned around to ensure that the rest of the world could see our unity. As if by being seen to be together, our sham would be made true. That's when I saw Clara.

'She was standing at the back of the small crowd. She had a photographer with her. As the priest came to the last words of the burial service, they moved forward. I tried to block Kay's view of them. I didn't want her to see them. And yet I made no move to stop them. Why didn't I, Rose? Why didn't I just kick them out there and then? Clara pushed on through the crowd – the young man with his camera followed. I turned away but could feel the pressure from behind – people being nudged aside, gasps of shock and dismay. At that point I was looking hard at the priest and he was looking hard at that small, white coffin. That terrible small, white coffin. I couldn't look at that – could never look at that, so I continued to stare at the priest. And then I heard Clara's voice next to me. She said something about my being a celebrity now and newspapers needing to know about my life. And I started to shake my head and whisper, "No, no, not like this." And I tried to focus on the priest – his face was thin and pointed, his face was like a scythe, like a reaper's scythe. But I couldn't stop shaking my head, and his face started to whirl before me but then I saw his expression change. His thin mouth came open and he raised his hands and then I heard this crash and screaming. Kay was screaming – her sister was screaming. I was screaming too. I could hear myself but it seemed that I screamed before I saw why. As I recall, that came seconds later when I had to look into that grave for the first time, look at the terrible white coffin – because Clara had fallen in on top of it.'

'Oh my God,' said Rose, clapping her hand to her mouth.

'Now do you see what I meant about absurd and tragic? You almost laughed there, didn't you?' He waved away Rose's denial. 'But you know you mustn't. Every decent human being knows they mustn't but for just a second, there was an embarrassed titter in the

357

crowd. She had pushed so far forward that the earth at the edge of the grave had started to give way. I didn't see her fall. When I looked, all I could see was this woman sprawled across the white wood. Her black skirt was up over her head. You could see her white lace underwear and this was in the days when women wore stockings and you could see her suspenders and the white chunks of thigh above the black stockings. Kay was still screaming and hitting out in all directions. The priest brought the service to an end. Two cemetery attendants came to help Clara out. She was sobbing, wailing, and limp like a rag doll. It must have taken a long time but I didn't see because invisible people, friends, family, were bundling us away.

'Next thing I knew, Kay was in a car with her sister, Martha, heading towards Martha's suite at the Grand Hotel, and I was standing alone by one of the funeral cars. Somebody must have decided that I should go home – to that goddamned villa – because I remember being in the library with all these shocked, scandalized, sobbing people. And then they were all gone but Kay didn't come back so I went upstairs to my piano. I must have played for hours. I remember wondering when Kay would come back and then ceasing to wonder and just playing and playing. It grew dark. I was playing a Beethoven piece – "The Tempest" – I could hardly see the keys and probably wasn't playing very well. But I didn't want to come out of the music. Do you understand that? I felt that if I stayed within that music I would be safe from everything. Then the doorbell rang. It must have been ringing for a long time. I ignored it – I thought that somebody must be downstairs to open it but I later learned that our housekeeper had gone into town to console Kay. They thought I didn't need consoling because I was playing my piano. The doorbell rang and rang. In the end I had to stop playing to answer it and it was just as I had feared. As soon as my fingers left the keys and the music stopped, all the horror of that day came flooding into that dark room. All those filthy dead leaves, all the

358

screaming, all the emptiness and silence afterwards.

'And still the doorbell rang. I was too numb to register that only a lunatic would bother to keep ringing. I went downstairs and opened the door. And there stood Clara. She had washed away the mud and leaves and changed her clothes. She was holding a letter. I didn't hesitate one second. I reached out and slapped her so hard on both cheeks that she went reeling to the ground. She was on all fours like an animal and dirty again, and still I wanted to hit her. I raised my hand but she held out this letter. She sobbed something about it being a letter of apology, about being too scared to say the words out loud. I took it and read it and as far as I could take it in, I sensed that it was quite beautiful. That the words she had chosen, like the music I had been playing, contained some comfort and truth. She was still on her knees. I lifted her up. Still I didn't want to accept her apology—'

'It *was* an accident,' said Rose. 'Not the photographer but the falling in the grave.'

'Was it? Maybe I thought so then. Now I'm not so sure. She was pushing. She always pushes to get what she wants, and pushes and pushes. There are lots of people like her in our world who use brute force to get what they want.'

'But she didn't get what she wanted – she fell.'

'She pushed herself. Anyway, once I'd pulled her to her feet on the doorstep of the villa I had an instinct to just close the door on her face and not accept that apology however beautifully written.'

'But it had been an accident so in a way you had to accept it.'

'Oh no I didn't,' said Leo. 'Kay was in shock. We hadn't even been able to throw earth or lay a flower on our own child's coffin. I should have sent her packing.'

'But you didn't, did you?' said Rose, reaching out to take Leo's hand. 'You forgave her. And you think I'm going to stop loving you for that?'

Leo withdrew his hand.

'Oh I forgave her all right,' he said.

Chapter Thirty-Eight

'Eat, *cara*, eat,' said Leo, pulling the plates of meat and the bread and cheese towards them. Rose made herself a sandwich.

'Aren't you eating?'

'Maybe some Mortadella later,' said Leo. He poured himself a glass of wine. 'This is not bad – you should have some more.' Rose held out her glass.

'So that's it?' she said. 'That's what you had to tell me? That's what you've been carrying around all these years?'

'You know I haven't finished,' said Leo.

'Oh but I wish you had.'

'After I'd pulled Clara to her feet, she wouldn't let go of my hand. She held on tight with those long, bony fingers of hers as if without me she would fall back onto the ground. She started talking about Beethoven, about the piece I'd been playing, about the healing power of music and how it had helped her when her own mother had died. She named the music that had brought her the greatest solace. Every piece she named was one that I would have wanted in times of great sorrow. At that point I managed to get my hand away, to break the physical contact but by then I was almost happy to talk to her. Kay and I had been so isolated in our sorrow, unable to reach each other. My only consolation has always come from music, and by that time Kay had decided that music, at least, the world of music and musicians, was to blame for all our woes. Had I not been singing *Giovanni* I would have spent more time with the child. Perhaps she had convinced herself that together we could have made little Antoinetta whole. Kay had found refuge in silence and I had found only loneliness.

'That same fierce bitter wind that had blown through the cemetery got up again. I kept thinking that this was the time to end the conversation, shut the door on her and go back to my music. I was about to bid her farewell – I didn't think I would ever see her again – when she said the fatal words: "My father is thinking of giving you a contract." She said that she was not supposed to say anything, that the old man was torn between phasing out his agency altogether or naming a successor and taking on new people. He had, she said, taken a shine to me but was bound by tradition and all sorts of cabals and machinations to take on the competition winners.

'The wind blew and blew. She was shivering with the cold. I asked her inside. There must have been some kind of reception after the funeral. All those shocked, sobbing people in the library must have been there in a formal capacity for the place was littered with empty coffee-cups and plates. I had been in such a daze I hadn't realized. I'd thought that they had come, like some Greek chorus, to provide wailing and commentary.

'I took her upstairs. Why? Why didn't I take her into the kitchen, give her some coffee? But no, without even thinking about it, I took her upstairs to the only room I had ever felt truly at home in. Since those days it has become like a little museum: original scores, composers' letters, statues. But back then when it was still a rented home it contained just the piano, and a long low *chaise-longue* under the window.'

'Can we continue this tomorrow?' said Rose. 'I'm so terribly tired and it's past midnight.'

'The room was dark,' Leo went on. 'I hadn't realized how dark. And a window had been open all the time I had been in there. I hadn't heard the wind then or felt the cold. I went in ahead of her to close the shutters and the window. I remember that the shutters were being blown so violently I had difficulty catching hold of them and pulling them to. I struggled for what felt

361

like a long time and all that time, I kept thinking, My poor damaged daughter is out in the storm, is out all alone in this wicked weather. And I realized that while I had been playing my Beethoven, some anonymous employee of the cemetery had shovelled earth onto her and that she was wrapped in blackness for ever.

'And the room was still dark. There has never been a light switch near the door and the only light comes from a lamp near the piano. For twenty-five years I've been meaning to change that but I never got around to it. Now I never will . . .

'I sat down on the *chaise-longue* by the window. My legs had given out beneath me. I had forgotten Clara. I wanted to put my head in my hands and cry but I couldn't. There seemed to be something so artificial, so operatic, about using gestures that I had learned in the theatre in my personal life, so I just sat. Until I felt this shadow alongside me. That's what it felt like at first – a shadow. She didn't move – just sat inches away in the dark. I remember thinking how discreet and gentle she was to just be there. I could hear her breathing and my own.

'And then I was inside her. I don't recall taking off my clothes or hers. I don't recall turning towards her or reaching out for her. All of a sudden I was naked and plunging into female flesh and warmth and softness.'

Rose put her hands to her ears, wishing that blackness and silence would come to this warm well-lit room. From where she sat she could see only the plates of German meat. Small beads of sweaty moisture had appeared on the gross, fat tongue. She thought she could even see traces of the thick blue veins that had once attached the tongue to the body. She shut her eyes and held her hands tight over her ears but still Leo told his one and only story.

'At first it felt wonderful, losing myself in all that warmth and wetness. It was a return to life, moving and thrusting and pumping. I was opposing all that frozen stillness. I hadn't fucked like that in years—'

'Stop it! Stop it.' Rose ran to the bathroom, threw herself down by the toilet bowl and vomited until she was heaving up nothing more than strangled air. When she looked up Leo was leaning over her. He wiped her mouth and ran his hands through the damp hair on her clammy forehead.

'I have to tell you, Rose—' Rose shook herself free of his grip.

'I can't believe it! I can't believe it! Your child was hardly cold in the ground and you – you fucked that cunt!' She could feel the cold, stinking rim of the toilet digging into the nape of her neck. 'You could get it up! Your child was hardly cold and you could get a hard-on and get your clothes off, and hers! And don't give me that bit about not remembering! You did it! It takes time, deliberation, to get clothes off unless the passion was so intense you just ripped them off. Was it, Leo? Was it? With Clara?'

'It had nothing to do with passion,' said Leo.

'You were inside her! Clara! Oh, I hate it! I hate it! She's held you naked in her arms. Everything I've longed to do with you, she's already done. Everything that I thought would be private and special, she's had. It destroys it all. She knows how your body feels. She's held your prick in her hands, in her body. I hate it! I hate her! I hate you!' Rose was sick again, on the bathroom floor this time. Leo had abandoned his attempts to hold her. Now he took a hand-towel, rinsed it in warm water and wiped up the mess.

'It was years ago. It was nothing to do with what we have.'

'Oh, sod it! All sex is the fucking same when you get down to it,' said Rose, still leaning against the cold, stinking rim.

'No it's not,' said Leo. 'That day on the *chaise-longue* under the window, I was still fucking away when I seemed to come out of the black tunnel of forgetfulness that I'd entered, and I realized that it was Clara's thin legs that were wrapped around me. For the first time I was aware of her bony chest underneath me. She was moaning and clinging. I felt I hated her, and myself even more—'

'But did you stop, Leo? I bet you didn't! I bet you came inside her! I hate it.'

'I was a young man,' said Leo. 'When it was over I hardly remember talking to her. We must have dressed in silence, then I just bundled her out of the room and down the stairs. I opened the front door. The wind had abated. I remember she turned and held up her face to be kissed but I took her hand and pushed her towards the gate. At that moment Kay and her sister arrived in a taxi.'

'Then Kay knows everything. You've been through this exact same scene with her,' moaned Rose.

'She never mentioned it. She has never mentioned it. At the very first moment, I was ready with any number of lies to cover myself. I wanted her to confront me but she didn't. Then as the weeks went by I was resolved to tell the truth but there was never a way into the subject. Twenty-five years went by and never a word has been said about that afternoon. But three weeks after the funeral I was given a contract by Clara's father. Kay didn't congratulate me.'

'Surprise, surprise,' said Rose. She had closed her eyes and now she felt that sleep might overwhelm her. There was nothing she wanted more than to drift into oblivion and shut out the blizzard, the miles of frozen barbed wire, the smiling policemen, the foul food and every one of Leo's words. She knew that she was still lying on the bathroom floor. She opened her eyes and, looking down, saw that her emerald dress was soiled with vomit. 'Poor failed wedding dress,' she sighed. And then she drifted off. At some point she felt herself being lifted from the floor. And then she was aware of her dress and bra being removed. Through a mist of sleep she saw Leo's hand holding a face-cloth and gently soaping down her face and neck and the top of her breasts. She was aware of the warm damp cloth in his broad hand. She could feel the soapy water on her skin and feel the cloth sweeping downwards. She knew that Leo's gaze was fixed on her breasts but even as the cloth circled her nipples, never once did his flesh touch hers. Then she was lying under the plump, white duvet in the apricot-coloured room. And then she plummeted into dense dreamless sleep.

Next morning the world seemed to Rose to have returned to normal. Someone was running a vacuum cleaner along the corridor; she could smell coffee coming from downstairs. She could tell without going to the window that the snow had stopped. Then she remembered.

When she went downstairs for breakfast, Leo was already sitting at a table by the window. He looked up from his *Deutsche Zeitung* and stood to welcome her. Then they both sat down in silence.

'It's stopped snowing,' said Leo. Rose didn't reply. She waited until a young woman had served them coffee then she said, 'At least now I know why you gave Clara a parrot.'

'I shouldn't have done that,' sighed Leo. 'I just wanted her out of my dressing-room.'

'Where did it come from?' said Rose.

'An ex-mistress,' Leo replied.

'So there were mistresses too?' said Rose.

'Of course.'

'Many?'

'Depends what you mean by many.'

'I'm exhausted already,' sighed Rose. 'Did you put me to bed last night?'

'Yes.'

'You undressed me?'

'I had to wash you first. You were in a terrible mess. I washed your face and neck and your breasts. They are beautiful.' He reached out to stroke her hand.

'Don't, Leo.'

Leo put his hand back on the newspaper.

'I sponged the front of your dress too – I hope it isn't damp.'

'It's fine,' said Rose. 'But everything else hasn't been put right just because you've unburdened yourself.'

365

'But it will be,' said Leo.

'I don't know about that. I think I need to go back to Füssen and be on my own to think.'

'I'll take you back to Füssen this afternoon if you want,' said Leo. And again he leaned across the table and took her hand in his. 'But come upstairs with me this morning. Lie down with me just once before you go.'

'What! After last night – you want me to make love to you as though nothing has happened?'

Leo shook his head. 'I want you to make love to me as though everything has happened. Don't you see, Rose, if you go away now, the images of me and – and her will grow and fester like they did with Kay. We need our own love-making to blot it all out. God, it was twenty-five years ago! What is it they say? That every one of our body's cells is renewed in a seven-year cycle. I don't even have the same skin!'

'I'm beginning to understand what Fritz meant about you. You've decided that you had to tell this ugly story and that once you did, everything would be clean and solved and that you could just proceed to the next phase of your plan without taking any account of my reactions.'

'I'm not that calculating. I didn't plan anything but I want you, Rose. I don't want you the way I wanted my mistresses, certainly not the way I wanted Kay all those years ago. I want you as – as – *come si dice*? – as my heart and body's companion. Come up to my room now, Rose. I'm not a young man – I don't have youth's faith in tomorrow.'

'Always this urgency! You're forty-eight, Leo. You may live another forty years. You don't have to charge ahead like a man pursued all the time. It's so ironic. When I first heard your voice I thought of it as a great comforter, as something solid that all the woes of the world could wash up against. And now—'

Someone had turned on a radio. Music filled the dining-room – music that evoked Otto, a flock of bullfinches in a snow-filled square in provincial

France, and a faith in the magic of journeys.

'The "Siegfried Idyll",' said Leo. The waitress heard him and stopped on her way to the kitchen.

'We play it every year on Christmas Day,' she said. 'Because that's when it was first played—'

'For Cosima's birthday,' sighed Rose. 'Even I know that but I think I'm sick of Cosima—'

'She was born in my town,' said Leo.

'You mean Bellagio? Is it still your town?'

But Leo hadn't heard. 'Listen to the tenderness in this, Rose. That one obnoxious man could contain such gentleness, such love. One day I will take you to Tribschen. We will go in winter when there's no-one around—'

'And find swarms of Japanese standing on the stairs where the orchestra stood,' smiled Rose. 'Besides, I thought you had no faith in tomorrow.'

'Ah, but music such as this can restore faith in anything.' He was gripping her hand again. 'I still want you to come upstairs with me, Rose.'

Rose withdrew her hand. 'I think we should be heading back to Füssen this morning before we get stranded by any more avalanches.' She stood up.

'As you wish,' said Leo.

'I think I do.'

'Then I think I'll sit and listen to the end of this.' At the same time he unfolded his newspaper, but when Rose turned to glance at him from the doorway, he was gazing out of the window, the paper untouched before him.

Alone in her room, Rose gazed at her reflection in the mirror. After Leo's impromptu bath, her hair had dried in uneven clumps and the evening's heaving and tears had left her skin sallow and shadowed. She rummaged in her handbag but she had never been organized enough to carry a make-up bag with her and she found only a lipstick. She was rubbing it into her cheeks in an attempt to give her face some colour when she noticed a piece of paper sticking out of the top of her handbag. It was Otto's one-page account of the

Ring, handed to her on the ferry and forgotten until now. She took it out and sat down on the edge of the bath to read it. She could make out only a few sentences.

Otto had written his account in the second person and Rose read: '*You will probably be bored by the story and find it pompous and inconsistent but in the music everything makes sense.*' Then the print smudged. Rose was too weary even to try to decipher it. She could make out just a few words in the last paragraph. '... *but the music speaks of redemption through love.*' Rose caught sight of her reflection in the mirror and saw her own wry smile before she was aware of the pity and envy that she felt for Otto, who came fourth in a competition once. How easy it was to believe in such grand concepts when you are a mere spectator in a red velvet armchair.

The bathroom door opened and Rose saw Leo's reflection behind hers in the mirror. Last night this man had washed her breasts. Now he came and stood behind her in the bathroom and put his arms around her shoulders. She dropped the tattered piece of paper and leaned back, resting her head on Leo's stomach. He stroked her hair for several long, silent moments and then he leaned forward and kissed the back of her neck.

'We must go,' she started to say.

'No,' said Leo. And he gathered her into his arms and carried her into the bedroom. Rose, who had always considered herself too plump, too stocky, too much for anyone to take on, found that all she was, flesh, bone, muscle, heart and soul, could be contained in Leo's arms.

And in the bedroom where the Christmas sun shone through the open curtains, she watched as Leo unbuttoned her dress. She could hear a train rattling along a track.

'There's a train—' she started to say.

'I saw it this morning when I woke up. It must run to Garmisch in one direction and Austria in the other.'

368

Her dress dropped to the floor. He unhooked her bra, let it drop to the floor, rubbed his hands gently across the tips of her nipples before reaching to remove his shoes and socks and unbuttoning his shirt.

'Then we are not cut off – the outside world has returned.'

Rose lay back on the bed and watched as Leo undressed. Now other sounds drifted into the room. She heard the sound of muffled footsteps and the swoosh of skis in the snow below. The bells rang briefly in the onion-domed chapel. Leo lay down naked beside her.

Clara. No, not now. Leo reached out for her, stroked her hair back and kissed her neck. Clara. No, he didn't do this with her. He took Rose's nipple into his mouth and stroked her inner thigh. He once lay between Clara's thighs. Now his hand became more insistent trying to part Rose's legs but there was Clara again – this third party lying between them as naked as Rose was. Rose wanted to look at the beautiful naked man that was Leo but all she saw in her mind's eye was Clara with her bony knees raised high and wide. Rose stiffened and drew her legs closer together. Leo raised his head.

'It was twenty-five years ago. That young man is dead or at least trying very hard to die.' He hugged her close. 'Oh my Rose, the only third party here is love. That doesn't always lie between two naked bodies, you know.' And again he rocked her gently but this time she could feel his warm body, his broad chest, the damp hair brushing against her breasts. Looking into his eyes she spread her thighs, drew her knees up and saw the room go dark as Leo moved to lie above her.

Chapter Thirty-Nine

After Otto's departure, Kay went upstairs and ran a bath. The hot water was as welcome as the freezing cold had been earlier. Kay lay in the warm water and wondered whether he had been real or imaginary, this ageless man whose soft lips had brushed her flesh. She looked down at her body. There was no sign of him there. She tried to remember his name and where he had come from but all she recalled were those lake-blue eyes and the smooth lips and soft tongue. As she had suspected for so many years, the lake had finally healed her. And as she lay in the warm water, Leo and the long-lost child seemed to plummet down into the irretrievable past. All the drama was gone from the story. Kay wanted no more of the intensity of feeling. She felt that she could sail for ever across the froth and foam of life.

When the phone rang an hour later it was the Pekinese's former owner.

'Can I stay with you for a few weeks after Christmas, *cara*?' said the count. 'The Eton affair didn't work and my house is sub-let and I have nowhere to go.'

Kay could think of nothing she would like more than to spend her days with this unthreatening, cultivated man.

'Of course,' she said, and decided to put him in the loveliest guest-room.

Before the lake man's visit Kay had been tempted to stay indoors ignoring the Christmas celebrations. Now she wanted to carry her secret into company. She consulted her diary and calculated that she could attend two invitations – a Christmas tea at a villa on the way into Como, and a late supper in the town itself.

And all of this without Leo. She could arrive when she wanted and depart when she pleased. And when she left it would be to return to her beloved lake which she now knew she must never leave.

When she dressed, it was with more than her usual care. She wondered whether she should contact Leo's lawyer and say that she was ready to talk. She was about to pick up the phone when she remembered that Christmas Day was not a day to discuss divorce settlements.

She started to make up her face in a mirror propped on the kitchen table. She liked to see her reflection in the bright stark light from the lake. She always took pleasure in what she saw but as she applied a thin layer of mascara, her fair face was suddenly thrown into shadow. The shadow was coming from the lake. Kay knew every nuance of light on Lake Como and could not explain this sudden darkness. She turned from her reflection and saw that a large boat had come so close to the window that it had blocked out the mountains. It was mooring at her deck. Kay leapt up and ran to the window. She was about to utter a cry of protest when she saw that it was the police boat that had been plying the waters that morning.

'Clara's got to be out of here by noon,' said Fritz.

'But she behaved quite well last night,' said Annaliese.

'She was not invited! Because of her my dearest friend went racing down the fire-escape like a criminal.'

'I love Leo dearly but he does tend to over-react.'

'I don't think so, Annaliese. I want her out.'

'But there are no flights to London on Christmas Day. I think that the airport is probably closed.'

'I don't care if she goes to London or Ougadoudou. I want her out of here.'

'I'll go and talk to her,' sighed Annaliese.

'No. I'll talk to her,' said Fritz and set off down the corridor.

Clara was sitting staring out at the rooftops. She had been subdued the previous evening because she had been expectant and then perplexed. All her conversations had taken place with her eyes fixed firmly on the door. Now, the gift for Leo lay on the dressing-table. Clara was feeling petulant and annoyed with her hosts for not living up to their promise – even if it was a promise that had sailed up to her via the kitchen drainpipe.

Fritz walked in without knocking.

'All right, Clara, you can start packing,' he said.

'But the doctor said—'

'I don't care.' He took her suitcase and threw it on the bed. 'I want you out of here by noon.'

'There are no flights to London!'

'Then you can go to Paris or Rome or even a hotel around the corner. I want you out of here!'

'I can't walk.'

'You did very well last night. And if you have trouble this morning, well, Clara, I suggest you crawl on all fours.'

He opened the wardrobe and threw Clara's clothes onto the case. Her precious silver dress caught on the handle and ripped.

'My best dress!' squealed Clara.

'Then pack it yourself,' said Fritz. 'I'm going to call you a taxi.'

'I'll tell the German Press,' said Clara.

'I don't care.'

'But I only came downstairs because I was feeling lonely. You don't know what it's like not having any family. I just wanted to join in the festivities. I really enjoyed choosing those gifts. I thought you liked your bottle of Bordeaux – didn't you?'

'Every time I look at it it will remind me of you, Clara. I intend therefore to give it to my gardener out at the lodge as an additional Christmas bonus.'

Clara started to cry.

'I'm unmoved by tears,' said Fritz. 'They might have worked with Annaliese or my more magnanimous

372

colleagues but I'm not known for my compassion. Pack your bags, Clara.'

'You have no idea, have you? Of what it's like to be born with such longings – for music and beauty and art. And to have no talents – no ability to create or perform. To be destined to just admire from afar.'

'But not far enough,' said Fritz. 'I'm going to call you a taxi. I expect to see you in the hall in half an hour.'

Clara hesitated for a few minutes. She wondered whether a last appeal to Annaliese would prolong her stay. But Annaliese was nowhere to be seen. Then she remembered the imminent arrival of the maestro's children. Clara disliked children. Within minutes she was packed and ready. She had decided to go to Vienna. A performance of *Fledermaus* and the New Year's Day concert in the Musikverein would carry her comfortably into the New Year. The previous evening had proved that she was now adept at walking on crutches and this was sure to bring her sympathy and the best seats. She had also decided that a handsome young German *Heldentenor* would be a suitable recipient for Leo's Christmas gift and she was sitting in the hall rewriting the label when Fritz appeared.

'Well now, if you're that keen to leave I'll call and tell the taxi to come at once,' he said.

'I'm still going to tell one of my journalist friends how badly you've behaved.'

'But they know I'm a heartless bastard,' said Fritz. 'So it won't be news.' The phone rang in the kitchen. Clara heard Annaliese's voice for the first time that morning.

'Fritz! Fritz!' And then she said something in urgent rapid German. Fritz turned and ran to the kitchen. He pushed the door behind him but Clara hobbled towards it and caught it before it closed with the end of her left crutch. Fritz was still talking to Annaliese. Clara couldn't hear or understand everything they said but she was sure that she heard the word 'Leo'. Then she heard the conductor speaking in Italian and guessed that he had taken the phone from Annaliese.

When Fritz hung up he turned to his wife.

'I'm not sure that we have to contact Leo immediately,' he said.

'But of course we do! That Italian detective said he could provide them with a preliminary identification.'

'But he doesn't have to. The parents will be flying in from the United States within a day or two. Why should Leo be disturbed when he's about to undertake one of the most important roles of his life? He can't go flying back there with only five days to go before the dress rehearsal!'

'I don't think the Italian police would understand your priorities,' said Annaliese.

'But the boy is nothing to him – if it is the boy – he's not part of his family – just some part-time employee. And anyway, why can't Kay identify him?'

'You heard what the man said – she's refused—'

'Can you refuse that kind of thing?' said Fritz.

'Well, Kay has. That's why they are looking for Leo. Kay sent them to us—'

'She always was frail,' said Fritz. 'I suppose Leo should be with her—'

'I've never considered her frail,' said Annaliese. 'Cold and selfish perhaps, but not frail.'

'Women never did understand Kay,' said Fritz. 'I suppose that's the fate of all great beauties—'

'Don't start that again—' said Annaliese.

'I suppose we should send for Leo,' Fritz repeated. 'If we could just string it out a few more days.'

'Tell the police he's cut off at the lodge and will contact them as soon as we can contact him,' suggested Annaliese.

'By that time, with any luck, the boy's parents will have arrived and it will be out of our hands.'

'Poor devils,' sighed Annaliese. 'Can you imagine flying across the Atlantic on Christmas Day not knowing if you are going to be faced with the drowned body of your own son?'

'I can't let myself imagine the death of a son,' said Fritz.

'What was his name? How old was he? Did you ever meet him?'

'John Tillson. He must have been about twenty-two or twenty-three. Leo introduced me a couple of times. He was one of those clean-cut, naïve American boys. Leo seemed to think he might have talent as a pianist and wanted him to play for me some time in the future.'

'And now he hasn't got a future—' said Annaliese.

'If it is him,' said Fritz. 'The body has been in the lake for over two weeks. They found no papers on it—'

'Well then—'

'But – John Tillson was due home in America last week and never boarded the plane.'

'Oh.' Annaliese and Fritz stood in the kitchen in silence until Annaliese said, 'Don't tell Leo yet. There is nothing he can do. And it will just serve to suck him back there, when for the first time in his life he seemed to be able to break away.'

'You mean with this new woman?'

'Rose? Yes, I liked her – at least the little I saw of her. We can hedge for time, Fritz – say that we haven't been able to locate Leo – give him a chance to get past the *première*—' Annaliese stopped in mid-sentence because Fritz was no longer listening to her but had walked towards the kitchen door and flung it open. Clara made no attempt to conceal that she had been listening at the door. Fritz raised his hand to slap her smiling face but Annaliese held him back.

'John Tillson is dead?' said Clara. 'Drowned? That beautiful villa must have a curse on it, don't you think?'

'We don't yet know that it is John Tillson,' said Annaliese.

'But if it is, how upsetting for Leo – the Press will link his name with the tragedy, just at a time when he needs to be concentrating on his new role—'

'The Press won't know,' said Fritz.

'Oh they will, because I'll tell them,' said Clara. 'I've got lots of journalist friends who would love a story like that. "Music student drowned at great opera

375

singer's lakeside villa." I'll call them as soon as I get to that hotel you're sending me to.'

'Well then, we won't send you to a hotel,' said Annaliese rapidly. 'You can stay on here a few more days.'

'Oh no she can't,' said Fritz.

'I wouldn't want to anyway,' said Clara. 'I thought the party was quite dull last night. You're not much fun when you're trying to be respectable, Fritz. I like you better when you're more relaxed – rehearsing your little sopranos in London.'

Fritz slapped Clara hard across the cheek. Annaliese didn't attempt to stop him this time. She had turned away from them both. Clara didn't flinch when Fritz hit her. She stared up at him and smiled. 'That's all right, maestro. The last time anyone slapped me like that, it was Leo. And it was half an hour before he fucked the shit out of me – love being very close to hate, I suppose.' She turned to Annaliese. 'But don't worry, Frau Annaliese – Herr Fritz isn't my type—'

'Leo never had you.'

'Ignore her, Annaliese,' said Fritz. 'She loves to spread crap like that around. Nobody ever listens.'

'Leo never had a piece of trash like you,' said Annaliese again.

'Oh yes he did. On the day he buried his daughter. She was hardly cold in the ground when he "had" me, as you so coyly put it.'

Annaliese turned to Fritz. 'I must not understand her English,' she whispered to her husband in German. 'I cannot be hearing what she says.'

'I told you to ignore her. She's a cheap little scandalmonger.'

'Oh he had me all right,' said Clara. 'So don't pretend you don't understand. In plain English, he fucked the shit out of me. I can prove it you know – I can tell you that he cries out in Italian when he comes. And I can tell you how big his cock is—'

'Get her out of here!' cried Annaliese, but Fritz was already pushing Clara out of the door.

'Don't listen to her, Annaliese. She's a compulsive liar – she's got nothing so she lives in a fantasy world. If it were true why did she wait so long to tell anyone?'

'Because I thought he might want me again—'

'He never wanted you,' said Fritz, dragging her towards the entrance. 'Even if a man does poke a piece of trash like you it's got nothing to do with want.'

'I waited and waited,' said Clara, ignoring him. 'I was patient. I kept that day like a beautiful secret—'

'A minute ago he screwed the shit out of you. Now it's a beautiful secret. Make up your mind, you wicked little bitch.' They had reached the front door. Fritz opened it and put Clara's case outside. Annaliese had followed them.

'I felt sorry for you,' she said as Fritz pushed Clara through the door. 'I was kind to you.'

Clara turned to face her. 'I thought that when things became unbearable with his wife, then he might come to me. The years went by – I knew he wasn't happy with her.'

'You never had a hope,' said Fritz. 'People just put up with you because of your father, because you had influence.'

'I know that, and I don't care. As long as I'm in the receptions and the first nights and the galas what difference does it make why or how I got there?'

'I wanted to help you,' said Annaliese. 'You seemed so lonely.'

'She's lonely because she doesn't value anyone for what they are. There are human beings at all your first nights and galas,' he hissed at Clara. 'Terrified, inadequate human beings but all you can see is the glory.'

'I valued Leo,' sniffed Clara.

'You don't know who Leo is,' said Annaliese. Outside a horn sounded.

'The taxi,' said Fritz, glancing out of the window. He rang for the lift and bundled Clara and her bags inside.

'I'll tell Leo about John Tillson,' said Clara, suddenly composed. 'I know the number of the hunting-lodge. I found it in your papers. I think he should know what's going on in his own home.' The doors slid shut. Annaliese and Fritz walked to the window and watched in silence until they were sure that Clara and her baggage had been driven away from their apartment block and out of their sight. As they walked back into their home, Annaliese started to weep.

'I don't know what to think. I can't believe that . . . that . . . of Leo. Not Leo and her.'

'I told you she's a liar,' said Fritz, but he was deep in some other thought, scowling and preoccupied.

'But if it's true?'

'It was years ago – what difference does it make now?'

'But it's disgusting,' said Annaliese.

'But it's not important now!' snapped Fritz. 'Don't you see we have to call Leo and tell him before she does, and she will, believe me – she'll call him.'

Chapter Forty

Two phone calls went from Munich to the hunting-lodge that Christmas morning. Twice a weary housekeeper explained that an avalanche had blocked the road and that no-one had been able to get through the previous evening. Twice she gave the number of the nearest hotel – the small inn where Rose and Leo lay.

They lay in the apricot room for all that morning and late, late into the afternoon. They forgot that there was a check-out time, that it was Christmas Day and that beyond the mountains Eva, Fritz, Annaliese, Daphne, Wagner, Wotan and his Walkyries awaited. In the early evening they dressed and made their way to a small Bierstüberl which had opened to serve the cross-country skiers who swooshed by on the paths through the trees. Leo wrapped his coat around Rose and held her close for warmth. They were the only people who walked.

They ate a poor meal of what Leo said was tinned ravioli. Rose said that she didn't care. They didn't linger but walked back through the pelting blizzard, their snow-covered silhouettes lit by the one lamp of the village street. Inside the apricot room, Leo closed the carved wooden shutters, lit the bedside lamp and pulled Rose back into the rumpled bed. They made love again and again. The phone started ringing in the room next door, Leo's room, at about ten o'clock. Two more calls had come in the afternoon when the landlady was passing by the reception desk with two large slices of Stollen for herself and her husband. She had transferred both calls to Leo's room but when he had ignored them, she had given up and returned to the warmth of the log fire and coffee and cake.

*   *   *

'You should have answered the phone,' said Rose. She lay with her head on Leo's chest, thinking what strange and wonderful things men's nipples are – to suddenly come across those small soft patches of dark pink flesh amongst all that muscle and damp black hair.

'It can't be for us – nobody knows we are here.' He had turned out the bedside light but the moonlight and the single village lamp shone through the cracks in the shutters. They could see each other quite clearly. And when he rolled over and entered her once more Rose saw that he was looking hard into her eyes. His eyes were so close to hers that they blended into one pool of deep brown just above her face. And even as she wrapped her legs around him and pulled him deeper into her she sensed, as she had sensed in London and Milan, that he had been seeking something in her face. And then she forgot quests and questions and even Leo's eyes in the joy of rubbing her cheek against his rough beard, of wrapping her arms around the sheer bulk of his broad smooth back, of feeling the warm hairs on his solid belly against her own soft flesh, of opening her legs wide as he pushed deep, deep inside her.

In the morning the phone rang again. Rose woke with the old familiar impression that she had been conscious for just a second when she heard the first ring but of course the phone had been ringing for a while and had woken her. Then there was a second unfamiliar impression as she became aware of Leo's warmth, of his black hair against her face, of the faint wonderful odour of sweat and cologne, and then, half sleeping, she felt Leo's embrace. The phone rang and rang.

'It must be a mistake,' said Leo, burying his head in the flesh of her shoulder and plunging deeper into Rose. The phone rang on.

'Something has happened,' said Leo and broke away from her. He picked up the phone. Rose heard the woman's voice, saw the rage on Leo's face, heard the woman's voice increase in volume, heard the name 'John Tillson' and the word 'dead'. Leo slammed down the phone.

She was still lying with her legs apart but in that one second that it had taken to pick up the receiver, Leo had withdrawn his whole being. Now he sat naked on the bed with his back to her. Rose drew her legs together and huddled under the duvet. With Leo's warmth gone she was suddenly very cold. Leo didn't turn to her but sat staring at the closed shutters. Rose didn't want to ask who had called. She stared at the naked back that in one night she had come to love so much, and waited until the silence became unbearable and then she asked the unbearable question.

Before Leo could answer, the phone started ringing again. They both stared at it. He made no move to answer it. There was the sound of hurried footsteps, first on the stairs then drawing closer in the corridor. They stopped outside the door and a woman's voice said in German that the call was urgent, that Herr Fritz Schreier had to talk to Leo. And all the time the phone rang on.

'I had better take this in the other room.' Leo turned to face her. Then he pulled on his underpants and trousers and gave a curt order into the receiver for the call to be sent to the room next door.

When he had gone Rose lay in silence and realized that she was very cold indeed. She looked at Leo's sweater but decided that donning his clothing implied far greater intimacy than lying naked with his erect penis deep inside her and the damp hairs on his chest clamped tight against her breasts. She left the sweater where it lay but got up and washed and dressed. She knew that Leo would not return to his place in the bed in the apricot room with the carved wooden shutters.

In the room next door Leo said, 'I know already, Fritz.'

'Then she got to you first. We called and called yesterday—'

'So did she. How did she know?'

'It's a long story. But I've been on the phone to Bellagio and I think I can arrange things so that you don't have to go down there – at least not until after the *première*—'

'Oh I have to go now—'

'No, no you don't. They wanted you to make a preliminary identification but you don't have to—'

'I have to go now,' repeated Leo. 'You see, I don't think this would have happened if I had been there.'

'Don't overestimate your own powers, Leo.'

'I hated that villa. I've hated it for twenty-five years but I've always feared that something would happen if I left it . . .'

'But he was only a part-time employee – if it is him – and it didn't happen in working hours so I don't think you have to worry about his parents getting some fool American idea of suing—'

'Have you spoken to Kay?'

'Yes,' said Fritz. 'Yes, I did last night.'

'And?'

'Well – to be honest, she is very, very upset. Annaliese and I couldn't understand it. I mean, wasn't he just some sort of houseboy?'

'He was like a son to Kay. There wasn't that much work to do but I kept him on because I sensed that she needed him—'

'Listen, Leo. You're due back here for rehearsals tomorrow afternoon. You've disrupted things enough wanting to do this thing – you can't go tearing off because of some houseboy.'

'I'll be there tomorrow. If I fly back today I can take care of any formalities, look in on Kay and still return to Munich tomorrow.'

'Call Kay first – see if you can delay things.'

Leo did call Kay. He called her as soon as he'd finished talking to Fritz to avoid the temptation of returning to Rose's warm, comforting body in the room next door. His conversation with his wife was brief and when he hung up he called Lufthansa and booked himself on the late afternoon flight to Milan.

When he returned to Rose's room, he found that she had dressed, opened the shutters and was sitting, waiting at the window-seat.

'I have to go back to Bellagio,' he said. 'One of my employees has been drowned.'

Rose watched in silence as he buttoned his shirt and pulled on his sweater. She gazed at his feet as he reached for his socks and remembered the strange, premature intimacy of that night in the dressing-room at La Scala. She knelt down and rested her head against his knees, stroking the pale flesh of his feet.

'Don't go back there,' she said.

'I must,' said Leo. 'He wasn't just an employee. He was a gifted young pianist. I didn't see much of him but he seemed like a genuinely good young man. They're still not sure it's him. They want me to identify his body before they go dragging his parents across the Atlantic.'

'Of course,' said Rose. Leo had pulled on his socks and was lacing his shoes. He has already left me, she thought, and felt humiliated to be kneeling at his feet. She stood up and walked to the window. 'Do they think he committed suicide?' she asked the pines in the forest and the chaffinches that hovered around a bird-feeder. 'I mean, why else would anyone be in the lake at this time of year?'

'My wife – er, Kay, swims in the lake every day – naked. I'm always embarrassed to tell people that last detail.'

'It makes her sound other-worldly,' sighed Rose. 'A beautiful naiad.'

'I think she's a little crazy,' said Leo. 'But I've never dared to say so because the response is bound to be that I made her that way.'

'And I suppose you feel responsible for this dead boy too?'

Leo came to stand alongside Rose. He stroked her arm and looked out of the window.

'It confirms all my fears about leaving that villa.'

'You're only going back for a day or two?'

'I hope so. Oh Rose, you don't know how much I hate that cold, silent house.' He pulled her to him. 'And just as I let myself love someone else for the first time in years, the place throws up a corpse.'

'The mad king,' said Rose. 'The mad king drowned and took his doctor down with him. Here we still sit in his kingdom and now we've got a body washed up on the shore.' Rose was filled with dread in the Bavarian room that was filled with sun. 'Oh Leo, don't get dragged down with that body. Don't go. Say you can't leave rehearsals. Don't go back there.'

'I must,' said Leo. 'I'm going to drive you back to Füssen – then I'll go up to Munich and fly home.'

'Home?' said Rose. 'What do you mean, home?'

Leo didn't reply.

An hour later they were in the Mercedes and driving along the road that led cross-country to Füssen. They drove for several miles in silence.

'It's the day after Christmas,' said Rose as they drove through yet another village of frescoed walls and onion-domed chapels. 'A day for renewal if ever there was one. Remember renewal, Leo?'

But his dark silhouette hunched lower over the steering wheel and they drove on in silence.

'You can drop me here,' said Rose as they drove past Füssen's pedestrian precinct. The Christmas lights were on but the streets were deserted. 'I want to walk a little bit.'

'Don't be ridiculous, Rose. You'll catch pneumonia.'

'Let me out here,' Rose repeated. 'I want to walk for a few minutes.'

'As you wish,' said Leo.

Rose stepped out of the car and pulled the shawl tight around her.

'I'll give you my sweater,' said Leo and started to remove his coat.

'It's not worth it for a hundred-yard walk,' said Rose.

384

'Of course it is,' said Leo, removing the sweater and holding it out.

'No, really, Leo. There's no point – not for such a short distance.' She turned to walk away. Leo drove alongside her. He lowered the window.

'Give me your address in London,' he said.

'Why would you need it if you're coming right back here?'

'To be sure I can always find you – just in case.'

Rose scribbled her address down on the envelope of the rental-car agreement.

'And the telephone number,' said Leo.

'Haven't got one.'

'Funny, wonderful Rose,' said Leo. 'You do intend to kiss me goodbye?'

'I don't like goodbyes,' said Rose.

'Please,' said Leo. Rose bent down and kissed the high wide forehead. For a second, Leo smiled the wonderful smile of trust and naïvety that she had seen when he had driven away from the hotel days, or was it years, earlier? Then he closed the window, scowled at the road ahead and was gone.

Rose stood in the empty street with the snow piled high along the edges and the Christmas lights flashing and winking for no-one but her, and watched the car grow smaller in the distance and watched it disappear and watched the space where it had been. She looked at the tyre tracks the Mercedes had left in the dirty snow and walked along inside them until the time came to turn off to the side-street where the hotel was situated. She turned away from those very last traces of Leo and went inside.

When she entered the hotel, Eva was sitting alone at the bar. Rose saw that she had been crying. The sight of Eva's red, puffy eyes shocked her but she could not bring herself to acknowledge the older woman's disarray. She had had enough of human distress for one day.

'Otto disappeared,' said Eva. 'He left a note, saying

not to worry, but I was sick with it for two days. And you took off without so much as a word!'

'There was an avalanche – I got stranded.'

'You don't have to make your excuses to me,' said Eva. 'Anyway, it was Otto who really scared me. I still don't know where he is but he just phoned in a message to reception.' She held out a piece of hotel notepaper.

'*The fight must always be against bitterness. Love Otto*,' was all it said.

Chapter Forty-One

Otto walked into the dining-room the next morning while Eva and Rose were eating breakfast. Rose turned and saw that Otto was carrying an overnight bag and hadn't shaved in a couple of days. She hadn't known that long, pale chin capable of sprouting stubble – but there it was, confirmed by the roughness of his skin when he leaned over to kiss her.

'I think it's time to go home,' he said to them both as he sat down and ordered a pot of black coffee.

'Where have you been?' said Eva. 'Disappearing on Christmas Eve – and sending the receptionist all those pretentious messages.'

'I didn't send the receptionist those messages, you silly old bag! I sent them to you via the receptionist.'

'Fight against bitterness!' said Eva. 'You'd have put your energy to better use telling me where you were.'

'The whole point of going was to get away from you!' said Otto. 'To stop being your failed little prodigy. The whole point was to get out into the real world and not be looked after by my smothering twin any more.'

'So where did you go?'

'I went on a winter journey, that's all. I rode around on some local trains and stayed in two-star hotels. And I didn't get lost. And the sky didn't fall . . . And now I want to go home. I want my records and my books and I want to just be Otto the travel agent – not Otto who might have been a singer – I'm tired of being that. In fact, Eva, I've been thinking that we might even do a bit of work on the house – make ourselves two separate apartments—'

'Why do you want to go messing around with the house?'

'Not messing around – increasing its value, Eva.' Otto laid his hand across hers.

'You want to install a separate kitchen and bathroom and live in them? On your own?'

'I'd only be upstairs. I'd invite you up for dinner—'

'For dinner . . .' Eva scowled down at the paper napkin that she had screwed up tight in her fist. After a long pause she said, 'But you'll still come in on the musical tours I've been arranging? I wouldn't be able to do them without you.'

'Of course I will,' said Otto and smiled at his sister for the first time since he had walked into the room.

'What about *Die Walküre*?' whispered Rose. 'What about Eva's gift? We will at least stay for that – won't we?'

'No,' said Otto. 'You see, Rose, you were right when you said that all we knew about life was acted out in front of us while we sat in our red plush armchairs. I think I want a rest from all of that for a while.'

'But you talked me into staying. You've mesmerized me with the beauty of the music and the singing. I would like to see it—'

'I'm sorry, Rose,' smiled Otto. 'But the agreement was that you would drive us around in return for your hotel bills being paid. If we decide to go home, well, you are honour bound to drive us.'

'But it's only a week away,' said Rose.

'I want to leave this afternoon,' said Otto.

They checked out of the Hotel Alpenhof at one o'clock. The manager came out from behind the desk and kissed Eva's hand. The twin sister stood outside the hotel entrance and stared off at the distant mountains while Rose wrote a desperate last note to Leo and left it with the receptionist. Otto loaded their bags into the back of the Escort and soon they were on the road that would lead them west towards London.

They made small talk all the long way home. Rose hadn't known that so many trivial, harmless topics of conversation existed. They talked of the difficulty of folding road maps, of the German habit of serving tea in a glass with a sachet of lemon juice in the saucer, of why *Lodens* have a dart in the back and of why Volvo headlights are always switched on. They said not a word about music. Otto and Rose never referred to their respective disappearances. Eva asked no questions. For all three of them the journey seemed endless.

The London snow was gone and in its place was a dank, mild English winter's day. They all noticed the litter that the recent thaw had revealed. Rose wondered why white snow should so soil the debris that it had enfolded but she was too weary to comment. They travelled most of the way in silence. Otto and Eva slept. The cassettes rattled around in the glove compartment. Rose recalled that they had left England to the sound of a funeral march but sensed that this new silence was more deadly.

As soon as they drove up to Otto and Eva's house, Rose knew that she must look for a new home. In her memory the house had been bursting with song and wrapped in snow. Now she saw how dilapidated it was. She stood and gazed at it while Otto and Eva unloaded the bags. They were happy to be home. They fussed and bustled. They talked of making tea and a fire. They didn't notice that Rose had tucked a copy of the *Evening Standard* under her coat. It was turned to the accommodation page.

She excused herself, saying that she had to catch up on her sleep, and went downstairs. The room that had once seemed charmingly eccentric now struck her as being ridiculous. And it was cold. She had been cold since those last hours in the room with Leo. She switched on a bar fire and feeling too old and heavy to climb the child's ladder to the bed below the ceiling, she pulled the pillow and duvet down and curled up and slept fully clothed on the floor.

She woke to find that she had kicked the duvet off and that one of her legs was blotched and red from being so close to the fire. The rest of her body was stiff

389

and aching from sleeping on the hard floor. She was very hungry. Her clothes felt clammy. The day outside was so flat and grey that she couldn't tell whether it was beginning or ending.

'I should have taken his sweater,' she said to the tiny room, as if Leo dalla Vigna would bother travelling across a continent to retrieve his clothes. But it would have given me something of his, thought Rose. And she started to rummage through her baggage for a piece of tangible proof that she had known this man. She had nothing – not a letter nor even a piece of paper with an address or phone number. All she found was the envelope containing Eva's gift of a ticket to *Die Walküre*.

When she stood up and pushed the duvet and pillow aside, she saw that two notes had been pushed under her door. She recognized Eva's writing.

'We knocked several times but didn't like to wake you. If you would like something to eat, come upstairs. This note was written at 12 noon on 28 December – Eva.' The second note just said, *'Ditto but at 5 p.m.'* Rose looked at her watch. It was eight o'clock. She had slept fully clothed on the floor for more than twenty-four hours.

She took a quick shower in the bathroom where neither the immersion heater nor the radiators were back on full power. Again she was cold, colder than she had been in years. When she had put on clean clothes, she didn't go upstairs but scribbled a quick note, thanking them for the offer, which she pushed through their door before escaping down the front path and into the town. At the end of that path in a gathering sleet a large man had turned to gaze quizzically down at her. Or had he? Rose had no proof. All she knew was that now he was gone, the street was empty. The returning commuters were just briefcase-bearing ghosts. The town was empty. The world was empty and her grasp on the whirling earth was unsteady.

She went into a pub, ordered a whisky, wallowed in

the warmth it brought her and thought: This is how they begin – the old women who push their lives around in Waitrose trolleys because the disappointments are too much to bear.

Hope returned with a bowl of soup and a glass of red wine. Leo will be as good as his word, Rose decided. He will call as he said he would. Or had he? She couldn't remember. Already he was slipping into the past. That great invisible barrier between now and then was the most insurmountable. Only days earlier she had kissed Leo's eyelids. But as soon as her lips had left the warm folds of his flesh, that moment had plummeted down as irretrievably into the past as – as the day of the funeral when Clara had held him in her thin, clinging arms. Already Rose was forgetting his face, his smell, the sound of his voice. Of course, the silence could be filled. With the purchase of a tape, Leo's voice could sing to her for ever.

But she knew that if he didn't return from Bellagio, the sound of his disembodied voice would be more than she could bear. Back in her room, she pulled out the silk dress and the woollen shawl and scanned them for a sign of Leo. As she buried her head in the fabric hoping to smell a trace of his cologne, she found a black hair. She fell back asleep that evening clutching it triumphantly in her hand.

She was woken the next morning by Otto knocking on the window. She had forgotten to pull the curtains and he was gazing down at her through the glass. Her first thought was for the strand of hair but her hand had unclasped during her sleep and it was gone. She wanted to feel around for it on the pillow but Otto's gaze inhibited her.

'Why are you on the floor?' He mouthed the words through the window.

'I felt suddenly too old to climb the stairs.'

'You'll catch cold,' said Otto to a woman for the second time that week. Rose let him in. He gazed at the small, cluttered room. 'It's not a very practical layout, is it?'

'Not if you're over twelve years old.'

'But it's all going to change,' said Otto. 'We sat down last night and worked out our budget and we're going to get the builders in to convert the house into two completely separate dwellings.'

'You didn't waste much time,' said Rose.

'At our age there isn't that much time to waste. Rose, I wanted to ask you – would you – if you . . . er . . . Would you consider . . .' He walked to the window and stared out. The tree that had sat so golden and definite in the middle of the lawn was bare now. Its leaves had all blown away and the stark, spiky branches looked to Rose to be incapable of ever holding anything as fleeting and uncertain as a leaf.

'What I wanted to say,' said Otto, 'is that there will be a place for you here – and would you consider – would you come into town with Eva and me this morning to help draw up some plans with the architect?'

'I couldn't manage this morning,' said Rose who intended to spend the day looking for her own flat.

'Fair enough,' said Otto, and Rose found herself disappointed in his lack of persistence. 'Anyway, I'll show you the plans when we get them.' His hand was already reaching for the door handle. Rose stared at him. He had shaved and was wearing the same royal blue cardigan and dark corduroy trousers that he had worn on the day she had visited the room. And yet he was very different.

'What's up, Rose?'

'That's it! Your syntax has changed!'

'What a funny thing to say,' said Otto.

'But it has. Ever since you walked back into the hotel in Füssen, your sentences have been – I don't know – simpler—'

Otto sighed and leaned against the closed french window.

'Trust you to notice,' he said. 'I was a bit theatrical before, wasn't I? A bit overblown – a bit high camp is what I think they call it these days.'

392

'You were wonderful, Otto. You were magical – you said things that most people never dare to say. Most conversation is so very dull. You were . . . But why are we talking about you in the past tense?' Rose reached forward and stroked Otto's gaunt cheek. 'Are you dead? You don't feel dead.'

'I must go,' mumbled Otto, pulling away from her hand and struggling to open the door.

'Was there any mail for me?' Rose called after him but he had vanished up the backstairs and gave no reply to her question.

Rose knew that it was too soon for any letter to come for her but she still checked the letter-box on her way out. The town was grey and dank. The day blew warm and cold. In the wind, Rose froze; in estate agents' offices she sweated. And all through the long dreary day she repeated to herself that this was sensible living, that she was behaving like an adult and making rational plans to hold her life together. At one point in the day, her tube train stopped at Covent Garden and she held on hard to the edge of the seat in order not to run out and up the escalators and towards whatever music that other singing house contained.

For three days she travelled around the town. She picked up some freelance translation work and visited two shabby studio apartments. She didn't see or hear Otto and Eva. By that third day she yearned for a voice, any voice except one, to reach down to that basement room, to fill her with joy and make her buoyant and light again. Practicality, allowing her head to rule her wayward heart, had left Rose so leaden that she abandoned all attempts to climb her child's ladder to bed and made a comfortable nest for herself on the floor.

On the fourth morning Otto arrived with the blue-prints. This time he didn't question her new sleeping arrangements but sat down next to her and spread the smudged white sheets out in front of them both. Rose had slept badly but at the sight of Otto she dared to hope that a letter had come. Otto brought only the blueprints. She rubbed her eyes and stared at them. So many lines, she thought. So much geometry and arithmetic to lock you into a nice, safe life of sorts.

'Do you understand all this?' she asked Otto.

'More or less. We've divided the house into two completely separate parts. Me up top because of Eva's knees. She'll have the ground floor and the basement.'

'And where would I go?'

'That's what I've come to talk to you about,' said Otto. He had flushed and was concentrating too hard on pointing his pencil at an incomprehensible smudge on the white paper. 'I wanted to ask you this the other day, Rose, but I didn't have the courage.'

'You're not scared of me, Otto.'

'I'm scared of what you'll say—'

'If you mean that there's no room for me in the scheme of things, I'll understand.'

'I mean just the opposite! I've worked it all out to make room for you – with me, Rose – upstairs. We'd have two floors, a whole new kitchen, a separate entrance—'

'With you?'

'I've thought a lot about all this, Rose. It's not a frivolous offer. I think that we could be comfortable together.'

'What do you mean?'

'I thought that we could – be together . . . I don't expect you to marry me but if you would then I'd prefer that, but if you just want a companion that would be all right too.' He was thumping his fist against the blueprint. Rose stared at the lines and calculations, at the squares and rectangles. This was what she'd thought she wanted: a blueprint for her frayed and unruly life. And now impractical, bumbling Otto had brought her just that. Rose was aghast. She stared and stared at the thin rigid lines, at the carefully thought-out structure, and thought she might suffocate. Otto talked on.

'I've thought and thought these past few weeks. Remember what I told you, Rose, in the Biffi Scala?

About not being, well – cut out for the sexual side of life. Well, I've found out that I'm not such a dead loss after all—'

'Where did you go on Christmas Day?' said Rose.

'I can't tell you. It doesn't matter anyway, but, Rose, I know that I could be a man – a husband. We get on – what more can we ask at our age? I'm never bored with you, Rose. You bring out something in me that Eva just squelches. We could be companions. I think that's more than most people get. I think we could content ourselves with that.'

Rose pushed the blueprint away.

'I don't know what to say,' she said.

'At this point people in films always say, "Then don't say anything – think about it."'

Eva knocked at the window.

'That happens in films too,' said Otto. 'But it's usually someone a bit more inspiring than my sister.'

'I heard that,' said Eva, stepping over the bedclothes and blueprints. She handed Rose a letter. 'This came for you this morning. I told Otto to bring it down but he must have forgotten.'

Rose saw the postmark. Munich. Not Bellagio. Not Milan but Munich. She wanted to cry, Hallelujah – I have been saved from the blueprints and the comfort and contentment, from the parallel lines and the squares and neat boxes, but she took the letter, said, 'I have to read this in private,' and ushered them towards the door. She saw the sadness on Otto's face and she avoided his eyes.

Alone in her room, Rose looked at the envelope for a long time. She studied the handwriting, the carefully copied address, the perfectly spelt name. She turned it over to see if there was a sender's name but the only clue was the German stamp and the postmark. She didn't rush to open the letter because she knew that once the words and realities that it contained came thronging at her, the joy of seeing her name in that bold and flowing hand would be diluted.

She even thought that she should wash and dress before reading it. She would tidy the room, buy early tulips, arrange them in a vase, spray perfume on her wrists and then she would sit down looking as untouchable as an Edwardian woman in a Tissot, and the letter would somehow miraculously conform to its surroundings – and not hurt her. But she couldn't wait that long. When she had read her name for the umpteenth time, her eyes lingering on the extravagant curved 'R' in Rose, she opened the envelope very slowly and unfolded the one sheet of paper inside.

'*Dearest Rose,*' she read, and paused and looked to the right-hand corner. In spite of the postmark the letter was headed Bellagio. No address, no phone number, no date – just the name of the beautiful lakeside town in capital letters. Rose went cold inside. She read on.

'*It was John Tillson's body that they found in the lake. I identified him last night. His parents are flying in tomorrow morning. He was an only child. Their gifted only child. Once the inquest on his death is over he will be buried at the churchyard in the village. I cannot understand why they do not wish to take his body home. I offered to cover the costs of transportation but they are religious people of the type that attach little importance to what happens to a body. And it was difficult to argue with them over the long-distance phone. The father kept saying that John had come into his own on the old Continent. The mother said that their shy lonely boy had blossomed. And now he is dead.*

'*My wife is very distressed. I think I told you that he was like a son to her. I have decided to stay here until after the funeral. I will fly up to Munich for the final rehearsals and the performances but I will come back here for the funeral. And probably for some time after that.*

'*I am so terribly tired, Rose. I slept for thirty hours when I came back from the police station. I must find my energy for Munich and yet I feel older than I have ever felt in my life. Of course, I am older than I have ever been in my life so I suppose I should not be surprised! Do you remember when I asked you if we had infinite energy for such things as love? You were so sure that we did but I fear that we don't, dear Rose. I think sometimes our hearts sink under the weight of the past.'*

Rose put the letter on the dusty piano lid. She wondered for a few brief moments if she could stop there – not read the next few paragraphs and just suspend herself and Leo in the past in that room in Bavaria with the low eaves and the roses on the door. If she never read the next paragraph the future would be easier to bear because the past would be contained in that room. But these were the dark, heavy days of the year. They left little room for escape or evasion. The bare tree in the courtyard bore witness to the truth that all must end, all must end.

'Did you ever have the feeling that there were some things that would always be accessible to you?' Leo's curving hand asked Rose. *'And others that you would never have no matter how much you might strive for them? I always knew that I would get celebrity, glory, whatever people see it as. I couldn't say so – it would have seemed like supreme vanity but I knew that for me it wasn't that difficult. I'd been given something and as long as I nurtured and treasured it, my only duty was to pass it on to the world. That was how I justified what happened with Clara. That's how I thought I was keeping my part of the pact I seem to have made with her that day – that's how I made peace with myself – I threw all my energies into my career, called upon all the nobler, more decent parts of myself to cancel out that black day and be worthy of what I knew I was going to attain. But this life is incomplete and I always sensed that I would never have one deep and abiding love. I am sure that you will, my beloved Rose – alas, I cannot be the one to give it to you.'*

Rose put the letter face down in the dust. As she had

read it, she had clamped her right hand tight across her mouth like a witness to a gruesome road accident. Her hand still in place and distorting her features, she walked to the window and pulled the dusty red velvet curtains tight shut on the day outside. When she turned back, the letter had fallen to the floor. Leo had written on the other side of the paper. She knelt down and read the last paragraphs.

'I want to say, "Let us write to each other.", "Come to see me after a performance.", "Let's meet for a drink one day." but if I let myself believe that I would ever see your lovely face again it would be impossible to say goodbye.

'And goodbye it must be. We have known each other for such a short time, and yet when I first saw you I felt that I had always known you, that yours was the face I had always looked for at every stage door, in every dull reception, in every applauding auditorium. I won't forget you, dear Rose. I now know that whenever I go out onto a stage to sing, that I sing for you. It is not much. What I do for a living takes only a small courage. Lives don't depend on it – empires won't fall because Leo sings badly. But it is the only thing I can give to you. I give it with all my love, dearest Rose. Goodbye.'

Rose sat for a long time in the darkening silence. She prayed that the broken old house would suddenly burst out in comforting song for her. But all was still. The music, all the glorious music of that winter, had stopped.

Chapter Forty-Two

'But if I never believed in your superstitious balance sheet,' wrote Rose, *'if I thought that life is endlessly renewing itself, that rebirth happens all around us every day, that you can serve your art to the best of your abilities and still have the right to love; and if I am the one with whom your life has so miraculously entwined, then surely my belief cancels out yours?'* She finished the sentence with a flourish. She had put her note in an envelope, written Leo's name lovingly on the front, when she knew with the utmost certainty that Leo would not read her letter. He had made his decision in favour of his work and his duty. There was nothing more to say. Soon he would move on from Munich. The letter might fail to reach him and fall instead into the hands of a secretary or a manager. Rose felt violated by all these anonymous people who now had access to a man who had decided never to see her again.

She opened another envelope, the one that contained Eva's forgotten Christmas present of a ticket to *Die Walküre.* The performance was the following evening.

Rose went back into the town and bought an airline ticket to Munich. She paid for it with a credit card promising money that wasn't in her account. She didn't let herself think of the debts and duties that awaited her if her trip to Munich failed.

Next morning she left Eva and Otto a note saying that she was visiting family, and flew to Munich. She rode the bus into the city, checked into a cheap hotel, flung her small overnight bag onto the bed and walked out into the fading day where the snow still lay

399

thick and mud-encrusted across the Max Josef Platz. She was convinced that Leo would somehow materialize before her in one of the dark, cobbled streets of the old town. Twice she thought she glimpsed him but both times she startled unsuspecting Bavarians who happened to have bought a similar coat. Disheartened and humiliated she walked back to the theatre and checked that his name was on the cast list.

It was. In her halting German, she asked the box-office clerk if Leo was definitely singing that evening. There was, she noticed, still a magic to be had in saying his name. When she asked if there was any way of contacting him, the woman scowled and said that the best she could do was to leave her name at the stage door, 'and he will contact you.'

'I know you,' said an elegant brunette who was standing behind her in the queue. She was about the same age as Rose. 'I saw you at *Don Carlos* in London.'

'Do you live here?' said Rose, who didn't remember the woman.

'No, I'm from Firenze,' said the brunette. 'But I drove up here to see the tenor.'

'Is he a friend of yours?'

'I wish! No, no, I just think he's wonderful.'

An older woman in a complicated Bavarian outfit of green suede and gathers, chained buttons and feathers, came to stand with them.

'You're talking about—?' She mouthed a complicated Italian name that sounded to Rose like Pollo arosto – roast chicken.

'No, no, not the baritone,' said the Florentine brunette. 'I come up here for the tenor.'

'Him! He might look the part but he shouldn't be singing Wagnerian roles.' Rose slipped away as the conversation became one that she had now heard many times before. She was halfway through the exit when they caught up with her.

'Come for a cup of coffee,' said the brunette. 'I like the chance to practise my English.'

'And I,' said the Bavarian.

400

Rose shook her head in refusal but they ignored her and followed her through the door. She turned right towards the Vierjahrzeiten Hotel and saw that she had acquired the two women who continued their conversation alongside her.

'Of course, Polloarosto is the greatest Verdi baritone,' said the Bavarian. 'For ten years I wait at the stage door. Every time I ask for his autograph but he never seems to recognize me.'

'The tenor recognizes me,' sighed the Florentine. 'At least I think he does. Once I went into his dressing-room in Vienna and he was getting ready to leave and going round kissing everybody and he kissed me! I think it was an accident. Have you seen his Siegmund?' She was addressing Rose directly.

'I beg your pardon?' said Rose.

'He sings it bare-chested. He's got a wonderful body – big square shoulders and nice golden hair. Of course he's happily married—'

'That's nice,' said Rose. They were walking past the Vierjahrzeiten. She had suddenly remembered that this was where Leo stayed. He could step out right there in front of her at any minute. And there she would be with these two fans. But perhaps she had become one of them and would merit nothing more than a polite smile of gratitude. She sensed that Leo was very close but inaccessible behind the barriers of his celebrity.

'She manages his business affairs so she's always around,' said the Florentine.

'Who?' said Rose.

'The tenor's wife.'

'I never even shaken hands with Polloarosto,' sighed the older woman.

'I doubt if a man like that would cheat on his wife,' said the Florentine.

'I never ever think about that,' said the older woman. 'I'm only interested in his woice. I got a wery nice husband and family. I'm interested in beautiful singing.'

'Of course, we all are,' said the Florentine.

Rose wondered if they would ever go. The three of them had wandered down a cobbled street and arrived in front of a large food hall.

'I need a sandwich,' said Rose and darted inside.

'They are expensive here,' said the older woman following her inside. 'I once saw Polloarosto buying kumquats in here.'

'They must be good for the voice,' said the Florentine.

'I said, "*Buon giorno*, Signor Polloarosto,' but he vas busy veighing them and didn't recognize me,' sighed the older woman.

'I once saw my tenor in a Neapolitan fish restaurant with his wife,' said the Florentine. 'She was feeding him oysters. The juice was running down his chin. She had his thigh between her knees. They must have an amazing sex life. His thighs are very hard and muscular. He once said in an interview that singing was like an orgasm.'

'Oooouw!' said the Bavarian and blushed.

'Must get a sandwich,' muttered Rose. She was no longer hungry and she wanted to lose the two women and collect her thoughts before she returned to the theatre and the peculiar situation of staring at Leo for several hours without him ever once seeing her. With the unwanted sandwich in her pocket and a promise to join the women for a drink in the opera bar, she headed away alone down a deserted street, thinking, If I linger too long I will become like them. What had Otto said to her on the empty vaporetto in Venice? You just want to fuck his voice. But I made love to him, Rose told herself. Or did I? She was no longer sure of anything.

She didn't leave a note for Leo at the stage door. She took out the letter that she had prepared in London and felt foolish and self-conscious as she reread words that had been written with such conviction and love. She knew that she could never push her way through the stage door huddle and deliver it into the hands of an anonymous doorkeeper, a man who must have greeted Leo's wife on other evenings – and delivered love-letters from other mistresses.

When she got to the theatre that evening the big Bavarian was waiting for her in the foyer. She led Rose downstairs to a crowded bar where she bought them each a glass of sparkling wine and a plate of finger-sandwiches.

'I don't really like Wagner,' she sighed. 'I only come because I have a prescription.'

'You mean subscription,' said Rose.

'Polloarosto vould never sing Wagner,' said the woman. 'He is a vonderful Italian. Of course, I know all Wagner because for years and years I have a prescription. Do you know *Walküre*? Vot it is about?' The woman was staring so intensely at Rose that she wondered if she would be awarded points for giving the correct answer. Then she remembered Leo's words.

'It's a farewell,' Rose quoted Leo.

'Vot a funny thing to say,' said the Bavarian.

When Rose took her seat inside the theatre she found that she was surrounded by empty space. Of course, these would have been Otto and Eva's seats but they had renounced them and were busy with more practical concerns. Rose suddenly knew that the reversal of roles was complete, that Eva and Otto had taken her by the hand and pulled her down into the black hole through which she knew she was still tumbling, only to climb back out, wipe the mud from their hands and move on. Then the storm music swept through the theatre and she forgot about her own life.

She knew that she had to sit through the yearning, ardent first-act encounter of Siegmund and Sieglinde before Leo's entrance in the second. Yearning seemed about right. Her interpreter's mind pondered the word, thought of equivalents in French and Spanish, and thought what an impossible, absurd state it was. To

403

yearn, to long for some unattainable thing, or some unattainable one. And she looked around at the intent German faces in the dark and thought how sensible they were to contain such impossible emotion within the safe, solid walls of their National Theatre.

That first act works itself up to such a fervour that Wagner must have known the audience would come roaring to its feet within seconds of the last notes. Rose took advantage of the roar to slip out and go upstairs where she thought she would be free of the large Bavarian and the yearning Florentine.

She found herself in a Wedgwood blue-and-white gallery with zealously polished parquet flooring. There were large mirrors at either end which confused Rose. She couldn't make out where the great gallery ended and the night and the city began. She started to wonder if the carved Wedgwood room perhaps stretched out across Munich, unfurling itself and its elegant inhabitants before apartment windows and the more mundane night-time activities of watching TV, ironing, sleeping or scratching.

A few minutes inside the gallery showed her that it had both an end and an order. Everyone was walking around in an anticlockwise direction. Rose had unwittingly become part of the parade. They went from blue, white and gold rooms to pink white and gold rooms and back into blue rooms. At some point in the procession Rose looked in a mirror and saw that the Bavarian and the Florentine were about to join the parade just behind her. The bell started ringing.

'Now ve vill see this big handsome Wotan!' bellowed the Bavarian.

'And *he's* got a beautiful wife,' sighed the Florentine. The neat circular parade started to fray at the edges as people returned to their seats. Rose tried to ignore the two women but they caught up with her.

'I see you have empty seats next to you,' said the Bavarian. 'Your friends don't come? Maybe ve sit next to you?' And she and the Florentine followed Rose down the aisle and sat in Otto and Eva's seats.

'Italian men are no good,' sighed the Florentine, studying a photo of Leo in the programme.

'They say dalla Vigna has the sex with womens in his dressing-room between two acts,' said the Bavarian.

All around her Rose could hear Leo's name. She sensed that they were waiting to witness his fall, that for most of them Leo was too successful, too ambitious and, this time, had pushed himself too far. Then Wagner's music roared in, heralding Walkyries and Valhalla and Wotan. And there was Leo. There was Wotan, grave and troubled – the flawed god with his eye-patch over his missing one eye.

'*Che bellissima voce*,' whispered the Florentine.

Rose could think only of the words in the letter: 'I now know that whenever I go out on to a stage to sing, that I sing for you.' She watched Leo as he sang the great monologues of the second act, watched his concentration, his transformation into the beleaguered god, and knew that he was singing for himself, for all the people in the auditorium, and that romantic pronouncements of the kind in the letter were a convenient salvo to smooth the way for his own departure.

And yet by the time they reached the rapturous farewell of the third act, his command of his art swept even Rose along with it. Leo was bidding farewell, but to what? To whom? Rose let the ocean of light that seemed to fill the orchestra and swell beneath Leo's voice carry her with it. For the duration of the farewell she submitted to the insistent ecstasy of Wagner's music. And she understood that Leo, who contained all this within him, needed nothing more. Mere human passion must seem a pallid, tawdry business after such rapture.

Leo kissed his daughter farewell, kissed Annaliese, the kind, pious hostess of that disastrous Christmas party, and strode away, with just one backward glance, through the flames that surrounded Brünnhilde's rock.

He had triumphed. The crowd forgot its earlier desire to see him fall and leapt to its feet. And although Rose knew that a crowd is an intangible, fickle thing, she thought, as he took his tenth curtain-call and single roses rained down on him, that this must be enough for any human being. A crowd can't listen to your heart beat through your winter coat or kiss your eyelids, but the Leo that walked through the flames had made himself as inaccessible and invulnerable as a god and could not need such small quiet things.

The crowd surrounded the stage door when Rose walked towards it with the Bavarian and the Florentine. She no longer knew what to say to Leo. During a moment when she thought her companions weren't listening, she asked the doorkeeper if it was possible to go up to the dressing-rooms. She would, she prayed, know what to say if she could talk to him on his own. But the doorkeeper said that unless her name had been entered on a list by Leo himself she could not go up. And the Bavarian overheard her request and said, 'Of course you vould not be on the list.' Rose hated her for her efficient use of the conditional. She could not know that, in order to attend John's funeral the next morning, Leo had left early by a side-door. Rose walked away from the theatre alone. Next morning she flew back to London. She never told anyone about the vain desperate weekend in Munich.

Chapter Forty-Three

Rose moved out of the house two weeks later. She had rented a one-bedroom flat in Staines. It was an easy commute into London and she would be close to her elderly mother. She had found a temporary post in a Spanish bank, replacing an old acquaintance who was on maternity leave.

Eva seemed unsurprised by her decision to leave. She didn't see Otto alone after the day that she received Leo's letter. Once or twice she sensed that he was watching her from behind a curtain, waiting, but most of the time the twins were busy carrying unwanted furniture and carpeting to a large skip that was now parked outside the house. When Rose gave her notice, Eva smiled her agreement and suggested that Rose help herself to any discarded object that might be of interest to her. Rose declined the offer.

The twins could afford to be in good humour. Eva's idea of cultural tours had been taken up by Otto's boss whose package tour income had fallen considerably. He invested money in the new programme and paid a pair of creative consultants to package 'little Otto' as the two young men insisted on calling him. They understood nothing of the subject of Otto's passion but they did understand that such depth of feeling so eccentrically expressed could make Otto a minor celebrity of the cultural travel circuit and a major source of income to them all. They encouraged him to wear velvet capes and wide-brimmed hats. They sent around a journalist to interview him for a leading music magazine. They planned to send the tours on the Orient Express and they suggested that Otto sing an introduction to the subject of his lecture from the dining-car. He declined this last suggestion.

Because Otto was busy with builders and blueprints, Rose could avoid seeing him alone. She knew that she must reject his proposal but could never find the right moment to tell him. Eva came and knocked on the door on the day after 'the day of the letter' wanting to know what Leo had to say. Rose didn't tell her but confirmed what the older woman suspected: that such irrational attachments are impossible and destructive. Eva smiled a rare smile of approval when Rose expressed her own intention of getting on with a more sensible life.

And so she moved. Daphne and Roger helped her load her possessions into their car one cold Sunday morning in mid-January. Eva kissed her goodbye. Otto waited by the garden gate, stood in the exact spot where Rose had first touched Leo and said, 'I suppose this is your answer.'

'I don't really know,' said Rose and put her arms round him and kissed him hard on the forehead. 'I think it must be.'

Otto nodded. Once again Rose wrote out an address where she could be found and handed it to the twins, although it was, of course, destined for a third party – a third party who would never ask where she had gone.

The weary winter drifted along. Rose made a few friends at the Spanish bank, chosen mainly from the few Spaniards who worked there. She was always glad to glimpse the noble Roman profile and high forehead of the vice president when he walked past her desk. She was comforted by the dark eyes of all her colleagues. She knew, but refused to admit to herself, that she would be looking for such arbitrary features – a greying beard, deep frown lines, even a navy cashmere coat – for the rest of her life. But she never, ever, listened to music.

One day when the space that Leo had filled became too empty to bear, she went to the Italian library and requested back copies of the *Corriere Della Sera*. She saw Leo's face on the third newspaper in the pile. He was standing at John Tillson's graveside. Kay was standing alongside him. Oh, how beautiful she is, thought Rose, and at the darkened desk in the musty office, she wept tears of envy. There is symmetry in this, she told herself. The circle is closed; they are reunited at a graveside. She saw but paid little attention to John Tillson's grieving parents who, not being celebrities, were of little interest to the newspaper and were only just visible in the background. The article said that the young man had died an accidental death by drowning. He had consumed a lot of alcohol and fallen on the icy quayside.

Because there was no-one else to talk to, Rose called her sister. They met in a quiet pub in the West End. Rose, who felt weighed down by silence and sensible living, blurted the whole story out to her sibling.

'You mean you slept with him? You slept with someone famous? How glamorous! How exciting!'

'No, Daphne, it wasn't glamorous,' said Rose. 'He was only a man – a very flawed man—'

'But women wait at stage doors for him. He gets standing ovations in all those romantic opera houses. You got into that world!'

'There really was nothing to get into – just people. That's all there ever is – a rag-taggle bunch of human beings. Anyway, even if there was a glamorous operatic world, I only got a glimpse – now the doors are closed to me for ever.'

'It was an irrational attachment,' said Daphne.

Rose suspected but didn't tell Daphne that irrational attachments carried many people through terrible lives; that the dull daily grind was made bearable by the image of a beautiful actress glimpsed on a stage or the hankering after an adulated rock star or even the love of a human voice. That should have been enough for her but she had made the one mistake of crossing the barrier between comforting fantasy and reality. When she had resisted that trip beyond the proscenium arch and into the dressing-rooms of La Scala, she had known that it would all finish here.

'But I loved him,' she whispered.

'It wouldn't have worked,' said Daphne, but her voice was gentle. 'Things like that have no chance in the real world. Can you imagine the two of you going round Sainsbury's together?'

'But I loved him,' whispered Rose.

Chapter Forty-Four

After John's funeral Leo invited the young American's parents to stay a few days at the villa. They refused. When Kay and Leo had picked them up at the airport they had also refused to come to their home, preferring to hold the polite, stilted conversations that the four of them would have in the overcharged décor and the overstuffed armchairs of the most expensive hotel in the town. Leo was glad of those conversations. They kept him and Kay at a comfortable distance from each other. When they did return to the villa, he slept in a guest-room, and when they talked it was of John. Kay had wept when he confirmed the boy's death. He held her in his arms until she said that she wanted to be on her own in her room. Then he went to the guest-room and wrote his letter to Rose. He posted it in Munich when he flew up there for a rehearsal.

After they said a final farewell to the Tillsons, they drove back home to the villa in silence. Leo dreaded the moment when they would be alone together in the house. Once the door had closed behind them, he busied himself with lighting a fire.

'John used to do that,' said Kay, watching him from the doorway.

'Mmm.' Leo was concentrating intently on the fire. 'You know I didn't know he drank,' said Leo. 'He didn't seem like a drinker. I've been thinking about it since I identified him.'

'He was an impetuous young man,' said Kay. 'That's the age when perfectly sensible kids do very dumb things. It explains why he smashed your statue,' she added.

'He did it?' The log had burst into flames. Leo had

been about to sit back and watch it with satisfaction. Now he turned to Kay. 'But what was he doing upstairs?' said Leo.

'Drunk?' Kay shrugged.

'Oh, my poor Kay—' Leo started to say but she held her hand up to stop him.

'I've made an appointment to see that plastic surgeon,' she said.

Leo made love to his wife that night. This time she didn't resist him, didn't wrap herself in silk. She even drew her slender legs up and clasped him within them as he entered her. But as he entered her his only thought was: this is what we should do now. Their love-making held no sense of homecoming or reconciliation for Leo. And when he had finished, Kay plunged almost immediately into sleep and he returned to the other bed and lay awake feeling lonely.

The weariness that had overwhelmed Leo since his return to the villa encompassed him again that night and when he did sleep, he slept until almost noon. He was awoken by the Pekinese which had climbed onto the bed with him during the night and, as the clock struck twelve, decided to climb onto his head. He groped for the dog and carried it downstairs with him. Kay had obviously been up for hours. She made him coffee. Once they had said everything there was to say about the dog, neither of them could think of another topic of conversation. The unresolved future oppressed Leo. He knew that he should suggest moving back. He decided that he would broach the subject after coffee.

He was halfway through an omelette when the doorbell rang. Kay ran to answer it. He sat quite motionless, a morsel of omelette on the fork in front of him. He was filled with an absurd, inexplicable sense of expectancy. He heard a man's voice and the sound of kissing. He walked towards the hallway and saw Kay standing with an elegant man in his late thirties. He looked like the kind of aristocrat that Leo often saw at first nights in Northern Italian towns. The man turned to acknowledge Leo but his attention was distracted by the Pekinese which hurled itself at his feet. With an apologetic shrug, the stranger bent down and scooped the dog up. Leo looked at his slender fingers with their three expensive rings and knew there was no chance of this man knocking any eyes out. Kay introduced the two men. Leo held out his hand. He heard Kay use the man's title of 'Count'. He saw that the Count had a suitcase which Kay was carrying towards the room that contained her precious tester bed. He excused himself and followed her.

'Who the hell is that?'

'I just told you.' Kay was folding back the white cotton sheets.

'You told me his name but who is he? What's he doing here?'

'He's Winston's father,' said Kay. 'I forgot to tell you he was coming this morning because *I* forgot all about it.'

'Winston's father? Winston's a fucking dog! How long is he staying? What's he doing here?'

'Indefinitely,' smiled Kay.

'Indefinitely,' bellowed Leo. 'Kay, this is not the time for house guests.'

'Oh, I think it is,' Kay smiled again. 'I think it most definitely is.'

Leo sat down hard on the spotless white sheets. 'I don't understand. I had no idea. Is that . . . is he the reason you've decided to get the plastic surgery – for some young, handsome man?' The sentence sounded absurd. He scanned Kay's face for a denial. She smoothed down the white sheet that surrounded his body.

'I'm doing that for me – for my own sense of aesthetics—'

'But who—'

'A friend – most definitely a friend. I don't think even my one flat chest would be manly enough for him,' said Kay. And for the first time in years, she laughed. Leo stared at her in astonishment. Then he

413

thought as he had thought so many times in the distant past: Laughter makes her even more beautiful. She is the most beautiful woman I have ever seen. But this time he also thought: It doesn't matter. It is of no importance.

'Why did we make love last night?' said Leo. 'I don't understand anything. You seemed to initiate it and I thought—'

'I wanted to prove to myself that I didn't need you in that way any more.'

'And did you?'

'Oh yes.' Kay sat down next to him. She patted his hand. 'You're too intense for me, Leo. I've come to understand that, by your standards, I'm superficial. What happened to me all those years ago should have added profound dimensions to my personality but, don't you see, they aren't there? They never were. Remember what the critics said back in Stresa? It was true. I like worrying about things like the colour of the curtains and the size of the rug for the hall. I can spend hours picking out a piece of jewellery. You have contempt for these things but they matter to me. I just want to skim the surface—'

'No, no, Kay. You think you do at the moment because of what happened to John. It's brought all the other business back, but when it passes you'll need—'

Kay was shaking her head.

'Poor old Leo. You're so locked into your world. Other men go to work and pilot planes, run companies, add up figures. You carry all this big operatic emotion around with you to earn a living and I'm just not up to it. It exhausts me.'

'But what about that – that man in there? I still don't understand—'

'He likes what I like. He understands the things that excite me. He is witty and light. Light. He is cultivated and not prone to intense emotion. Next week he's going to introduce me to David Hockney.'

'Swimming-pools,' snorted Leo.

'I like swimming-pools,' smiled Kay.

'But I still don't understand. I thought that with John's death you'd need – you'd need my company – me.'

'Always you, Leo.' Kay got up and opened the window. 'I wasn't quite right for years, I'll admit that, but the lake cured me.'

'What?'

'The lake cured me. I can't explain. I always knew it would and it did.'

'It killed John,' said Leo.

'Swallowed up innocence. Oh yes, that it did, but in one of nature's extraordinary circles it healed me.'

Leo put his head in his hands. 'Do you want me to leave?'

'No.' Kay laughed again. 'There's not going to be any problem of male rivalry. You're hardly ever here anyway. What do *you* want?'

Leo looked out at the lake, started to reply, and with that old familiar flick of the head that chased away all unbidden thoughts and feelings, despatched his first instinctive thought and said, 'I want to go to work. I want my music.'

'See? I knew that within a couple of days you'd be itching to get back to *Die Walküre*.'

'Do you want to come?'

'Can you get two tickets?'

'Does he like opera?' Leo waved his own words away. 'Oh, *they* always do.'

'No crass generalizations now,' said Kay. She had walked to the door. 'I shouldn't leave the Count alone.'

Leo continued to stare out at the lake. Little of what Kay had said made any sense to him but it was her truth. And she had laughed more in the last ten minutes than in the previous ten years. She was still standing in the doorway and when Leo stood to leave the room, she went back and smoothed down the soft white sheet at the spot where he had been sitting.

He left for Munich the following morning. He was relieved to learn that the Count always slept late and

415

that they would not bump into each other in dressing-gowns over cups of coffee. Kay walked with him to the Mercedes.

'I will always look after you,' he said as he opened the car door.

'I know that.' She kissed him on each cheek. He kissed her on the forehead.

'Go back inside,' said Leo. 'It's snowing again. You'll catch cold.'

She stood in the shelter of the front entrance and waited to wave to him. She felt deeply sorry for the dark, solitary figure of her husband as he climbed into the car. Poor Leo, she thought, who must always scale the precipices and gaze into the abyss. Kay was happy to have nothing more to think about than the choice of a restaurant for lunch.

Leo felt sorry for Kay as he turned to wave goodbye to her diminishing figure in the doorway. But he knew that his sympathy was unfounded and he was glad when the car rounded the bend by the snowy wood and he could close his eyes and try to think of nothing but his music. In Munich he went straight to an orchestral rehearsal with Fritz and by the time he fell into his bed in the Four Seasons he was too tired to think of anything except the stray bars of Wagner that still drifted in and out of his brain.

Throughout his stay in Munich, he would feel little need to venture beyond his hotel room and the theatre. At one point during that stay Rose passed in front of his window in the company of a large Bavarian woman and a small passionate Florentine. He was lying on his bed at that moment, fully clothed and staring at the ceiling. She was just a hundred yards away from him.

Chapter Forty-Five

At the end of February Rose had a miscarriage. She hadn't been aware that she was pregnant until the painful moment when she ceased to be. A Spanish secretary from the bank accompanied her to the hospital. The young woman kept crossing herself and crying until Rose told her very firmly to stop.

When it was all over and she was cleaned and sedated and propped up on white pillows in a narrow bed she asked for a telephone and called Eva. She couldn't have said why she turned to the surly twin sister but there was no-one else to whom she wanted to talk. Eva brought her a shocking pink azalea and two packets of digestive biscuits.

'You'll have to do something about the circles under your eyes,' she said, pulling up a chair and sitting alongside Rose.

'Not for the moment,' sighed Rose.

'You had them back in Bavaria. I noticed but didn't like to say anything. It's the trouble with you Latin types – you don't wrinkle as much but you go sallow. There's a concealing cream that covers them up. I saw it on the Boots' cosmetics counter.'

'Sod everything,' said Rose. 'Sod it and fuck it.'

'You can have another one,' said Eva.

'Never will,' said Rose. 'Never will,' and she cried and cried until Eva told *her* very firmly to stop.

'I should have stuck closer to you,' said Rose.

'I usually sat in the front seat,' replied Eva. But Rose meant that she should have stayed closer to Eva's view of the world. She should have kept her eyes on the highways and the hypermarkets. By travelling in Otto's snowbound universe, seeking the ghosts of the

417

nineteenth century, hearing only the siren song of the old world's singing houses, twentieth century Rose had slipped into the ways of those days. But she had forgotten that in the old world loving so unconditionally invariably produced life.

'Otto is outside,' said Eva.

'You didn't tell him?' said Rose.

'Of course I did,' said Eva. 'You knew I would – he's my brother.'

'I feel such a fool,' said Rose, when Otto came in a few seconds later. He had obviously been listening at the door and taken his name as a cue for his entrance.

'Oh my poor dear Rose, this is so awful. How can you stand it?' He sat down hard on the side of her bed. 'Life is such a pointless fucking exercise, and yet when it just gets cancelled out like that . . .' He blew his nose on a tissue from the box by the bed. 'Why do we bother? Why do any of us bother? It's nothing but pain from start to finish, nothing but disappointments, failure, misery and pain.'

'Not all the time,' said Rose.

'All the time, from start to finish, nothing but misery!' cried Otto.

Rose was still groggy. Otto had sat down against her left thigh and she could feel it going numb. She closed her eyes.

'I was quite ecstatically happy for most of this winter,' she said.

'And look where it got you!' cried Otto. 'It always ends in tears. Nothing lasts, nothing holds.'

'Something endures,' said Rose, her eyes still closed.

'What? Tell me what?' Otto blew his nose again.

'I haven't any idea,' mumbled Rose. 'But if someone came in here right this minute and offered to put me painlessly to death, I wouldn't let them, and I'm as miserable as I've ever been in my life – so something must endure.'

'Fear of the unknown, that's all,' sniffed Otto.

'If someone came in here and offered to put *him* down painlessly, I might give it some serious thought,' said Eva. 'When do they come round with tea?' She walked out into the corridor to look for the tea-trolley. Once she was gone Otto said, 'You'll have to tell him.'

'No I won't,' said Rose, opening her eyes and trying to sit up.

'But you must. If you don't, I will.'

'No, Otto.'

'Why not?'

'Because there is nothing to say. A few hours ago there was something and neither of us knew. Now there's nothing so what's the point of getting in touch with the poor man and saying, "By the way, you almost got a second crack at fatherhood. In the end it came to nothing but we just thought you might like to know." It all came to nothing, Otto – nothing.'

'Then I was right two minutes ago, nothing ever comes to anything.'

Rose closed her eyes again. 'No, that wasn't quite what I meant. Look at your life lately. It's changed. I saw your interview in that travel magazine.'

'That's all silliness. All very trite and frivolous.'

'But it's brought in some money, some new acquaintances, even a bit of celebrity.'

'It's not quite up to opening the season at La Scala, though, is it?' smiled Otto.

'I bet that isn't exactly a barrel of laughs.'

'But it might just, for a second, bring you close to a musical summit. I'll never know how that feels.'

'I thought you'd lost some of your interest in music – you don't listen to it that much any more.'

'I do!'

'But you'd stopped when I moved out. Perhaps that's what made it so easy to go – the silence. I hated that sudden silence.'

'But it wasn't silent,' said Otto. 'I couldn't breathe if I didn't have my voices and my Verdi and Wagner and Mozart—'

'The house was so silent the day the letter— I mean, the week after we came back. One day all the music stopped and suddenly everything looked weary and shabby.'

'I bought a discman!' cried Otto. 'It's a portable thing for listening to compact discs. I knew the builders would be coming and crashing and bashing around so I bought this thing to listen to my music in peace.'

'I didn't know that,' said Rose. 'I stopped listening to anything at about that time—'

'You're mad,' said Otto.

'Dear Otto.' Rose was tumbling into sleep again. 'It was that kind of conviction that attracted me to you.'

'You're mad and stupid,' said Otto. 'Just because of one man you can't lock yourself out of a whole world—'

'A world that rejected me,' murmured Rose.

'One man rejected you,' said Otto. Rose lay and cried again with her eyes still closed. 'I too could have sulked twenty years ago because it really did reject me. The truth was I wasn't good enough. I could have gone off in a corner and become all critical and vicious the way some people do but look at what I would have missed.'

Rose dozed as Otto spoke. She wondered if she were perhaps absorbing his words in the way that some language teachers had once deemed it possible to learn vocabulary and grammar by running a tape as one slept.

'The first time I ever heard Caballé that night in Nice when we thought the chandelier would fall – the applause went on so long. And Callas in *Lucia* in Berlin. Riches, Rose, invisible riches and I will contain them for ever . . . that's what I am. I never had a family and yet in a way they are my family. They fill my head, keep me company when I'm lonely, give me energy when I feel old and weary; with luck one day, there I'll be sitting in the plush velvet seat you are so contemptuous of and I'll die while they are singing to me—'

'Nothing to hold on to,' muttered Rose.

'I don't need it. You see, Rose, once you understand

that what actually makes you happy isn't necessarily what other people tell you should make you happy, well, you've learned one of life's great lessons.' His voice faded for a moment then he added, 'I suppose men who enjoy wearing women's underwear feel much the same way.'

'Nothing to cuddle, nothing to talk to,' said Rose.

'You could always reconsider my offer.' Otto fingered the pages of a newspaper that lay on the bed. The last light of the short day was fading behind his shoulders.

'I can't do that, Otto,' said Rose, struggling to stay awake. She propped herself up against the pillows and smiled at him. 'I do love you. I always had an expectancy of grandeur in your company. For a long, long time I got it all wrong. I thought it was chandeliers and applause and marble staircases. But it's you – just you.'

'Then reconsider, Rose – please.'

'You know love doesn't work like that. I wish it did.'

'I don't know anything about that sort of thing. I keep telling you that.'

'Well, it doesn't. Trust me. It doesn't, it doesn't.' She was sinking back into unconsciousness. When Eva returned with a tea-tray, Rose was asleep, so the twins opened a packet of biscuits and sat in silence staring at her.

'She should get her hair touched up,' said Eva. 'There's a lot of grey coming through.'

'Give her time to get better,' said Otto.

'She shouldn't let herself go,' said his sister.

'You did,' said Otto.

'I'm different,' said Eva. Otto nodded in agreement.

'I wish she'd had that baby,' he said after a long silence. 'Imagine if it had inherited that voice.'

'We could have been godparents,' said Eva. 'I'd have liked that.'

'Perhaps we should tell him,' said Otto. 'Send a note to wherever he is, have him call us—'

'No, not unless she says so,' sighed Eva. 'It would be pointless.'

Chapter Forty-Six

A year went by. Rose got a better job that involved occasional travel around Europe. She was glad to have chosen to live so near to the airport. She painted the flat in a shade of apricot that took her weeks of searching through colour samples to locate. Daphne said that she would have been better off with the more neutral magnolia but Rose had found the shade she wanted and devoted an autumn weekend, locked up on her own, to painting the walls.

This new winter brought no snow. A dank, mild, humid English Christmas delivered itself to the flat in Staines and the house in south-west London. On the day of the winter solstice Rose invited some friends from the Spanish bank to her home for a paella. She took too long choosing the wine, forgot to buy saffron and mussels, and when the four Spaniards arrived, was in the steamy kitchen surrounded by pots and hacking at an undercooked chicken. The two women salvaged the meal; the two men opened the wine and took her into the apricot sitting-room where they talked about soccer. Rose was grateful to spend a whole evening speaking Spanish and she was disappointed when her guests left at eleven o'clock because of torrential rain and a long drive back into London.

That last hour of the shortest day in the year seemed endless to Rose. The women had left the kitchen immaculate and when she had rinsed the two remaining brandy snifters there was nothing else to do. She didn't want to read; she had grown to hate the television. She had never dared to follow Otto's example and console herself with music, but as the clock hands trudged from five-past to ten-past eleven, she took out the old vinyl records of *Don Carlos*. For a long time she stared at the label, then she put the disc back in its sleeve and went to bed where she lay awake for a long time full of envy for the Ottos of this world who can find solace in something so intangible. Rose knew that it would never be enough for her.

She was woken at seven o'clock by a ringing phone. It was Otto. She hadn't spoken to him since the end of summer. In autumn the opera season is at its peak and when they had last met he had been preparing to accompany a 'Music of the Winter Palaces' tour to Moscow and St Petersburg.

'Do you know what time it is?' she started to say, but she was too happy to hear his voice to be angry.

'Such excitement, Rose!' said Otto. 'We're having our Christmas party tomorrow and we've got a very special guest.'

'Oh really,' said Rose, thinking . . . but no, no, even Otto wouldn't be that tactless . . . and fate wouldn't be that kind.

'We meant to get in touch with you before but we've been so busy. You will come – it'll be mince pies and mulled wine and all those other dreadful Christmas things?'

'But who will be the guest?'

'Pieter Marinski – he's a young Russian tenor. You must have heard of him.'

'No, no I haven't.'

'But you'll come? It will be our only chance to get together before Christmas. The theme will be Verdi in Russia. You know he went to St Petersburg for the *première* of *The Force of Destiny*? Got himself all kitted out in a fur coat and took his own food supplies along – I'll be giving out his recipe for risotto.'

'Who else will be there?' Rose was uneasy with the inevitable circle that was being traced before her.

'Just the usual old trouts, some new people who've joined as a result of the opera trips—'

'Is that all?' said Rose.

'Well, yes, almost.'

'What do you mean, almost?'

'Well – Clara might come. She was one of the first to recognize this young man's talent and—'

'Then I can't come, Otto,' said Rose.

'But you must. You can't sit out there in some God-forsaken suburb letting yourself get all withered up by bitterness.'

'I'm not, I'm building a life for myself—'

'That doesn't preclude a trip to our house, does it?'

'Of course not, but not tomorrow.'

'Yes tomorrow, most definitely tomorrow. It's Christmas – it's Verdi. Fight bitterness, Rose, or you'll rot away from the feet upwards like that hotelier in Venice.'

For a moment Rose didn't know what he meant. She had sought not to think about Venice for almost a year. When she started to protest that she wasn't bitter, Otto was already saying goodbye and that he expected her at seven o'clock.

Because she feared the bitterness that had settled upon her, Rose took up Otto's challenge and decided to attend the Christmas party. She took a long time choosing her clothes; she rinsed her hair a dark, almost auburn, blonde and put on more make-up and perfume than usual. She arrived an hour late. The front door was open. Otto had finished his talk and was ladling mulled wine into a row of glasses on the kitchen table.

'I'd given up on you,' he said.

'We thought you were Clara,' said Eva.

'Why Clara?'

'Because she said she'd be late. Her fiancé is conducting a concert at the Festival Hall and—'

'Her fiancé?' said Rose.

'Oh yes. She's getting married next month. Didn't Otto tell you?'

'I didn't think Rose would be interested,' said Otto.

'I'm not,' said Rose, helping herself to a glass of the warm wine. 'Who is she marrying?'

'A young Hungarian conductor she met on some

yacht off the Sardinian coast last summer,' said Otto.

'I'm amazed,' said Rose. 'How did she—' She had been about to say, 'How did she do it?' but stopped herself in time.

'Life moves on,' said Eva. 'People change, things happen.'

'Of course,' said Rose, for whom life had stopped one January day almost a year earlier. 'What's he like?'

'You'll see when they get here,' said Otto. 'But let's not talk about her – tell me about you, Rose. What's been happening with you?'

Since very little seemed to happen except in her dreams, Rose could think of nothing to say. She was relieved when the doorbell rang. Otto went to answer it. She heard Clara's voice in the hallway, followed by a heavily accented male voice. They didn't come into the kitchen but went into the main room where Rose heard cries of greeting in incomprehensible languages. She remembered that she hadn't even bothered to feign an interest in the young Russian tenor. She poured herself some more wine, reapplied her lipstick and made her way slowly to join the party.

Nobody noticed her arrival. The room was full. Otto's old trouts were there, dusty and rickety as ever, but they were outnumbered by younger people with louder voices, more contemporary clothes and faces. Otto's lifelong passion had become fashionable. Most of the people were thronging around one corner where Rose could see Clara and a very handsome man of about thirty-five. They had brought a case of champagne. From where Rose stood, she could see that the frosty bottles were perfectly chilled. They gave off a faint mist as the handsome young man popped them open. Rose had a sudden longing for champagne and the lightness that went with it, but that corner of the room seemed a long way away and was dauntingly young and exuberant. The Russian tenor had linked arms with the Hungarian and was singing a folk song. Glasses were filled and refilled. There were sudden inexplicable bursts of applause.

425

'He's very handsome,' said Rose to Eva who was gathering up empty plates on a tray. 'And very young.'

'And why not?' said Eva. 'It's always been perfectly acceptable for older men to have younger women so why not the other way round?'

'Oh, you're quite right,' said Rose. 'I suppose he's had quite a struggle, being from the east.'

'If you mean, "is he after her money?" he's got plenty of his own,' said Otto, who had reappeared from the hallway. 'And he seems to be extraordinarily nice.'

'Then why Clara?' Rose shut her eyes and sat down on a nearby armchair. 'I shall never understand life, ever.'

'Perhaps true love has changed her,' said Otto, refilling her glass. 'Isn't it supposed to do that?'

Rose didn't reply. She finished the wine and went outside, down the stairs to sit on a damp seat under the beech tree. The night was a mild, humid English winter's night and she could sit for a long time without feeling the cold. She noticed that Eva had replaced the red velvet curtains in her old room with the long promised floral prints. When the wind got up, she went back inside to the kitchen. In the sitting-room someone was playing a piano. The tenor was still singing. The small crowd was still applauding.

Clara came into the kitchen carrying a half-full bottle of champagne. She saw Rose, swayed slightly and held up the bottle and a glass. Rose stared back at her but Clara didn't notice. She poured a glass of warm champagne and handed it to Rose.

'Be here till bloody dawn,' she muttered and sat down at the table opposite her. Rose realized that Clara hadn't recognized her. She *was* very drunk. She spread her arms out on the table, rested her head on them and dozed. Rose sat, mesmerized by the sleeping, quite innocuous presence of the cause of so much heartache. She noticed the large emerald on Clara's ring finger and thought of her beloved silk dress and another table in a restaurant on a winter's night in Milan.

Clara sat up with a jerk and consulted her watch. 'Be here all night,' she said.

'Have him take you home,' said Rose.

'Can't do that. Won't come. Won't do anything he doesn't want to. Fucking men never do.' She closed her eyes again but she wasn't sleeping. A few seconds later she said, 'Father wouldn't either.'

'Wouldn't take you home?' said Rose. Part of her wanted to get out of the kitchen and away from Clara, for she knew that all that Clara represented was being dragged up from deep inside her and that the fragile peace she had made with pain might not survive this clammy night. And yet she remained mesmerized by the bony, dark woman before her.

'Wouldn't do anything he didn't want to. Even when he knew he was dying and he knew I knew – he wouldn't let me near him. Not for six weeks – six whole fucking weeks.'

'But he must have seen you during that time,' said Rose.

'Not once. Not once,' mumbled Clara. 'And all because I went to a poor babe's funeral. He punished me for that, for going to a funeral.' She closed her eyes again. 'Ever see Maria Callas?'

'No,' said Rose.

'Haven't lived.'

The linguist in Rose noted that drink had drowned Clara's pronouns. The rest of her was struggling with dates, lapses of time, trying to align Leo's story with Clara's drunken ramblings.

'When did you last see your father?' She heard herself utter the title of a Victorian painting. The words sounded absurd but she repeated them. 'When did you last see your father?'

'February the eighteenth, 1973.'

Rose recalled that Leo's child had died in March.

'Did you speak to him on the phone after then? Or write to him?'

'Wouldn't answer – begged him to see me, pleaded, wouldn't, wouldn't . . .'

427

The Hungarian had come into the kitchen. Rose watched with a dull pain in the pit of her stomach as he wrapped a coat around Clara's shoulders, whispered endearments and escorted her to their car. But as soon as they were gone, she rummaged in a drawer, found paper and pencil and wrote down the dates of Clara's tale and alongside them the dates of Leo's. Then she sat in silence and stared at the written proof of what they, what she and Kay and Clara, had all really known all along – that there had been no pact, no false claim to glory – Leo had done it all on his own.

She reached for the phone but as she raised her finger to dial the number she realized that there was nowhere to call, no-one to tell. Leo had gone, had decided to go, and deliberately left her no means of contacting him.

'Oh, my Leo,' she sobbed to the empty kitchen. Always the doubt hovered that the reasons for his departure were colder, more complex, than his last letter had stated. Always there was the fear that after that one brief coming together he would have gone anyway.

The Russian tenor was singing a solo. Rose recognized the aria from that last lost winter. She couldn't have named it, couldn't have even said where she heard it, but for the first time in almost a year she sat and listened to music. When the Russian stopped, there was applause, people murmured 'Encore' and names of other arias, and within a few seconds he was singing the piece again. Rose tried in vain to identify it, then realized that she didn't need to know its name or from where it came. It was quite, quite beautiful in itself. And it brought back to her the winter that she had sought to forget.

Sitting in the empty kitchen, she remembered horse-faced Annaliese and fierce Fritz, a Bulgarian baritone shaking his fist at the audience, a soprano whose voice felt like a cascade of pearls; she remembered the fat chorists, the invisible orchestra players, the adoring fans at the cold stage doors, the besotted homosexuals, a star-struck German policeman in a Bavarian blizzard, and the blasé, the greedy and the inspired who all came together in Verdi, in Wagner, in Mozart. And a year, a lifetime, away, an old woman with a walking-stick had wept with Isolde. What had Leo said? Once you really hear this music, know it, you will have taken into yourself the equivalent of a Sistine Chapel or all of Shakespeare and you will carry it within you for ever. It strengthens you for whatever life may bring.

Rose decided to join the small group in the next room. But by the time she had folded away the precious piece of paper and picked up her glass, they had turned to singing carols. The Russian was dozing against a piano leg and Eva was looking at her watch. Otto saw Rose and beckoned her back into the kitchen.

'We haven't had time to talk,' he said. 'You must come to tea next Sunday just you and us. We'll talk about our travels. I'll show you our photos of St Petersburg—'

'All right,' said Rose. When she left the house a few minutes later, the group was singing 'In the bleak midwinter', but nobody seemed to know any of the words, and as she walked away down the path in the muggy, drizzly night it was to the accompaniment of 'In the bleak midwinter la la mm la la.'

Chapter Forty-Seven

The next Sunday Eva baked a cake and took it up to Otto's flat.

'No, Eva, no,' he said when he opened the door and saw her standing there with the iced cake on its bone-china stand. 'That's not what I had in mind – you meant well but it's all so Women's Institute.'

'Sod you, Otto,' said Eva, whose syntax would never change.

Otto pulled her inside the flat, shut the door and pushed her towards the living-room.

'I've been given a second chance, Eva,' he said as he sat her down on the sofa. 'Things have to be different. I don't quite know what I'm doing but I can't do some prissy tea – not this time, not for Rose.'

'I suppose I'm not welcome,' said Eva, reaching for her cake.

'Of course – come up and see the slides of Russia but don't stay too long.'

'Sod you, Otto,' said Eva, and carried her cake back downstairs.

Rose didn't come. Otto waited an hour, two hours, then went out to a phone-box and called her number. He got a recording, saying that she had been called out of town on urgent business.

He returned to the flat. Eva heard his footsteps on the stairs. A few minutes later she heard the sound of crockery smashing against the wall. She ran upstairs and knocked and called but he didn't answer. Late into the night Eva could hear him sweeping books and records off the shelves. She knew the layout of the flat so well that she could tell that he was working his way systematically through everything that he treasured.

She heard him send the books and records tumbling to the floor, heard the tearing and crashing, heard the glass on precious photos shatter. After a while she could stand it no more and she sat with her hands over her ears until, at almost midnight, the noise stopped.

Rose was in Munich. She had found the last place on a cheap ski charter. Everyone else on the plane was dressed in phosphorescent oranges and blues. They all seemed to belong to large noisy groups. Rose sat in silence with a small overnight bag tucked under her feet. From time to time she took out the crumpled piece of paper with those long-distant dates and read it and reread it.

She had studied those dates so many times in the week since Otto's party that the paper had torn in two and had to be put together with Sellotape. She hadn't thought of rewriting it. She took the paper into work, studied it during her lunch-hour and she concluded that Leo should know. She told herself that there was no hope that this new knowledge would bring him back to her; she was simply, she told herself, a servant of the truth.

Then she had set about locating him. She bought a music magazine and studied the cast lists of the four greatest singing houses: La Scala, Vienna, the Met in New York and, with the deepest hurt, Covent Garden itself. Leo's name was nowhere. She scanned the cast lists of Paris, Munich, Zurich, Hamburg, Berlin, Naples, Rome, Florence, San Francisco, Geneva, Turin, Genoa, Venice, Sydney, Chicago, Barcelona, Buenos Aires, on and on she searched, and not once did she see his name. When she reached the end of the lists, a chill ran through her as she realized that he could have died and no-one would have told her. She rarely read newspapers and Leo was not a celebrity who interested the mass media. Of course, she told herself, Otto would have told her. He would not have been able to contain himself. No, no, Leo was alive but she could not know where he was because she knew nothing of his daily existence. She tried to imagine him somewhere, in a hotel room, in a restaurant, a dressing-room, walking across a deserted piazza at night. Surely lovers maintain such invisible bonds? Surely some telepathy must exist with a man so intensely, albeit so briefly, loved. None did. With another icier chill, she realized that she could only picture Leo in the past.

When she had read those cast lists a second and third time, she saw a name that she did recognize – Hartman. Annaliese was still singing and still in Munich. She and Rose had met for no more than a few minutes but Rose remembered the plain woman's smile of welcome in the stairwell and her minute of prayer in her home, and placed her faith in Annaliese. She took three days to gain the courage to call the Nationaltheater. Each time she reached for the phone her heart pounded so hard in her chest that she couldn't hear herself speak. When she did make the call she was told that Annaliese was not available and that she should leave a message. She left three messages and got no reply. She called a fourth time and asked first in English and then in faltering German if Annaliese was there. An anonymous female voice had said, 'She sing tomorrow, she sing tomorrow.'

Tomorrow was Saturday. Rose had got the last seat on the ski charter. She had a return ticket booked for a flight that left at midnight on the Sunday. She told herself that she could do what she had to do and be back at her job, tired but discharged of all responsibility, on the Monday morning.

When she landed in Munich, she couldn't see out of the window because one of the brightly clad men was staring out. He turned to her and said, 'Incredible snow! Even down here!'

'Thank God,' said Rose. And for a few seconds as she gazed past his shoulder at the white fields beyond the runway, she believed that everything here had lain in wait, unmoving, unchanging, for her return.

She left the luminous blue and orange people and

432

took the bus to the train station and walked from there to the Nationaltheater at the Max Josef Platz. She thanked the Fates that it was Wagner again and that the performance, therefore, started at tea-time. She waited in the cold by the stage door, watching all the anonymous people who had access to Leo's world, and searching for the familiar face of Annaliese.

The soprano was the last to arrive. She pulled up in her own car. Somebody from inside the stage door leapt out and took her place at the wheel. Annaliese ran in, clutching a garment bag and muttering in German about taxis and weather. She was accompanied by a small, bald man and a young woman. They blocked Rose's access to the singer. She saw the moment when Annaliese would pass before her without even knowing she was there. She held out a hand and clutched at the soft suede sleeve of Annaliese's green coat. The older woman turned, irritated, and then she recognized Rose.

'Annaliese, please, I have to contact Leo,' said Rose. 'It's urgent.'

'*Auf Deutsch, auf Deutsch*,' said the soprano. 'I no time – need time for English.'

'Leo, *wo ist Leo*?'

'*Die Jagdhütte*,' said Annaliese. She squeezed Rose's arm. 'I am so late. Fritz boys all sick with flu. We talk after. Come back here.'

'I'll try,' said Rose who herself had even less time. 'Is Leo all right?'

Annaliese shrugged. 'We talk after.' She smiled and turned to leave.

'Can you give me the address of this – this Jagdhütte?'

Annaliese muttered an instruction to the small, bald man, said, '*Später, später*,' to Rose and started down the corridor. Rose had one more question for her.

'Is he – is he with his family or . . . ?' She translated her question into her poor German. Annaliese paused, turned, smiled and said, '*Allein, allein*,' and was gone. The small man was writing the address in capital letters.

433

'How do I get there?' said Rose. 'Is there a train station near by?'

'Change at Garmisch,' said the man. 'Then a taxi for ten kilometres.'

'And what is a Jagdhütte?'

'A hunting-lodge,' said the man.

Rose went straight back to the train station. She noticed nothing of the journey to Garmisch. She could think only that for once life had had the good grace to wait, or at least put itself back into the same place as last year. She had been given what the Americans would call a rain check – except in this case a snow check was more accurate. Here they were where they had left off in the snow *en route* for the hunting-lodge – except that this time Leo had gone on ahead. At Garmisch there was no connecting train that evening but Rose didn't care. She decided that a morning arrival would be better and wandered out into the snow to look for a hotel, swinging her bag and singing to herself as she stumbled on the ice.

Next morning she ate an early breakfast and had an hour to kill before the first train came through. She walked into town, past the ski shops, the casino and the coffee-houses. She wandered into a frozen, formal garden with a shuttered pavilion at one end. A sign at the entrance said 'Kurpark'. Rose decided that this must translate as 'Curepark' and still in the buoyant mood of the previous day said out loud, 'If I stand here long enough, will *I* be cured?'

As she rounded a bend on the only path in the frozen garden, an old couple came into view. They both wore the traditional Bavarian green and walked arm in arm under a dark green umbrella flecked white by the falling snow. The sight of these old lovers so comfortable in their own context was like a punch in the stomach to Rose – all the buoyancy of the morning was gone as she watched them walk ahead of her. They were no hybrids these – they knew where they came from, had surely shared the same childhood landscapes, were linked by language, food, weather, even the shape and smell of an old school building, stored away in mutual memory. They were not two strangers who had just once come together over so many gulfs.

Still she took the train and journeyed on, travelling in the daylight through those pine forests of last Christmas Eve. When she arrived at the nearest village, she found that there were no taxis and that the only way to get to the lodge was to walk five miles through the snow. Before she set out, she stopped at a small coffee-house, sat down at a window-seat and ordered a hot chocolate. And she saw Leo and a laughing young brunette come out of a baker's across the street and get into a Mercedes.

Rose sat in the window-seat for another hour. She stared after the Mercedes as it drove towards the mountains and then she sat and saw nothing of the Sunday morning bustle that passed on the pavements outside.

When she did leave the café, she too turned towards the mountains. She had persuaded the owner to keep her overnight bag behind the counter but although she had nothing to carry she dragged her steps out of the small town and onto the pine-bordered road. She had lost the wings of hope that had carried her this far.

'I lost self-delusion – that's all,' she told herself as she scrambled up a steep hill. 'I had twelve hours of it – and now it's gone. But it has nothing to do with why I came.' She could not let herself think about the laughing brunette. For the first mile, she did try to recall the face of the young woman who had waited outside the La Scala dressing-room and even convinced herself that it was she who had gone ahead with Leo to the hunting-lodge. Then she realized that it was of no importance. 'Only my pride is hurt,' she repeated to herself as the hill levelled out and the road stretched ahead of her. 'Only my pride is hurt.' And soon she shortened this to, 'It's just pride – what's pride?', turning the phrases into a marching rhythm that carried her almost three miles and an hour into her journey.

All energy left her in that next, penultimate mile. The road had climbed upward again and to keep on the flattened, gritted snow, she had to skim the edge of the barbed wire. Halfway along, it caught her coat and ripped the sleeve. She unhooked herself and took the time to rest. She was sweating hard and she knew that her cheeks were glowing and that her hair was damp. She wished for long legs like Daphne's to carry her the last mile. She wished to be safe and sensible like Daphne. She resolved that her own irrational behaviour would end with this last journey. Never again would she love like this. Never again would she feel so desperate and driven and vulnerable. Never again would she be at the mercy of another wayward, difficult human being.

At the top of the hill, she saw the hunting-lodge – it was the only building in sight and lay next to a small wood behind a frozen brook. Smoke was coming from the chimney and for a moment the scene seemed to be as innocent and comforting as a picture in a book of fairy tales. Then she remembered the brunette, imagined Leo building the fire to warm her, and wished for witches and spells and poisoned apples.

A sign saying 'Fussweg' pointed away from the road and led through the forest. Rose followed it, calculating that it was a short cut down to the lodge and grateful that it went through the trees and spared her the sight of that spiral of smoke. 'Just pride – what's pride?' kept her going. From time to time the trees would shudder and shed their snow with a gentle sigh. 'Just pride – what's pride? – shoosh,' said Rose and the trees.

Then the forest ended, the trees slipped away behind her and she was at the gate to the lodge. All courage left her as she looked hard at the frescoed walls, the sloping roof and the open shutters. She decided to write a note, push it through the door and make her way back. She had no pen and the only paper was that tattered sheet on which she had written the two dates and their corresponding events. She stood by the gate, tired and sweating, all noble intentions forgotten and not a notion of what to do next.

Leo saw her. He had been standing staring out at the mountains when he sensed a small moving figure at the far limit of his peripheral vision. He turned to look more closely and knew immediately who it was. Rose was still standing, quite lost, on the other side of the gate when he opened the door.

'Leo!' Rose saw the tall figure standing in the shadows of the doorway. She pushed open the gate and made her way up the path. She couldn't see his face until she was within feet of him. He looks greyer, graver, than before, she thought. Oh his hair was still black, as was most of his beard, and she could see his dark brown eyes now, but 'grey' and 'grave' were the words that came to her. Grey, grave – awful words. She was almost at the door. He was wearing a dark sweater and had his hands in the pockets of his grey trousers. At some point as she crossed those last few inches, those hands should have moved, should have reached out towards her but they remained hidden in his pockets. She had been sure that he was smiling when he opened the door but now he just stared at her. And he was surrounded by music – not his music, not the music he made, that was part of him, but by jangling, abrasive electronic sounds that were coming from a radio in the upper part of the house.

'Rose,' he said. Still he stood in the doorway, hands in pockets. 'You should not have come – not here, not like this.'

'You could at least look surprised to see me.'

'I am,' said Leo and ushered her inside. He stood well back as she passed in front of him. Even their bulky winter clothes did not touch. He led her into the room where the log fire was burning. She followed him, confident that the room would be empty for she could hear the brunette moving around upstairs. Leo

437

closed the door behind them and motioned towards an armchair. 'You're all frosty – you need a towel,' he said and left the room for a few minutes. She heard him go up the stairs and open a door. The awful music grew louder and with it came the noise of a running shower. Then the door closed and he came back downstairs. Rose was staring at the fire imagining the comfortable intimacy between him and the naked dark woman in the bathroom, when he placed the towel on the armrest beside her.

'And take off your coat,' he said. But he made no attempt to take it or even show her where to put it, so she slung it awkwardly over the other armrest where it dripped onto the rug and the edge of the hearth. She thought again how grey and grave he looked, and how wary.

'And why did you come?' He leaned forward very slightly. There was a loud ticking clock somewhere in the room. She could not bring herself to look away from him and locate it. Off in the distance she could hear geese honking. He was waiting for her reply. All she had to do was give it, explain in a few brief sentences the purpose of her journey, and then she could leave. It would all be over and he would remain in this warm and beautiful lodge with the dark woman who was wet and naked just a few feet above their heads.

That woman must have come out of the bathroom for the noise of the radio increased.

'I can't talk with that row going on,' said Rose.

'I hate it too,' said Leo. He walked to the door and called up the stairs, 'Mariella! *Basta!*'

'Does she live here?' asked Rose, with a sudden absurd hope that the brunette was perhaps a maid or a housekeeper.

'No – neither do I.'

'But she stays overnight?'

'Just last night – I wasn't expecting visitors.'

I only got one night, thought Rose, but she said, 'I was told you were alone. Otherwise I wouldn't have

438

come. Annaliese told me where you were and she said you were alone.'

'You saw Annaliese?'

'For a couple of minutes yesterday. Just long enough for her to tell me where you were and that you were—'

'Alone.' Leo shrugged.

'Why aren't you singing, Leo? I looked in cast lists all over the world. What are you doing here?'

Leo stood up and walked back to where he had been standing when he had seen Rose.

'I couldn't stand the – the . . .' He snapped his fingers as if to summon the English word out of the air. '*Il clamore*. I'm sorry, I don't speak English much these days—'

'Why not? Where is Kay?'

Leo ignored these questions. His attention was fixed on that one Italian word. He repeated it, '*Clamore* – how do you say this in English?' He had turned to look at her but the white winter light in the window behind him dazzled Rose and prevented her from seeing his face.

'Clamour?' said Rose.

'Clamour. I had to get far away from the clamour. After that Wotan in Munich I didn't know where to go. All that work, then such ecstasy to sing, all that applause, and then emptiness. I didn't know where else to go to get away from all those surface feelings – those big circles.' He traced a circle with his right arm.

'Is that a surface feeling?' Rose pointed to the ceiling where the radio had been turned on in another room.

'Oh yes, very much,' said Leo. 'But sometimes necessary.' He sat back down in the chair. 'You still haven't told me why you came.'

'And you didn't tell me what happened to Kay.'

'It's a long story.'

'I'm used to your long stories,' said Rose. And Leo almost smiled. She waited for him to go on. He said nothing.

'I'm used to your long stories,' she said again. 'But the last one you told me was incomplete.'

'How is that?'

She told him about her encounter with the drunken Clara, tried to explain the dates and their significance and rummaged in her bag for the piece of paper. She handed it to Leo. His fingers brushed hers as they took it. It was the first time that they had touched in a year. He felt in his pocket and brought out some reading glasses.

He wasn't wearing those last year, thought Rose. She noticed a few grey hairs at the opening of his shirt and thought, Grey, grave . . .

He read the paper slowly, folded it and handed it back to her.

'So you see,' her voice sounded too young, too hopeful, 'you did it all on your own.'

'Yes,' said Leo and she saw in his face that same quizzical look that she had seen in London and on the street in Milan, as though he was seeking something in her face. Then it was gone and he said, 'From the moment I saw you, I knew you held something for me.'

'And that was it? Just that? I'm some sort of heavenly messenger destined to deliver you of a truth?'

The grandfather clock ticked on. The young woman in the room upstairs had turned off the radio. Rose could hear her steps going around closing doors. Soon she would come downstairs. The restless geese were flying round and round outside. Rose could sense the shadow they cast over the white light in the window as they swooped, first one way then the other.

Rose watched Leo and waited.

Then something in her rebelled against waiting. She had not lost a child, had her life stopped, travelled all this way to leave all the answers in his hands. Rose sat on in silence but she was no longer waiting. She had made *her* decision. There remained just one obstacle.

'Where is Kay?'

'Still in the villa,' said Leo. 'Living with a count.' He took his glasses off and wiped them. 'A homosexual count – they go to auctions and lunches.' He put a question mark after the word 'lunches' as though he had never heard of such a thing.

'A lot of women are very comfortable with homo-sexuals,' said Rose.

'So I am told,' said Leo. 'I will never understand people, ever.' He rubbed his fingers into the deep frown lines at the top of his nose.

'Where do you live now?' asked Rose. She hated this check-list of questions but she sensed the approach of the young woman upstairs and she needed to know this one last answer.

'In that same apartment in Milan but I'm buying a house near Parma. I sign the papers next week.'

'Going home,' said Rose. 'Back to the earth, back to Verdi.' At the mention of his old hero, Leo relaxed and smiled that same naïve smile that she had first seen outside the hotel in Füssen.

'And you, Rose. Tell me about you – what are your plans?'

By asking about her future, he had tacitly answered yes to that earlier question that still hung between them: Was my only purpose to deliver you of a truth? He was despatching her off into the world. But Rose no longer cared. She was no longer dependent on his reply. She had made her decision.

Rose knew that the average mortal has little access to moments of luminous, incandescent truth. Such moments are glimpsed for a second then carried away on the tide of daily existence. Rose had just experienced one such moment. Now she had to respond to it.

Light footsteps echoed on the staircase. Leo swore to himself in Italian, walked into the hallway and closed the door behind him. Rose heard a car on the driveway, the sound of a rapid embrace and the front door opening and closing. She waited for Leo to return. When many long minutes later, he still hadn't appeared, she went to the window to see if he was in the garden.

The geese had stopped swooping and honking overhead and were flying towards the horizon. Two men had appeared in the field next to the forest. Rose heard shots and saw two of the geese plummet to earth.

'You shouldn't have been so indecisive,' she whispered through the glass pane.

She waited several more minutes for Leo. There was no sound of him in the hallway and she wondered in a moment of panic if he had perhaps ridden away in the taxi. She was about to go out of the warm, safe room and look for him in the rest of the house when he walked in carrying a pile of logs.

'The fire was almost dead,' he said and heaped them onto the embers.

'I just saw two geese get shot,' said Rose. 'I never saw that before – a living thing – shot out of existence.'

'This *is* a hunting-lodge,' said Leo.

'But you don't hunt?'

'Of course not.' He sat back in his chair on the other side of the fire. Rose was still standing at the window, watching the hunters and their dogs as they approached the dead birds.

'I am grateful that you came so far to tell me this,' said Leo. 'But I meant everything I said in my letter, Rose, and I still do. I didn't write it on an impulse. I sat up all one night trying to find the English words.'

'You did a very good job,' said Rose.

'After I met you I tried to imagine what it would be like to have a new partner. I'd always had Kay – off in the distance perhaps, but in a way I respected her independence. I looked around at my colleagues and their wives who are always there, like Siamese twins, like nursemaids, and I knew then that people like us who perform, who pretend to be God but behave like puppies wanting the whole world to love them, we consume others with our selfishness—'

'I wouldn't have let you consume me.'

'I know and I didn't want to but it had already started just as before. Do you know why I offered to pay for John's body to be flown home? Not out of any

442

great concern for his parents but for my own selfish reasons, because I couldn't stand the thought of being back at that cemetery. And those imbecile Americans wouldn't listen. So there we were again, graveyards and coffins and young death. Round and round, endless circles.'

'So now you are going home to Verdi?'

Leo nodded. 'I'm preparing some master-classes. I think for a while I want my life to be as flat as the land around Bussetto.'

'Back to Verdi?' Rose repeated.

'Yes, yes. That's what I said.'

'Far from the Wagnerian summits?'

'I suppose so,' said Leo. 'I hadn't thought of that.'

'I wouldn't have thought of it on my own,' said Rose. 'But last winter when I heard so much music that my life was changed for ever, someone said to me that Wagner can take us to such ecstasy that ordinary life is almost unbearable afterwards, whereas Verdi, like Shakespeare, reconciles us to the earth, to our miserable human condition, makes us noble in our despair.'

'That's quite a speech, Rose,' laughed Leo.

'Alas, none of the thoughts are mine.'

'But they are all true – I didn't know where to go after that *Walküre*. In a way I was glad to have the duty of going home. I walked out of the theatre after all that ecstasy and all that exhaustion, and thought, I can die now.'

'But you didn't. And in Hohenschwangau, when you had the choice, you chose the humbler family residence and rejected that cold, looming dream castle on the hill.'

'You mustn't see meaning where there is none.'

But all Rose could see at that moment was the middle-aged man who sat in front of her and she saw that there were no living legends, no myths, no great invulnerable sources of comfort and security. There was just Leo who had no solutions, who was as perplexed by life as she was.

'Perhaps, but choices reveal character,' said Rose.

'And you are much, much better than you think.'

'*Basta! Basta!* Enough of me.' Leo got up and walked back to the window. 'You still haven't said what you are going to do. What are your plans?'

Once again he was sending her away.

'Well, first I'd like you to call me a taxi. I have a plane to catch at midnight.'

'Tonight!' He scowled out at the snow.

'What else should I do? This isn't a holiday.'

'No, no, of course not. Then I will call for a cab.'

He started towards the door but stopped as he reached for the handle.

'That wasn't what I meant by plans, Rose.'

'I know.'

Then he was gone, back in the hallway, and she heard him say, '*eine halbe Stunde*', and knew that the taxi would be there in half an hour.

'Half an hour,' Leo said when he came back into the room. He clapped his hands together, then let them drop to his sides, smiled at Rose and said, 'You could have stayed a little longer and eaten something.'

'I don't want to miss my plane.'

'No, no, of course not. Would you like to drink something while you're waiting?'

'No thanks.'

'So, Rose! Tell me about your life, your other plans.' Again he rubbed his hands together but, away from the stage, Leo could not feign emotion for long and soon the falsely boisterous hands had disappeared into his pockets and he was staring hard at Rose.

Again the words 'grey' and 'grave' drifted up to her. Slowly, slowly, the sentence had been forming in her mind. Daphne had been wrong. Eva and Otto had been wrong. Irrational as this attachment might be she knew now that she would love Leo until one or other of them lay in that grey old grave. Now she had to voice the decision that she had taken fifteen long minutes ago.

'I'm moving to Parma.' She was trembling when she said it and could hardly look at him.

'What!'

444

'I'm moving to Parma.' Now she looked straight at him.

'When did you decide this?'

'About fifteen minutes ago,' said Rose.

'But you can't!'

'Oh I can. It's in the EEC you know, so it's quite straightforward.'

The doorbell rang. Again Leo swore to himself in Italian but this time when he went into the hall, he left the door open. The two hunters stood in the front doorway. They held the dead geese out to Leo. Their cheeks were red, they wore feathered caps and dark green knickerbockers with thick woollen socks rolled up around the knees. The dead geese dripped blood onto the doormat. Both men looked proudly at the geese and shyly at Leo.

'*Per il maestro*,' said the shorter man.

The freezing outside air filled the hallway. The two men looked past Leo at the fire. He hesitated, looked at Rose and said, 'You must come by for drinks tomorrow.' He accepted the dead geese and closed the door.

'That was kind of them,' said Rose.

'But wild goose is awful,' whispered Leo, as if the two men might still be within earshot. 'Tough and tasteless. And look, they are bleeding all over Annaliese's floor.'

'Well, put them in the kitchen,' said Rose, and followed Leo and the trail of blood towards the back of the house.

'I don't know what to say, Rose,' said Leo once the two thin corpses were laid in the sink. 'I've never encountered a situation like this.'

'It's not your situation so there is nothing for you to say.'

'I don't understand.'

'I'm not asking to move in with you, Leo. I don't think we will ever live together. I doubt if there is a happy, domestic ending for us. Independent of you, I'm moving to Parma. True, if you had said that you were moving to the Congo, well, then I'd have gone there too. It would have been less convenient but I'd have managed—'

'Crazy Englishwoman,' said Leo but he was laughing in spite of himself. 'Be sensible, Rose. What could you do in Parma?'

'Teach English, push old contessas around in wheelchairs, add Italian to my languages and do some more translating work. Oh, there's plenty to do and I want to do it on my own but not too far away from the possibility of seeing you. It's all very satisfying for your operas to end tragically but I don't intend to be a romantic old Englishwoman with just memories.'

'But are new starts possible at our age?'

'You'll have to answer that one on your own,' said Rose. 'Speaking for myself, well, I've told you what I intend to do. Once I'm settled perhaps we'll bump into each other from time to time. I plan to start by having a front-row seat in all your master-classes. I'm sure you can teach even a non-musician like me something—'

'Oh, I can find my way around Verdi's world and Wagner's,' sighed Leo. 'But I don't seem to understand much of this one.'

'Neither do I. But I do know that I've lived life before you and I've lived life without you, and I don't like either. I know I'll always share you with the music and the dead composers and that there will always be people giving you geese and staring, and beautiful dark women in upstairs bedrooms, but even if we only meet at the market buying our cheeses—'

'What would you know about buying Italian cheese?' said Leo.

'I'll learn,' said Rose, who could picture the market as she spoke. She did not tell Leo that those words 'grey' and 'grave' had refused to leave her since she had walked up the path and that she had understood that they could not be ignored, that older lovers must acknowledge them and know that their time is short and getting shorter. Instead she centred her thoughts on that market, saw its colours and textures, its reds and yellows and greens, its daily promise of rebirth in a world that for her had been without colour or taste for one long year.

'From time to time you will buy me a coffee in the piazza. Is there a piazza in Parma? But of course there must be – what's it called?'

'Piazza Garibaldi,' said Leo. He had folded his arms and was leaning against the sink watching her.

'Good – then weather permitting, we'll have coffee in the Piazza Garibaldi. Then you'll go to your home which I'm sure is some big old villa with far more rooms than you need, and I'll go to my small, easy-to-manage apartment.'

'But perhaps not every time,' whispered Leo.

Rose hadn't heard him.

'Should we have any sort of relationship – it will surely have more chance of surviving if we each go back to our own homes.'

'But not every time,' Leo repeated. This time Rose did hear him.

Behind his shoulder out in the twilight, a large lone bird was winging its way home above the forest. It flew towards the frozen land with grace and certainty. Rose couldn't be sure that it was a swan. She couldn't bring herself to look beyond Leo and stare at the silhouette as it faded into the dusk, but she decided that for her current purposes a swan it would be.

THE END

A SELECTION OF FINE WRITING
AVAILABLE FROM BLACK SWAN

THE PRICES SHOWN BELOW WERE CORRECT AT THE TIME OF GOING TO PRESS. HOWEVER TRANSWORLD PUBLISHERS RESERVE THE RIGHT TO SHOW NEW RETAIL PRICES ON COVERS WHICH MAY DIFFER FROM THOSE PREVIOUSLY ADVERTISED IN THE TEXT OR ELSEWHERE.